A
TIMELESS
Romance
ANTHOLOGY

OLD WEST
COLLECTION

A TIMELESS
Romance
ANTHOLOGY

CARLA KELLY
SARAH M. EDEN
LIZ ADAIR
HEATHER B. MOORE
ANNETTE LYON
MARSHA WARD

OLD WEST
COLLECTION

Interior Design by Rachael Anderson
Edited by Annette Lyon, Kelsey Allan, and Jennie Stevens
Paperback edit by Cassidy Wadsworth
Cover image # 170729465, Shutterstock.com

Published by Mirror Press, LLC
http://timelessromanceanthologies.blogspot.com
E-book edition released May 2014
Paperback edition released October 2014
ISBN-13: 978-1-941145-30-2

TABLE OF CONTENTS

OTHER TIMELESS ROMANCE ANTHOLOGIES

Winter Collection

Spring Vacation Collection

Autumn Collection

European Collection

Love Letter Collection

Summer in New York Collection

Silver Bells Collection

All Regency Collection

Californa Dreamin' Collection

BREAK A LEG

by Carla Kelly

Other Works by Carla Kelly

Mrs. McVinnie's London Season

Reforming Lord Ragsdale

Summer Campaign

Miss Milton Speaks Her Mind

Miss Grimsley's Oxford Career

The Admiral's Penniless Bride

Mrs. Drew Plays Her Hand

Her Hesitant Heart

My Loving Vigil Keeping

The Spanish Brand Series:
The Double Cross
Marco and the Devil's Bargain

BEFORE THE STORY BEGINS

By August of 1882, Hospital Steward Colm Callahan, 34, had decided he was bored with army life. Perhaps it was just life at Fort Laramie, which used to be interesting during the Great Sioux War. That conflict had ended when most of the hostiles were trundled onto reservations. Someone had definitely waved a white flag and declared the war over when Sitting Bull and his ragged band had left Canada and surrendered at Fort Buford in 1881.

The end of the Indian Wars had turned the grand dame of the Plains into a backwater garrison. Arrow wounds and amputations had given way to catarrh with copious phlegm (hacks and coughs to laymen) and the occasional case of diarrhea—neither very interesting. Women of the garrison still gave birth, but the post surgeon managed without help from his hospital steward. Thanks to nearby hog ranches, willing sporting women, and soldiers ripe for a spree, the clap would never go away. Venereal disease was as constant with the army as bugle calls.

On the average morning now, Colm handled Sick Call with little or no interference from his post surgeon, Captain Dilworth. After nineteen years of army medicine, Colm knew when something warranted the more specialized attention of the post surgeon, and in those cases he summoned the surgeon from the breakfast table accordingly. When it was just catarrh or the dry heaves, he left Captain Dilworth to his newspaper and toast.

Colm handled Sick Call, which meant admonishing any malingerers trying to put one over on the Medical Department, physicking those who needed it and sending them back to the barracks for rest, or hospitalizing the promising few. His reports were done by 10 a.m. and left, squared away, on Captain Dilworth's desk.

Then what? A steward could only count linens, roll bandages, and inventory the pharmacy so often. There was seldom anyone stiff and cold in the dead house to embalm. Lately, Colm found himself upstairs, staring out the window. Situated on a bluff, the hospital commanded a view of the whole garrison.

Depending on his mood, he would look in the direction of the iron bridge—out of his sight—which still saw traffic to the Black Hills, even though the major gold strikes were ancient history now. The Shy-Dead Road, the storied route from Cheyenne to Deadwood, was traveled mostly by law-abiders now. Worse still, rumor hinted that soon the cavalry would be withdrawn, leaving Fort Laramie with infantry only. Colm could almost hear the death knell for the Queen of the Plains.

More profitably, Colm might look out the windows that faced the parade ground. He watched children walking to school, which was held in the newly completed admin building by the Laramie River. Soon mothers with prams would stroll the wooden boardwalks, chatting with one another. That domestic sight sometimes sent him into melancholy, as he remembered desperate days in 1876 and '77, when troops came and went and war waged all around. Fort Laramie looked as gentrified as a Midwestern town now. Great Gadfreys and all the Saints!

If Colm was lucky, he might catch a glimpse of Ozzie Washington, easily the prettiest woman on the post, or so he reckoned. Depending on who might be ill among the officers' wives, the lieutenant colonel's wife was kindly inclined to send Ozzie, her servant, with a tureen of nourishing broth or a loaf or two of bread to the House of Affliction.

Ozzie was not a time-waster. Bowl- or basket-laden, she moved at a clip that set her hips swaying so nicely. She was grace personified, moving rapidly but with the dignity of her race. Once—perhaps on a dare from one of the lieutenant colonel's children—Ozzie had set a bushel basket square on her head and worn it the length of Officers Row without mishap. During Reconstruction days in Louisiana, he had seen women of color carry goods that way. So much grace and symmetry had impressed him then and did so now with Ozzie.

Always the observer, he had noticed how nicely the races had mingled for at least a century in New Orleans, producing graceful women of café au lait skin called mulatto or the regrettable "high yaller." He had admired them because they were so different. Ozzie's hair was wildly curly to a fault, and her skin was more olive than coffee, but her nose was straight and her lips at least fuller than his.

To say he admired Ozzie Washington was to minimize the matter. He was no expert, but Colm thought he loved her. He had met her seven years ago, in 1875, when the Fourth Infantry was first garrisoned at Fort Laramie. The Medical Department had assigned Colm permanent duty there—barring field emergencies—so he had ample time to watch the movements of various regiments. Ozzie stood out because the hospital had been plagued with endless winter ailments, and then-Major Chambers, commanding, ordered her there to help.

Help she had. Ozzie had no fear of the pukes or runs and did exactly what the surgeons required. She never complained, and she kept her mouth closed when other women on similar assignments objected long and loud.

During a welcome lull in sheet changing and basin dumping, Colm had mustered his courage and asked her how she remained so calm. She had given him a kind look, the sort of glance women reserved for the young and the addled, and said in her velvet voice, "Suh, if I didn't help, who would?"

She was right. Colm assured her that he was no sir, just a hospital steward. She nodded with understanding but everlastingly called him *suh*. He quit arguing about it, because he liked the languid way one word glided into the next when she spoke.

Ozzie Washington was exotic to Colm Callahan, who himself was an orphan from New York's bleak Five Points slum, a drummer boy with the Irish Brigade, and had become an impromptu hospital steward at Gettysburg, when he had no choice—much like Ozzie.

Her kindness stood out more than her beauty. He remembered an endless night in 1876 when the post surgeon had stretched out onto the table in his operating bay to grab a nap. Colm had slumped to the wall in the corridor, weary nigh unto death of 36-hour days. With a tap on his shoulder, Ozzie had handed him a cup of tea and an apple already sliced, then sat beside him. When he forgot to eat, she had put a slice in his hand. So kind.

Once he had mentioned her to a friend, a corporal in the Third Cavalry, tentatively expressing himself. The corporal had looked at him in shock.

"You know what she is," the man had said, then said it anyway—a word Colm heard all the time and had probably said a few times himself; everyone did. After that day, he never said it again, because it wasn't a polite way to talk about someone as thoughtful as Ozzie Washington.

Any fears the corporal would blab to others that the Irish hospital steward was enamored with a maid of color ended at the Battle of the Rosebud, when the corporal died. Colm had never chanced his feelings again; he kept his thoughts about Ozzie to himself. He was too shy to ever act on them.

Still, during moments like this at the window, he wondered what he would do when the Fourth Infantry was ordered somewhere else and Ozzie went along as Mrs. Lieutenant Colonel Chambers' trusted maid. When that happened, as it inevitably would, all he had left was resignation, leaving the army far behind. Another encounter with Ozzie would be more punishment than a shy man deserved.

ALSO BEFORE THE STORY BEGINS

Dzzie Washington knew it was time to visit the post office. Three weeks had passed since she had given her letter to a private in A Company, Fifth Cavalry, and asked him to mail it for her when the troop reached Fort Russell in Cheyenne. He'd never asked questions, because he couldn't read, and she always gave him a dime for her errand. He would mail the letter she had addressed to Audra Washington, Fort Laramie, Wyoming Territory, which would arrive back here in a week or so.

The first time she had mailed herself a letter, the Fourth had been garrisoned in Fort Concho, Texas. Lieutenant Colonel Chambers, then a captain, had checked the mail, staring a long time at the envelope.

"Audra Washington? Who do we know named Audra Washington?" he had joked.

"My real name is Audra," Ozzie had said.

He hadn't handed the letter to her until he teased her about a beau, which made her smile. She had no beau. Even when the Fourth had been garrisoned with one of the colored regiments, she never had one; she was too white for those men, even if they were former slaves too. The corporals and sergeants of the white regiments considered her too dark for them. There would never be a beau.

She never wrote herself more than four letters a year. When the day's work was done, she would make herself tea and open the letter she had written to herself. "Dearest Little Audra," she always began, as if this letter were from her mother, an illiterate woman who had been sold away from her, screaming, when Audra was only five, and sent to an East Texas cotton plantation. In these letters, this mother she barely remembered was living as a seamstress in New Orleans, with her own shop and an elegant clientele.

As the years passed, Ozzie wove an intricate fiction of carpet baggers and a fine man who courted her widowed mother, leaving her his fortune when he died of yellow fever. Her letters to herself were fabulous, and a welcome treat, because she had no one and would never have received a letter otherwise.

Mrs. Lieutenant Colonel Chambers was always happy to have Ozzie make the trip to the post office. While it couldn't be said that Hattie Chambers was lazy, it could be said that she cared not to exert herself, especially in high summer when the wind blew, as it invariably did in Wyoming Territory. Ozzie knew the trick of weighting the hem of her dresses with fishing lures or lead shot, the better to fool the wind.

Seventeen years in the employ of the same family meant that Ozzie had them all well trained. The Chambers' children had been trundled off to relatives in the East for schooling, which meant that life in the lieutenant colonel's quarters was simple. When her chores were done, she was at her leisure to walk to the post office.

She tried to time her visit with the probable appearance of Hospital Steward Colm Callahan, but lately he had been less cooperative. Either the post surgeon was picking up his own mail, or the dratted man had given Suh other duties.

She always thought of Steward Callahan as *Suh*. Face red, he had told her once that he was no gentleman, so she needn't refer to him that way. She had been just brave enough to continue calling him *Suh*, until he no longer objected. After that non-introduction, they had settled into the familiarity of frontier service, nothing more.

Ozzie admired the way he looked, even if his nose did peel in the summer and he was too vain (or busy) to coat it with zinc oxide, as some of the other light-skinned men did. He burned and peeled regularly, which detracted in no way from his admirable height and high cheekbones, which gave his face a thin look. His eyes were a surprising brown rather than the expected blue. In a moment of rare candor for a man so reticent, Suh had remarked that her eyes were lighter than his. The fact that he'd noticed flattered her.

He once told her how much he enjoyed the gentle flow of her Louisiana accent, but she never worked up the nerve to tell him that she liked the clipped cadence of his New York speak with just a hint of the Irish. That his grammar was impeccable, even though he admitted his early years were spent in a ghastly orphanage, hinted something else: he was as ambitious as she was.

Her own ambition had been borne of desperation. Maybe someday she would tell Suh about those dark days as the war was ending. Thinking back, she knew that the time a war was winding down was the worst time of all.

While it was true that the port of New Orleans had been liberated by Yankees early in the game, coloreds on the state's northern plantations had lingered in slavery. Ozzie thought she was twelve when the other slaves had simply dropped their tools or untied their aprons and walked off the LeCheminant plantation with not a word spoken. She remembered feeble protests from Madame LeCheminant and her daughters. What could they do, with all of the white men gone fighting in Lee's army?

Ozzie was young, so she'd stayed and found herself saddled with all of the house chores the others had done. When it became too much, she knotted her other dress in a tablecloth, along with her rosary and an ebony-backed hairbrush she'd swiped from Lalage LeCheminant, a child her own age, whose companion she had been. Lalage been the first to call her *Ozzie* because she could not pronounce *Audra*.

At twelve, Ozzie had slung her tablecloth luggage over her shoulder and left the house just after dark, when the haunts were out, which she did not believe in, being of a practical mind. A kindly man of color with a load of chickens trussed for market handed her up beside him in his cart and shared his sandwich with her.

He told her to find a Yankee woman to work for, that the best place was the U.S. Army encampment where he was headed. When they arrived outside New Orleans two days later in the early-evening rain, he helped her down and pointed to a row of houses, Officers Row.

She knocked on the first door, tried to introduce herself, and received a swipe with a broom for her pains. At the second door, she introduced herself, recited her skills—some exaggerated, some not—and did not leave even when Mrs. Captain Chambers closed the door politely on her. She shivered on the porch through the night and was still there in the morning when Captain Chambers looked out the window and saw her, chin up and eyes determined, a child.

He let her in, and she'd been their servant ever since. Ozzie Washington worked hard at every task assigned her and saved her modest wages, which were paid every other month when the army was paid. She never looked back.

Maybe it was time to put that money to use. She'd liked the look of Cheyenne—it was more refined since the early days, when the hell-on-wheels Union Pacific crew went through. The days were gone when she could knock on a door, look both desperate and determined, and find work. She had true skill now in dressmaking.

Any day, she would bid the Chambers *au revoir*, catch the southbound stage at the Rustic Hotel, and land herself in Cheyenne. Every town of any size had a seamstress or two. She could find work with one of the dressmakers, see where the land lay, and start her own business.

Any day.

WHERE THE STORY ACTUALLY BEGINS

"Things are slow, Callahan. If I have to treat one more case of clap, I'll take to drink," Captain Dilworth announced one morning.

Colm was far too wise to say that he alone had treated those so afflicted, because it was a homely duty beneath the notice of the post surgeon. As for taking to drink, Captain Dilworth was already lurching down that road. Again, Colm was too wise to mention it.

"Captain, are you thinking about a bolt to Cheyenne?" he asked instead.

"I was thinking more in terms of Omaha with the missus. We'll catch the UP in Cheyenne and spend a week there. Can you manage? I expect no trouble."

Yet again, Colm was far too experienced to suggest that the nature of medicine often meant a nasty surprise now and then, something beyond the official duties of a hospital steward. But who was he kidding? In the absence of post surgeons, Colm had extracted arrows, set bones, pulled teeth, prescribed probably useless medicine, done a successful shoulder resection because *someone* had to, and had even delivered a stubborn baby.

11

"I can manage, sir. When are you leaving?"

They had been through this conversation several times since Captain Dilworth had arrived three years ago. Colm had worked with better surgeons before, and worse ones. He could handle a hospital in a backwater garrison for a week.

The Dilworths were gone in a day, which made Colm Callahan happy; he liked being in charge. He had stood by his favorite window, looking down on the venerable fort below. "Bring it on, Old Girl," he boasted.

A day later, Colm Callahan wished he hadn't tempted Asclepius, the Greek god of medicine. That day began long before days should, with banging on his door by a frightened first-time father, a lieutenant of cavalry with the Fifth. Colm was pulling up his suspenders before the man finished knocking.

"My wife isn't due for confinement for another six weeks, but . . . but, there's water everywhere!"

So there was. When Colm arrived, Mrs. Lieutenant looked as frightened as her husband; he had two youngsters to calm down. He sent the lieutenant running down Officers Row to the Chambers' quarters with a note for Ozzie. Five minutes later, she arrived, and the calming began. Ten minutes later, the sheets and Mrs. Lieutenant were changed and the mother-to-be was back in bed. In another twenty, there was an addition to the dependents at Fort Laramie, a little one who looked almost as surprised as her parents.

"Nothing's ready!" the mother wailed.

"Heavens," Ozzie said so calmly. "All we need is a bureau drawer and some toweling." She turned to Colm. "Or should we put this little one close to the kitchen range, Suh?"

"My thought precisely," Colm said, happy he had been so wise to summon Ozzie.

While Ozzie laid a fire in the wood stove and pulled up a chair padded with a quilt, Colm cleaned the infant. "We'll keep her warm by the fire for a few days," he explained.

"She's a wee one and could use a boost. Happily, 'tis summer. And what will you name her?"

Soon Eugenia Victoria—so much name for one so small—had gathered herself into a compact bundle and slept, warm, before the open oven door. When all was calm at the lieutenant's, and Sergeant Flaherty's wife was in firm control there, Colm thanked Ozzie. With a nod, she started back to the Chambers' quarters. He stood a moment looking at her, a smile on his face.

That night, he managed forty-five minutes of sleep before the bugler sounded Sick Call. Luckily there was only a bilious stomach and a hacking cough to deal with before the next emergency, an ankle avulsion caused when a soldier-turned-carpenter (the army hated to pay for experts when privates existed) fell off a partly shingled stable roof.

His comrades carried the private to the hospital on a stretcher as he moaned and clutched the offending ankle. The private timed his arrival with the appearance of a baker's assistant who had spilled hot grease on his forearm. Colm sighed and wrote another note, sent with one of the stretcher men. By the time Ozzie arrived, the owner of the avulsed ankle was certain that amputation lay in his immediate future, and the baker's assistant had fainted when Colm touched his arm.

Sensible Ozzie. "Where do you need me the most, Suh?" The sparkle in her eyes betrayed her amusement, but she looked serious enough to satisfy the patients.

Without thinking, Colm put his hand on her shoulder. "The ankle thinks he's facing amputation at his hip and sure death. Calm him down while I take care of the burn."

She went to her duty while Colm made no attempt to revive the burn victim. Better to clean and prod while the man was in a far better place.

Burns in the second degree, he thought as he went to work. Out of the corner of his eye, he saw Ozzie remove the avulsed ankle's shoes. She wiped the man's face with a damp cloth, all the while keeping up a soothing conversation. Soon he was silent, caught in Ozzie's web. What a gift.

When the burn victim was resting with a cold compress on his arm, Colm pulled up a stool and sat by Ozzie's patient, whose eyes filled with terror again.

"By the Merciful, steward! Don't take off my leg!"

"Wouldn't dream of it," Colm said. "But I'm going to poke a bit. The pretty lady will hold your hand."

The pretty lady did so, freeing Colm to let his experienced fingers roam around a rapidly swelling ankle. "Wiggle your toes," he commanded, and the private wiggled. *This little piggy*, Colm thought. "Once more."

The private looked at him expectantly, but when Colm just sat there, the dread returned.

"Not a break in sight, private," he announced, putting the man out of some of his misery. "There's an avulsion, though, which means a little piece of bone has been tugged away by the ligament. We'll treat it with RICE."

The soldier stared at him. "Rice?"

"Aye, lad." Colm ticked off four fingers on his hand. "R-I-C-E: rest, ice, compression and elevation. And no more roofs, d'ye hear? I'll send a note to the sergeant."

"Yes, sir!" The private closed his eyes with relief, certain he had stared down death.

After the man was resting, iced, compressed, and elevated, Colm promenaded from the ward to the entrance with the woman who had come to his aid twice today. He walked as slowly as he could, although he knew Ozzie had other duties. He was too shy to ask her to return later if she could, but he needn't have bothered.

"I'll be back this evening to sit with your patients," she said. She peered closer; clearly more was on her mind.

"Go ahead," he said, wishing she would reveal her undying love.

No luck. "Suh, do you think you should telegraph Fort Russell for some help? At the very least, where's your hospital matron?"

"Home with lumbago," he said and made a face. "As for telegraphing, I don't think conditions here will get much worse."

Things did get much worse a half hour later, after Mess Call. As the hospital matron hauled her bones up the hill to prepare lunch, the bugler sounded Sick Call, something that never happened at one o'clock in the afternoon.

Captain Dilworth had left his medical bag in his office. Colm grabbed it and was out the door in seconds. He ran down the hill toward a crowd gathered by the post traders' complex.

From its off-colored front wheels, he recognized the ambulance as the vehicle that had left for Cheyenne only that morning, carrying mail and several officers bound for court-martial duty. Colm worked his way through the crowd to the sergeant on patrol, a usually genial Irishman like himself who looked anything but genial.

"Colm, dear boyo, we came across the Shy-Dead stagecoach just past the iron bridge, tipped on its side." He gestured to a piece of canvas from which booted feet poked out. "Couldn't do anything for the driver." He pointed again, further inside the ambulance. "Here's your real patient."

Ever cautious, Colm raised the canvas. The driver's head was cocked at an odd angle, but Colm rested his fingers against his neck anyway. Nothing. He shook his head.

"Come, come, young man, I am yet alive!"

Colm stared in surprise at the huge voice that boomed from an older man of somewhat ordinary dimensions. He wore a suit that could be called flashy—odd in a man of obvious mature years. Colm looked closer. The man's cravat was a strident shade of green that would give a statue a headache. Stuck through it was a cravat pin in the shape of tragedy and comedy masks.

15

"Lysander Locke, *the* Lysander Locke, awaiting your good offices, sir!" the man boomed again. "I do believe I have broken my leg."

"I . . . well . . . let me look." Colm moved farther into the ambulance.

Colm felt the leg. The man was entirely correct. Lysander Locke's tibia appeared to be at odds with the world. To Colm's relief, the skin was still intact.

Lysander Locke watched Colm's gentle prodding with a real air of detachment, even as he sucked in his breath. "Say it isn't serious and that I can be on my way to Deadwood, where an engagement awaits to perform *King Lear* in three days."

Colm smiled; he couldn't help himself. The man spoke in such theatrical tones, with a certain flourish. He was worlds braver than the avulsed ankle resting in the hospital.

"It is most certainly a broken leg, so Shakespeare will have to wait a few weeks."

Lysander Locke put the back of his hand to his forehead and closed his eyes. "Young man, the show must go on!"

"Not in the next three days."

His hand still on the broken leg, Colm took a good look at his patient, doubting that Fort Laramie had ever seen such a man. "Otherwise, how are you?"

"A little shaken, my good man, but none the worse for it," the man announced. "I am Lysander Locke, late of Drury Lane and Covent Gardens, and a noted tragedian."

Not one to hide your light under a bushel, Colm thought, amused.

Lysander Locke had an accent, but Colm didn't think he would have placed it so close to England. But never mind. Here was a man with a broken leg, even though Captain Dilworth had assured him that nothing would happen while he was in Omaha.

The medical department does not pay me enough, Colm thought as he scribbled another note to Ozzie.

16

"Let's get up the hill," he told the driver as he crouched next to his newest patient.

With a passing private's help, Colm loaded the corpse onto a stretcher and left him in the solitude of the dead house, located behind the hospital and next to his own little quarters. The same stretcher moved Lysander Locke into the hospital's operating bay, if such Colm could call a place where no one had operated in recent memory.

Thank goodness Ozzie arrived so promptly. Without a word, Colm handed her one of his own aprons, which circled her waist and then some.

"Are you game, Ozzie?" he asked when she stood outside the operating bay, looking indecisive. "We'll need to cut away his trousers and smallclothes. I don't want to shock you or anything . . ."

Maybe this was a stupid idea. Holding patients' hands was one thing, but asking her to assist an operation quite another. "Or maybe I should do this myself."

"I'm no shrinking violet, Suh," was all she said as she crooked her arm through his and towed *him* into the operating bay.

Indeed she was not. Ozzie did everything he asked, all the while delicately covering the actor with a sheet. Praise all the saints and the Almighty that the fracture was a simple one. Just the right amount of chloroform on a square of gauze put the patient out so Colm could go to work, rotating and straightening, comparing the two legs, tinkering until he was satisfied.

"You're as good as Captain Dilworth," Ozzie said, holding the leg still while he splinted it. "Probably better. You've done a lot of this, haven't you?"

Maybe he was feeling cocky because the whole matter went so smoothly. Whatever the reason, he told Ozzie about the night on the battlefield five years ago at White Mountain. He had assisted Captain Sternberg, who operated by feel in the dark, because Nez Perce sharpshooters kept targeting their kerosene lamp. "We both worked on that man and saved him, all in the dark," he concluded as he finished splinting. Plaster would come later.

"You're a hero, Suh."

"Just a hospital steward. Pull him toward you a bit."

When he finished, they rolled the table into the wardroom. The avulsed ankle and burned forearm watched with some interest as the two of them gently lowered the actor into a bed.

"I'll sit with him until he comes around," Colm said. "The matron promised to return with food for him, but I have my doubts." He looked at the lovely woman beside him, who was watching the actor. "Ozzie, I do need you."

"Then you have me, Suh," she said quietly. "Mrs. Chambers will manage."

"It'll be more than a night or two," he said, doubtful again.

"She'll manage," she replied so softly, touched his shoulder, and left the ward.

He watched her walk away, embarrassed that he had boasted about that battlefield surgery. It was all true, but he had never been a man to toot his horn. He couldn't help wondering when she would get tired of helping him.

"*That* is a lovely woman."

Colm looked around in surprise. The stentorian voice, which could probably blow out the back wall of a theatre, was considerably weakened, but there was no mistaking the dramatic timbre.

"You're among the living again," Colm said, putting a hand against the old gent's chest. "Firm beat." He touched his two fingers to his wrist. "True there."

To his further surprise, the actor grabbed Colm's wrist and inexpertly felt for a pulse. "Lad, are you smitten by that pretty lady?" He closed his eyes. "When I feel better, you must tell me everything."

18

When pigs fly, Colm thought, not sure if he was amused or exasperated. *Gadfreys, was he that obvious to a man coming out of anesthesia?*

As it turned out, Ozzie didn't have to exert any pressure on her employer. She explained the situation, and Mrs. Chambers barely heard anything beyond *actor*.

"Do you think he might perform for us when he is better?" she asked. "We could hold such a party."

"It'll be a few days until he is lively enough," Ozzie hedged. "Surely you can arrange for a corporal's wife to help you while I am busy at the hospital." She delivered the clincher. "It's for the good of the regiment."

Mrs. Chambers was no slouch and no kinder than most penny pinchers. "If you will promise her the wages I would have paid you."

"Yes, indeed," Ozzie replied, secretly amused.

As she hurried to her little room to gather up an apron that fit, and her extra dress, Ozzie stopped a moment to pat her hair here and there, then wonder how long she might have to stay at the hospital. It would be a pleasant change from garrison tedium, if nothing else. She patted her hair a little more.

All was calm in the hospital when Ozzie returned. She hesitated in the corridor, wondering if Suh really needed her. She sniffed the air. He needed her.

She peeked into the kitchen. There he stood, stirring madly at a pot from which a burned smell rose like gas in a Louisiana swamp.

"I'm hopeless," he said. "The books say patients should have a low diet of gruel and tea, but for the life of me . . ." He took the pan off the hob, looked inside hopefully, as if something might have changed, and sighed.

19

Without a word, he handed her the wooden spoon, turned around and bent over, which made Ozzie whoop with laughter. Soon, he laughed, too.

"Help me?" he asked simply, straightening up. "I have eggs, milk and cream." He looked toward the pot. "We'll forget the farina."

Ozzie carried the offending pan to the dry sink and left it there to suffer third-degree burns. "We may have to throw out that pan altogether," she said. "I will cook for you all."

Suh put his hand to his heart and staggered backward. "Thank the Almighty." Perhaps he had learned something from Lysander Locke, Shakespeare tragedian. "'We,' she says. 'We.' She's not leaving me alone to suffer."

Ozzie wiped tears of merriment from her eyes. "I am going to make scrambled eggs and flapjacks."

"That's not a low diet."

"Honestly, Suh, how can anyone get well on gruel?"

"So I've tried to tell any number of post surgeons in the past decade, with no success." He looked around elaborately. "But Captain Dilworth isn't here, and those men are hungry."

"Then stand back and let me cook," she said. "Any vanilla? Dare I ask for maple syrup?"

"You dare, indeed." He pointed out the objects in question. "I will retreat to the ward and assure the broken leg, burned arm, and avulsed ankle that good food will arrive shortly, and that I had nothing to do with it."

Smiling, she went to work in the hospital kitchen, grateful for the matron's lumbago. The kitchen was well stocked and quiet. Ozzie found herself humming as she made flapjacks, that staple of army life but with a touch of vanilla. They went into the warming oven while she scrambled eggs and added cream, something even the Chambers didn't see in their kitchen too often. Medical rations were far superior, as long as amateur cooks weren't allowed to roam at will.

"Suh, you are a forlorn hope in the kitchen," she said to the eggs, which were getting all glossy, as good scrambled eggs should.

She found a small cart on wheels, so it was with her own Louisiana flair that she rolled dinner into the ward and witnessed the eagerness of hungry men.

Poor, poor Mr. Lysander Locke. His eyes were half open in the same sickroom stare she recalled from times of illness in the Chambers household. She was hard pressed to remember a time she had ever been bedridden. Sick, yes, but that meant nothing on a plantation, unless you were white. She looked at the peaceful men lying there, wondering why others were born to serve.

"Pancakes and scrambled eggs, gentlemen," she said, certain that three of the four had never been called *gentlemen* before.

The hospital steward's relief was nearly palpable, to Ozzie's delight. As Colm helped the avulsed ankle into a sitting position, the burn looked on with interest. "I can't remember when I last saw maple syrup," he declared, pushing himself upright.

Soon the soldiers were eating. Ozzie voiced no objection when the burn asked permission to douse even his eggs in maple syrup.

Lysander Locke was more of a challenge. As Colm struggled to help him sit up, Locke sighed in a most theatrical way.

"You'd better lend a hand, too, my dear miss," the actor said.

She obliged, quietly pleased when Colm twined his fingers with hers and offered a firmer foundation to a man more substantial than the usual run-of-the-mill soldier. They hauled Lysander Locke upright. If the steward kept his fingers twined in hers a little longer than a casual observer may have thought necessary, Ozzie still had no objection.

Their heads were close together too. Colm Callahan smelled strangely of camphor, which puzzled her. Camphor?

She gently released her grip on Colm and stepped back, but Lysander Locke plucked her sleeve. "Do I ask too much, my dear, to ask you to feed me? I feel so weak."

Ozzie looked at the steward, who nodded. His eyes were full of concern and made her wonder if she had become entirely too cynical at the advanced age of twenty-eight.

Mr. Locke is not at death's door, she thought.

"I dislike eating alone," her patient said as she tucked a napkin under his chin. "Is there enough for this fine young man too?" he asked, indicating Colm.

"Yes, Suh," she said. "We'll need another plate."

That fine young man took the cue and hurried to the kitchen, returning with two plates and forks. "There's enough for all of us," he said, taking his share and dishing a plate for her. "We can take turns feeding him."

They did. Before long, the actor was regaling them with stories of fame and fortune in Drury Lane, and then Broadway. But it wasn't entirely about him. After the scrambled eggs were gone, he paused in his narrative.

"Laddie, you have a faint accent that places you in New York City, and perhaps somewhere more removed."

"Aye," Colm said. Ozzie smiled as he blushed. Such a shy man. "The farther removed is County Kerry, which I left at the tender age of five."

"Thence to the teeming metropolis of lower Manhattan?"

Colm nodded, his expression more serious. "You needn't know any more."

"But I wish to," Lysander Locke said. He indicated Ozzie. "And so does this fair damsel, who saved us from starvation. By the way, my dear, what is your place of origin?"

"A plantation in Louisiana," she told him. "It belonged

22

to the LeCheminant family, but it might be in the hands of a bank now, or maybe a Yankee scalawag."

"I see no regret," Colm commented, his eyes lively.

"None from me, Suh."

She could have told him much more, but she didn't need his sympathy, and she didn't know the actor well enough to need his, either. As a house slave, she had been treated kindly enough, discounting the times Madam LeCheminant took after her with a hairbrush when Ozzie had talked back to her daughter. She still had scars on her back and neck.

Lysander Locke looked at them. "Here I am, stove up and wounded and relying on you both to entertain me, but you're struck dumb!"

Ozzie glanced at Colm and started to laugh, just a quiet one, because she had been taught years ago to call no attention to herself. But she couldn't help herself when Colm turned away, his shoulders shaking. She laughed louder, until she was leaning against the iron footboard of the actor's bed.

"*What* is so funny?" Lysander demanded finally, with all the careful enunciation and drama he probably saved for the stage.

Colm recovered first. "It's this way, sir. Speaking for myself, I've never considered myself an entertainer." He turned his smile on Ozzie. "Miss Washington? Have you ever been asked to entertain someone?"

"I have, Suh," she said, her voice soft. As she braved a glance at Colm Callahan, she saw a flicker of understanding in his eyes. Where it came from and how, she did not know, but it gave her courage to continue. "I was the personal slave and entertainer of Lalage LeCheminant, who was five years old, my age. If I couldn't entertain her, I got the hairbrush for my pains."

Colm's smile vanished. She'd said too much and turned to go, but he touched her elbow. That was it, nothing more.

She had long suspected that Colm Callahan may have had a less-than-pleasant childhood of his own. Too bad she would never be brave enough to ask about it.

She recovered as gracefully as she could, looking down at the little watch pinned to her bodice. "Dear me, Suh, I think your other patients need more flapjacks." With all the poise she could muster, she pushed the cart down the row toward the other men.

Colm seated himself so he could at least pretend to listen to Lysander Locke and still keep an eye on Ozzie Washington. He already knew that the actor could carry on a conversation requiring little from the listener save the occasional *aye* and nod.

Locke was saying something about the importance of being in Deadwood within a day or two as Colm watched Ozzie finish serving flapjacks and retreat to the kitchen.

"I will have you know that I once served in the Swiss Guard and saved Pope Pius from assassination by cutting a man's throat with my teeth."

"Aye, sir," Colm said, which earned him a balled-up napkin thrown at his temple, followed by a theatrical laugh aimed at the back wall.

"Ah ha! I could have told you I was Judas himself, and you'd have nodded," Lysander Locke declared with triumph. "You're not paying attention. You're a goner, did you know?"

"I . . . what?" Colm asked, embarrassed.

Locke's voice turned into a stage whisper. "Laddie, I know a smitten man when I see one."

Colm sighed, deciding then and there not to reenlist in September. When even a moth-eaten old actor could see right through him, it was time to take up another line of work in a distant city, perhaps Constantinople. Colm waited a moment, knowing his good humor would return. It did, but not as soon as usual.

"You're right, sir," he said, knowing it would be foolish to argue with a patient who would be gone in a week or less. "I've admired Ozzie Washington for years, but—"

"You've made no move because she is a woman of color?" the actor supplied.

Colm started in surprise. "Not at all!" he exclaimed, wanting to brain the man with a bedpan for such an observation. He was tired; that was it. How had he gotten himself into this discussion?

"Then why are you wasting time?"

Colm opened his mouth to make some stupid reply, then closed it. "I have things to do," he mumbled and left the ward. In the hall, he leaned against the wall and closed his eyes. What had happened? He was precise and efficient for 364 days a year, until the 365th, when an actor showed up with a broken leg.

"Are you all right, Suh?" Ozzie had such a lovely voice, and she even sounded concerned.

He could have made some noncommittal reply— yesterday, he probably would have—but something had changed. He just wasn't certain what. The earth's axis hadn't shifted, and as far as he knew, no out-of-control meteor raced toward Wyoming Territory. He could go upstairs and busy himself with something, except that he didn't want to. He wanted to stay in the corridor with Ozzie.

"Suh?"

"Never been better," he told her, and it might have been true. Deep breath. "You know I need help. Ozzie, I'm about to fall asleep." He shifted to look her in the eye. "Am I asking too much of you?"

Bless her heart, she knew just what he meant. Trust a woman to know.

"We're going to take turns here," she said, and he heard some uncertainty. "I sort of wish you would be closer than your quarters, in case something happens, but I know you need to sleep."

"Let's do this: While you're in the ward, I'll sleep on the cot in Captain Dilworth's office." No point in standing on overmuch ceremony. "I . . . I changed my bed linens yesterday, so you can sleep in my house while I'm awake in here."

She nodded, practical as he was. She turned to say something when a moan came from the ward. Ozzie's eyes opened wide in fright, but then she giggled. "He's such an . . . an actor," she whispered, leaning toward Colm. "I'll see what's wrong."

He nodded, content to let her do his dirty work, because he was a most typical man.

She returned a moment later. "I have been requested to keep Mistuh Locke company," she said. "You, Suh, get to wash the dishes."

"And I shall," he said. "Then I will go to bed. I'll take the cot in Captain Dilworth's office while you watch in the ward."

A worried frown appeared between her eyes. Impulsively, he smoothed it down. "If anything happens, just knock on Captain Dilworth's door. I won't be far."

She gave him a relieved smile, which warmed his heart.

Before sitting beside the actor, Ozzie did her own ward walk, something she had seen Suh do. The private with the avulsed ankle was full of flapjacks and settling himself down for the night. When she rested the back of her hand against his forehead, he opened his eyes.

She glanced at the chart hanging at the foot of his bed.

"Is everything all right, Private Henry?" she asked. "If you need something, just call me."

He nodded and closed his eyes.

Private Jones with the burned forearm was in some pain. "I'll ask Steward Callahan if there is something—"

A mighty crash of pans came from the kitchen.

"You may want to trade places with the steward for a few minutes," Private Jones suggested. "He doesn't shine around crockery."

She laughed and took his suggestion. With some relief, Suh turned over the dishes to her. "Let me measure powders any day," he muttered as he hurried from the kitchen.

He returned sometime later as she made her last swipe of the dish towel around the last plate. "My timing is exquisite," he joked. "I've administered powders and done bedpan duty," he said, ticking the items off on his fingers. "Two out of three are asleep, and you must listen to the actor for a while. G'night."

He tipped an imaginary hat to her. A moment later, she heard the door to Captain Dilworth's office close.

He had left a kerosene lamp on the table in the corridor, a hospital lamp with four slatted sides for varying degrees of light. On the back of a blank prescription, she found a note. *Take this with you,* Suh had scrawled.

Ozzie closed two of the slats and carried the lamp into the ward. Feeling like Florence Nightingale at Scutari Hospital, she held it high and satisfied herself that the privates slumbered. Lysander Locke was wide awake. She pulled up a chair, made herself comfortable, and asked him why he couldn't sleep.

"I am an actor. We are always awake in the evening. Curtain comes down at ten of the clock."

"And then you sleep?"

"No, no. I smile graciously at well-wishers, remove my makeup, then toddle off to a nearby chophouse. In New York

City, I take a hansom cab to Delmonico's."

She couldn't overlook the wistful tone in his voice. "It's been a while since New York City?" she asked, then could have bitten her tongue, because it sounded so heartless.

Lysander Locke sighed. Maybe he was more tired than he wanted to let on. "Far too long, my dear," he said. "Denver wasn't quite the cultural center I was led to believe."

He didn't say it with any self pity, but Ozzie knew what he meant. She could have made some offhand remark, but something had happened between them. She wasn't certain just what, but maybe it was her turn to talk. She took a deep breath.

"I know how that feels. Freedom is nice, but it's not all that easy."

Her words, softly spoken, seemed to hang there like mist. She gathered her nerve and looked at Mr. Locke, wondering what he was thinking.

He gazed back, his eyes so kind, even though she knew he must be in pain. "How did freedom come to you, Miss Washington?"

She told him about borrowing courage from some unused source to finally walk away from the LeCheminant plantation. "I think I was twelve. My mother would know for sure, but she was sold into East Texas when I was five."

You can't possibly want to hear this, she thought and started to rise. There must be something she could fold, or put away, or straighten, and this man did need his sleep.

He put out his hand, motioning down, so she remained where she was. "Sold? Your mother?"

Ozzie nodded, startled that her eyes should start to brim. She knew she would never find her mother, though she thought about her every day. "She was a house Negro. Maybe she made Madame LeCheminant angry."

"Your father?"

Ozzie shrugged. "Monsieur LeCheminant."

Mr. Locke made a sudden noise that didn't sound in the least theatrical.

"Never mind, Suh! That was life in the South."

Through the years, she had given the matter some thought. Maybe Mr. Locke would find it interesting. "I don't know for certain, but I do know this: whenever a new baby with light skin was born in the slave quarters, some house slave ended up on the auction block in Shreveport. Madame LeCheminant was not a kind woman. I have scars." She stopped, certain she had said too much. "Well, Suh, everyone has scars. Some show and some don't."

When Lysander Locke spoke, his voice shook. "Did you . . . did you choose your last name?"

"I did," she declared with pride, then looked around, fearful she had spoken too loudly. Private Henry shifted positions, but Private Jones continued to snore.

"I gather your choice wasn't LeCheminant?" the actor teased, but gently.

"Never," she said emphatically, but quieter. "Some chose Jackson, or Lincoln, or Jefferson. Others gave me all sorts of suggestions, but I wanted to choose something for the first time in my life. Washington freed his slaves. I like it."

"So do I, Miss Washington, but why Ozzie?"

"It's really Audra," she said with a laugh. "My mother named me, but Lalage LeCheminant called me Ozzie." How much of the truth did the actor need? "I insisted that my name was Audra and got the hairbrush for being impertinent. I'm used to Ozzie now."

"Do you never use Audra?" he asked. "It's lovely."

"Well . . ." She hadn't planned to tell him, but it was late, and she was tired. Maybe talking would keep her awake.

The two slats of the ward lamp gave off such a comforting glow. She could almost imagine herself sitting in front of a fire in her own parlor, if she had one.

"I pretend to get letters from my mother." For just a moment, the sorrow of the whole thing grabbed her. She had not seen her mother in twenty-three years; why should it matter now? She would have stopped if she hadn't seen such interest in the old actor's eyes. "I . . . I address it to Audra Washington and send it to myself."

"Right here?"

"I give it to a soldier heading to Cheyenne, or maybe Omaha, and he mails it from there. Or he may be going to Billings, in Montana Territory." She touched his hand. "Or even Deadwood! That way, I'm never quite certain when it will come back. Sometimes . . ." She paused again, hoping he would not think her foolish. "Sometimes I even forget, and the letter is almost a surprise. As if . . ."

"Your mother actually sent it," Lysander Locke finished. "You're a remarkable lady, Miss Washington." His voice was lower now, the words strung out. His eyes closed.

"Do you receive other letters, my dear?" he asked when she thought he slept.

"Who would write to me?" This was becoming too serious; she had to turn the conversation. "Mr. Locke, how does *your* mail keep up with you?"

He yawned. "My mail? I don't get much mail either."

It had never occurred to Ozzie that there were others like her. "You hear from your family, don't you?"

"What family?"

"Well, I mean . . ."

He opened one eye. "I devoted myself to Shakespeare."

She couldn't think of anything to say to his artless declaration, mainly because she could not fathom anyone choosing such a life on purpose. How odd, how sad.

"Maybe someday you will settle down and have a family," she ventured cautiously.

No answer. She peered closer, hoping he would forget this entire conversation. Ozzie sat in silence as his breathing became regular and deep. *Poor man*, she thought as she stood.

Suh had draped Mr. Locke's clothes over the foot of the iron bedstead. Moving quietly, she took his suit coat and shook out the wrinkles, or tried to. The material wouldn't cooperate. She looked closer. The wool was cheap, even though it looked good from a distance. His bright green cravat had been creased and folded many times. How many cravats did Mr. Locke possess, or was this his only one? She put the coat on a peg reserved for patients' clothing and wet her fingers to smooth out the cravat.

He had a shabby little suitcase; perhaps he had other trousers. She gave the suit her critical appraisal: shiny wool with what looked like bits of filler fabric woven in.

"Mistuh Locke," she whispered, "fortune has not smiled on you lately."

Ozzie had seen better shirts in those rummage sales so dear to the hearts of army personnel. Since officers had to pay their own freight from garrison to garrison, any move of significance meant rummage sales to help lighten the load. She had acquired her second-best petticoat that way, as well as the shoes she wore now.

After a good wash, she could turn the cuffs on Mr. Locke's shirt. His stockings were hopeless, with holes in each heel, but she had yarn and could knit him another pair, considering that she'd be spending nights sitting in the ward so Suh could sleep a little.

She contemplated the matter as she walked up and down the little ward, stopping for a while beside the private with the burned arm. He moved restlessly, even though he was asleep; his arm surely pained him. She hesitated at first then took his good hand in hers, stroking it until he settled into deeper sleep again.

She returned to her chair beside the actor, wondering how on earth he would fare in Deadwood, Dakota Territory.

She had heard some of the garrisons' wives whisper about what a sinful place it was, with gambling, dance hall girls, and women of the night. She could not picture *King Lear* in such a place.

Are you telling us the truth, the whole truth, and nothing but the truth? she thought, then sighed. Who would lie about Deadwood?

She must have dozed, because she woke up to a light hand on her shoulder. Was it already two o'clock? Startled, she looked up to see Suh holding a finger to his lips, his eyes lively even in the gloom. He looked more chipper than a man should with so little sleep, but Ozzie knew he was used to the twilight life of a hospital steward.

"Everyone alive?" he asked, bending close to her ear.

"Suh, you see them in the same state you left them," she retorted, enjoying his little joke—and the way his breath warmed her ear and set off prickles down her spine.

He pointed to the door, and she followed. The door to Captain Dilworth's office stood open, and moonlight streamed into the corridor. A portrait of poor President Garfield still hung there. Any day now, someone from Washington, D.C., would surely remember to mail a portrait of President Arthur.

Tired now, she stood next to President Garfield, glad to turn the patients over to someone who could do them more good than she if they woke.

"How long should I sleep?" she asked.

"Until Mess Call." He made a face. "Wish it could be longer, but you know my kitchen skills."

She just smiled.

"I'll tend to Sick Calland then make sure our patients are buffed and sparkling before I turn them over to you again," he joked.

"And?" she prompted, when he seemed to hesitate.

"Ordinarily, I'd let you take another rest before Noon

Mess, but I have to attend to the corpse in the dead house."

"Glory, Suh, do you *embalm*, too?"

"I am a man of amazing talents, Ozzie. Learned that skill in the war, as well as others."

Suh took her arm and guided her to the side door, opening it onto a moonlit path. "Enough of that indelicate subject! I'll wait right here until you go inside." He indicated the two little buildings, pointing to the left. "That's mine. The other one's the dead house." He chuckled. "Don't mix them up."

She stopped halfway down the path and took a few steps back toward him. He met her, a question in his eyes.

"Suh, I wonder just how successful Mr. Locke really is. His suit looks like it's made of shoddy, and why on earth would anyone in Deadwood want to see *King Lear*?"

"I've been wondering that myself," he replied. "D'ye think he's putting on an act for us?"

She shrugged.

"If he wakes up with the chickens, I'll see what I can learn. Go to bed, Ozzie. You've been more than kind."

True to his word, he watched her until she stood on the porch of his quarters. His solicitude touched her. It wasn't more than a stone's throw to his quarters, but there he stood until she turned the doorknob.

"Lock the door," he called. "This is still an army garrison."

He had left a lamp burning in the small parlor. Even though she was ready to drop from exhaustion, Ozzie took the lamp and peered into his even smaller kitchen, which was tidy to the point of appearing unused. Considering his culinary skills—something he obviously *hadn't* learned in the war—she figured he ate his meals in the hospital, when the matron wasn't suffering from lumbago.

The other room was his bedchamber, with its narrow bed, three-drawer bureau, and a wash basin with a scrap of mirror at Suh-height for shaving. His night table had a lamp and two books: *Les Misérables* and the U.S. Medical Department Annual Report, more well-thumbed than Jean Valjean's tale of woe and redemption.

No pictures hung on the walls in either room. The only thing she had noticed was a calendar of fetching, round-bottomed women in the kitchen. Suh had no more family than she did, a realization that saddened her.

Her eyes closed, Ozzie stripped down to her shimmy and crawled into bed. It was lumpy in all the right places, but the pillow smelled of that mysterious camphor. Her last thought was that she would have to ask him why on earth camphor.

Everyone slept, giving Colm time for the paperwork so dear to his heart. He discovered it was less dear than usual, mainly because he was picturing Ozzie Washington asleep in his bed. He was an organized, rational, intelligent, and efficient man. Even during those fraught days at the age of fourteen, when he stood beside his commanding officer in K Company, 69th Regiment of the Irish Brigade, drumming out the commands to direct soldiers into battle, he had not flinched or failed anyone. And here he was at thirty-four, a non-commissioned officer commanding some respect—mooning over a woman.

Dashed good thing I told her to lock the door, he thought in disgust. *I am an idiot.*

He was also disgusted with himself, too shy and ill-equipped to even make an attempt to court Ozzie Washington, as much as he wanted to. Life in an orphanage after his father had run off and his mother had died, then the army at fourteen, had promised him no childhood and no way to learn about the finer things.

Years had passed. The press of hospital work, the constant turmoil of fighting, and vast distances had meant no furloughs. The relative isolation of hospital life, and his neither-fish-nor-fowl rank as hospital steward, left him dangling in the vast gulf between enlisted society and the officer corps.

He belonged nowhere and to no one, and the sad fact chafed him raw. He was too shy to speak to Ozzie Washington of anything beyond commonplaces. He, Colm Callahan, organized man of considerable responsibility, didn't know where to begin.

The ward was still shrouded in shadow, but Colm needed only one slat of light to assess his patients. He stood at the foot of the avulsed ankle's bed, amused to see Ozzie's careful handwriting—a contrast to his almost-doctor scrawl—listing each hour she had looked at the man and his condition.

My dear Ozzie, you are nearly as precise as I am, he thought. Private Henry slumbered on, just the way Colm wanted to find him at five o'clock before Reveille.

Private Jones was a different matter, tossing his head from side to side, the portrait of early-morning discomfort that Colm always associated with burns, his least-favorite injury. The soldier wasn't quite awake yet, so the hospital steward pressed his hand on the private's forehead. In a few minutes, he slept again. Funny how just a touch could calm. Some imp sitting on his shoulder suggested that he try touching Ozzie to see what happened. The thought made him roll his eyes.

As he sat with the private, thinking he might have to debride the burn when the light was better, Colm glanced toward Lysander Locke. The actor watched him with what appeared to be considerable interest. When Private Jones drifted deeper into sleep, Colm tiptoed to Lysander Locke's bed and sat down. After a whispered conversation—at least as quiet as a man with vocal pipes like an actor could whisper—and a moment with the bedpan, Lysander appeared disposed to talk.

"She took good care of me. Uh, sergeant?"

"No. Just Steward, or you may call me Callahan. Captain Dilworth does."

"No first name?"

"Not in the U.S. Army." It was early in the morning; maybe Colm could be forgiven for wishful thinking. "I can't recall the last time anyone used my first name."

He didn't say so for the actor to frown and feel sorry for him, but Mr. Locke did look touched at his pronouncement.

"That's wrong, my boy. What does Miss Washington call you?"

He shrugged, glad that the gloom of early morning hid his blush, if the warmth of his face was any indicator. He thought about it and suddenly realized that he had a nickname with Ozzie alone, their private name. "She calls me Suh. I told her I wasn't a gentleman and shouldn't be addressed as Sir, but that's what she calls me."

"I like it."

"So do I."

There. He had said enough. His failure at doing what probably eighty percent of the population did by finding a mate was *his* problem, and not one to share with a bedridden, broken-down actor. He made as if to rise, but Mr. Locke put out his hand. Colm sat down. There was no reason for the man to take an interest in him, but that was what he appeared to do. Right or wrong, Colm couldn't deny feeling flattered.

Lysander Locke leaned forward like a conspirator, so Colm did too.

"Did you know that her real name is Audra?"

He didn't. Audra. *Audra.* Just exotic enough to match her olive skin and beautiful eyes. He listened as the actor regaled him with information about Ozzie's early life, obviously gleaned during a late-night conversation bearing some resemblance to this early-morning one. None of it was anyone's business, but Colm wanted to know more about the woman sleeping in his bed.

He listened, amused and then touched, to learn of Ozzie's letters to herself. He couldn't remember a time he had ever received correspondence from anyone except the U.S. government, and he admired Ozzie's resourcefulness.

But here was the old gent, clapping his hands softly, demanding attention. "I have an idea! *You* could write her a letter. Think how surprised she would be."

"Oh, I . . ."

Lysander Locke was a professional at riding over someone else's conversation, if Colm could call his own mumble actual conversation. "Think how much you owe her. Just a note of appreciation."

Colm sat back. It *would* be a surprise for a lovely lady, just a note and a penny stamp.

"Have you ever received a letter?" Locke asked.

Colm laughed, then looked around when Private Jones stirred. "And who would write to an orphan from Five Points?"

"Surely you made friends in . . . did you fight in the war?"

"I was only fourteen when I ran away from St. Agnes," Colm replied. "Enlisted as a drummer boy with the 69th."

"No friends, no comrades in arms?"

It had been a long time; he nearly didn't falter. "One died at Fredericksburg and the other two in a wheat field at Gettysburg."

Thank goodness Private Jones started to groan; Colm had a perfect excuse to tend to someone who needed him and avoid more questions.

"Didn't mean to interrupt your conversation," the

private gasped between rapid breaths.

"Easy now," Colm said, happy to devote his attention to something he was familiar with. Letters? He had decided years ago that they were for others.

Colm removed the loose bandage, and the private sucked in his breath. Eyes wide, he stared at the mess that was his own forearm.

"No fears," Colm said. "I'll have you fine in a few days."

And he would. Colm had seen the same worried look on other men with burns. Speaking low and keeping his explanation simple, he told Jones what he would do for the burn to heal properly. "A little morphine will make it easy enough to bear. A few more days, and I'll send you back to the bakehouse."

"To work?" the private asked, uncertainty in his voice.

"To rest. Don't you have quarters off the storeroom? Perfect place to recuperate." Colm rested his hand on the private's shoulder. "Trust me, laddie. I've seen worse."

By the eternal, he had. How curious that he had found his life's vocation in a burning aid station on the second day at Gettysburg. After his commanding officer ordered him to beat retreat through the wheat field, then sank to his knees with a minie ball between his eyes, Colm had done the sensible thing. He beat retreat as ordered, then unhooked his drum and left it there in the wheat field. He took up his other duty as stretcher-bearer and carried out a wounded lieutenant, only to have him burn to death when the nearest aid station took a direct hit from a cannonball. The ether exploded into fireballs, and Colm dragged out the wounded, his own hair singed and stinking.

He went back in, and that made all the difference. When the battle ended two days later, he could debride burns, hold retractors, and throw in a simple suture. He never went back to find his drum, and no one in the Irish Brigade complained.

"Steward?"

Startled, he looked down at his patient. "Sorry, I was doing some rare remembering." He patted the man. "Can you rest now?"

The private obediently did as he was bid. Colm looked back to see Lysander Locke's eyes on him, maybe with admiration in them. With a sigh borne of too little sleep and more recollection than he wanted, Colm again sat beside the actor's bed. To his chagrin, Lysander Locke had not lost the thread of their whispered conversation.

"Well done, Callahan. Do I gather that you have never received a letter either?"

"You gather right, except for memos from the Medical Department." Colm started to say something else equally inane, but he sniffed the air instead. Good Gadfreys, was that sausage? He couldn't imagine anything less suitable for a low diet, but since Captain Dilworth was not there to enforce the prescribed nutrition for sick men, he, Colm Callahan, was not about to quibble.

"I think I'll check on breakfast," he said to the ward at large. He rose, but Lysander took his hand and tugged it.

"I think you should surprise her with a letter." He gave Colm a calculating look. "Even a shy man can write a letter."

Colm smiled at his patient—Mary and Joseph, but Locke was nosy—and sauntered down the hall to the kitchen.

With the same concentration that he devoted to medical matters, Ozzie was subduing a rank of fat sausages.

"Where in the world did you find those?" he asked by way of greeting.

She pointed to the ice chest. "You should inventory *that* sometime."

She wore a different dress, and had tried to curb the exuberance of her hair, tying back the mass of curls with a bit of elastic midway up the back of her head. The effect, while disorderly, struck him as charming. He cleared his throat, and screwed up his courage—a different kind of courage than what he had shown on the nighttime field at Fredericksburg, or the Gettysburg aid station.

"I owe you a thousand thanks," he said.

She turned around with a smile. "You need me," she said simply, then immediately returned her attention to the sausage, which made him suspect she was shy too.

Perhaps putting trust where she should not, Audra handed Colm the long fork and told him to keep turning the sausage. Meanwhile, she prepared oatmeal and stirred it, standing close to him because it wasn't a large kitchen range.

Audra stopped. Her face was warm, surely from the steam spiraling off the porridge. She took a step away from Colm Callahan, who stared with fierce concentration at the sausages.

When the porridge was subdued into the occasional glop glop, Audra set it at the back of the range and found some brown paper so Colm could spear out the sausages to drain them.

"You sleep all right?" he asked.

"Never better. Except . . ."

"It's a lumpy bed," he said, apologizing for his mattress.

"It's not that. The lumps are in the right places." She transferred the porridge to individual bowls and sugared it well, wondering why she couldn't leave well enough alone and say nothing more.

But he was looking at her, curious and interested. "Colm, I mean Suh, why does your house smell of camphor? It's all over your pillow."

She put her hands to her face, amazed she had mentioned something as intimate as a man's pillow. *You are merely curious*, she reminded herself. "I . . . I sniffed it on you yesterday, Suh."

The range must have been hotter than she thought, because Colm was red faced too. At least that much color would never show on *her* face.

He chuckled then, apparently deciding not to be embarrassed. "It's this, Audra: I know it's silly after all these years, but the smell of blood makes me queasy. When the bugle summoned me to the ambulance yesterday, I didn't know what I would find, so I dabbed camphor on my upper lip. I can't smell anything else with camphor there. D'ye mind?"

She shook her head. "I just wondered why." She opened her mouth and closed it, wondering why she was turning so nosy.

"Go ahead," he said.

"You called me Audra." There, she said it. Audra waited to feel nervous or embarrassed, but she did not. Maybe she could tell this man anything.

He gave her the kindest expression, even though his face flamed now. "Blame Lysander Locke." The lilt to his voice was more pronounced, as though he was conscious of every word he spoke to her. "What did he do but tell me all about you this morning, how . . . how you were beaten when you told that little girl your name was Audra and not Ozzie."

"I've never told anyone before," she murmured, wondering what it was about the actor that drew out her secrets. Maybe it had been the late hour. "No one wants to hear such things."

He continued to look at her, measuring her in some way. "It's no shame," he said finally.

To her amazement, he turned around and pulled his woolen shirt out of his trousers and lifted it high enough to show wicked-looking scars on his back. "I was not the most obedient orphan at Saint Agnes," he said as he tucked his shirt in again. "You're not the only one, Audra. Why us?"

Shocked, she willed herself to calm, with no idea how to reply. There was no need to say anything. Mumbling something about checking on the corpse in the dead house, Colm hurried from the kitchen.

Her mind in turmoil over what had just happened, Audra served breakfast silently.

Serving, always serving, she thought, distressed with herself at time a-wasting. For the first moment in her parched life, she allowed herself to think of fixing breakfast for just one man, of eating with him, and discussing this and that, as she had seen the Chambers do for years. She knew she wanted those things, but Colm had to make the move. It wasn't something women did, and certainly not maids of color.

She shook her head when Lysander requested that she visit with him and retreated to the kitchen. She banged the dishes around, blaming them for her misery. She took out her irritation on herself—over the shy hospital steward she loved, with the whole unfair universe—by sweeping the floor with impressive vigor.

"Stop it, Audra," she muttered and leaned the broom against the wall.

"Beg pardon?"

Suh stood in the doorway.

"I was talking to myself," she said, monumentally dissatisfied with herself.

"Sounded more like a rare scold," he replied with a half-smile. He cleared his throat, and the now-familiar blush rose up his neck from his uniform collar. "Audra, I'm sorry I pulled up my shirt like that. Where have my manners gone?"

Tears filled her eyes. "Maybe I needed reminding that mine was not the only hard life."

"That's not why I did it," he said, coming closer. "I wanted you to see that you and I are not so different. Neither of us had a childhood. I know you're tired, but please watch our patients. I have to embalm that poor coachman." He left, but the camphor lingered in the room.

Audra dabbed her eyes and returned to the ward, skipping Private Henry, because two of his bunkies must have sneaked away from a work detail to visit the sick and afflicted.

Private Jones lay staring at his bandaged arm, chewing on his lip. Audra sat beside his bed. "You'll have a scar, but that's all," she assured him.

"I have a sweetheart . . ."

"She'll still love you," Audra teased.

He shook his head. "Bet you never met such a coward."

"Burns are difficult." She paused, then had to ask, "Do you get many letters from her?"

He grinned, looking happy for the first time since his arrival. "Every week, without fail. In fact . . ." He glanced over at the party on Private Henry's bed. "Could one of you miscreants go to the post office to see if I have a letter?"

One of the "miscreants" gave him a friendly thumbs up, stood, and sauntered out the door. He was back in ten minutes, waving two letters. He dropped one in Private Jones' lap and handed the other to Audra, along with a folded note.

"Mrs. Chambers flagged me down and gave this to me," he said. "She had fire in her eyes."

"Oh, dear."

Audra knew the letter was from herself, but she stared at her familiar handwriting a moment, wondering why on earth she had ever thought a fictitious letter from a mother she barely remembered could make up for the real thing.

I have been living in shadows, she thought, tucking the letter in her apron pocket, determined not to look at Private Jones and his real letter.

Mrs. Chambers' familiar scrawl leaped out at her when she unfolded the note. "The Fourth is moving out in four days for Fort Assiniboine, Dakota Territory. Ozzie, we must pack! Only this day and night at the hospital!! That is all!!!"

"No," she said out loud. "I can't go. I *won't* go."

Embarrassed, she looked around. Private Jones was deep in his letter, and someone in Private Henry's traveling circus had broken out a deck of cards. His face placid, his eyes kind, Lysander Locke watched her. She was on her feet even before he gestured to her. She sat down and handed him the note.

He read it and handed it back. "Regiments move around all the time, Miss Washington."

"Yes, but—"

"You'll make new friends there." He folded his hands on his belly. "I always do when I travel from theatre to theatre."

"But I don't want to leave."

"Put away the cards, lads, or I'll put you on report. Faith, now, who's leaving?"

She couldn't help her tears at Colm's familiar voice. Quiet on his feet, his eyes exhausted, he stood by Private Jones' bed, rolling down his sleeves.

"I'm leaving," she said, handing him the note as she leaped up and ran into the hall. She looked around. There was nowhere for her to go. Colm had to sleep, and she had promised to stay. She hurried up the stairs and sat down on the top tread. For years she had worked and moved with no complaints, but now it was too much. She put her head on her knees, wishing to be somewhere else, but desperately wanting to stay right here at Fort Laramie.

Why had she ever offered to help Colm Callahan? All she had done was discover just how much she loved him and how impossible that was. The man was shy, and she was a woman of color. She shivered against the knowledge that nothing would ever change in her life. Was this freedom?

"It's too much, isn't it?"

She looked down the stairs to see Colm looking up.

"I'm just tired," she told him. That was no lie. She would never tell him how she had tossed about last night, teased by the odor of camphor, wondering how long it was possible to love a person before he could be decently forgotten.

There now, Audra, he has enough to do without worrying about you, she scolded herself. *Brace up.* When she thought she could, she stood up. Colm was so tired, he looked like he was swaying on his feet. He didn't need her drama. It was time to give her greatest performance.

"You're the one who has had too much to bear," she said, keeping her tone light. "It's your turn to sleep, or . . . or . . ." She laughed and nearly convinced herself. "Or you'll end up in the dead house."

"It won't come to that, but I could use a nap," he admitted, even though the worried look didn't leave his face.

"A nap of about five hours," she insisted.

"All right, all right."

Silent, she walked down the hall with him as he reeled off instructions.

Check: the sergeant of the guard was sending a wagon to take the coffined stagecoach driver to the fort cemetery. "We haven't heard from the Shy-Dead office yet, so we'll bury him on the end, where they can retrieve him, if need be."

Check: Private Henry was released to ride in the same wagon and park his bones back in the barracks. "I'll check him tonight. He's with the Fourth, so he'll be packing soon too."

Check: He would take a good look at Private Jones' forearm, decide whether to debride the burn, then send him on his way rejoicing tomorrow.

Check: After that, Lysander Locke would be their only patient, and little trouble. Just this night, and he'd release Audra to the Chambers again. "If the hospital matron still isn't spry, I can get one of the barracks cooks to send us what little Mr. Locke and I will need."

Check: Captain Dilworth would be back in two days, according to the telegram remembered at last by one of Private Henry's partygoers. "If I were a wagering man, I'd bet that nothing at all will happen after he returns."

Then he ran out of steam. "I've got to sleep, Audra."

"No lunch?"

"Later." A wave of his hand and a click, and the door to Captain Dilworth's office closed.

Working silently, her jaw clenched against tears, Audra made vegetable soup and sandwiches from leftover sausage for the patients, and for Private Henry's friends, too. Lunch was followed in short order by the arrival of the sergeant of the guard and his minions. The coffin left the dead house, taking Private Henry, too, perched on the coffin with a pair of crutches and looking more cheerful than when he'd arrived a day ago. He even blew her a kiss, which demanded a smile, however forced.

Private Jones slept the sleep of the blissfully content, letter in hand, so Audra could not ignore Lysander Locke anymore. She sat beside him at last, content at least to rest her feet.

When she thought she could look at him, she gave her attention to the actor, wanting to hate him, because he had told Colm Callahan what she had said. She had bared her soul to an actor, of all people, telling him her real name, of the letters from her mother, of her dreams about a clothing shop in Cheyenne.

But she was too generous of heart to be angry with the old busybody. All she saw when she looked at him was a shabby man down on his luck, heading to what couldn't be a good venue for Shakespeare in Deadwood. He was at the end of his career, and it didn't look sanguine. She realized with a tug at her heart that she was looking at herself in thirty years, and probably Colm Callahan, too. Alone.

"Mr. Locke, why have you never married?" she asked.

"It's the man who does the asking, so you have the advantage. Was there never a pretty actress?"

"Plenty of those," he said, reminiscence in his eyes. "My dear, I gave all for the theatre, and the theatre is a jealous mistress."

"Suh, will you be lonely later?"

He looked her in the eyes. "No lonelier than you, Miss Audra Washington."

They sat together through the afternoon, Audra knitting a pair of socks for the actor because she feared he had no others. Her dusty heart began to heal a bit as, using different voices, he read *A Midsummer Night's Dream* to her and Private Jones. It was a lovely performance, something from Fort Laramie to treasure in her heart. She wondered how much longer the Grand Old Dame near the junction of the Platte and the Laramie would be around, because the frontier was closing. Everything was changing, and she was helpless before circumstance. She even tucked away the dream of her own dress shop in Cheyenne, because she was too tired to make any more effort.

She prepared more flapjacks and eggs for supper and was finishing the dishes when she heard the door to Captain Dilworth's office open. She thought Colm might come into the kitchen, but she heard his footsteps on the stairs. When he came down, he looked in the kitchen.

"I saved some for you."

"You are a peach, Audra," he told her. "I'll eat after I give these crutches to our actor to practice with. I can't do anything else for him, and there is a stage leaving for Deadwood tomorrow morning."

"I'm worried about him," she said. *And about me. Oh, yes, me,* she wanted to add.

"I needn't do any more for him here. He's ready to go." He brightened up. "And now, my dear Miss Washington, you have earned a good night's rest."

Colm did not see Audra in the morning. Still complaining loudly, the hospital matron puffed her way up the hill and reestablished ownership of the kitchen. Private Jones had been a total stoic as Colm tweezed away bits of burned skin, dabbed saline solution, and wrapped the burn in damp gauze. He knew his handiwork was equal to or better than anything Captain Dilworth could do. From a determined drummer boy in a burning aid station at Gettysburg to a competent hospital steward had been the education of nearly twenty years. He knew he could pass the state medical examination in Wyoming Territory, and he liked the high plains.

It's time, he thought. *No more reenlistments.* Mine company doctor, Indian agency doctor, railroad doctor, small-town doctor—he could choose.

After Sick Call, Colm sent Private Jones on his way, aided by the other baker's assistant and bolstered by Colm's promise to visit twice a day to change his dressing.

Quietly competent in all things, he arranged for a horse and buggy to take Lysander Locke, Shakespeare tragedian of Drury Lane, Broadway, Denver, and Deadwood to the Rustic Hotel down on the flats. He needed no urging to accompany the old toot.

They hadn't long to wait. They sat together in companionable silence, both of them with their faces raised to the morning sun. Soon August would become September, and all bets would be off as winter peered around the corner. By cold weather, the Fourth would be shivering in drafty barracks at Fort Assiniboine.

Maybe I'll set up practice in Green River, Colm thought. *It's an ugly town, but even ugly towns need physicians.*

He glanced at Lysander Locke, worried for him. "I owe you such a debt," he said, as the Shy-Dead stage came into view. "Could I . . . could I loan you some money? I'm worried that Deadwood won't—"

"Stuff and nonsense," Lysander Locke interrupted. "Actors always land on their feet." He chuckled as he looked down at his plaster cast, new that morning and whittled down to walking size. "Shake my hand, boy, and do what you promised."

Colm took his time writing the perfect letter to Audra Washington. Maybe there was enough of the Irish rascal inherited from his scamp of a father to make it easy to declare himself to the loveliest, best woman he knew. He hadn't enough courage to ask her in person, but he couldn't be the first man in the universe who ever proposed via the U.S. mail.

The hospital was blissfully empty, tidied just so, with every bed sheet squared away, pillowcases creaseless, and floors swept. After the matron left, he bathed in the fort's only actual bathing room, soaking and thinking. That night, he slept like a virtuous man in his lumpy bed.

In the morning, he put on his best uniform and left a note on Captain Dilworth's desk, informing him that he was not planning to reenlist in September. He had done his duty well enough.

He ambled down to the Rustic Hotel, thinking that Captain and Mrs. Dilworth might like some help with their luggage. They did. He smiled to see that Mrs. Dilworth had two hatboxes she hadn't left with, and she wore a smart new traveling coat.

They hitched a ride with the mail cart, which let them off in front of the surgeon's quarters.

"I suppose the Fourth is packed and ready," Captain Dilworth said.

"Leaving tomorrow, sir."

Since he had been so helpful, Captain Dilworth invited Colm inside. Over malt whiskey that made Mrs. Dilworth frown, Colm described his patients, saving the best for last.

"We even had an old, run-down actor on his way to

Deadwood. Broke a leg, but we didn't shoot him." Funny how malt whiskey loosened his tongue.

"Name of . . .?" the post surgeon prompted.

"Lysander Locke, Shakespeare tragedian," Colm declared, striking a little pose.

Captain Dilworth gaped at him. "Holy Hannah, you're joking."

"Who would joke about someone named Lysander Locke?"

Captain Dilworth started to laugh. He leaned back and howled at the ceiling while Colm stared at him, suddenly sober.

"Rundown old actor?" Dilworth said when he could speak. "*The* Lysander Locke?"

"Aye, captain," Colm said, smelling a rat.

"To Deadwood, you say? That I can understand."

Colm just stared.

The captain must have decided that his hospital steward needed some enlightenment. "Lysander and Abigail Locke and their two sons own the best theatre in San Francisco."

"But he's alone and nearly destitute!"

"Hardly. He's a rich man with a talented family! They have performed before Queen Victoria, I hear, and a president or two."

"But he was shabby and going to Deadwood," Colm insisted.

The captain leaned forward and whispered, so any road agents within forty miles wouldn't hear him. "He owns a gold mine there called The Merchant of Venice. He was probably just checking on his business interests. Apparently he is eccentric that way."

"How in the world do you know all this?" Colm burst out.

"Mrs. Dilworth reads all the gossip in *Frank Leslie's Illustrated Weekly*."

Colm wasn't a man to surrender without a fight. "He told us—Audra Washington and me—that he had no family, and he led us to think that he was one step from ruin."

"Callahan, he's an actor," Captain Dilworth said, his eyes lively.

Colm sat back as understanding washed over him. *And he has convinced me to be brave and propose to the woman I love*, he thought. *He preyed on my sympathy until I knew I didn't want to be a lonely man like him. The old rip! He probably did the same thing with Audra.*

He had one more question. "Do you know . . . Is he really English?"

"Ames, Iowa."

Colm stood. "I've been fair diddled," he said with a smile. "Excuse me, sir, but I have a letter to deliver."

It was only a few steps down Officers Row to the sutler's store and adjoining post office. The sun was warm, and it was a good day to whistle, which caused a head or two to turn. He took a deep breath when he looked in the store and saw Audra standing there with a letter in hand.

God is good, he thought to himself.

He waited until she walked the few feet into the adjoining post office, a closet-sized box with an iron railing. He cleared his throat, and she turned around.

Wordless, terrified, he held out his letter, the one with all the love in his heart on two close-written pages. She took it as she handed him a letter.

This wouldn't do. He looked at the sutler, who watched them with some interest.

"Mr. London, is the enlisted canteen open yet?"

"Too early, Steward," he said with a smile.

"Could you . . . could you let me have the key? We'll only be a few minutes."

Mr. London handed it over. Colm took Audra by the arm, but that suddenly wasn't close enough. He put his hand on her waist, and with a sigh, she sort of melted into his side. Mr. London's back was turned, so he kissed her cheek.

The canteen was dark and cool, smelling of stale beer, trapped smoke, and spittoons that needed attention. It was no place to propose, but that was army life. Silent, he sat them both down. Her breath came a little fast, but he didn't think she would hyperventilate. If she did, he could find a paper bag for her to breathe in.

Her fingers shook, but she took out his letter and spread it on her lap. He took out her letter and did the same. He read quickly and let out a deep breath. Maybe it was worth a lifetime's famine to read "beloved" and know he was the one beloved. His clinical mind almost suggested to him that "adore" was over the top, but for once, his heart overruled his brain.

She finished first. "Yes, Suh," was all she said, but it said the earth, moon, planets and a galaxy or two.

No expert, he kissed Audra Washington. She kissed back, no expert either. They were both in good health; they had years to improve.

In the cool of the enlisted men's canteen, he told her of his plans to take the medical boards in the fall, and to find a little town that needed him in a territory with nothing but little towns. "I've saved for years. I can set up an office."

"I've saved too. We can have a house with running water."

She was on his lap then, both arms around him, head pressed to his chest, where his heart was doing things that, in a big city, would have landed him in a cardiac ward.

"I wish . . . I wish we could tell that dear old man. Would you mind . . . If Deadwood doesn't work out for Mr. Locke, we could find a place for him with us, couldn't we?"

"Certainly."

Lysander Locke could wait. Colm Callahan wanted to kiss Audra Washington a few more times before Mr. London got curious. Maybe they could honeymoon in Deadwood. Colm did like to check up on his discharged patients.

ABOUT CARLA KELLY

What to say about Carla? The old girl's been in the writing game for mumble-mumble years. She started out with short stories that got longer and longer until—poof!—one of them turned into a novel. (It wasn't quite that simple.) She still enjoys writing short stories, one of which is before you now. Carla writes for Harlequin Historical, Camel Press, and Cedar Fort. Her books are found in at least 14 languages.

Along the way, Carla's books and stories have earned a couple of Spur Awards from Western Writers of America for Short Fiction, a couple of Rita Awards from Romance Writers of America for Best Regency, and a couple of Whitney Awards. Carla lives in Idaho Falls, Idaho, and continues to write, because her gig is historical fiction, and that never gets old.

Visit Carla's website: CarlaKellyAuthor.com

THE SOLDIER'S HEART

by Sarah M. Eden

Other Works by Sarah M. Eden

Seeking Persephone

Courting Miss Lancaster

The Kiss of a Stranger

Friends and Foes

An Unlikely Match

Drops of Gold

Glimmer of Hope

As You Are

Longing for Home

Hope Springs

For Elise

ONE

Nebraska Territory—June 1865

How does a man go about introducing himself to the woman of his dreams without making the situation excruciatingly awkward? Gregory Reeves had pondered that question across five states. As near as he could tell, the feat was impossible.

He'd begun tackling the problem by rehearsing a direct approach. "Good day, Miss Bowen. I am Gregory Reeves, and I am relatively sure I am in love with you." Somehow that was both awkward and unintentionally insulting.

He'd practiced a more subtle approach as well. "I am Gregory Reeves, and I know you rather well, though we have never met." That had far too ominous a ring to it.

"Your late brother was a friend of mine who read me your letters. I grew quite fond of you and have now come to fulfill a promise I made to him before he died. Also, I've come to care for you deeply." That speech had the benefit of being truthful with the enormous drawback of dredging up her very personal loss, his nosiness at having read her letters, and the decidedly uncomfortable revelation that he'd fallen in love with her without having ever met her.

He stood on a dirt path running past the humble farm he'd been told belonged to the Bowen family, feeling like a complete fool. He'd had a month to sort out what he meant to say but still didn't know. Yet he couldn't simply turn around and leave.

"Gregory, I need you to promise me," Josiah Bowen had said the night before the Battle of Antietam, "that if I don't live to see the end of this war and you do, that you'll look in on Ma and Helene. They're on their own, you know. I'm afraid for them."

Josiah had very nearly survived. Only one more month, and he would have been on his way home to his family. Instead, Gregory stood on the road in his place.

"I could always tell her the bit about her brother and the promise I made without admitting to all the rest."

He'd taken to talking with himself during the arduous journey to Nebraska. There'd been no one else to keep company with. He'd actually found himself to be decent company, which made him suspect he'd spent too much time alone.

Gregory brushed at the dust covering his Union uniform. He wished he'd had the time or money to purchase some new clothes. He looked as tired and raggedy as he felt, and that likely wouldn't do his cause a bit of good. He was a stranger to these people, and he was showing up at their door looking like a vagabond. They might simply bolt the door and pretend they'd never seen him.

Putting off the inevitable was the coward's way out. Gregory was a lot of things, not all of them positive, but he was no coward. He marched up to the porch and rapped soundly on the door. As he waited, he took a moment to look things over. The house didn't appear neglected, but it clearly could use a bit of work. The porch posts needed sanding. A few of the floorboards appeared loose. The whole place needed a fresh coat of paint. Gregory could see to all of that, though without money in his pocket, he'd have to find creative ways to pay for the improvements.

He raised his fist to knock again but stopped with his hand midair when the door pulled open. The sight that met him drained the air from his lungs—a woman stood, watching him. Her golden hair sat in a soft bun at the nape of her neck. Her light-blue eyes shone with intelligence. She had Josiah's fair coloring and assessing air, with an undeniable femininity. For a moment, he forgot how shabby he looked and simply stared. This was Helene, the woman whose letters had captured his heart.

"Well, now, it's past time for you to have shown up," Helene declared firmly.

"It is?" Gregory could hardly have been more confused. He hadn't sent word ahead. She couldn't possibly have been expecting him.

"Come on, then." She stepped through the door and out onto the porch. "I'll show you where to get started."

"Where to get started?" He watched her continue past him and down to the ground out front. She was even more beautiful than he'd imagined over the past two years. Coming face to face with her tied his tongue hopelessly.

She looked back, a bit of impatience in her expression. "There's plenty to be done, and you're late."

Gregory couldn't manage any words. Something in the firmness of her tone and the unyielding nature of her posture had him simply following after her.

"The ladder is just inside the barn," Helene said, motioning toward that very building. "The gutters need cleaning out. When you've finished with that, several of the eaves have come loose and need to be nailed back in place. You'll find a hammer and a bag of nails in the barn as well."

He was happy to help, but he couldn't at all make sense of the situation. She seemed to have been anticipating his arrival, which wasn't at all possible. Only Josiah would have guessed at his destination, but neither of them had discussed the agreement since that long-ago battle. Gregory doubted Josiah had mentioned it to his family.

"That ought to keep you busy for the remainder of the day," Helene said. "I'll call you in when it's time for dinner."

"I think there's been a mistake, Miss—"

"The only mistake I am worried about is hiring you to do work around here, as you don't seem inclined to get at it." She held his gaze without a hint of uncertainty. She was clearly no wilting flower in need of rescuing. "Must I find someone else?"

He shook his head mutely. He didn't at all want to be sent off when he'd only just arrived.

"What's your name?" she asked.

Somehow his name emerged almost as a question. "Gregory." She'd thrown him so entirely for a loop, he couldn't quite piece words together.

She gave a quick nod. "Do your work quickly and well, and you'll have plenty of time to settle in after dinner before it grows dark."

"Yes'm."

Helene's determination, combined with his own fumbling feelings, rendered him rather useless. He really ought to explain who he was and why he'd come, but his heart was pounding too hard in his mind for any thoughts to form. He'd kept his wits through some of the worst battles of the Civil War but had fallen apart under the assessing gaze of Helene Bowen.

She turned toward the house but didn't take more than a few steps before stopping and looking at him once more. Though her shoulders remained squared and her expression stayed every bit as firm, something in her eyes had softened.

"I can see by your uniform that you served during our long years of war."

"I did, ma'am," he answered.

"I know this job won't pay anything beyond a place in the barn and food to eat, and I'm sorry for that," she said. "Those who fought to keep our Union strong deserve better than that, and I hope you'll find it."

In that moment, he realized two things. She had mistaken him for a hired hand she'd apparently arranged for, and, beneath her demanding exterior, Helene was every bit as good as he'd believed her to be.

As it so often did, embarrassment paralyzed his mouth. Only a nod emerged in response to her kind words. She gave him a quick, small smile, sending his heart soaring.

Quick as that, she returned to the house, and he was left standing in the yard, trying to decide what to do. He couldn't simply leave. He'd not yet fulfilled his promise to Josiah. More compelling still, he wasn't ready to give up on his goal of getting to know Helene better.

He'd vowed to help the Bowens, so he'd do just that, starting with the gutters and eaves. Then he'd find out what else needed doing and do it. Should the man originally hired come around, Gregory would simply send him off. If Helene needed a hand around the place, he'd offer his own. And somehow along the way, he'd find the means of making a good impression on the woman who'd long since found her way into his heart.

TWO

Helene pushed the kitchen door closed and stood there a moment, attempting to catch her breath. The man whom her neighbor's aunt's neighbor had recommended had been described as a hard worker and a trustworthy one, a man she needn't feel nervous to have about the place. She'd known little else about him.

This Gregory was tall. His shoulders filled out his uniform. Though his thick, unkempt whiskers and dirty, heavily worn clothes gave him the look of a drifter, his eyes were sharp with unmistakable intelligence, and his posture was anything but threatening. And, yet, there was something about him that made her just a bit jumpy, though not in a fearful way.

She looked out the curtained window, eying Gregory as he stepped from the barn with the ladder under his arm. He'd set straight to his chores, which was a good sign. He might not have looked the way she'd expected, but he was doing the work. By the look of his uniform, he'd seen a great deal of battle. Josiah's clothes had likely been just as stained and ragged. Helene's heart dropped at the thought of her dear brother. She hoped his passing had been quick, that he'd not suffered long.

But it wasn't *her* sadness over Josiah that still had her worried most, but her mother's. Helene pulled the curtains closed, then moved from room to room, doing the same in each. After two months of supporting her mother against the weight of grief and loss, she didn't dare risk the sight of an army uniform sending Mother right back to the pit of despair.

"Who's that man behind the house, Miss Helene?" Bianca asked as she stepped into the kitchen. The girl fiddled with the ribbon tied in a bow on the end of her long braid. "I've never seen him before."

"His name is Gregory, and he's been hired on to do a bit of work."

Bianca was apparently satisfied with that answer. She climbed onto the stool at the counter and began peeling carrots. In the six months since Bianca and her brother Liam had come to live with them after the death of their parents, both children had done any work asked of them without complaint. Helene was grateful for that. It was no secret that she and Mother had taken the orphans in because the house was in need of some extra hands. She despised how heartless it sounded, but she couldn't deny the truth of the reasoning. Had the children resented the motivation behind their acceptance, her guilt would have grown tenfold.

"Is Liam still pulling weeds in the garden?" she asked Bianca.

"Yes, Miss Helene. And once he's done, he'll bring in the string beans from the cellar like you asked."

She watched Bianca work, wondering for perhaps the hundredth time if there was something she might do to help the children feel a little more at home. Their parents had died only a half year earlier, and grief still hung heavy in the children's eyes. She didn't mean to replace their family by any means, but neither did she want them to feel like mere guests or, worse yet, hired hands.

Pounding echoed from outside the house, no doubt Gregory beginning the repairs.

Bianca paused in her peeling. "What's Mr. Gregory doing out there?"

"Cleaning gutters and securing the loose eaves." Helene dropped the sliced carrots into the pot of simmering broth, then fetched a few potatoes and set to peeling them. "Tomorrow we'll find something else for him to do."

"He's coming back?"

Helene nodded. "We've hired him on for the rest of the summer."

"I didn't see him 'cept at a fair distance," Bianca said. "Is he handsome?"

Helene gave the question a moment's thought. "I couldn't really tell, honestly. He has such thick whiskers . . ."

"And such thick dirt," Bianca added with a dimpled grin.

"Exactly. Perhaps underneath all of that, he is quite devastatingly handsome."

Bianca sighed. "Wouldn't that be quite the thing? A handsome prince in disguise."

Helene remembered all too well the tendency she'd had at Bianca's age to dream of such things. She was grateful Bianca had retained that innocence despite the difficulties she'd already endured in her life. "Mr. Gregory may very well be handsome, but I am almost certain he isn't a prince."

"No. He's a soldier." Bianca's brow pulled in thought. "I hope Mrs. Bowen don't see his uniform. Soldiers always make her cry."

"Let us hold our breath and cross our fingers and pray a bit that Mrs. Bowen doesn't peek outside." Helene had been doing all three ever since opening the front door and finding a soldier standing there.

"I don't want her to be sad," Bianca said. "She is always so kind to me."

Helene gave the girl a grateful smile, having learned early on that Bianca didn't care to be hugged.

Liam came in the back door. "There's a man pounding nails into the eaves," he announced as he set a small basket of string beans on the counter near Helene.

"He's Mr. Gregory," Bianca said. "He's been hired on to do chores around here."

Liam turned accusatory eyes on Helene. "I done the chores you asked me, and I can do more, too. You needn't pay someone to do work; you've got me."

"And I am infinitely grateful for both you and Bianca," Helene assured him. "You are already working very hard and doing so very much. And I will need your help, along with his, in the fields as harvest grows nearer. Having a hired man is in no way a sign that I don't think you capable, only that this farm is larger than you and I can work on our own."

Liam's pride still appeared to be a bit wounded. Helene didn't know how to convince him that his tireless labor over the past six months was enough.

"I've not given any of your chores to Mr. Gregory," Helene said, "as I know you'll see to them. He's taking on the odd handful of things neither you nor I are responsible for but that need doing."

Liam nodded and looked at least somewhat appeased. "He's a soldier, you know. Mrs. Bowen won't like that."

Helene stirred the simmering soup. "I'll ask him to wear something other than his uniform tomorrow. With any luck, Mrs. Bowen won't spot him today."

Liam returned to his chores shortly after that. Bianca remained in the kitchen helping Helene with dinner preparations. Bianca had been quiet and withdrawn when she'd first come to live with them, but she'd since grown more comfortable. She was a regular chatterbox now.

The remainder of the late afternoon passed against a backdrop of pounding nails. Helene looked out the windows now and then, and never once saw Gregory lazing about.

Not long before dinner time, Mother descended the stairs. "Liam has been nonstop at whatever he's pounding on out there." She rubbed at her temples as she spoke.

Helene regretted her mother's headache but breathed a sigh of relief at the knowledge that she hadn't peeked outside and seen the soldier working on the house.

"The work will be done in but a moment," she promised her mother. "And most of it is being done at the back of the house. The front parlor will be relatively quiet."

Mother nodded and moved in that direction.

"Go see if you can lift her spirits a bit," Helene said to Bianca. "She looks a bit frazzled."

Bianca hopped off the stool in front of the sink and dried her hands on a rag. "And I won't tell her the man's a soldier," she promised.

"Thank you, sweetie."

Mother was exceptionally fond of Bianca, and the dear girl rather idolized Mother. Helene needn't worry about either one when they were in each other's company. She slipped out the back door to the porch, looking around for Gregory. He was not far off, standing atop the ladder, sweeping out a gutter.

"Mr. Gregory," she called out.

He came down the rungs as she approached. "Just 'Gregory' will be fine, Miss Bowen," he said.

She nodded her agreement. "Dinner is ready. I'll dish some out for you while you put the ladder and such away."

He hesitated. "I haven't finished all the work you gave me. Not for lack of trying, I promise you. There were a great many more loose eaves than you likely realized."

She waved off his apologetic declaration. "I know you worked hard. You can pick up where you left off tomorrow."

"Yes'm."

Somehow the humble tone of a servant didn't at all fit him, but neither did it sound feigned. Had he once enjoyed greater status than he currently claimed? The war had been unkind to so very many.

She met his gaze and was struck by how very fine his eyes were. Beyond that, there was a sincerity in them that put her instantly at ease, something she was not at all accustomed to. Living alone, other than for her mother, had taught her to treat strangers with wariness and to watch closely for any signs they weren't trustworthy. But Gregory gave her no such worries.

"I hope this request won't sound too presumptuous." She pulled her shawl more closely around her shoulders, trying to block the fierce wind.

"You won't know if you don't ask." The response was both teasing and entirely sincere.

"I wondered if you might be willing to not wear your uniform tomorrow."

He looked surprised but not offended. What a relief to know he didn't immediately assume the worst. "It's all the clothing I have."

"Well, that does leave us with something of a predicament. You see, my brother fought for the Union, and he did not survive the war." She made the explanation quickly, not entirely trusting the steadiness of her emotions connected to Josiah's death. "My mother's grief is still very raw, and I worry that her seeing your uniform would be a painful reminder for her."

Even beneath his thick whiskers and dirt, she could see empathy pulling at his features. "If I am making difficulties for you, I will understand. If you'd rather I go—"

"Oh, no. Not at all." She set her hand on his arm, intending to add emphasis to her words. But the connection set her heart to a quick staccato rhythm. She snatched her hand back, confused at the unexpected frisson of awareness. After all, she didn't even know this man.

"Then I'll try to think of a way to not upset your mother with my appearance," Gregory said. "And I'll put these things away as you requested, as well as thank you for the meal."

She smiled a bit. "Perhaps you ought to hold off thanking me until you've tasted it. You may consider yourself ill paid for your labor."

"I am quite certain that will not be the case."

For a man in such a state of dinginess, who lived from one odd job to the next, he spoke with a decidedly educated accent.

He pulled down the ladder and carried it toward the barn. Helene remained on the porch, watching him go. Everything about his appearance and situation ought to have inspired at least a little wariness. Why was it, then, that she felt pulled to him instead? There was something almost familiar about him. He'd not indicated that he knew her, and she was certain she didn't know him.

The question spun about in her mind as she dished out a bowl of soup and spread a layer of butter on two thick slices of bread. It was not a fancy meal, but it would be filling for him. She stepped back through the door to bring it to him just as he stepped onto the porch.

She held the soup bowl and plate of bread out to him. "I would normally invite you to take your meal in the kitchen, but I've not yet worked out how to appease my mother's emotions should she catch sight of you."

He nodded his understanding. "I am sorry I don't have anything else to wear. I truly do not wish to cause you or your mother any distress."

As quick as a flash of lightning, Helene had an idea. "Wait here a moment," she said and spun about, moving swiftly back into the house. She hurried up the stairs and to the trapdoor in the attic floor, then opened it and climbed the ladder that led up. She swatted at the swirls of dust twisting in the air all around her and crossed to a small trunk pushed into the corner.

The hinges protested as she lifted the lid. She'd bought the trunk and all of its contents at a rail station three years earlier. It had been abandoned, and the station manager had been happy to be rid of it for a pittance. She'd hoped the odds and ends would be useful as scrap fabric or for making a quilt. Fortunately, she and her mother had not yet cut down the man's shirt and pair of men's trousers inside.

She pulled them out, flicking them unfolded. A quick survey told her they'd likely be a bit too large for Gregory. But too big was far preferable to too small. They were nothing fine or fashionable, but she felt absolutely certain he would appreciate them just the same.

Helene tucked the garments under her arm and closed the lid of the trunk once more. She had the attic shut up in no time and quickly made her way toward the stairs. She stopped in the hallway and pulled open the linen closet. She took a towel and washcloth from the shelves, then bent low to pull a cake of soap from the small bucket of them kept in the corner.

Her hands and arms full, Helene returned to the back porch. Gregory didn't see her when she first arrived, too intent as he was on eating his soup and bread. Her heart ached at the obvious hunger in his posture. How long had he gone without a true meal?

"I have a few things," she said, stepping over to where he sat on the back step.

His eyes met hers, then dropped to the various bundles she carried.

"Please do not take this amiss, but I've brought you some soap." She sat on the step. "I thought you could use a bath."

Far from being offended, he laughed, and the sound was deep and rumbling. She couldn't stop herself from grinning. He had a wonderful, joyous laugh.

"I am not at all offended," he said, his tone light and amused. "Believe me, I am well aware of how bad I smell."

She set the soap, towel and cloth on the porch, then laid the clothes across her lap. "These are some old clothes we happen to have inherited. I am positive they will be too large for you, but it *is* a change of clothes, and that must be a welcome thing."

"I haven't worked enough to have earned a change of clothes," he protested.

"Then consider them a loan," she said, though she fully intended to find a way of making him keep them.

"You would do all of this for a stranger?" It was not shock or accusation that colored his words, but an unmistakable, tender degree of approval.

She could feel her cheeks heat. Fair skin never was good at keeping secrets. Unable to account for the feelings this particular stranger inspired in her, she covered the confusion with a lighthearted reply. "I am doing it for myself, if you must know. These items mean I no longer have to endure the smell of you nor the sight of your raggedy attire."

He laughed again, just as she'd hoped he would. "I am happy to oblige. When next you see me, you'll hardly recognize me, I'll be so clean."

"I look forward to not recognizing you."

Gregory finished his bowl of soup, sighing contentedly. "I don't think I worked hard enough to deserve such a good meal, Miss Helene, but I assure you, I'll work that much harder tomorrow."

"Don't think I'll go easy on you simply because you told me a sob story about not having even a change of clothes. I mean to work you hard this summer. You'll be so tired of laboring in the fields that you'll be begging for another line of work."

"I look forward to begging," he said, echoing her earlier quip.

She watched him walk back to the barn. Something about him had awakened in her a sense of longing, as though she'd known him before and had lost him, only to have him return to her again. He intended to spend the evening cleaning himself up. She intended to spend as much of the night as possible straightening out her own jumbled feelings.

THREE

You should have told her who you really are.

He'd had a few opportunities. She'd sat beside him as he'd eaten dinner. She'd spoken with him for a time before that. But both times, his tongue had been tied. He was continually struck by how very pretty she was, which was a bit intimidating on its own. But to know who she was, to have been granted a glimpse of her character through two years' worth of letters, made the situation overwhelming.

Gregory had washed himself in the creek, even taking time to shave. He hadn't cleaned his appearance in a few weeks, so his beard had been scraggly and thick. He could use a haircut but knew his limitations too well to attempt to give himself one.

The clothes Helene had given him were a bit large, as she'd predicted. They were also a far sight cleaner than what he'd been wearing since the war ended. He transferred the suspenders from his uniform trousers to the pair he had on now, grateful he wouldn't find himself with his pants puddled about his ankles at an inopportune moment.

He carried his shaving kit, towel, soap, blanket, and folded uniform back to the dim barn. He'd slept in his share of barns over the past eight weeks, most of which had smelled far worse than this one. Helene must have worked herself to the bone day in and day out to keep up with the running of an entire farm with only her mother to help. She'd managed to keep up with the mucking and caring for the animals.

"You're Mr. Gregory?" a voice asked, which sounded like a child's.

Gregory scanned the barn but didn't spot the source. "I am," he answered. "And who might you be?"

A blond head popped up over the side of the horse stall. By the look of the boy, he was somewhere near twelve or thirteen. "I'm Liam Milner."

"Do you live near here?" If Helene had a child living out of her barn but wasn't aware of it, he intended to let her know.

"I live in the house," Liam said. "With Mrs. Bowen and Miss Helene and my sister."

"Are you kin to them?"

"My sister and I only have each other for kin, but the ladies took us in when our folks died."

Gregory didn't think Helene had written anything about that to Josiah. "How long ago was that?"

"I ain't gotta answer all your questions," the boy insisted. "How long are you staying around to work?"

"If you don't have to answer my questions, why do I have to answer yours?" Gregory set his armful on a nearby stool.

"Because I'm the man of the house around here." Liam stepped out of the stall. "I won't have you sniffin' about the place if you're a no-good, low-down snake."

The boy had gumption; he'd give him that. "In exchange for your honesty, I'll give you a straight answer. I don't know how long I'll be here helping around the place, but I'll work for as long as Miss Helene needs me to."

Liam strutted right up to Gregory, eying him with unflinching confidence. Gregory liked the boy all the better for it. An orphan with a sister to look after needed to be tough and sure of himself.

"Have you got ideas where Miss Helene is concerned?" Liam asked. "'Cause she's not the kind of woman who goes about kissing every hired hand who comes around."

"That is a good thing," Gregory answered, "because I am not the kind of hired hand who goes about kissing every woman he works for."

Liam was unimpressed with the witty turn of phrase. "I've half a mind to believe you, Mister. But don't think that means I like you being here."

"I was thinking when I came in to the barn just now that whoever looks after it does a fine job," Gregory said. "Is that you?"

Liam's chest puffed out with pride. "Miss Helene says she doesn't know what she'd do without me."

That was likely part of the reason the boy disliked Gregory's being there. "I'd wager this entire farm would fall apart without your help. You be sure to let me know if Miss Helene gives me a job to do that you feel ought to fall to you. I'm not familiar with running the place like you are."

Liam nodded. "That'd work. I can tell you what we need you to do."

He'd smoothed Liam's ruffled feathers a bit. Somehow, over the time Gregory would have in Nebraska, he needed to find a way to make his case to Helene, something that would not be nearly so easy.

FOUR

"That blasted, no good soldier." Liam slammed the kitchen door behind him.

He usually returned from his morning chores in a quiet mood. She knew she oughtn't find his irritation amusing, but she couldn't help a small smile.

"Firstly, do not slam doors," Helene said. "Secondly, you told me just last night that you had decided that Mr. Gregory wasn't such a terrible person after all. What did he do to change your mind so entirely?"

"He milked my cow!" Liam tossed himself into a chair, absolutely fuming. "I told him last night that I do a fine job with my chores. That I'm a hard worker and don't need him doing my work. And he said he believed me." Liam shook his head, lips pulled in tight. "But then he went and did my milkin' like I'm a laze-about little child. And he's gathering eggs, meaning Bianca ain't gonna have nothing to do neither."

Helene sat in the chair near him. "I would wager he simply doesn't understand that doing your chores is so important to you." She didn't entirely understand why Liam clung to that so much. "I'm certain that once he realizes as much, he'll not take over your chores again." She would insist he didn't.

As if fate meant to force the conversation, the kitchen door opened. It could be no one but Gregory. Helene steeled her resolve—he must be made to understand Liam's concerns—and looked up in the direction of the door.

It was, indeed, Gregory, but quite a different Gregory than the one who'd worked about the place the day before. He looked like an entirely different person. His clothes were clean, though ill fitting. The dirt and raggedness was gone. And he'd shaved. Heavens, without the scruffy beard, he looked years and years younger. Bianca had predicted he was a prince beneath his whiskers. Prince or not, he was shockingly handsome.

Only with effort did she tear her eyes away, her gaze settling instead on Liam. He folded his arms across his chest and refused to look in Gregory's direction. Helene had been too young when her brother was that age to know if unrelenting petulance was a normal thing for a twelve-year-old boy.

"Good morning, Miss Helene," Gregory said, setting the bucket and basket on the countertop.

Helene rose from her seat. "If you have a moment, I would like to have a word with you."

Her abrupt and stern request didn't faze him in the least. It spoke well for him. She'd known any number of men who wouldn't abide a woman confronting him with any degree of self-assurance.

"Of course, Miss Helene. Would you mind, though, if I speak briefly with Liam first?"

Her eyes darted from Gregory to Liam and back again. She sensed nothing at all threatening in Gregory's bearing. Liam even seemed the tiniest bit intrigued. And allowing

Liam to sort out his own difficulties would serve him well in the future.

"Certainly," she said and motioned for him to do so.

He turned to Liam. "I realized as you left the barn a moment ago that by milking the cow, I had inadvertently stepped on your toes. I ought to have realized that the chore was yours, or at least have asked. My presence here is meant to be helpful, not disruptive. If you have some time later this morning, I'd appreciate your letting me know which jobs are yours so I don't make the same mistake again."

Liam gave him a begrudging look of acceptance. "What about Bianca?"

"Your sister?"

Liam nodded. "She has chores too."

"As I said, I'm here to help in whatever way is welcome. I won't take over any of Bianca's work if she'd rather I didn't. And I'm certain Miss Helene has plenty of odd jobs for me to do." He looked over his shoulder in her direction with a smile equal parts camaraderie and uncertainty.

In that moment, she felt an odd sort of kinship with this man she hardly knew. Gregory's patience with Liam and his willingness to do what he could to smooth the boy's ruffled feathers spoke to his kindness.

"There is always work to be done," she told Gregory. "I'd wager you'll be sorry you offered to do it all after I put my list together."

His eyes twinkled with merriment. "I'm not afraid of hard work, Miss Helene. Never have been."

"Glad to hear it." She most certainly *was* glad—more so than she would have expected to be. Wariness had been her characteristic response to most strangers of the male variety. Oddly, almost miraculously, Gregory—Good heavens! She didn't even know his surname!—didn't inspire even a drop of worry.

She told herself she'd be quite careful. "Just wait until

the fields need constant work," she warned him amusedly. "We planted a larger crop than usual this year. You'll be quite busy."

His eyes held hers for a long moment, neither of them looking away. She'd always been rather partial to dark eyes. "Well, I'd say between Liam and me, you'll have quite a bit of help."

She smiled, both at the promise of his help and at his understanding that Liam needed the recognition. "I don't know what I would have done these past months without Liam and Bianca."

Much of the seriousness melted from Gregory's expression. "I haven't met Miss Bianca yet, or your mother. I hope to have that privilege at some point."

"You'll be joining us for dinner tonight, here in the house. You'll meet them then."

"Are you certain?" he asked. "I don't wish to be a bother."

"No bother at all," she insisted. "Now that you're not in uniform, Mother will be far less likely to fall to pieces at the sight of you."

One corner of his mouth twitched upward. "Is that your way of saying I clean up nicely?"

"That wasn't what I meant, but it's true just the same."

He chuckled, and the sound echoed around the room in waves of warmth. "I do believe that is the finest compliment I've been paid in years, Miss Helene."

As he crossed the kitchen and pulled open the door, he whistled a jaunty tune. He glanced over at Liam. "Don't forget to come find me to let me know about those chores of yours," he said, then stepped outside, pulling the door closed behind him.

Helene stood rooted to the spot, watching the now-empty doorway. If Gregory was always so pleasant in the morning, he would be a joy to have around until harvest.

"I know what that look in your eyes means," Liam said.

She shook off her distraction and turned her gaze to the boy, who was watching her from the table.

"You're goin' moony on him, ain't you?" It wasn't an accusation so much as an amused declaration.

"I've no idea what you mean." She turned quickly to the basket of eggs, intent on losing herself in making breakfast.

The sound of chair legs scraping the floor told her that Liam was on the move. "I'll find out everything I can about him then let you know if he's a blackguard or a lay-about man or anythin' like that."

"I appreciate the offer, but—"

"Don't go saying you're not sighing over Mr. Gregory. I've got eyes, haven't I?"

"I hardly know him." She set her cast-iron skillet on the stovetop. "He seems nice, I will grant him that, but there is nothing beyond that."

Liam didn't answer. After a moment, his silence pulled her eyes toward him once again. His eyes narrowed. She set a hand on one hip and dared him to contradict her.

But issuing a dare to a twelve-year-old boy is not always a wise thing to do.

"I knew it," he said firmly. "I'll let you know if he ain't worthy of you, Miss Helene."

"You are getting mighty far ahead of things, Liam."

He shook his head. "The way you two're looking at each other, I'd say I'm just in time."

FIVE

*T*he way you two are looking at each other. Helene mulled Liam's words over all through dinner that night. *You two.* Though she had no intention of confessing to a twelve-year-old boy that she was inexplicably drawn to this stranger who'd come to work for her, Helene knew it was the truth. But Liam seemed to think that Gregory was nursing a similar instant attraction.

Was that reason to feel flattered or worried?

She watched Gregory throughout the evening. He was quiet during their meal but grew more talkative in the parlor afterward; Mother had insisted he join them there. Bianca was rather in awe of him, watching his every move, hanging on his every word—a common affliction for almost-eleven-year-old girls when faced with a decidedly handsome man. But Gregory was kind to Bianca, offering praise when he learned that Bianca had prepared the string beans.

Mother discovered quickly that Gregory was from Massachusetts, which explained why he spoke so differently from the men in Nebraska who'd lived away from the East most, if not all, of their lives. Mother spent most of the evening quizzing him on the places he'd seen and the people he'd known. They had, after all, lived in Massachusetts many years themselves. They discovered no mutual acquaintances, and, to Helene's relief, neither Gregory nor Mother spoke of Josiah. Mother never held up well when speaking of her son.

Liam gave Gregory the cold shoulder, but the man didn't press for acceptance. He was an easy and unobtrusive addition to their family circle.

The same scene played out the next night and the next, continuing as the week went on. Gregory quickly became a natural and easy part of their lives. Helene grew more comfortable in his presence yet felt more anxious as well. He wasn't a threat or a danger; she knew that on an instinctive level. But he left her unsettled in a way that made her heart turn about inside her chest every time he entered a room. All she had to do was spot him at a distance through the kitchen window, and a nervous kind of excitement warmed her veins.

On his tenth evening spent at the house with the family, Gregory chose to sit directly beside her on the parlor sofa. Helene told herself not to put too much store in that, but her heart didn't entirely listen. She'd resigned herself to the knowledge that she'd fallen rather head over heels for this man she hardly knew. She was sensible enough not to entirely lose her head over him, but she was also vulnerable enough to hope he felt something for her—anything remotely resembling her own preference.

Gregory leaned closer to her and lowered his voice. "Bianca let me in on a little secret."

A secret? Helene's heart stopped. Surely Bianca hadn't made the same discovery her brother had regarding Helene's feelings for this man. "What secret is that?" she managed to whisper.

"It seems Liam is quite an accomplished musician."

Relief surged through her. She could even look at him

without feeling as though she were ready to crumble—although the realization that he sat so very close set her insides fluttering. "Liam plays the guitar," she acknowledged. "He is quite good at it."

Gregory motioned across the room with a quick twitch of his head. "I convinced him to play for us tonight."

She was impressed. "How did you manage that? He doesn't generally like to play, and I can't say that you are his favorite person."

He smiled. Oh, how that smile made her feel like giggling despite being well past the age when such a thing was even remotely acceptable. "I posed my invitation as something of a challenge," he explained. "The poor boy couldn't resist."

"That was underhanded, Gregory." She smiled through the half-hearted reprimand.

"Perhaps." He leaned lazily against the sofa back, his arm outstretched along the top. "But he's so determined to prove his worth through work that he seems to have lost the ability to enjoy himself."

Helene sighed in dismay at the truth of that statement. She'd tried so hard the past six months to help Liam feel at home, but he never seemed truly at ease. "I don't know how to convince him that he's wanted and appreciated without working himself to the bone."

"It may be that hard work is something he values in himself."

There was undeniable wisdom in that. She watched Liam as he tuned his guitar and wondered for perhaps the hundredth time if she was hindering more than helping him. She'd never been a mother but now had two children in her keeping. Her own mother had spent much of the past months too distraught to offer any insights.

Gregory's arm slipped from the back of the sofa down around her shoulders. Her heart thudded as he pulled her closer to him. "I can see that you are fretting yourself into knots over this," he whispered. "But let me tell you this: Liam speaks highly of you when it's only the two of us out working. He's far too protective of you and Mrs. Bowen to be anything but dedicated to you both."

Some of the ever-present tension in her shoulders eased at his words. She leaned a little against him. "They've lost so much in their short lives. I don't want to add to their burdens."

"You are a good woman, Helene Bowen, just as I thought you were."

A deep sigh surged through her at his compliment. She'd been more or less on her own since moving west with her mother three years earlier. Josiah had been off fighting in the war then. The uncle they'd come to Nebraska to live near had moved farther west shortly after they'd arrived. Gregory's soothing company was a balm to her lonely soul. How long she'd waited for someone to enter her life whom she could trust.

She sat beside him, with his arm about her shoulders, perfectly content for the first time in years. She couldn't predict where their connection would take them. Perhaps she'd find reason over the long growing and harvest seasons to keep him at a distance. Perhaps she would discover in him a soul mate, someone who would stay around even after his employment was over. She didn't know which it would be but chose in that moment to simply enjoy his company and hope for the best.

Liam had, apparently, finished tuning his guitar. He launched into a jaunty, fast-paced tune. Bianca tapped her feet in time to the music, smiling contentedly.

Mother stepped up to the sofa, a steaming cup in her hand. "Coffee?" She held the mug out to Gregory.

"Thank you, Mrs. Bowen." He accepted the cup with a smile. As Mother walked to her rocking chair by the mantle,

Gregory turned to Helene. "She didn't bring you any coffee, but you're welcome to this cup if you'd like."

"I'll never sleep tonight if I drink coffee this late," she answered. "But thank you for offering."

Gregory settled into his corner of the sofa, coffee in hand and his free arm still around her shoulders. He wouldn't do that if he weren't at least a little bit interested in her. Would he?

Don't think about this too hard. Just enjoy it.

Liam strummed through a couple of tunes, his expression lighter than Helene remembered seeing in all the months he'd been here.

"Do you know 'Old Dan Tucker'?" Gregory asked at the first lull in music.

Liam smiled and began playing the song.

Bianca clapped her hands gleefully. "I love this one."

Gregory grinned at her. "I never could resist a golden-haired angel." He set his coffee on the end table and stood. Helene immediately missed his one-armed embrace.

He crossed to where Bianca sat and held out his hand. She jumped up and took his hand. Gregory danced her around the room, spinning her about. The two of them laughed and smiled. Helene pulled her feet onto the sofa beside her and watched the magic Gregory was weaving over Liam and Bianca.

Her eyes met Mother's. A soft smile touched Mother's lips as her gaze returned to Gregory and Bianca. Helene sighed and watched him as well. What joy he'd brought to their lives.

"Play 'Lorena,'" Bianca said to Liam when the dance had ended. "Play it, and I'll sing."

Helene had never heard Bianca sing; it seemed they were in for a night of firsts.

As Liam strummed the chords to the slower, lilting tune, Gregory turned to where Helene sat and offered the same wordless invitation he'd extended to Bianca. Her heart flipped about. She slipped her fingers in his and allowed him to pull her to her feet.

Bianca sang with feeling, "'Oh, the years creep slowly by, Lorena. The snow is on the ground again . . .'"

Gregory pulled Helene into his arms and led her into a slow and meandering dance. He hummed the tune as they wove around the room. The song was one Josiah had mentioned in his letters. Its lyrics of loss and longing spoke deeply of the lonely soldiers thinking of their loved ones far away.

Who had Gregory longed for?

She looked up into his eyes, bracing herself to see mourning and sadness there. But his gaze was firmly on her, with nothing but contentment and enjoyment in his eyes.

"We sang this song every night of the war," he whispered, pulling her ever closer. "I like it far better when dancing with you than I ever did sitting about a fire with a bunch of scraggly soldiers."

She laid her head on his shoulder and closed her eyes. How she hoped he was as upright and honest as he seemed. She was quickly growing quite fond of his company. Her heart would break if he proved a disappointment.

SIX

The promise of an evening with the family, and most especially with Helene, gave Gregory a healthy dose of motivation for his day's work. The hours flew by. He hardly noted his own exhaustion, filled as he was with the anticipation of seeing her again. He no longer felt like a stranger interrupting the family's life but almost as though he was part of it. He could only hope that, given time, such would truly be the case.

The heat of July hadn't dampened his enjoyment of Nebraska. Three weeks had flown swiftly by since his arrival. Three weeks exactly. He'd excused himself from this night's gathering in the parlor, having his laundry to see to, but his thoughts were in the house.

He couldn't know for certain what Helene's feelings for him were. The air sparked and jumped when they were near each other. She danced with him anytime Liam played music for the family. She let him put an arm around her shoulders when they sat on the sofa. That all seemed like good signs to him. Yet she didn't seek out his company nor send him longing, lingering glances. She'd certainly never said anything that would convince anyone that she had feelings for him.

He scrubbed his trousers more vigorously against the washboard. A man ought to respect a woman's feelings for him, or lack of feelings for him. He meant to do just that. But the uncertainty was eating at him. He had half a mind to simply ask what she thought of him, but he wasn't certain he was ready to hear a negative answer, so he opted not to chance it.

You're a coward, Gregory. You know that.

He bent over the wash basin in only his tattered uniform trousers; he was washing all the rest of his clothing. The necessary state of undress had led him to choose a more isolated spot along the river for his work. The loneliness of it was helpful on two fronts. First, he needn't worry about being embarrassed at his appearance, and second, he wouldn't be interrupted while sorting through his confused thoughts.

It'll be awkward, but you need to talk to her, find out where she stands. And somewhere in all of that, you really do need to tell her your history with her family.

He wrung out the excess water in his work trousers. Laundry was far from his favorite chore, but he had more than adequate motivation to keep at it. Helene wasn't likely to think of him as anything other than the hired hand if he walked about with half of the dirt in the fields caked all over his clothes.

He snapped the trousers open once more, then hung them over the rope he'd strung between two trees along the riverbank. He turned back to begin washing his socks, but stopped at the sound of footsteps. An instant later, Helene rounded the corner.

Her eyes pulled wide. His did the same.

Good heavens, I'm only in my trousers.

"Miss Helene, I'm sorry I—"

She turned away enough to no longer be looking directly at him, but her profile was fully visible, as was the blush stealing up her cheeks.

"I wasn't expecting anyone to be coming this direction," he explained. "You said you meant to spend the evening sewing with your mother and Bianca."

"I had intended to," she said, still looking at the river. "But those two are like peas in a pod, and it became quickly apparent that my presence wasn't needed. I'm sorry to have caught you unawares and for any embarrassment it has caused."

She was worried about *his* embarrassment? He could see that he'd caused her a great deal more embarrassment than he felt. "Both of my shirts are drying on the line. I'm afraid I haven't the means of making myself more presentable just yet."

She smiled a little. "We seem to be enacting our very own comedy of errors." She glanced at him for a brief moment. "I wish you had told me you needed your clothes laundered. I would gladly have thrown them in with the family's washing."

He shook his head at that. "I'm not here to make more work for you."

Her eyes were on him again. "What is it you *are* here for?"

"To help," he said.

Her gaze remained firmly locked on his face—searching, almost. "Is that all?" she whispered. "To work?"

It was the perfect moment, the ideal opportunity, to explain it all. He couldn't have asked for an easier means of making his confession. "I wanted—I wish to—" He couldn't seem to find words, that hadn't happened in Helene's presence since his very first day at the farm. He forced out a deep breath, holding his hands up in a show of frustration.

"It is amazing how awkward conversation becomes when one isn't wearing a shirt."

She smiled a little, color rushing to her cheeks once more. "You also aren't wearing shoes."

"Somehow that's not quite as disconcerting," he muttered.

"Would you rather I leave?" She sounded disappointed at the prospect.

For a moment, he considered asking her to go. Cowardice appealed then. But he needed to have the conversation with her, as inopportune as the situation was. "I'll just fetch my coat from the barn."

"I don't wish to put you out."

"Not at all." He took a single step toward the barn, but turned back when he realized she might walk away while he was gone. "I'll be back directly."

"You had better be. Your socks are lying there all alone beside the wash basin, crying out to be cleaned."

He made quick work of rushing to the barn, where he snatched his wool uniform jacket. When he returned, Helene sat on a log near the wash basin.

She looked up as he approached. "It's far too warm for such a heavy coat."

He sat at the basin again and grabbed his socks. "It's either this or a wet shirt."

"Or no shirt at all," she added with a smile.

"Which is only helpful if my goal is to make certain you neither look at nor talk to me." He scrubbed quickly at his socks. He'd never been alone with her before, and he didn't want to waste the moment with laundry. "How long have you been in Nebraska?"

"Almost five years." She looked out over the river. "I didn't care for it at first. Everything was so different from Massachusetts. But I fell in love with the quiet and openness. And the people are so friendly."

"You've taken on a lot of responsibility with such a large farm to run." He kept on scrubbing.

"It's small by comparison to many farms around here." She turned a little, so she looked more in his direction. "Now that the war is over, where do you mean to settle?"

"I haven't decided yet." He stood and hung his socks beside the rest of his drying clothes.

"Perhaps you'll fall in love with Nebraska, as well," she said. "It is a very nice place."

She didn't wish to be rid of him. That fact argued firmly in favor of her caring for him, or at least not disliking him. "I have enjoyed Nebraska, although I haven't been here in the winter. Is that season likely to change my opinion of the place?"

She smiled. "I'd better not tell you; you might leave now."

"The winters are quite cold in Massachusetts," he reminded her.

But she shook her head. "It's not the same kind of cold here."

Gregory sat beside her on the log. "The only trees growing around here are along the river. Do you chop them for fuel?"

"We do gather driftwood, but we don't cut trees. We'd quickly be out of them if we did."

"Then what do you burn?" He had a sudden, horrible picture in his mind of her freezing through bitter winters.

"Sunflower stalks. Straw, sometimes. We burn a lot of buffalo chips." Her nose crinkled adorably. "That is one of the few things I don't like about living here."

He slipped his hand around hers. He'd done so before, but the experience hadn't grown any less enjoyable. "Do you need me to start gathering chips?"

"Mother and Bianca do that. They've already begun, actually. It's an urgent task from the first thaw of spring until the snow is too thick for gathering."

"They can't possibly enjoy that." He rubbed his thumb over the back of her hand.

"No, but it's necessary." She held his gaze. "I'm glad you came, Gregory. We—I enjoy having you here."

"I fought for a lot of years, Helene." He held his breath to see if she'd object to him calling her by her Christian name. She didn't. "I can't say that there were many things about those years I enjoyed. It's been a fine thing these past weeks, being here with you and your family. I'm glad I came as well. I am very, very glad."

"I'm sorry I interrupted your laundry," she said quietly.

"I'm not."

"My company is preferable to a washboard's?" She smiled a bit coyly. "I'm so relieved."

"Are you attempting to force a confession? To get me to admit that I spend my days eager for your company? That those short hours I spend with you each evening are the highlight of my day?"

Color stained her cheeks, but she didn't shy away from the compliment. "Do you know what it is I look forward to?"

He inched closer to her, their legs brushing against each other on the log. "What is it you look forward to?"

"The evenings you dance with me."

His heart had begun to thrum inside him. He'd imagined this so many times—courting her, working to convince her to love him. His efforts, it seemed, weren't failing.

"I'm not a very skilled dancer," he admitted. "I'm grateful you overlook that."

"I think you're a fine dancer." She leaned toward him and pressed the lightest of kisses to his cheek. "And a fine man."

Gregory couldn't quite piece two thoughts together. She'd kissed him. On the cheek, yes, but she'd kissed him.

With a quick smile and an ever-growing blush, she stood. "I need to get back to the house," she said. "I'll see you tomorrow, Gregory."

"Good night, Helene."

"Good night to you as well."

SEVEN

The next morning Gregory was still in a state of inarguable shock. Helene's kiss hadn't left his thoughts. And with the memory came hopes of kissing her more fully. He'd lain awake most of the night in the loft, with thoughts of her lingering in his mind, torturing him.

During his years serving alongside Josiah, he'd imagined her as something of an angel. The reality was far better. An angel was something distant and unobtainable; Helene was very real and lovely in the best of ways.

And she had no idea who he actually was.

He had mentioned his surname during conversations with Mrs. Bowen, but no one seemed to have made the connection. He knew Josiah had written home about him, but Helene and her mother hadn't seemed to have pieced those things together with the man he was. He ought to have confessed that first day, or at least shortly thereafter. But things had moved quickly. He'd been up to his ears in work, struggling to win Liam's trust and prove himself worthy of Helene's. Next thing he'd known, he'd passed three entire weeks under a hidden identity. There was no easy way to explain things now.

He walked up the last row of crops that he needed to check before lunch. Liam was one row over, doing the same. The boy had been in something of a dark study all day, his quiet, pensive mood matching Gregory's.

"I set the lunch pails up against that fence post," he told Liam and received a silent nod in response. They were quite the team.

A moment later, they were seated side by side in the minimal shadow cast by the thin fence post. Liam ate silently. Gregory did the same as he set his mind to his dilemma.

Good morning, Helene, he silently practiced a greeting for the next day. *The sky is clear. The stalls are mucked. And by the way, I was your brother's best friend in the army. I apologize for not mentioning that sooner.*

That sounded ridiculous.

Dinner was wonderful. Don't tell your mother, but I was with your brother when he died.

That was even worse.

He'd simply have to look her in the eye, admit he hadn't been entirely forthright, and hope she forgave him.

He watched a few wisps of clouds lazily creep across the sky. The crops were growing fine. The most urgent repairs had been made to the house. Other than his looming personal crisis, the situation wasn't entirely bad.

Liam sat slouched forward, his mouth set in a line of contemplation.

"What's weighing on your mind, Liam?"

The boy shrugged, not looking up at him.

"It's only you and me and the crops. You may as well take the weight off your mind. No one here is going to look down on you."

Liam smiled a little. "Are you certain the crops won't judge me?"

"Relatively certain."

Liam finished off his sandwich and leaned back against the fence post. "Last night, I broke a plate."

All of that pouting over a broken plate? "And you're upset because you're embarrassed about it? Or because you were punished?" Gregory couldn't imagine Helene lashing out at the children.

"Miss Helene doesn't punish us, not like some people would with orphans they had to take in."

"I don't think Miss Helene sees you or Bianca as someone she 'had to take in,'" Gregory insisted.

Liam nodded quite seriously. "She and Mrs. Bowen have been good to us."

"So what is it about the broken plate that's upset you so much?" Gregory took another bite of his sandwich.

"I didn't tell her I broke it," Liam muttered. "I didn't want to get in trouble. But she found the broken bits."

Gregory was beginning to piece it together. "So you ended up in trouble anyway."

"More trouble," Liam answered. "She said from my first day here that lying was the one thing she wouldn't abide."

"Did you lie to her about the plate?"

Liam shrugged with one shoulder. "I just didn't tell her, not on my own. She says leaving off the truth is a lie."

A lump formed in Gregory's throat. Helene viewed lies of omission in the same light as outright falsehoods. That did not bode well for him. "Was she quite upset with you, then?"

"She was mostly disappointed." Liam's brow pulled low. "I hate it when she's disappointed in me."

"I would rather hate that myself."

He'd never have the chance to prove himself worthy of her affection if she felt she couldn't trust him. What chance did he have now of building any kind of relationship between them?

He and Liam walked the rows throughout the

remainder of the afternoon, pulling weeds and checking the crops. Gregory was tied in knots inside. He had to confess the entire thing to her that very evening. He didn't relish the idea.

Just so long as she gives me a second chance. Even if he had to fight his way back into her good graces, he'd be happy. But in his bones, he felt certain that the day wouldn't play out in his favor.

"How are you at splicing rope?" he asked Liam when they'd finished up in the fields.

"I know how," Liam answered. "But I ain't fast."

Perfect. "There are two short lengths hanging up near the tools at the back of the barn. Start on the splicing, if you would. I've a bit of business to see to up at the house."

Liam headed in the direction of the barn, and Gregory set his footsteps determinedly toward the house. The time for full disclosure had come.

He opened the kitchen door and stepped inside. "Helene?"

Bianca looked up from the table. She smiled at him.

"Good afternoon, sunshine," he said in greeting.

"Afternoon, Mr. Gregory."

"Is Miss Helene about?"

Bianca nodded. "She's in the parlor. She and Mrs. Bowen have a visitor."

That complicated his plan a bit. He'd peek inside and ask if he could have a minute of her time once she was available. He found her in the parlor as Bianca had said he would.

Mrs. Bowen and another elderly woman Gregory didn't recognize sat on the sofa with Helene in a nearby chair. The older women looked up at him.

"Forgive me," he said. "I don't wish to interrupt."

Helene slowly turned. Gregory fixed a smile on his face in anticipation of seeing one on hers. But there was no smile.

Not even a hint of one. Instead, anger crackled in her eyes, sending him back a step. Her mouth pressed into a tight, tense line.

Gregory looked, wide eyed, from Helene to Mrs. Bowen and back a few times. "What's happened?"

Mrs. Bowen and their visitor looked at him in obvious confusion and displeasure.

"Have I done something?"

Helene stood with palpable dignity. "May I speak to you a moment?" she asked. "In private, please."

He nodded, a feeling of foreboding settling over him. Helene sailed past him, her chin held at a determined angle. Gregory followed in her wake. Helene spotted Bianca in the kitchen and changed her path. She pulled open the front door, went through, and came to a stop on the front porch.

Gregory pulled the door closed and stood on the spot, bracing himself for whatever was about to come his way.

"Who are you?" Helene demanded.

He hadn't expected that. "I beg your pardon?"

"Mrs. Jamison"—she motioned quickly in the direction of the house—"arranged for the farmhand I hired for the summer, the man I thought was you. But she says that that man was thrown from a horse a month ago and wasn't able to come."

Gregory's heart dropped to his boots. His ruse had been revealed before he'd had a chance to confess.

"But you," Helene continued, "let me believe you were the man I'd hired."

"Helene—"

"Miss Bowen," she corrected. "Now, who are you? Answer me truthfully."

"I am Gregory Reeves, just as I always said I was."

She was shaking her head even before he finished. "You know perfectly well I'm not asking what your name is. You allowed me to believe you were the man I'd arranged to work here, someone whose character had been vouched for by someone I trusted. Tell me now who you are and why you are here."

He'd wanted to make the confession. The time had come for it, though this was not all how he'd hoped to go about it. "I'm Gregory Reeves, lately of the United States Army, where, like most soldiers, I was known by my surname—Reeves. They all just called me Reeves."

Her brow pulled a moment, but then her eyes pulled wide and her mouth fell open in the tiniest of Os.

"I served with your brother," he continued, though he was certain she'd already begun to piece together his identity. "He was my very best friend. He read me all of your letters because I didn't receive many myself. He asked me to come check on you and your mother if he didn't live to do so himself."

She blinked a couple of times, her gaze vague and distant. "Josiah sent you?"

"In a manner of speaking, yes."

She paled, and he felt an urgent need to reach out for her. The gesture, he knew, would not be the least welcome. He kept his arms at his sides and pressed on.

"I intended to tell you as much on that very first day, but you set me to work so quickly, I didn't have the opportunity."

Her eyes flashed once more. "Do not blame this on me, Mr. Reeves," she warned. "You have had three weeks to tell me the truth, but you spent that time lying to me instead."

He stuffed his hands in his trouser pockets. "You're right. I have no excuse, no good explanation. At first I didn't say anything because I told myself I could explain later. Before I knew it, it *was* later, and I was caught up in the tangle of my own omission."

She folded her arms and all but glared. "Did you ever intend to tell me the truth?"

He nodded meekly. "That was my purpose in coming up to the house so early this evening."

"You'll forgive me if I have trouble believing that. The fact of the matter is that I'm having trouble believing *anything* about you."

He had anticipated his confession creating tension between them. But he'd lost her faith in him entirely. His heart fell at the realization.

"I can abide a great many things, Gregory Reeves, but dishonesty is not one of them."

He nodded. "I understand."

"You can take your dinner on the back porch tonight just as you did your first evening here."

"Yes'm." He didn't know if that meant she intended to send him off in the morning or not. He wouldn't blame her if she never spoke to him again. He'd come to care for her even more over the past three weeks but, with his own cowardice, had ruined his chances.

EIGHT

"So, Gregory is Josiah's friend Reeves." Mother didn't seem so much distressed by the revelation as intrigued. Mrs. Jamison had long since gone. Dinner had been served—with Gregory noticeably absent— and Helene had pulled her mother out to the back porch to make the revelation. "I must confess, I feel a bit foolish for not having sorted that out on my own."

"But how could you have? He didn't tell us anything about his connection to Josiah or his real reason for coming."

"Well, no, he didn't." Mother tapped her bottom lip with one finger. "But I do think he was quite honest about who he was, other than that bit of information."

"That 'bit of information' seems rather important, doesn't it? He pretended to be the hired hand sent over from the Jamisons' aunt's farm. He never told us the truth."

"He should have, I agree. But he told us his full name, which, if we'd known the name of the man the Jamisons were sending, would have solved the riddle from the beginning."

Helene had been chastising herself for exactly that lack of oversight over the past couple of hours. She'd been inexcusably irresponsible in not making absolutely certain she knew the identity of the man she'd hired, who would live on her land and interact with her family.

"Still, he should have been honest with us," Helene said.

"Oh, I agree. Even with the awkwardness of explaining things after realizing we were mistaken, he ought to have done so." Mother looked out at the barn. "What do you intend to do now?"

Helene sighed and leaned against a post. "I don't know. It is a little late in the season to try finding a replacement, and he has done good work. Liam and Bianca like him. Aside from his glaring omission of information, I'm rather fond of him myself."

"'Rather fond'?" Mother raised a doubtful eyebrow.

"Considering I'm not certain whether I can even trust the man, 'rather fond' is all I can feel at the moment."

Mother stepped up beside Helene and set a comforting arm around her shoulders. "I do wish your father were still with us. If he had lived, perhaps you wouldn't struggle to trust men so much."

"Are you saying I should forget this entire ordeal and go on as we were before?" She didn't think herself capable of that.

But Mother shook her head. "That man misled you," she acknowledged. "And you have every right—indeed, a responsibility, even—to make absolutely certain he can be trusted."

"Then where does that leave things? I don't know how to move forward."

"Were I in your shoes, Helene, I would march myself over to the barn and start over. Begin again with the knowledge of who he is. Allow him the summer and harvest season to be himself and prove to you whether or not he's worthy of your regard."

She took a shaky breath. "What if he isn't? My heart has been breaking all day. I don't know if I can bear two or three more months of this."

Mother gave her shoulders a squeeze. "If he proves himself to be someone you cannot love, the pain will pass, and you will move on. But if you don't find out one way or the other, you'll spend *years* wondering."

Mother was right, but that didn't make the prospect easy.

"My heart was so very ready to fall in love with him," she confessed. "Now my head won't allow it."

"Perhaps your love story, should there prove to be one, won't be an uneventful stroll through a flowery meadow. It doesn't need to be. And you don't need to know the ending now. You simply need to go make your beginning."

Helene solidified her resolve. "It seems I have a bit of business in the barn." She spoke as firmly as her uncertainty would allow.

"That's my brave girl," Mother whispered. "I'll go sit with the children."

They walked in opposite directions. Helene didn't allow herself to look back, afraid her determination would fail her. She marched through the open door in the side of the barn.

Before her eyes had fully adjusted to the dimness inside, Gregory's voice broke the silence.

"Hele—Miss Bowen. Is there a problem?"

He approached from a nearby stall, watching her with worry.

Even though they were quarreling, he was still concerned about her welfare. She truly wanted to believe he was the good and honest man she'd thought he was.

"I've been thinking over our current situation," she said.

He grew very still, watching her closely.

"I think we should start over again," she continued. "We should make a new beginning, but an honest one."

"I would like that very much," he said. "Though I hardly deserve the second chance."

"That is when a person needs it most."

He nodded, eagerness mingling with hope in his expression.

Helene took a fortifying breath. "Good evening," she said. "I'm Helene Bowen. I should warn you that I'm stubborn, sometimes to a fault. I've been accused more than once of being bossy. And I have a very difficult time trusting people, though I am willing to keep trying."

He looked immediately relieved. Helene swore she could see a weight lifted from him. Her opinion mattered more to him than she would have guessed.

"I'm Gregory Reeves, and your brother was the best friend I've ever had. He read me your letters because I seldom received any, and in so doing, allowed me to be part of your family. I came here not only to fulfill a promise to him, but because I wanted to meet you. I'm not perfect—far from it, in fact—but I hope to prove myself trustworthy. And regardless of what you decide about me in the end, I promise to work hard, and I'll stay as long as you wish me to."

A smile began tugging at her lips. "I would very much like you to stay," she admitted.

"Do you really mean it?"

"I really do."

He slipped his fingers around hers and pressed a kiss to the back of her hand. "Thank you, Helene. A hundred times, thank you. You won't regret this."

"I don't intend to."

He kept hold of her hand. His expression was the one of a man who'd been granted a last-minute pardon.

She didn't know how their future would play out, but in that moment, she could not doubt that he sincerely cared for her. If he were indifferent, her willingness to begin again wouldn't matter to him at all.

She leaned closer, raising herself up on her toes. "Prove me right, Gregory," she whispered.

He held her gaze with his beautiful dark eyes. "I intend to."

His free hand cupped the side of her face, holding her gently. He pressed the lightest of kisses to her lips, one undemanding and gentle. Not a kiss of time-tried passion, nor one to seal a vow, but one of hope.

They were making a new beginning with a world of possibilities ahead of them.

ABOUT SARAH M. EDEN

Sarah M. Eden is the author of multiple historical romances, including *Longing for Home*, winner of *Foreword* magazine's IndieFab Gold Award and the AML's 2013 Novel of the Year, as well as Whitney Award finalists *Seeking Persephone* and *Courting Miss Lancaster*.

Combining her obsession with history and affinity for tender love stories, Sarah loves crafting witty characters and heartfelt romances. She has twice served as the Master of Ceremonies for the LDStorymakers Writers Conference and acted as the Writer in Residence at the Northwest Writers Retreat. Sarah is represented by Pam van Hylckama Vlieg at Foreword Literary Agency.

Visit her website at www.sarahmeden.com
Twitter: @SarahMEden
Facebook: Sarah M. Eden

HIDDEN SPRING

by Liz Adair

Other Works by Liz Adair

Counting the Cost

Cold River

The Mist of Quarry Harbor

Spider Latham Mystery Series:
Snakewater Affair

The Lodger

After Goliath

Trouble at the Red Pueblo

ONE

Susannah stepped out of the cottage where she lived alone. Pulling a pair of gloves out of her apron pocket, she gritted her teeth as she put them on, steeling herself for the long and painful walk ahead. She wrapped one of Wesley's large bandanas around each hand, picked up the enamelware milk jugs, and set off down the lane.

By the time she got to the fence that divided the upper and middle pastures, she had to stop and set her burdens down. As Susannah flexed her hands, Sweetie, a fawn-like calf and the solo resident of the middle pasture, came over to see her.

"Don't you stare at me with those big, sad eyes," Susannah said. "The milk isn't for you. You can thank Mama Brown for that. She's lined up customers for every day of the week."

As she picked up the jugs and continued, Sweetie followed on the other side of the fence. "That's a hard-hearted woman," Susannah told the calf. "'You've got to go back to your own place and get on with your life,' she said to me. So I told her, 'I don't have a life anymore.' And I don't. I don't have a husband. I don't have any money, and I'm stuck here in Arizona Territory, a place thirty years behind times. It's 1890, for heaven's sake, and here I am, walking a mile to town every day carrying these stupid—"

Susannah set the milk cans down again and stared at Sweetie as an idea started to form in her mind. The heifer was four months old. Two gallons of milk wouldn't be too much of a burden for her to carry. Susannah just needed something to make a set of saddlebags. She picked up her skirts and ran back toward the house.

"Don't go away," she called over her shoulder. "I'll be back."

Slamming through the front door, she ran through the kitchen-parlor-dining room, into the bedroom, and pulled down the ladder that went to the loft. After scrambling up, she hefted the cases of Wesley's books out of the way. Behind them was the battered trunk that had served as her hope chest when she'd married a little over a year ago.

Susannah opened the trunk. She didn't pause to touch the rosebuds she'd embroidered on the chambray nightgown for her wedding night. Nor did her gaze linger on the wedding picture stashed between dishtowels and bed linens. She dug to the bottom, unearthing the quilt Ivy Patterson had given her. Though Susannah liked the bright reds, blues and pinks in the nine-patch quilt, she had never liked Ivy Patterson, so she smiled grimly as she pulled it out and tossed it over the loft railing. She slammed the lid shut and moved the boxes of books back in front of the trunk, then headed to the ladder to climb down.

At the top of the ladder, she paused. Reaching over, she opened one of the boxes and took out a slim volume, all she had left of her dead husband. She traced the embossed letters as her lips formed the words of the title: *Hidden Spring, Poems by Wesley R. Brown.* On impulse, she slipped the book into the pocket of her apron and finished her descent.

She grabbed the quilt and sewing box, then went to work at the kitchen table. With the aid of a spool of carpet thread, a stout needle, and a pair of scissors, she folded and stitched the quilt into a crude and colorful set of panniers so that when it would hang over Sweetie's back, each side would have separate pockets for two one-gallon milk cans.

"I think this will work," she announced to the empty room. "If I walk beside her and hold it on her back, it should be fine."

She put her sewing things away and picked up the saddlebag, but she had hardly gotten out the door before the thought hit her that she should have some way of leading Sweetie. Instead of heading to the pasture, Susannah went to the lean-to behind the house. Half of the shed was used as a milking parlor. The other half was for storing garden implements and grain.

After pulling open one of the double doors, Susannah waited a moment for her eyes to adjust to the dim interior before scanning the tools and tack hanging on the wall. There it was—a halter with a rope attached. She grabbed it off its nail and thought to put some grain in the bottom of a bucket. Then she ran to the pasture, where an unsuspecting Sweetie was cropping grass.

Susannah let herself in the gate and hung the quilt on it. "Halter first," she instructed herself, shaking the bucket. "Here, Sweetie. Want some nice oats?"

The calf came willingly, brushing her damp muzzle on Susannah's arm as she investigated the intriguing sound from the pail.

Susannah set the oats on the ground and, while Sweetie's tongue was busy scraping up the tasty morsels, worked to undo the buckle. Bending over Sweetie's head as the calf pushed the empty bucket along the grass, Susannah managed to put the halter on and get it fastened.

She stood back and examined her handiwork, breathing hard from the exertion. The halter didn't look quite right. The ring to which the rope attached was on the side instead of the bottom, and she had never seen an extra loop stick out like this one did. But when she pulled on the rope, the calf responded, and that was good enough for now.

"Come on, girl." Susannah led the heifer to the gate, where she hung the quilt over Sweetie's back. The calf's only reaction was to turn her head and sniff at the fabric.

"Now for the milk." Susannah pulled on the rope. Sweetie followed through the gate and over to where the jugs sat by the side of the lane. Loading them in the pockets was a bit tricky, but the calf stood still, and soon the colorful patchwork panniers were bulging and balanced.

"I'm just a little farm girl takin' my wares to market," Susannah said, adopting the local drawl, so different from her own Boston accent. "Come on, Sweetie. We're goin' ta town."

The calf obliged by keeping pace beside her at a good clip, even when they passed Sweetie's mother in the lower pasture. Lady, the Jersey cow Mama Brown had insisted Susannah buy with what remained of Wesley's inheritance, raised her head and ambled over to the fence. Susannah kept the rope in her left hand and her right on Sweetie's withers to make sure the quilt didn't shift.

Susannah's place at Hidden Spring was nestled at the head of a box canyon. Water welling up inside a cave at the base of a high sandstone cliff spilled into a stream that flowed down the widening valley, creating a swath of green in this mostly brown, high desert part of Arizona Territory. The track that led from the house to the main road skirted the pastures and followed the line of the rocky bluff.

About the time she turned onto the road to Masonville, the feel of the book in her apron pocket, which was bumping against her thigh, reminded Susannah of her favorite poem.

She tried to recite it but couldn't remember how the second stanza began. Letting go of the quilt, she pulled out the volume of verse and fumbled it open to the second page.

"Listen, Sweetie," she said and began to read aloud.

Love, thou art like the waters
That flow to Hidden Spring,
Coming from afar, unnoticed,
Unheralded, yet you bring
With you, life.

Love, thine eyes are blue as rivulets
That pool along the way,
Thy hair the color of the sun,
Whose streaming, golden ray
Doth warm the earth

Beauty follows in thy wake,
And dormant dreams revive.
Souls shriveled by mundane cares,
In thy sweet presence come alive
And blossom.

Susannah held the book next to her heart and closed her eyes, picturing Wesley as he'd first read the poem to her in the Pattersons' parlor. The family had been out, so Susannah had an evening off and permission to use the room. The flickering fire created highlights in Wesley's black hair as he bent his head to read the poem. Then he knelt before her, pressed the paper into her hand, and asked her to marry him.

The lead rope ripped from her hand. Susannah's eyes sprang open. Her arms swung out to steady herself, but the calf's hind legs caught the book squarely and sent it sailing. The next time Sweetie kicked, it was Susannah who went sailing.

Hitting the ground, she shrieked as she watched the saddlebags slide off Sweetie's rump and fly through the air as the calf kicked them. They landed in a multi-colored pile in the middle of the road. When she tried to get up, pain struck her midsection, slashing through like a rusty knife. She lay back down, her eyes following the calf as, calm now, Sweetie turned to investigate the colorful heap, still holding the milk she was taking to sell in town.

"Oh, Sweetie," she moaned. "What have you done?"

"Are you all right, ma'am?"

Susannah tried to rise up on one elbow to see who had spoken, but a sharp pang forced her to lie back down. Blinking, she squinted at the man bending over her, but the morning sun behind him was in her eyes. In spite of the glare, something about the shape of his head and the blackness of his hair was so familiar that her heart skipped a beat. "Wesley?"

TWO

The stranger knelt beside her. "No, I'm not Wesley. I'm Douglas."

Susannah turned her face away, embarrassment and disappointment making her chin quiver. Why did she still do that—think she saw him in familiar places? It had been six months.

Wesley was dead. He was never coming back.

"Can you sit up?" the man asked. "I hate to see you lying in the dirt." He slid his arm under her shoulders.

She allowed him to help her to a sitting position but then shook him off. "I'm perfectly fine. I can get up by myself."

"Are you sure?" He stood, dark eyes fixed intently on her.

Susannah considered a moment. Her skirt was tucked under her, so standing up would be a two-stage affair. Then there was the problem of the pain in her ribcage. She relented. "If you will give me your hand, I would appreciate it."

He reached out, and she grasped his right hand with her left. The calluses on his palm and the sureness of his grip reminded her of Papa Brown, and somehow that made her feel better. Holding her right elbow tightly against her ribs, she used the strength of his arm to get to her knees and then to her feet.

She released his hand, but he seemed reluctant to let go, retaining the smallest amount of pressure so that her little finger trailed over his fingertips.

She felt color rising to her cheeks, and because she didn't know what to do with her hands, she brushed off her skirt. "Thank you, Mr. . . .?"

"Cooper," he supplied. "Douglas Cooper. And you are . . .?"

She examined him before answering. How could she have thought he resembled Wesley? He was taller than her husband had been, with broader shoulders and a more muscular build. His jaw was square and shadowed with black stubble, and there was a rough patch on one side of his face that had the look of a brush with smallpox.

"My name is Susannah Brown." She gestured toward the mouth of the canyon. "I live at Hidden Spring." She reached out to pet Sweetie, who had come over and was leaning against her thigh.

"You're married to Wesley Brown?" Douglas grinned, and his eyes moved to the wreckage of the saddlebag experiment heaped in the middle of the road. "I might have expected Wesley to be involved in that some way."

"What a despicable thing to say! What a malevolent creature you are." Susannah marched to the quilt and grabbed one corner. She had intended to whisk it into her arms and do a grand exit, but whisking was not an option. Not only did it hurt to bend over, but the locking tops of the cans had apparently done their jobs. The pockets she'd made were sufficiently snug, so the two gallons of milk were still where she'd put them.

Douglas laughed. He bent down and picked up his hat. "I lost this when I piled off my horse trying to get to you," he explained and added, "You and Wesley should get along just fine. I bet you spend evenings practicing long words."

Still clutching the blanket, Susannah turned away, not wanting this stranger to see her tears. His guess had been too accurate, for she and Wesley indeed had spent many an evening working on vocabulary, delighting in the color and texture that words gave conversation.

"Here, let me help you with that." Douglas picked up one of the milk cans by the handle.

She turned further away from him, winding herself into the quilt. With the corner she had in her hand, she dabbed her eyes.

Douglas pulled the milk jug out of its pocket. "You know, this is quite clever. As tame as that calf is, it might have worked just fine."

Susannah gritted her teeth. She still wouldn't look at him. "Don't patronize me."

"Miz Brown, I don't even know what that means." He pulled the quilt and unwound her. "I think your patchwork saddlebags must have slipped back and hit that calf in the flanks, made 'em buck. Shoot, that's how they get the broncs to buck at rodeos—tie a strap around their flanks."

"Fascinating," she murmured, but she still held onto the corner.

"Tell you what. How about I deliver your milk for you today?" He tugged on the quilt, and Susannah let go. "You head on home with your friend here." He indicated Sweetie with his thumb. "Tend to your bruises. Take it easy."

Susannah watched as he reinserted the jug into its pocket and carried the quilt to a sorrel horse standing with its reins on the ground. Bunching the quilt at the middle, he hung it in front of the saddle and tied it on. He picked up the reins and gave her a searching look. "You be all right walking home alone?"

"I'm not alone." Susannah couldn't repress a small smile. "Sweetie is with me."

He answered her smile. "Where do I take the milk?"

"One gallon goes to Pattersons. They live on Elm Street, the big yellow house with columns. The other goes to the Browns. They live on—"

"Wesley's folks? I know where they live. The Pattersons, too." He mounted his horse and patted the quilt. "I'll get your outfit back to you."

"Leave it at the Browns. I'll get it from them."

"Fair enough." He touched the brim of his hat.

Susannah watched him ride away, her eyes lingering on his straight back and broad shoulders until she felt the dampness of Sweetie's muzzle on her arm. "Yes, my friend," she said to the calf. "We don't want to stand in the road all day." She picked up the lead rope and started back to Hidden Spring.

With every step, a dull ache radiated though her torso, and she hadn't gone a hundred feet before she stopped. "You know what?" she asked her bovine companion. "We're halfway to town right here, and I think a cup of Mama Brown's willow-bark tea would do me a world of good."

Taking Sweetie's silence as assent, Susannah turned again toward town. Seeing that Douglas was still within shouting distance, she wondered if she should call him back and tell him that she'd deliver the milk. "I'll just let him do it," she told Sweetie. "His horse must be a slowpoke, though. I would have thought he'd be halfway there by now."

When they reached the scene of the fracas, Susannah stopped. "Wait a minute. We need to pick up the book, which you so rudely kicked out of my hand."

Like the lane from Hidden Spring, this road marched alongside a line of sandstone bluffs. It was merely a wide track through a broad expanse of sagebrush, but here and there, the occasional nopal cactus or yucca plant asserted a spiny presence. Susannah stood in the middle of the road, making a visual sweep of the whole area, then dropped the lead rope and tramped around among the brush. But there was no sign of the book.

"Well, isn't that something." She stood, hands on hips, and scanned a full circle one more time. "What could have happened to it?"

She picked up the calf's tether and began walking toward town. "Lucky for me, I have 499 more copies," she said. "Come on, Sweetie. I'm looking forward to that willow-bark tea."

THREE

By the time Susannah arrived at the Browns', she was hot, sweaty, and feeling a little weak in the knees. Though early May, the sun blazed from a sky the color of azurite, and cottony tops of cumulus clouds peeked above the hills to the north.

Masonville had been settled by hardy souls coming to Arizona Territory in 1863. Designated county seat, it had blossomed in a modest way with the coming of silver mines and the railroad in 1880. Now it had a settled, prosperous air.

Susannah turned right on the first street she encountered and walked to the last bungalow. The Browns' house had a well-tended lawn bordering the little-used front door, but Susannah headed for the back, passing the orchard and the garden along the side of the house. She led Sweetie to a corral beyond a grape arbor and put her inside.

She recognized the sorrel, tied to a post by the back porch with the quilt still hanging in front of the saddle. Walking by it, she paused at the door. She didn't live here anymore. Not since four days ago. Did that mean she should knock, or should she just walk in?

She tapped the screen, then opened the door and walked through the sleeping porch. With her hand on the kitchen door jamb, she paused and blinked at the sight before her.

Papa and Mama Brown sat at the table, coffee in front of them. Douglas Cooper leaned against the sink, a saucer in one hand, a steaming cup in the other. Deep in conversation, they had apparently not heard Susannah enter.

"What if we hadn't been here?" Mama Brown was saying. "What if we were dead, like Wesley?"

Douglas answered. "Then I would live with that regret the rest of my life, just like I regret—" He glanced at the doorway and stopped when he saw Susannah. He straightened and set his cup and saucer in the sink. "Good afternoon, Miz Brown."

Papa Brown stood and held out his arms. "Susannah! How good to see you. Are you all right? You're a little peaked." He smiled with his familiar stooped shoulders and his kind, lined face.

After the frustrations of her morning and long walk, her father-in-law's welcome felt like a safe harbor after a storm. She walked to him and laid her head on his shoulder, closing her eyes at the comfort of his embrace and the smell of the familiar odor of horses and hay. She sighed, but when his arms tightened on a tender spot, she flinched.

"Ouch." She pulled away.

"What's wrong?" Papa's voice held concern.

"She tangled with a calf out on the road," Douglas said. "Which reminds me—I've got your milk." He walked past them to the back door.

Mama Brown's dark eyes moved from Susannah to Douglas's retreating form. "What's he talking about?"

"I met him on the road to town just after Sweetie kicked me."

Both Mama and Papa Brown simply stared, so Susannah explained. "I fixed up a saddlebag so Lady's calf could carry the milk. It must have slipped back to her flanks." She touched her ribs under her right breast. "She kicked me right here."

Her mother-in-law got to her feet. Tall and slim, she wore her black hair braided forward with the long plaits pinned like a crown on top of her head. It gave her a regal, no-nonsense air that was somehow comforting. "Come into the spare room, and let me see it."

When Susannah had stayed in that room during the first six months of her widowhood, she'd thought of it as the spare *tomb*. She followed her mother-in-law and closed the door behind her. "I thought maybe a dose of your willow-bark tea would help with the pain."

"I'll brew some, but first unbutton your dress."

Susannah did as she was bidden, stripping off her bodice, corset and chemise. She found herself looking at her nude torso in the mirror, and she blushed as she remembered Wesley cupping her breast and murmuring, "Your stature is like a palm tree, and your breasts are like its clusters." He said he was quoting from the Bible, but the words sounded more like something from his book of poems.

"Let's see now. Where did . . . never mind. I see the bruise." Mama Brown probed the area with gentle fingertips, apologizing whenever Susannah winced. Then she helped her back on with her chemise and picked up the corset. "I don't think you've broken a rib. It will probably be sore for a few days, but that's all."

Susannah raised her arms so her mother-in-law could hook the fasteners. "Mama Brown, who is that man out there?"

"What man? You mean Douglas? He's my son."

Susannah blinked. She would have been less surprised if

Mama Brown had said the man in the kitchen was Billy the Kid. "But he said his last name was Cooper."

"It is. His father's name was Adam Cooper."

Susannah was too stunned to say anything.

Mama Brown hooked the last fastener. "Adam died of smallpox when Douglas was two."

"Smallpox? But they've had a vaccination for that forever. It's compulsory in Boston. Has been since 1843."

"Adam didn't hold with vaccinations."

Susannah pulled on her bodice. "Wesley said he had a brother named Sonny." The notorious Sonny who had to leave town suddenly after almost killing a man in a barroom fight. All of a sudden, Billy the Kid seemed not so far-fetched.

"We always called him Sonny, but he goes by Douglas now."

As she buttoned her dress, Susannah remembered the scene in the Browns' kitchen last week when her in-laws said it was time for her to go back to her own place at Hidden Spring. Cringing at the memory of how she had acted, she blurted, "I'm sorry for what I said to you last week."

"What was that?"

"I said you didn't know how it feels to lose someone, to be left alone."

Mama Brown took her by the shoulders. "Then remember this, Susannah. You can love again. You *will* love again."

Susannah closed her eyes and shook her head.

"Let's get you some willow-bark tea." Mama Brown opened the door to the kitchen, and they went out.

Douglas was back again, coffee cup in hand. "I put the milk in the spring house."

"Thank you, son." Mama Brown took a tin out of the cupboard and shook some of the contents into a cup. She poured in hot water from the kettle and handed it to

Susannah. "Let it steep for a few moments. Sugar's on the table."

Susannah took the cup and sat, stirring the wood chips and watching the water take on a yellowish hue. She looked up to find Douglas's eyes on her and quickly returned her gaze to the tea. What was he looking at? Didn't he know it was impolite to stare?

No one spoke for a moment, and then Papa Brown broke the silence. "Has Lady started giving more milk now that she's on better pasture?"

"She has. I may have to get more milk pails."

"And more customers," added Mama Brown. "You'll have a tidy little business if all goes well."

Douglas took a sip of his coffee. "And if Sweetie cooperates."

Papa Brown stood. "I think that's mighty clever of you to make that calf into a pack animal. I'd like to see the saddlebags you made. Come on out and show them to me."

Susannah was shy about having her father-in-law see her handiwork, but she followed him out the back door and through the porch. The erstwhile quilt hung on the top rail of the backyard pen, a bright splash of color in a sepia landscape.

Mama Brown had followed them out. "Wasn't that Ivy Patterson's wedding present?"

Susannah smiled. "It was, but Ivy was so mad at me for stealing Wesley from her that she gave us something she found in the attic. I doubt she would even remember it." She fingered the quilt. "It gave me the idea of calling my business Patchwork Dairy. I like the colors. I think it'll draw attention."

"It'll draw attention, all right." Douglas came to stand by his mother. "Especially when it's slung over that calf and you've got the halter on sideways."

"Do I? I thought it looked strange."

Papa Brown let himself into the pen, caught the calf, and fixed the halter so the rope was tied in the right place and the odd-looking loop was gone.

"Thank you, Papa Brown. You're such a gentleman." Susannah threw a meaningful glance at Douglas, but he had his hands in his pockets and was concentrating on grinding a dirt clod to powder with the toe of his boot.

Papa Brown put the saddlebags on Sweetie and stood back. "If you'll fix a strap to come around front and keep the whole outfit from shifting back, I think you'll be fine."

"I've already got something figured out," Susannah said. She looked up at the approaching thunderheads. "I'd better be getting back home. Do you have your empty milk can?"

"I'll get it." Mama Brown headed for the house. "And I'll get you some willow bark to take with you."

Half an hour later, Susannah was on her way home. The rain loomed closer, and a cooling breeze had sprung up. The dull throb in her ribcage was gone, and the saddlebags held two extra milk jugs Papa Brown had found on a shelf in the spring house. Mama Brown's comment about a *tidy business* started wheels in Susannah's brain churning ideas all the way home.

When she arrived, the rest of the day was spent in chores. She braved pounding rain to bring Lady up from the lower pasture, then braved it again to carry the evening's milk to the cave that hid the frigid spring. When she finally made it back to the house with two buckets of water to do the washing up, she was dismayed to find the roof leaking. Sighing, she found the vase Wesley had brought home after they'd discovered the hole in the roof. Back then, sitting on the settee with his arm around her, she had thought the sound of water dripping into the blue ceramic urn was magical. Now she wished he had spent the money on tar to fix the roof. She plopped the vase on the floor and went to make a fire to heat the kettle.

After washing the strainer and buckets, she brewed a cup of willow-bark tea and drank it with a piece of bread and butter for supper. Then she spread Ivy Patterson's quilt on the table and began working on alterations, adding a sash that would tie in front and hold the quilt from slipping back. When she was finished, she put on her nightgown and braided her hair. Then she got in bed and blew out the lamp.

She lay there listening to night sounds as she waited for the sheets to warm. The rain had stopped, but the plink-plink-plink of water dripping in the living room continued. She heard the plaintive cry of a night owl and then the reassuring sound of Sweetie moving about in the pen next to the lean-to. Pulling the blanket up around her ear, she curled up on her side, looking forward to having Wesley with her again in dreams that seemed so real she hated to wake each morning.

She finally drifted off to sleep, but it wasn't Wesley who came to see her. It was a dark-haired man with a rough patch above the black stubble along his jaw line. He watched her over the rim of his coffee cup and assured her that he was a gentleman.

FOUR

Susannah woke to sun streaming in the window and the sound of Lady bawling next door. The Jersey had spent the night in the milking parlor, since it had seemed cruel to send her out into the pouring rain. Susannah would have to face cleanup for that bit of kindness, but she didn't mind. She was anxious to get the morning chores done so she could get to town to start implementing her new ideas.

Not pausing to fix her hair, she pulled on a work dress and the stout shoes she wore around the farm. She built up the fire and put the kettle on before going out to put Sweetie in the upper pasture. "Eat quickly," she called as she closed the gate. "We're going to town today."

She took time to open the middle pasture gate for Lady before trotting back to the house. By the time she got there, the water in the kettle was warm. She poured it in a basin and picked up a rag. "You'll like this, Lady," she murmured. "No cold water for you."

The Jersey was standing at the trough when Susannah opened the double doors, and it only took a moment to throw some grain into the manger and lock her in the stanchion. Grabbing a bucket, she sat on the stool and rested her forehead against the cow's warm, silky side. She dipped the cloth into the water, washed the udder, and then reached for the two back teats.

"I've gotten pretty good at this," she said as milk streamed into the bucket. "You wouldn't know that I've only been milking for two weeks, would you?" She paused to consider a moment without breaking rhythm. "Actually, *you* would know, but I think anyone else would think I'm an old hand."

Lady shifted her weight and sighed, and Susannah chuckled. "Is that a comment? Hold on. I won't be too much longer."

She worked silently, watching the bucket fill. When she had stripped the last of the milk into the pail, she set it aside and undid the stanchion. Lady backed up, turned, and sauntered out into the sunshine, heading down the lane toward the middle pasture, where the gate stood open for her.

Susannah fed the chickens before she carried the milk outside, glancing to see if Lady had turned into the pasture. The sight of a rider atop a sorrel horse at the middle gate caused a fluttering in her chest and then dismay because her hair was still in braids and she wore old work clothes. She ground her teeth at the thought. Why should she care if he saw her like this? It was just Douglas Cooper. She would be polite for the sake of Mama Brown.

She watched him close the gate and turn the sorrel in her direction. Tossing her head, she continued on into the house. Politeness didn't mean she had to wait on the doorstep.

Inside, she strained the milk and poured it into gallon jugs, ready to go to the spring. She set the dishpan on the table and was busy washing the milking things when Douglas knocked at the door.

"Come in." As she turned away to hang the strainer on a nail, she heard the screen open, and a flutter returned to her chest. She frowned as she turned around to face him.

Neither of them spoke. His eyes raked her over from head to toe, and her chin came up as she met his gaze. "Good morning, Mr. Cooper. Thank you for closing the gate."

"Don't mention it." Still he stared.

"To what do I owe the honor of your visit?"

"Beg pardon?"

"Why are you here?" She picked up the kettle and began to scald the milk bucket.

Finally he looked away. Casting his eyes around the room, he apparently spied a straight-back chair and moved toward it. Unfortunately, the blue vase sat in his path, and he kicked it over. "What the devil?" He watched water spreading across the floorboards. "What's that doing on the floor?"

Nettled, Susannah set down the kettle, crossed over to pick up the vase. "Is that any of your business?"

He didn't answer but stood, hands on hips, examining the ceiling. "Got a leak in the roof?"

"I repeat, is that any of your business?"

"Could be." He walked to the chair and sat.

"Won't you sit down?" Susannah set the vase on top of the cupboard.

He leaned back and smiled. "Thanks for the reminder that my manners need improving. I'll not argue with you there. In fact, that's why I'm here." He gestured toward the other chair. "Will you please sit too?"

Susannah glanced at the clock on the shelf. Her morning was slipping away.

"It will only take a minute. Please."

She sat.

He clasped his hands in his lap and looked down at them. He cleared his throat.

Susannah looked at the clock again. "Mr. Cooper . . ."

He held up one hand, still not looking at her. "This is harder than I thought."

She waited. She could see a pulse beating at his temple.

Finally he lifted his eyes. His face was pale and his expression very serious. "I'm sorry." He spread his hands. "I should have fixed the halter for that calf instead of making fun of how you had it."

Susannah frowned. "You came all the way out here for that? Why?"

He turned around to look out the door as if checking for a getaway route, then rubbed his hand along his jaw. "I spent sixteen years fighting against everything Nathan Brown tried to teach me, and I've spent the last five learning that I shouldn'ta been fighting. I shoulda been listening and learning." He shrugged. "Yesterday, he fixed the halter for you. I shoulda done that."

Susannah didn't know what to say. It was her turn to look at her hands.

He cleared his throat again. "I'd like to fix your roof."

She shook her head. Then she met his eyes, softening her refusal with a small smile. "There's too much to do around here. If I let you do that, you'd find something else and ask to do that, all to atone for a wretched halter." She stood. "Besides, Wesley's folks—your folks—want me to be able to take care of myself."

He stood as well, stuffing his hands in his pockets. "Then hire me to do it."

She laughed. "I don't have money to pay someone to fix it. If I did, it wouldn't be leaking."

"Feed me supper," he said. "I'm staying at Gertie's Boarding House. I don't think I can face another meal there today."

"You'll repair the roof if I feed you supper? Isn't that like buying a pig in a poke? You don't know what kind of a cook I am."

"You couldn't be worse than Gertie. Is it a deal?" He put out his hand.

She was going to refuse, but the look in those dark eyes wouldn't let her. She shook on it.

He took a deep breath and exhaled. "Well, that went better than I expected."

"Am I such an ogre?"

He cocked his head. "I'm not sure what that means."

"A monster. Am I a monster?"

His dark eyes were serious. "No. You're not a monster. You're—" He paused, then shrugged. "I've never been good with words." Turning, he walked to the door. "Five o'clock? Six o'clock?"

"For supper? How about half past five?"

He nodded and lifted his hand in farewell. When he'd gone out the door, she moved to the screen and watched him walk to his sorrel and mount, noting again the straight back and broad shoulders.

She turned away to finish washing the milk things, her mind busy with ideas for supper. As she considered the merits of noodles compared to dumplings, she became aware that he was whistling as he rode away. She recognized the tune.

It was "Oh, Susannah."

FIVE

Two o'clock that afternoon found Susannah and Sweetie in front of the office of Archie Patterson, Attorney at Law. As she stood in the street gathering her courage, Ivy Patterson stepped out and closed the door behind her. Dressed in a pink dress with leg-o-mutton sleeves and a slight bustle, Ivy carried a pink parasol.

"Good afternoon." Ivy's lips moved into the straight line that Susannah had learned was her rendition of a smile.

"Hello, Ivy."

"Making your rounds, I see." Her former employer's daughter came down the steps and paused a moment to finger the fabric of the quilt. She examined the pink taffeta flowers Susannah had snipped off a party dress and attached to Sweetie's halter. Only when Ivy touched the matching taffeta sash, sewn to the quilt and tied in front in a huge bow, did Susannah remember that the dress had been a hand-me-down from the Pattersons when she worked for them.

"Very clever." Again the straight-lined smile before Ivy continued across the street.

Watching her go, Susannah realized she had been holding her breath. She exhaled, tied Sweetie to the hitching post, and pulled a copy of Wesley's book out of her apron pocket. Straightening her shoulders, she climbed the two steps to the boardwalk that ran through the two-block business district, and she opened the door of the law office.

As she came in, a balding, middle-aged clerk sat at his desk behind the railing and looked over his spectacles. "Hello, Mrs. Brown. I haven't seen you in a long time."

"Good afternoon, Mr. Taylor. Is Mr. Patterson available?"

"He's in his office. Knock first."

Susannah pushed through the gate and approached the heavy wooden door. Her heart began to pound, and she wiped her hands on the skirt of her dress before tapping.

"Come in." The words were clipped, businesslike, assured.

Susannah pictured the small, carefully groomed man on the other side of the door, forced a smile on her face, and turned the ornate brass knob.

Archie Patterson looked up as the door swung open. He didn't return her smile. "Susannah."

"Good afternoon, Mr. Patterson."

"You've come to see me?" He pointed to a chair.

Susannah sat on the edge and crossed her ankles.

"Well?"

Thinking that learning to milk was infinitely easier than door-to-door selling, she plunged ahead. "I was wondering if you'd be interested in buying a copy of Wesley's poems." She held up the book.

Mr. Patterson actually recoiled. The corners of his mouth turned down, as if he'd bitten into something sour. "Why would I want to do that?"

"I heard you tell Judge Nesbit that Wesley was a talented poet."

"Wesley was a damned fool, always mooning around in a velvet jacket and a silk scarf and fancying himself to be Lord Byron. At the time, Ivy was sweet on him, so I put a good face on it." He narrowed his eyes. "You were a parlor maid in my house and, as such, were not supposed to listen to conversations."

"Actually, Mrs. Patterson always called me a governess." Susannah's hands began to tremble. She clutched the book so tightly her knuckles turned white, but she went bravely on. "The volumes are gilt-trimmed and are only eighty-five cents."

"That's too much by eighty cents." He reached in his pocket and tossed a coin onto the desk. "I'll give you a nickel."

Susannah stood. It was all she could do to keep her voice steady. "I regret that I cannot accept your kind offer. Thank you for your time."

She turned and intended to sweep out of the room, but Douglas Cooper stood in the doorway, looking urbane in a well-cut three-piece suit. The shock of seeing him—and having him witness her humiliation—turned her knees to jelly. He must have sensed it, or maybe he noticed the blood leave her face, because he stepped forward, took her free hand, and supported her elbow.

"Good afternoon, Miz Brown. I hope you are well."

"Good afternoon, Mr. Cooper. I am, thank you."

Still supporting her, he walked her to the door. "Shall I accompany you to your next appointment?"

"That won't be necessary. You obviously have business with Mr. Patterson. Good-bye."

As she fled to the outer office, she heard the attorney say, "Cooper! Welcome. Shut the door."

Susannah was grateful that Mr. Taylor wasn't at his desk, and even more grateful that the boardwalk was empty. Seeing the sorrel tied to the hitching post next to Sweetie, she ran down the steps and slipped into the safe haven between the two animals. With shaking hands, she stowed the book in the saddlebag, then put an arm around the calf's neck. "Oh, Sweetie. What an awful day this is."

She took a deep breath. "Wesley wasn't a damn fool," she said. "He was kind and generous and a very good poet. You would have liked him very much."

Sweetie rubbed her head against Susannah's bosom.

"Thank you for that comfort," she said. "Look, you're losing a flower. I'll fix it, and then we'll go see if Gertie wants to buy milk from Patchwork Dairy." She tied the pink flower back to the halter and unhitched the lead rope.

Patting the sorrel on the neck, she murmured, "Tell Mr. Cooper thank you." Then she led Sweetie to the end of the block, where a white, two-story house sat, ringed by a picket fence. A sign hanging from the porch roof proclaimed this to be Gertie's Boarding House.

Susannah stopped in front. "I don't know if I can take two rejections in one day."

Sweetie stood still, but one ear swiveled.

"We could go on home and come back tomorrow. I have someone coming for dinner, you know."

Sweetie turned her head toward the back door of the boarding house.

"Oh, all right. We'll go see Gertie. But don't come bawling to me when she says something awful to us."

Susannah led Sweetie down the lane along the side of the house, and as they reached the back porch, Gertie herself stepped out, carrying a pan of water. Redheaded and ruddy cheeked, she laughed as she saw her visitors. "Who you got there, Queen of the May?"

"This is Sweetie. She's going to be the second cow I milk at Patchwork Dairy."

"Looks like it'll be a little while." Gertie threw the water on a flower bed next to the house.

"It will be, but I'm just starting out. With one cow, I've got more milk than I've got customers. Do you need someone to supply you with nice, rich Jersey milk? It's got lots of cream in it."

Gertie scratched her ample bosom. "Jersey milk, eh?"

"With lots of cream."

Gertie opened the screen and called inside. "Lucy, don't you stop stirring. If it scorches, I'll have your hide." She scratched again, obviously considering. "Would you sell me just cream?"

"How much do you need?"

"As much as you've got to spare."

Susannah grinned. "I can do that."

"You'll probably want to do some figuring, see what you need to charge, but I'll pay what's fair." She opened the screen again. "And if you were of a mind to make cottage cheese with the skim milk, I'd buy that from you too."

"I'll see what I can do."

"Mind you, I'm only doing it because you've got such a purty young heifer there, all done up in flowers and bows."

"I'll bring you some cream tomorrow." Susannah backed away. "Thank you."

"You're welcome." Gertie waved the basin and stepped inside. "Lucy, stir!"

Susannah led Sweetie back toward the road. "How could you ever have doubted?" she asked, tweaking one of the flowers. "You let Mr. Patterson scare you. Don't ever do that again." She rubbed the calf behind the ears. "Now let's go home and fix dinner. How does chicken and dumplings sound?"

SIX

Douglas arrived a little early. Susannah didn't hear him ride up, but she heard him put his horse in the pen beside the lean-to and then heard him climbing onto the roof.

She dropped dough into the boiling chicken broth for dumplings and wiped her hands on her apron. Walking outside, she shaded her eyes and looked up. "You're not going to start that right now, are you?" she called.

He rose from a crouching position. "Good afternoon, Miz Brown."

"Supper's almost ready."

"Just wanted to take a look, see what I'll need to fix it. I'll bring supplies out tomorrow." He walked over the ridge and disappeared from view, reappearing moments later from behind the house.

"The flashing around the chimney has gone to pot," he explained. "I'll bring some sheet lead tomorrow and replace it."

"Will it be expensive?"

He smiled. "Very. It will probably take two or three suppers to pay it off."

She laughed. "You drive a hard bargain. Won't you come in?"

As he followed her in the house, she paused, looking at the ceiling. "That leak was nowhere near the chimney. Are you sure it's the flashes?"

"Flashing," he corrected. "Yes, I'm sure. Water gets in one place, but it runs across to another before it finds a hole to get through." He looked around. "Boy, it's hot in here. You got the windows open?"

"You can't cook without heat," she said.

"What's it going to be like in July?"

"I hate to think, but I have to heat water."

He grabbed the two straight-back chairs and carried them to the door. "You need a summer kitchen."

She watched him push the screen open with one of the chairs. "What are you doing?"

He called from around the corner. "Let's eat out under the old-man pinyon."

"Where?"

"Bring the breadboard and come out back," he called.

She pulled it from its slot and followed. "Why do you call that tree the old-man pinyon?"

He moved a keg sitting under the eaves over between the two chairs. "Because it's so old. Grandpa Brown cut the lower branches so we could eat under it."

She regarded him a moment before handing him the board. "Do you mind that Wesley inherited this place?"

"It's the way it should have been. Wesley was blood kin."

"But—"

"Grandma Brown didn't forget me. I got her wedding ring." He placed the breadboard on the keg. "I think we're ready."

They worked together to transport dishes and food to the outdoor dining area, and soon they were having supper under the shady bower.

"It's nice and cool back here," she said.

"That's because there's a breeze blowing down the ravine."

"What ravine?"

He pointed to the right. "You can't see it because of all the brush. Might be a good thing to clear it away. If a fire got started up on top, it would come barreling down like the midnight special."

Susannah had greater matters to talk about. She leaned forward and fixed her eyes on his. "Why didn't you tell me yesterday down on the road that you were Wesley's brother?"

"Half-brother." He adjusted the position of his spoon. "Why didn't you tell me you were Wesley's wife?"

"Widow." She leaned back. "I guess I was angry because of what you said about him."

"Which was?"

"You thought he'd made the saddlebags. You were making fun of him."

"An old habit of mine. He liked colorful things. Used to wear a red coat."

She felt her cheeks getting warm. "It was claret colored."

"I suppose it was." He smiled. "But it wasn't all one-sided, you know. He would tease me back. Said I had no sense of style."

"That sounds like him," she murmured.

"It was true. Still is."

She shook her head. "You looked very nice today in Mr. Patterson's office."

"A lady I knew took me in hand, taught me a few things." He passed his plate for a second helping, and she spooned it on for him.

"About Mr. Patterson," Douglas said, cutting the

dumpling with his fork. "When I opened the door, he was saying that you'd worked for them. Somehow I can't picture you as a servant."

"You can't? May I remind you that I'm a milkmaid?"

"You're a businesswoman. Quite a difference."

"Is there? I'm working harder now here than I ever did at the Pattersons'."

"How did you end up there? If you don't mind my asking."

She sighed. "The short version of a long story is that I was left an orphan when I was sixteen. My mother died when I was born. My father was a scholar, a lecturer at Boston University. He died of tuberculosis."

"I'm sorry," he said.

"I had no family. We had a library full of books but very little money, and I had no skills fit for earning a living."

"But how did you get from Boston to Masonville?"

"The Ladies' Aid took me as a project. They advertised in church magazines that I would work for room and board." She brushed a pine needle off the table. "The Pattersons were the first to respond. Next thing I knew, I was on a train bound for Arizona Territory."

"It has to be different from the life you knew."

"Completely. But Wesley made up for every loss."

"I see." He picked at a paint fleck on the breadboard. "I saw Ivy Patterson today."

The antipathy Susannah felt at hearing Ivy's name on Douglas's lips surprised her. "Oh?"

"Haven't seen her since she was fifteen." He smiled to himself, still worrying the paint. "She asked me to supper."

Susannah stood. "Don't think you're beholden—"

"I don't." He looked up. "Would you let me help sell your books?"

Her brows drew together. "What do you mean?"

"You're trying to sell them to the wrong people. You need to find a market back east."

She sat down again. "How am I going to do that?"

"Put an ad in an eastern paper. Make it sound, oh, I don't know, exotic."

"Exotic."

"You betcha. And expensive. How much do you make on a book if you sell it for eighty-five cents?"

She cleared her throat. "A nickel."

"Charge a dollar and a half."

"A dollar and a half! Who would pay that?"

"Lots of little old ladies. I know someone who will put an ad in the *Troy Morning Telegram* for you. That's in New York."

"Is this the same person who taught you how to dress?" But before he could answer, she held up her finger for silence. "Hear that?"

"All I can hear is a cow bawling."

"That's Lady telling me it's milking time." She stood and started gathering dishes. "Your folks are very wise, you know."

"How's that?" He grabbed the chicken pot and the breadboard, and they headed around to the kitchen.

"They knew I wouldn't come back to life for my own sake. They practically forced me out here and gave me a creature that depends on me to get up and do something twice a day."

"You wouldn't come back to life?" He opened the door for her.

She nodded. "I wanted to die. Tried to die. For months after I lost Wesley, I either slept or sat in a dark room, holding his coat. The claret-colored one." She smiled up at him.

"I can't believe that."

"It's true." She put down the dishes, took the basin from its nail, and poured in water from the kettle. "Could you go open the gate? Can't keep Lady waiting."

"Yes ma'am."

He strode out the door and down to the pasture while she carried the basin and milk bucket out to the shed. After swinging the doors wide, she stood inside and watched him follow Lady as she ambled up the lane. The sun had already dipped behind the bluffs, cooling the air and turning the horizon periwinkle.

She murmured her thanks for bringing in the cow, then slipped into her milkmaid routine. Once, she glanced up to see him leaning a shoulder against the barn door, watching her.

"You could feed the chickens and gather the eggs," she remarked and smiled to herself as he complied. *Handy fellow to have around.*

He proved as much again when he helped her take care of the milk and wash up. Susannah brought a lantern as they carried the cans to the spring. Though outside it was dusk, inside the cave would be completely dark.

Walking into the cave from the warm outside air was like walking into Jack Frost's lair. The frigid pool began about ten steps beyond the mouth of the cavern and spread from wall to wall, reaching back about sixty feet. Shallow and flat for a little ways, the bottom quickly dropped to a dangerous depth.

Susannah held the lantern up as Douglas placed the milk cans in the water.

"You've got three gallons in here already," he said. "Your customers aren't keeping up."

"Gertie's going to buy cream and cottage cheese from me."

"Where did you learn to make cottage cheese?"

"I haven't yet. That's next on my list."

He laughed out loud. "You are fearless. Ask my mother. She knows."

"I will." She shivered. "It's cold in here. Let's go

outside." Unconsciously, she reached for his hand as she turned to leave the cave.

Moments later, she realized what she'd done. Her cheeks grew warm with embarrassment, but she didn't know how to gracefully get out of the situation, because he'd laced his fingers through hers.

She stopped in the middle of the path. "Douglas?" She hated how she'd become breathless, and she scolded herself for getting herself into this predicament and acting like a schoolgirl.

With great resolution, she raised her hand, bringing his with it. "I didn't mean to do this. I don't know why I did."

"I do." He chuckled and brought her hand to his lips, kissing the knuckle of her pinky finger. "But don't worry. I'm not interested in being proxy for a ghost."

He released her and continued to stroll back to the house.

Feeling like a deflated balloon, she walked beside him, the hand that had held his suddenly empty and barren. She wished it weren't so dark so she could see better. She needed to kick a rock down the path. Instead she said, "For someone who has trouble with big words, you rolled that one off your tongue pretty easily."

"What do you mean?"

"*Proxy*. That's not a word in everyone's vocabulary."

"I own a few mining shares. It's a word you hear quite often at shareholders' meetings."

At the house, she held the lantern as he saddled his horse. Neither spoke until he was astride.

"What time do you want me here for supper tomorrow?" he asked.

"Same time, unless you'd rather have supper with Ivy."

He ignored her remark. "I'll come early and fix the roof. Can you have that advertisement written?"

"I suppose so."

LIZ ADAIR

"Remember: exotic and expensive." He touched the brim of his hat and clicked his tongue to the sorrel.

Susannah watched as he rode beyond the circle of her lamp and was swallowed by the night, though she could still hear the sound of his horse's hooves growing fainter.

And then, floating through the warm evening air, came the whistled tune of "Oh, Susannah." She smiled as she walked back to the house.

She went to bed, curling on her side and waiting for the comfort of the covers' warmth. Closing her eyes, she anticipated sleep and Wesley's visit. Tonight of all nights, she longed for a return to what Hidden Spring had been to them, an Eden where they spent the days making love and reading poetry, lost in the pleasure of words and each other.

Wesley didn't come. She slept soundly and dreamlessly and woke the next morning out of sorts and on edge. A phrase dodged around the frontiers of her memory, one she knew was important but couldn't recall. She frowned as she heated water, as she went down to open the gate for Lady, as she washed the cow's udder. It was only when she was on the stool, forehead against the Jersey's side and listening to the sound of each stream hitting the bottom of the bucket, that the phrase came to her. It repeated over and over in time to the splash of the milk:

I'm not interested.
I'm not interested.
I'm not interested.

SEVEN

Heading home after deliveries that afternoon, Susannah heard a wagon approaching from behind. She led Sweetie to the side of the road to let it pass, but it stopped beside her. Looking up, she saw Douglas on the wagon seat and recognized Cookie, Papa Brown's horse, in the traces.

"Good evening, Miz Brown. Would you like a ride?"

"Are you on your way to Hidden Spring?"

"Sure am. Tie Sweetie on behind." He sprang down and transferred the quilt-saddlebag from the calf to the wagon. "Four gallon jugs," he said. "You get many more customers, and you're going to have to get a bigger pack animal."

He walked around the wagon, pulling the brim of his hat down to shade his eyes as he watched a rider approach from town. "Afternoon, Bobby," he called, smiling.

The rider didn't answer until he was abreast. He stopped his horse, tipped his hat to Susannah, then looked at Douglas. "Dummy? Is that you?"

"People don't call me that anymore." Douglas's tone

was friendly, but his smile grew rigid when a muscle in his jaw tightened.

"Uh, sorry." Bobby shifted in the saddle. "I hear you're one of the big shots looking to reopen the Silver Jack. Hear you been to college in New York and everything."

"I'm not a big shot," Douglas said. "And I'm here to see if we can pump water out cheap enough to make reopening pay."

"You gonna be hiring?"

Douglas climbed onto the wagon box. "Come see me at the mine. My office is by the old timekeeper's shack."

"I'll do that. Thanks . . . Douglas." Bobby raised his hat to Susannah. "Ma'am." He kicked his horse and trotted on down the road.

Susannah watched him go. "Who was that?"

Douglas picked up the reins and slapped them on Cookie's back. "Bobby Schumacher. He was in my grade in school."

"What did he call you?"

He looked away. "I'd just as soon not talk about it."

Something tightened in Susannah's throat, like she was going to cry. She looked away as well, and they rode in silence to the Hidden Spring intersection. He made the turn but stopped the wagon in the shadow of a bluff.

"I couldn't read," he said.

"Beg pardon?"

He fiddled with the reins. "I attended through the eighth grade, and that last year, I was still reading with the second graders."

Susannah looked at the man beside her. His shoulders slumped, and he rested his elbows on his knees, holding the reins in slack fingers. Such a different face from the proud, almost arrogant one he had been showing her. Her heart ached for him, and she touched his wrist.

"Oh, Douglas," she whispered.

He shook her off with an almost imperceptible flick. "I don't need pity. You asked; I answered. My folks called me Sonny, but the kids called me Dummy because I couldn't read."

"But you—he said you went to college."

"It was a polytechnic institute."

"Whatever it was, how could you do that if you couldn't read?"

Douglas clicked his tongue at Cookie, and they continued up the lane. "I learned."

"When? How?"

"I found a lady to teach me." He chuckled. "Her name was Mrs. Smithers. She was eccentric and had a houseful of cats. And bad plumbing. I fixed the plumbing, and she fixed my reading."

"Just like that?"

"No. Not just like that. It took a year—to fix the reading, not the plumbing. I wanted to give up lots of times, but she was determined."

"Was that in New York? How did you end up there?"

"After I left school, I went to work at the Silver Jack. They were fighting the water then, trying to stay ahead of the underground streams in lower levels." He looked at her to see if she understood.

She nodded.

"I worked with a man by the name of Mr. Rathbone for six years. He taught me all he knew about water, but in the end, we couldn't keep the mine dry, and they closed 'er down."

"Then what happened?"

He pushed his hat to the back of his head. "Mr. Rathbone took me with him to mine headquarters in Troy. They wanted me to go to school, become a hydraulic engineer, but there was that one problem."

"You couldn't read."

"That's the one."

They were passing the middle pasture, and Susannah pointed. "I need to put Sweetie in."

"I'll do it." Douglas set the brake, hopped down, and let the calf loose in the field. Back in the wagon, he handed the flower-decked halter to Susannah and picked up the reins.

"Wait a minute," Susannah said. "You said you left because they closed the mines. I heard that you left because you almost killed a man in a bar fight."

Douglas threw back his head and laughed. "Is that what people said?"

She nodded.

"I did rough up Zeke Russell pretty good the night before I left, but he was still on his feet last time I saw him."

"But you never wrote to your family. You simply disappeared."

"I didn't write because I couldn't. Didn't know how. And after I learned—" He stopped the wagon at the house. "I just can't put what's in my heart on paper." He climbed out and walked around to help her down. "I'll fix the roof while you get supper, and then I need to get Papa's rig back to him."

"You mean you're leaving right after supper?" Susannah tried to keep her disappointment from showing.

Douglas looked up from the rope he was uncoiling. "I don't want to leave Cookie standing too long." He tied the horse near the watering trough, unloaded his tools, and set a bucket of tar to melting over a small fire.

Susannah went inside and made supper out of leftover chicken and dumplings, adding some early peas she'd carried home in her apron pocket from Mama Brown's garden. She skimmed cream from last night's milk, set it aside to go over home-canned peaches, and poured the rest into a pitcher.

As she carried chairs out back, Susannah glanced up at Douglas working on the roof with the deft motions of a craftsman. Her eyes lingered on the way his shirt pulled tight across his back as he crouched down and the way his black hair fell forward over his brow. He looked up and caught her watching; she turned away to place the chairs under the pinyon tree.

Moments later, she heard him come down the ladder. "Almost done," he said.

"So's supper."

He appeared a moment later with the tar bucket, and as he effortlessly scaled the ladder again, she went back to setting up supper. By the time everything was ready, he was finished, and the tools and ladder were put away.

"I'll just wash up," he said, rolling up his sleeves. "May I use some of your hot water?"

Susannah nodded and sat waiting under the pinyon, enjoying the coolness of the breeze as it blew down the ravine.

He returned, pausing at the corner of the house to button his cuffs, and then he came over and sat opposite. "It smells tasty. Thank you, Miz Brown."

She ladled chicken and dumplings into a shallow bowl for him. "My name is Susannah."

"I know."

"Why do you call me Mrs. Brown? You could say we're family."

He picked up his spoon. "You could. Or, you could say that we have a business arrangement, and that with my being a single fellow out here alone with you every evening for supper, it's better if I don't start using your Christian name."

"But that arrangement will be over at the end of the week."

"Well, as to that . . ." He sat back, eyes twinkling. "How would you like to have water piped from the spring to the house so all you had to do for water was turn on a faucet?"

Her brows shot up. "Could you do that?"

He grinned. "Easy as pie."

Susannah clapped her hands in delight, and they spent the rest of the meal talking about the project. Every time she thought of a new way it would make her life easier, she voiced it, and when he climbed into the wagon to go home, she was still listing them.

"I'll be able to fill the tub on wash day so much more quickly," she said.

He picked up the reins. "You already said that."

"Did I?" She put her hands in her apron pocket. "Oh, I forgot. Here's the ad you wanted me to write. To sell Wesley's poems."

He took it from her and stowed it in the pocket of his shirt.

She backed away. "Tomorrow evening, then?"

"Yes." He touched the brim of his hat and clicked to Cookie, and the wagon started down the lane.

Susannah followed behind, heading to the middle pasture where the Jersey grazed. By the time she made it to the gate, Douglas was passing the fence line at the end of the lower pasture. She undid the latch and watched the wagon disappear behind a screen of willows, standing for a moment to listen intently before she called Lady in.

There it was, floating on the warm purple haze of the evening air—the sound of a whistled "Oh, Susannah."

EIGHT

Susannah and Douglas settled into a comfortable routine. He would arrive about an hour before supper and work until she called him in to eat. As the days lengthened, he worked after they ate as well, sinking an intake port into the spring and laying pipe from there to the house.

"We'll worry about getting it in the ground before cold weather," he said. "For now, let's just get the water flowing."

It took two weeks of work, but one evening he called her out of the kitchen to a standpipe by the watering trough. "It's ready," he said. "Will you turn on the tap?"

She did so, and cold, clear water gushed out of the faucet. "Oh, Douglas! That's the most beautiful sight I've seen in a long time." She turned the handle off and then on again, grinning up at him. "It's wonderful." She stood on tiptoe and kissed him on the rough patch on his cheek.

He bent down to stow his tools in a satchel. "Just paying for my supper. Glad it pleases you." He spoke without looking up.

"It pleases me enormously. And speaking of supper, it's

ready." She walked with him back to the kitchen, and while he washed up, she said, "I've got another batch of cottage cheese for you to try." She handed him a spoon and lifted a dish towel, revealing a crock of snowy curds bathed in cream.

"Looks good." He put a spoonful in his mouth.

She waited as he closed his eyes, and she smiled as the corners of his lips curled up. "How is it?" she asked.

His eyes opened. "Right on the money. Can you make it like this every time?"

"That's the challenge." She handed him a kettle to carry out to the pinyon tree and picked up a pan of biscuits. "The trick is in heating the curd. Slow and low is the secret."

All during supper, they talked about the next project. He wanted to make her a summer kitchen, but she felt it would be better to get the piping in the ground before the summer rains started. And she'd have liked a shelter in each pasture before then too.

"You're the boss," he said, and for the next three weeks, he worked at getting a ditch dug parallel to the water line. When the pipes were underground, he brought Papa Brown's wagon, and they went up on the bluff to cut cedar poles for the shelters. It took a week to get all they needed, and another two weeks to get the shelters built.

The day after he finished, he brought Susannah a piglet. "He's the runt of a litter that Bobby Schumacher had, but he'll grow if you feed him the whey from your cottage cheese."

Susannah was delighted and named him Percy. While she did the evening milking, Douglas fixed the pen beside the chicken coop so the piglet couldn't root underneath and get out. As she finished, he came into the milking parlor. She handed him the pail while she undid the stanchion. "I'm staying in town after my deliveries tomorrow, so supper may be late."

"Oh?" He moved aside for the Jersey to go out the door.

"It's my anniversary. Wesley's and mine. I'm going to the cemetery."

He nodded and carried the pail into the kitchen, setting it on the table. As she followed, he pulled a folded paper from his pocket and handed it to her. "I almost forgot this. I'll go put Lady in the pasture."

He went out the door, and she opened the note, finding another paper inside. She read the letter and then the enclosure before trotting down the lane to meet him on his way back.

"Somebody sent a postal money order for a copy of Wesley's book?"

"Looks like."

"We've been so busy, I forgot about the ad." She looked at the letter again. "You make me believe anything is possible."

He smiled down at her as they walked to the house. "Likewise, I'm sure."

NINE

The cemetery sat on the far edge of town, a dusty patch of land surrounded by a barbed-wire fence and sprouting sagebrush, wooden grave markers, and tombstones. Susannah arrived late afternoon and tied Sweetie to a post.

She hadn't visited the graveyard for well over two months, not since moving back to Hidden Spring. It felt a little strange, like when she returned to the Browns' when it wasn't home anymore. She used to talk to Wesley when she came, but now that seemed strange too.

She pulled a tumbleweed, a vigorous bit of green sprouting from the dun-colored earth covering her beloved—or the beloved of the girl she had been last year. She didn't feel like the same person now.

A sound behind her made her look around, and her heart beat a staccato rhythm as she recognized the rider dismounting his horse. "Hello, Douglas." She took a deep breath as he came toward her.

"Do you mind if I'm here, too? I haven't visited since I came back."

She shook her head, and he stood quietly for a moment, staring at Wesley's headstone.

"I don't know how he died," he said. "Mama mentioned blood poisoning, but she wouldn't talk about it."

"It got pretty awful before the end."

"I'm sorry. I shouldn't have brought it up."

"That's all right." She flapped her arms against her sides. "It was so stupid. It started out as a blister on his foot."

"A blister?"

"He spent most of the money he inherited from Grandma Brown on publishing his poems. That was to be our income, you know." She folded her arms and looked at her shoes. "He caught a ride to Tucson and tried to sell some there, but nobody would buy them. He couldn't find a ride all the way back, so he walked the last twenty miles. I often wonder—" She stopped and closed her eyes.

"What do you wonder?"

"If he didn't die of a broken heart. You know, from the rejection."

Douglas put his hands in his back pockets and kicked at a dirt clod. "I don't think you die of a broken heart," he said quietly. "Rejection can break your heart, but you end up living with it."

They stood in silence for a moment, and then he said, "My father is buried here too."

"Where?"

"I'll show you." He led her down the row to a grave with a wooden marker.

Susannah deciphered the faded writing, then did some math. "She must have remarried pretty soon after he died."

"She did. Maybe because a good man came along."

Susannah nodded. "And because a little boy needed a father?"

"Maybe. Too bad the little boy didn't appreciate his good luck."

The bitterness in his voice made her look sharply at him. "What do you mean?"

Douglas took his hat off and ran his hand through his black hair. "Nathan Brown is as good as they come, but I never could forgive him for not being my father." He gestured toward Wesley's grave with the hat. "And I couldn't forgive Wesley for being all the things I wasn't."

"Because he could read and you couldn't?"

"I guess." He sighed and put his hat back on. "Papa—Nathan Brown—wanted to adopt me, wanted me to carry his name, but I wouldn't have it. I was sure he was ashamed of me, so I went around being angry and raising hell."

"Like the barroom fight?"

"Yeah. Who wants a son who gets in trouble all the time?"

She turned and began walking toward the gate. "You're not getting in trouble now, are you?"

He laughed as he walked beside her. "Maybe. Just a different kind of trouble." He nodded toward the sorrel, tied by Sweetie. "Want a ride home?"

"If I ride, you'll have to walk. I'm used to walking."

"We can ride double."

She looked down at her skirt, and he added, "You can be in front. Hook your knee over the horn like a sidesaddle. You'll be fine."

She nodded, and he lifted her into the saddle. While she shifted to get her right leg positioned correctly, he tied Sweetie's lead rope to the rear saddle string. Then he swung up behind the cantle and turned the sorrel toward Hidden Spring.

As they rode, Susannah was very aware of his proximity, of his arms around her as he held the reins, and of his chest as she leaned against him for stability. Her whole world shrank to the places she felt his touch—her arms, her back, where his cheek rested against her hair. Neither of them spoke, and when they finally arrived at the house, he silently dismounted and reached up for her. She unhooked her knee and put her hands on his shoulders, looking into his dark eyes as she slid off.

When her feet touched the ground, he didn't move away.

"Susannah . . ." His voice had a husky timbre. He stood so close, she could feel his body heat.

She touched his face lightly, fingertips grazing over the rough patch on his cheek, feeling the texture of the stubble on his jaw line. She felt his arms encircle her, pressing her to him, and as she ran a hand through his raven hair, she knocked off his hat. Ignoring the loss, she put her arm around his neck and raised her mouth to his. Feeling the moistness of his lips, her own parted, and she abandoned herself to a flood of hunger and desire, things she hadn't felt for such a long time. His breathing quickened, and she could feel his pulse under her fingers at his temple, beating in time with her own.

When his lips moved to her cheek and then to her hair, she held him close and murmured, "Oh, Wesley."

He stiffened. He pulled away, and she opened her eyes. He was still breathing hard, but he wasn't looking at her.

"Douglas? What's the matter?"

He didn't answer but shook his head as he bent to pick up his hat. He slapped it against his knee to get the dust off.

"Douglas?"

"The devil of it is, you don't even know."

Realization began to dawn. She had called him by the name of her dead husband. Susannah's eyes widened, and she covered her mouth with her hands. "Oh, no. I didn't mean it. You know I didn't mean it."

Douglas began untying Sweetie's lead rope.

Susannah tugged at his shirt. "Douglas, please listen to me."

"There's nothing for you to say. You already said it." He turned to face her. "It's another case of Wesley being everything I'm not, and there's no way I can compete with a dead man."

She shook her head, tears running down her face. "That's not the way it is."

He gave the watering trough a vicious kick. "Have you thought about the life you'da had with him? When the money ran out, what would you have lived on?"

She *had* been thinking about it lately, and the fact that he voiced questions she had been reluctant to speak put her in a defensive mode. "That's none of your business!"

"How could he leave you like this, working from dawn to dusk, carrying buckets of water from the spring? I'll bet he made sure you had plenty of those useless books. I'll bet you have stacks of them."

She covered her ears. "I'm not going to listen to you say hateful things about him."

He replied, but with hands over her ears, she couldn't hear. She could see the angry expression on his face, though, and it took the starch right out of her. She walked to the house and sank onto the porch, and when she looked up, he was astride the sorrel.

He touched the brim of his hat. "I won't stay for dinner. In fact, I'll be eating at Gertie's from now on. Good-bye, Miz Brown." He kicked the sorrel to a lope.

"Douglas, wait!"

If he heard her, he didn't respond, and he didn't look back as he rode down the lane and out of her life.

TEN

Though she felt like holing up in her dark bedroom as she had when she lost Wesley, the sound of Lady announcing the discomfort of a distended udder made Susannah get out into the early morning sunlight and accomplish something. She milked the Jersey. Took care of the milk. Fed the chickens. Made cottage cheese. Slopped the pig. Walked to town to make her deliveries.

Each night, as she ate a solitary supper, she realized how lonely it was without Douglas, and every time she turned on the tap and got running water, her heart ached for the man who'd made it happen.

A week after the visit to the cemetery, she met Ivy Patterson in town. Susannah would have avoided the meeting, but Ivy popped out of the back door as she was handing the milk jug to the Pattersons' cook.

"Why, Susannah Brown. Are you ailing? You look positively haggard." Ivy wore a dress of lavender cotton lawn, her dark hair piled high and ringlets falling artfully over one ear.

"Good afternoon, Ivy." Susannah wished she could leave right then, but the cook had gone to get the milk money.

Ivy checked her image in the back door windowpane. "I suppose you know that Wesley's brother, Douglas, has been having supper with us every day this week."

"Why would I know that?"

"Family connection."

"He doesn't live with his folks. I rarely see him."

"Oh?" Ivy raised one brow. "Fanny Miller saw you riding double out by the cemetery last week."

"Douglas gave me a ride home." The cook appeared. Susannah gratefully pocketed the coins and turned to go.

Ivy stepped in front of her. "When he was here yesterday, he mentioned to my papa that he's thinking of marrying."

Susannah felt blood drain from her face. She put a hand on the door jamb for support.

Ivy cocked her head. "I swear, Susannah, you look positively ill. Do you need a drink of water?"

"No thank you, Ivy. I'm fine." She pushed past and untied Sweetie, who was tethered to the fence. Walking as fast as she could, Susannah kept her head down, lest someone see her tears threatening.

It was hard enough to think that she had lost Douglas, but that he would marry Ivy Patterson was too much to bear. Reaching Main Street, she turned at the corner by the courthouse and ran straight into a man as he stepped off the boardwalk into the street.

She didn't realize who it was as she apologized for the collision. He must not have known either, for when Douglas turned to face her, his eyes got wide. They stood for what seemed an eternity, neither speaking, gazing at each other.

Finally he spoke. "Afternoon, Miz Brown. Are you not well?"

"I'm fine." But though she mouthed the words, no sound came out.

Silence again.

He gestured toward the courthouse. "I just came to town to fill out some forms. I'm getting ready for something I'm fixing to do." He held up an official-looking document, complete with a seal.

She moistened her lips and tried again. "Ivy told me."

"Did she? She wasn't supposed to—" He frowned. "Never mind." Touching his hat, he turned, bounded up the boardwalk stairs, and entered the general store.

"Come on, Sweetie," Susannah murmured. "Let's drag our broken heart home." She glanced back at the merchant's door and saw Douglas watching her from the window.

The walk back to Hidden Spring was the longest it had ever been, even longer than that first day when she'd had to carry two milk pails the whole way. Towering, black-bottomed clouds approached from the north, and she quickened her pace, not wanting to get caught in the rain.

"That would really complete my day," she told Sweetie.

By the time she reached the lower pasture, the sky had turned inky. Thunder rolled across the canyon as jagged lightning bolts connected to the bluffs. Susannah took the saddlebags off and put Sweetie in the upper pasture.

"Don't be frightened," she said. "If you were up on top, you might want to worry, but lightning won't strike down here."

She did the evening chores early, but even so, she had to light the lantern to see to wash up. She wondered whether to leave Lady in the shed overnight but figured it would probably be another dry lightning storm like the one they'd had last week. The shelter Douglas had built would protect her if it rained. She gathered the eggs and fed the chickens, noting they were roosting early, heads tucked under their wings. After mixing whey into the pig mash, she filled Percy's trough, and as he smacked his lips over it, she scratched his bristly back.

When everything was finally done, she retreated to the house and got ready for bed. She braided her hair, blew out the lamp, and lay there, feeling the cool breeze blowing down the ravine. She was grateful for the diversion of lightning flashes and the window-rattling thunderclaps that followed, because they took her mind off the image of Ivy standing at the altar with Douglas.

She finally fell asleep, only to be awakened sometime later by Percy's high-pitched squeals. The storm seemed to have passed, but the moment Susannah opened her eyes, she knew something was terribly wrong.

ELEVEN

She couldn't see anything because of the darkness, but a choking smoke filled the air, and a dull roar filled her ears, sounding like wind rushing down the canyon.

With shaking hands, she found matches and lit the lamp. Turning up the wick, she carried the lamp outside. It was a moonless night, but the house had an orange halo behind it. Fear clutching at her heart, she ran past Percy's pen to the back. Flames flared up from the ravine, and a blast of hot air hit her like an oven.

Percy's squeals were more frantic now, and Susannah dashed to the gate. Fumbling in the dark, she used precious moments figuring out how to undo a latch she'd opened without thinking every other day of her life. She held the gate wide and called the pig, but Percy was nowhere to be seen.

The roaring in the ravine was getting louder now, the crackling of pine and cedar adding to the noise. Smoke burned her eyes and made it harder to see. Holding up the lantern, she headed for the source of the keening cries and found the pig in a corner. She quickly set down the lantern, then grabbed his hind legs and dragged him out the gate.

"You're on your own now," she called as she pushed him toward the lane.

Embers rained down from the sky—beautiful, glowing fireworks floating on the wind and landing all around. Some lodged on the cedar shingle roof of the house and began burning so brightly she didn't need the lamp she'd left in Percy's pen.

Putting one arm over her nose, she raced to the chicken coop. She found the birds packed tightly against the wall, making plaintive cooing sounds. Holding her breath and squinting through streaming eyes, she gathered an armful of hens, ran outside, and flung them into the air.

Just then, the old-man pinyon turned into a thirty-foot torch.

She dashed back in, the light in the coop much brighter than before, making it easier to see the three remaining chickens. She grabbed them and ran.

She didn't stop running until she reached the upper pasture. Sinking to the grass, she watched as the house and everything she owned went up in flames.

It didn't take long for the house to burn to a skeleton. The loft crashed down, sending a cloud of sparks into the breaking dawn. After that, though fires continued to flicker, they were smaller, more localized blazes and not the massive conflagration that had engulfed the house.

A small squawk reminded Susannah she still cradled three hens. She set them down and leaned against a fence post, trying to calculate what she had lost. All her clothing. All her savings. She wiggled her bare toes and added shoes to the list. She didn't even have a milking bucket.

About that time, she became aware of the sound of a horse approaching at a gallop. The morning was now light enough that she could see as far as the lower pasture. Was it a sorrel? Her heart hammered in her chest.

She stood and watched the rider approach. Something about the way he sat his horse told her it was Douglas, and when he called her name, she ran down the lane.

They met at the middle pasture fence line. Douglas dismounted while the horse was still moving and held his arms wide. She ran to him, felt herself folded into an embrace, and immediately began to tremble.

She couldn't restrain the shaking or the wave of sobbing that swept over her. He didn't say anything, just held her close until she regained control. Finally she spoke. "It came so fast. If Percy hadn't woken me, I'd still be in there."

He gave her his handkerchief. "Bobby Schumacher told me there was a fire burning on the bluff, and I was afraid it had traveled down the ravine."

"It did." She wiped her eyes. "I barely had time to save Percy and the chickens."

He touched a hole in her sleeve. "I can see how close. You've got charred places all over your nightgown. I should've cleared out the brush instead of building those shelters."

He put his arm around her waist, and they walked to where the remains of the house still smoldered. The only recognizable thing left was the cook stove. "When we build again, we'll have a summer kitchen," he said. "And running water. And indoor plumbing."

"Sounds wonderful, but how can that happen when you're going to marry Ivy?"

His jaw dropped, and he turned to face her. "Where did you get that idea?"

"From her. She said you'd been talking to her father about marrying."

"I talked to him about changing my name."

"*Your* name?" Susanna thought about that a moment. "I can understand how she'd get the pronoun wrong, but why do you want to change *your* name?"

"For Papa. To say I'm sorry."

"Oh." She smiled. "He'll like that."

He poked a pile of smoldering debris with the toe of his boot. "I'm sorry about the things I said that day after the cemetery."

"You were right when you said I had boxes of Wesley's books. That's a pile of them still burning over there. They're all gone now."

"I've got one."

"Where did you—" She laughed in realization. "You picked it up the day I met you."

He nodded and began to recite, "'Love, thou art like the waters that flow to Hidden Spring.'" He wouldn't look at her, but his voice was warm and full of expression as he went through the whole poem.

When he finished, she said, "For someone who learned to read late, you do pretty well."

He shrugged. "I read that poem every night before I go to bed."

"Even this last week?"

"Especially this last week." He dropped to one knee. "Love, will you change your name to mine?"

"Um, if you're going to be Douglas Brown, I wouldn't be changing my name."

"Hadn't thought about that." He stood and took both her hands. "Then say you'll marry me."

"I will."

He kissed her long and hard then, and she kissed him back, shedding the black heartache of the last week along with the ties to her widowhood.

"Oh, Douglas," she sighed.

"Oh, Susannah," he murmured as he bent down to kiss her again.

ABOUT LIZ ADAIR

New Mexican native Liz Adair lives in Kanab, Utah, with Derrill, her husband of 50 years. A late bloomer, Liz published her first Spider Latham Mystery just as AARP started sending invitations to join.

After writing three in the Spider Latham series, Liz moved into romantic suspense with best-selling *The Mist of Quarry Harbor*. She took a break from suspense to write *Counting the Cost,* a novel based on family history. The book won a 2009 Whitney Award and was a finalist for the Willa Award and Arizona Publisher Association's Glyph Award.

Cold River, a romantic suspense, followed, and now Liz is set to bring Spider Latham back to solve a mystery set in southern Utah's red rock country, titled *Trouble at the Red Pueblo.*

Liz is a member of LDStorymakers and American Night Writers Association, and she chairs the annual Kanab Writers Conference.

Visit her blog at SezLizAdair.blogspot.com.

THE SILVER MINE BACHELOR

by Heather B. Moore

Other Works by Heather B. Moore

Esther the Queen

Finding Sheba

Beneath

The Aliso Creek Series

Heart of the Ocean

The Newport Ladies Book Club Series

The Fortune Café

ONE

1885—Leadville, Colorado

The Leadville church congregation had exactly nine eligible men. Well, ten, if Lydia Stone considered her new boss the marrying kind. But Mr. Erik Dawson was not the kind of man she could ever imagine kissing . . . And kissing would be required if she were to become a married woman before she turned the spinster age of twenty-seven.

The heavy-set reverend of the Leadville congregation closed his sermon, and the choir started to sing. Lydia twisted her hands as the melody rose. As a young girl, she'd loved singing, but those days were over. Her father had been the one to teach her the hymns. After he died, Lydia hadn't sung much. It was just too painful. God would have to be happy she was even at church.

She caught sight of Mr. Dawson sitting one pew in front of her to the far left—his back ramrod straight, as always. Lydia didn't have to see his eyes to remember that they were deep green—like the shady side of a pine tree.

Green eyes that could freeze a bear in its tracks. Over the past two weeks, Lydia had heard plenty of stern words from Mr. Dawson to his employees. She doubted that any of the miners cared for their boss, and she was certain he cared nothing for them. Like most of the mine owners in Leadville, profit was his only concern.

Lydia could respect a stern businessman, yes, but not a hypocrite. She'd heard rumors about Mr. Dawson being sweet on a woman from one of the brothels. Though Lydia tried not to give much credit to gossip, having been the target of old gossips before, she knew there was always a grain of truth in rumors. The fact that Mr. Dawson was at church actually shocked her—a man who frequented the brothel had no place for his black heart inside a holy building.

The only thing that gave Erik Dawson away as being the tiniest bit human was how his natural curls had fallen out of position, especially with his hat off, as it was now. Lydia forced herself to not steal a peek at the dark curls above his starched white collar.

Lydia had been an employee of the Dawson Mining Company for a full sixteen days, but already in that short amount of time, she'd narrowed down her list of eligible men. She'd been to church twice and decided that's where she had to pick from. Plenty of unmarried men worked in the silver mines high in the Colorado Rockies, but not many were churchgoers, preferring instead the atmosphere of one of the many saloons strewn along Main Street.

Another of the bachelors sat by her—Mr. Parker—close enough she could tell he'd washed up before crossing the church's threshold. That detail was important to Lydia; church attendance and cleanliness were at the top of her list of required attributes for a potential husband. Although Mr. Parker's hands were grime stained from working in the mine. Lydia had seen miners scrub their hands with the harshest lye soap, only to have it make very little difference.

Lydia swallowed back her distaste for things that weren't clean. If she were to marry a miner, she'd have to put up with stained hands. She moved her attention from Mr. Parker and focused once more on the choir. Two of the eligible men were singing—Mr. Roberts and Mr. Brown. Mr. Roberts was a bit short for her taste. What would it be like to kiss a man a tad shorter than she? Would she have to lean down? Her face flushed at the thought, and she looked away from Mr. Roberts. The other eligible bachelor in the choir had the reddest hair Lydia had ever seen on a man, or anyone, for that matter. Yet his name was Mr. Brown.

Mr. Brown also sang louder than all of the other choir members, reminding Lydia of her father—not a good thing. The choir launched into a rendition of one of her father's favorites, and Lydia's eyes stung with tears.

Lydia blinked rapidly and drew in a breath to calm herself. She diverted herself from the swelling music by glancing discreetly about the room. Mr. Janson sat in the row ahead of her boss. Mr. Janson was a bit craggy in the face— perhaps he'd had the pox as a child—but he was kind and soft-spoken.

How did such a gentle man endure such a harsh work environment? Mining was hard labor, and unless you had ownership in the mine, the pay wasn't enough to support a family. Men shared rooms in boarding houses, scrimping and saving until they could get enough money to move on. Rumblings of a strike for higher wages were part of everyday gossip.

Lydia's eyes flitted to Mr. Dawson again. He'd joined in the singing—all of the congregation had except for her. As the music assaulted her heart, she went over her mental list of requirements a husband would need to possess. They were quite specific—as well they should be.

Her mother had been the one who encouraged Lydia to apply for the secretary job, saying, "You'll find yourself a hard-working, ambitious man up at Leadville. Just make sure he's a family man and goes to church and that he has eyes only for you."

Lydia's mother's advice had never gone astray. Not when Lydia had been engaged to Roger *or* to Thomas. Her mother had been right about both men . . . neither had fulfilled her mother's five requirements. Thankfully, Lydia's hometown knew only of her engagement to Thomas. And the engagement to Roger had been very brief. Two failed engagements, however, were enough motivation for her to leave an all-knowing small town for a bigger one and make a fresh start.

Her gaze stopped at Mr. Bartholomew, who sat on the right side of the church, his eyes fastened on the choir. He wasn't singing either, but he seemed absorbed in the music. His suit was far from new, yet it was clean . . . a mark of a conscientious man. Plus, he kept his hair short and his face shaved. For those reasons, she added him to her list.

The hymn came to a merciful close, and as Reverend Stanley prayed in dramatic tones for the souls of the "good citizens of Leadville," Lydia took another peek at Mr. Dawson. His head was bowed, but his eyes weren't closed. In fact, from the corner of his eye, he was peering at *her*.

Heat rushed to Lydia's face, then spread all the way to her toes. She lowered her head, snapped her eyes shut, and squeezed her gloved hands together. Even with her eyes closed, she could see Mr. Dawson's green ones in her mind, along with the slight upward turn of his mouth and the way his curls had escaped their careful Sabbath grooming.

Oh, laws. Someone please save me from the embarrassment of being caught staring at my boss. If the reverend hadn't still been praying, and Lydia hadn't feared causing a disturbance by hurrying out of the church, she would have left then and there. If only to escape what was surely a very amused Mr. Dawson.

TWO

Erik Dawson leaned against the outside wall of the church, waiting for the reverend to finish talking to the departing members of the congregation. For two years he'd been coming to this church, and for two years the reverend had rejected Erik's requests for aid. But this new reverend had been here only a month, so Erik hoped to persuade the man to help his sister.

The Colorado mountain air seemed especially thin today, or maybe it was Erik's growing awareness of his new secretary, Lydia Stone. He'd caught her looking at him more than once during services, and he didn't know what to make of it. Miss Stone hardly paid him mind at the office. She went about her business in silence, totally absorbed in her work, as if she were afraid to make any demands.

Of course, Erik was no stranger to women looking at him. In fact, he'd experienced quite a few disreputable ones throwing themselves his way—that was part and parcel of spending time at his sister's brothel—but Lydia Stone was different. It seemed she'd finally taken notice of him, although they'd spent hours together over the past two weeks, working in close quarters.

She was pretty enough, and definitely grown up enough, to have a husband and a brood of children of her own. Why she was single, and working in a rabble-rousing mining town, mystified Erik. She wasn't widowed and didn't seem particularly destitute—that much had been clear from her application. It all made Erik curious, even though he didn't want to be.

The last thing he had time for was a woman.

Managing his silver mine and keeping track of his sister took up all of his physical time and emotional energy. Not to mention that the combination of Erik Dawson and women seemed to always end badly. His mother had left their family when he was nine, and his father drank himself into a stupor, disappearing two years later. Erik's childhood sweetheart had up and kissed Teddy Jennings—his biggest enemy. Without their parents, his only sister, Margaret, four years his senior, had tried to support them. But she had no education, and no one would hire her to clean or watch children. It seemed their father had burned every possible bridge.

In the end, Margaret had fled to a brothel to feed him.

And that was how she paid for Erik's private boarding school. It wasn't until he was sixteen that he discovered where the money had really come from, and then he was so horrified he dropped out.

That's when they'd had their terrible fight. Margaret had fled town, and Erik had spent the next fourteen years working in mines across the country, trying to find his sister. He found her more than once, but each time she turned away his offer of support. Erik was determined to rescue her from her life of debauchery, settle her in her own home, and show her that she didn't need to sell her body to earn a living.

At least, not anymore.

When Erik had learned that Margaret and her group of ladies had established themselves in the booming mining town of Leadville, he investigated in advance. With a bank loan in his favor, he bought out a few small claims. Miraculously, those mine shafts revealed rich ore deposits only a few more feet down, more than the seller had known about. And thus, Dawson Mining was born.

Erik still visited Margaret several times a week in an effort to persuade her to leave. So far, she'd refused. And now she was ill . . . seriously ill, if Erik was to believe the doctor he'd hired to examine Margaret.

Consumption, the doctor had said, and the thin mountain air wasn't helping.

Margaret said she knew she was dying, but she didn't care. She wanted to stay with her "ladies"—the women had become like family to her.

That fact sat like a bitter pill inside Erik. His sister preferred the life of a paramour over a clean home where he could provide for her. If only he could get a reverend in to hear her confession, then Margaret could relieve her guilty conscience and begin the road to change.

The congregation leaving the church had thinned, and Erik hoped it would only be a few more moments before he could petition the new reverend. Then Lydia Stone stepped out of the church and shook the reverend's hand. She smiled up at the reverend, her cheeks faintly flushed, and Erik felt a twinge of envy. Ridiculous! The reverend was a portly, older man, certainly not someone Lydia could be attracted to. But she had never smiled like that at the office. And never at Erik.

Of course, any proper woman wouldn't give him a second glance if they knew about his sister's living. If there was any word to describe Lydia Stone, it was *proper*.

Her gaze moved from the reverend's to meet his. Her eyebrows lifted in faint curiosity, but she looked quickly away. She stepped past the reverend, and Erik straightened to speak to her. "Good afternoon, Miss Stone."

For a moment, Erik thought he saw a spark of interest in her calm, gray eyes. But maybe he was mistaken. She nodded, he nodded back, and she stepped off the porch and walked away.

Mr. Janson came out of the church next, a tall, lanky fellow. He bid farewell to the reverend then hurried after Miss Stone.

Erik let out a sigh, unsure why it was disheartening to see a man try to capture Lydia Stone's attention. It was nothing new. Every miner entering the office practically tripped over his heavy boots after coming face-to-face with the gray-eyed woman.

Finally, the reverend was alone, and Erik followed him back into the church. "May I speak to you in private?"

Reverend Stanley turned, his thick brows arched. "Of course, son. Do you need to confess?"

Erik flushed. "No, I have a special request to make, if you don't mind. It's for my sister."

The reverend clasped his large hands together, waiting. But by the time Erik was halfway through explaining his sister's plight, Reverend Stanley was already shaking his head.

"Please, sir," Erik said. "She's very ill, and I need her last days to be ones of peace."

"If she's not accepting of the good word, I cannot force her." Reverend Stanley spread his hands wide as if he were completely helpless.

Erik let out a breath, trying to keep his frustration and anger at bay. It was the last thing he wanted to do—to coerce or bribe. But his sister's soul was the most important thing to him. "I will make a sizable donation to the church."

The reverend's eyes widened. He was silent for a few moments, the only sound reaching a passing wagon. Finally he said, "Can she travel? Come here tonight after dark?"

Erik's heart sank. Getting his sister to leave the brothel would be near impossible in her condition, and especially if she knew of the destination. But if that was the only way the reverend would speak with her, he'd figure out how to bring Margaret.

THREE

Lydia had agreed to go on a walk with Mr. Janson on Sunday evening after supper. Yet almost as soon as they started, she profusely regretted it. Strolling down one side of Main Street had been more than enough, but they still had to return to her rented room over the bakery at the other end of the town.

Sunday night was always a wild time in Leadville. The saloons were open, with virtually every miner in attendance. Easy women stood in groups outside of the saloons, smiling and flirting with the male passersby.

The sight of such casualness made Lydia shudder. She'd been eyed more than once by bawdy miners, which caused her to tighten her grip on Mr. Janson's arm. She hoped he wouldn't take her actions for more than what they meant.

Yet that wasn't all. Mr. Janson might be gentle and kind, but women seemed to be his weakness as well. He'd actually stopped when a woman wearing a low-cut dress, displaying her ample bosom, had called to him from across the street. Plainly, that woman couldn't have cared less that Mr. Janson had a lady on his arm. And the woman was good and drunk.

Mr. Janson tried to escort her across the street to speak to the brazen woman.

Lydia's face heated thoroughly. "I'll wait here, thank you," she said, when in fact, she should have demanded he take her home then and there. If she were braver, she'd have up and left. But she was too nervous to walk back alone; too many drunken men were about, if the shouts and laughter coming from the saloon across the street were any indication.

"She seems to have an urgent question. Maybe she needs my help," Mr. Janson said. "I'll be back shortly."

Lydia pressed her lips together and nodded her reluctant assent. Mr. Janson didn't waste a moment hurrying across the dusty street. The sun had set awhile back, and the sky was navy, cut by the glow from the collection of saloons with their fancy gas lighting. Lydia pulled her shawl tightly around her, warding off the cool breeze, as she ignored the stare of a man walking by.

She scooted to the side of the boardwalk as the stranger lumbered past. His steps weren't quite steady, although his gaze was—and it was on her. The man continued on his way without saying anything; Lydia exhaled in relief. She looked over at Mr. Janson again, who was leaning against the outside wall of a saloon, talking to the woman.

What on earth? Could Mr. Janson really be that daft? And was she so foolish as to wait for a man talking to a . . . *prostitute*?

Lydia fished out a folded piece of paper that she kept in her bodice and opened it. Mr. Janson's name was number four on her list. With the stubby pencil from her handbag, she crossed his name off with three lines to ensure that it was properly crossed out.

She started walking along the boardwalk, ignoring every greeting and jest directed at her. She made eye contact with no one, and even when she heard Mr. Janson calling after her, she didn't stop.

Not until she saw Erik Dawson did her step come up short. He was exiting a building next to another saloon. Lydia didn't need to see the dangling wooden sign creaking in the wind above the door to know her boss had just exited a house of ill repute.

So the gossip was true. Before she could avoid being seen, Mr. Dawson caught her gaze. Lydia knew her face must be flaming bright red, but his expression surprised her. Where she would have thought he'd be embarrassed, or defiant, at having been seen both at church and at a brothel in the same day, all she saw on his face was sadness. Possibly grief.

And it was for that reason she didn't start moving again until he'd turned and crossed the street without further acknowledgment of her. Which was just as well. Her heart pinged at the thought of what could have possibly made Mr. Dawson so upset. Perhaps his favorite prostitute had found someone younger and more handsome. She gave a derisive laugh.

And then she felt foolish; she'd once considered that man for her eligible list. He was lightly penciled in as number ten, pending her ability to discover whether the rumors were true. As disappointment burned through her, confusing her thoughts, she felt even more foolish. She hadn't held any particular affection for him. Why did she now feel such profound regret? As soon as she reached to her room, she'd cross his name off too.

"Miss Stone," a man called behind her.

She realized too late that Mr. Janson had caught up. She exhaled and turned to face the man who'd been a terrible companion.

"Where are you going?" he asked, coming to a stop and trying to catch his breath.

"Mr. Janson," Lydia said, keeping her voice firm, although she felt anything but. She had to practically crane her neck to look up at him, he was so tall. "You are no gentleman. You abandoned me on the street with drunken men all about, in favor of a woman of ill repute."

"She only wanted to know—"

Lydia held up her hand to stop him. "It doesn't matter. I would appreciate it if you did not call on me again." Anger pulsed through her. How much more could her heart could endure in a single night? Turning, she walked as rapidly as her heeled boots would allow.

Mr. Janson called out, "Miss Stone . . ." But his voice died away.

She kept her chin lifted and gazed forward with smarting eyes. It appeared that no one was whom he seemed tonight. If she hadn't witnessed her boss coming out of the brothel, she would have continued to doubt the rumors. Thank goodness she'd been able to find out Mr. Dawson's and Mr. Janson's true characters so quickly.

As she walked, she ignored the squeeze of disappointment in her heart. Instead, she thought of the other eight names on her list. She hoped there wouldn't be any terrible secrets about them to be discovered. She didn't know how many more surprises she could tolerate.

FOUR

"Damn," Erik muttered. "Double damn."

First, his sister had refused to listen to reason. He'd groveled to the reverend for nothing. Then Lydia Stone had come marching down the street. Her wide eyes had said what she must think of him . . . But he didn't have time to worry about that. He had to get back to the church and let Reverend Stanley know that his sister wouldn't be coming tonight after all.

He just hoped the reverend would have an extra measure of compassion, as befitted a man of his profession, and agree to visit the brothel. Erik moved to the alley across the street, where he'd left his wagon. He didn't want any of Margaret's friends to alert her that he'd brought a wagon into town to take her to the church before he could talk her into it.

Erik smoothed back the mane of his ever-patient horse, Rust, then climbed into the wagon. He pulled onto Main Street, letting the horse clip along at his own pace. Sunday night was busy in town, as if all the miners and their women were trying to get every last moment of the weekend in before work started at dawn the following morning.

As he traveled along the street, he recognized a few men, although there were probably more of them he should have recognized, but he was used to seeing them covered in dust. It had taken nearly two years to get the men to trust him. Being the manager and owner of a mine was delicate business. Men had threatened to strike at other mines, asking for higher pay and fewer hours. Erik wondered when discontent would reach his mine.

The profit in silver mining was rising, but each raise in pay had to be considered carefully. Erik had seen boomtowns rise to the top for months only to become ghost towns before the year was out. Often when miners banded together and went on strike, managers would fire the strikers and bring in a new group of men willing to work for the contracted pay. Erik had decided long ago that when the price of silver went up, he couldn't pay his men more, because when the price inevitably came back down, they'd refuse to take less pay.

Rumblings throughout Leadville had increased over the past couple of months. Union leaders were becoming more vocal, and one of the larger mines had already endured a strike. It had lasted about two days, until a new group of men was brought in. By then it was too late for the former employees to get their jobs back. Erik had hired about a dozen of those displaced miners, but even though his mine was doing well for its size, he couldn't afford to hire any more men.

He had found it necessary to hire a secretary, though, if he hoped to get any sleep at night. He'd been working from dawn until well into the night just trying to keep up with the paperwork and other demands of the mine. He hadn't expected a woman such as Lydia Stone—beautiful, statuesque, calm—to apply for the position.

Erik pulled into the churchyard, and his heart sank as he thought of the task before him. He despised begging, but he'd have to do some more. Light spilled from the small windows of the rooms built onto the back of the church, where the reverend lived. Erik climbed down from the wagon, tied up the horse, and walked to the rear door, then knocked.

Moments later, the door opened, and Reverend Stanley welcomed Erik into the small parlor. Looking past Erik, the reverend said, "Your sister's not here?"

Erik felt himself redden. "She's in a difficult temperament."

The reverend closed the door against the night's chill and motioned for Erik to take a seat.

Erik sat on a small, velvet-covered sofa that had seen better days. He didn't wait to make his request. "I know this may be unprecedented in your experience, but I would be much obliged if you would accompany me to visit my sister."

The reverend lifted his thick eyebrows. "If she is not willing to come here, then my arriving at her brothel won't change her mind. You cannot force someone to change, Mr. Dawson."

Erik looked at his clasped hands. Of course he couldn't force Margaret to change . . . but if she could see that someone other than her brother cared about her soul, her heart might soften. She might accept help before it was too late.

"Mr. Dawson," the reverend said in a quiet voice. "I am truly sorry. I am. It's always difficult when a family member turns away from the light. The only thing you can do for her is pray."

Erik's eyes burned. He felt his last hope slipping away. Was a miracle possible for his sister? Knowing he was on the verge of becoming desperate, he thanked the reverend and left, feeling too raw to pursue anything more tonight.

It wasn't until he was driving back home that he remembered the look on Lydia Stone's face. Stunned, condemning. Again, Erik cursed. A mantle of self-pity fell over him, and he spent the next thirty minutes allowing himself to wallow in the whys of his life.

Why had his mother left him? Why had his father died? Why did his sister have to resort to selling herself? And why, after he had proven his ability to provide for her, did she insist on remaining in her profession?

He dried his eyes with his sleeve, and when he reached his house he jumped down from the wagon, boarded the horse, and prepared to face what was sure to be a long, sleepless night.

FIVE

By the time Lydia unlocked the office door in the morning, she had made up her mind. She would treat Mr. Erik Dawson as any good employee would treat her boss: with kindness and deference. What he did on his own time—at a brothel, no less—was not her business. She'd crossed his name off her paper the night before, then had awakened plenty of times throughout the night with the disconcerting image of his sad eyes, and then had finally climbed out of bed before dawn streaked the sky, resigned to having a disagreeable day.

She had to keep her chin up. As a woman of nearly twenty-seven, working as a secretary in a bawdy mining town, she had limited options. She had to be realistic. Her husband-to-be would not be perfect, although he'd certainly be better than the likes of Mr. Dawson and Mr. Janson. Stepping into the cold office, she crossed the room to light the wood-burning stove, reviewing her list of requirements in her mind.

Hard-working, churchgoing, and having eyes only for you.

Perhaps Lydia could cross off *churchgoing*. Last night, after witnessing the behavior of Mr. Janson and Mr. Dawson, she knew that church attendance obviously did not prove a man's moral character.

Lydia opened the stove's metal door and propped up a few pieces of kindling against the wood already laid inside. She struck a match and lit the kindling, then warmed her hands by the flickering flame as they grew. Ash drifted from the stove, but Lydia's mind was elsewhere. When the office door opened and shut, it startled her out of her thoughts.

"Good morning, Miss Stone," Mr. Dawson said behind her.

She took a deep breath. "Good morning." And then she turned. He was standing close—close enough for her to see his green eyes. To see that they were still sad. For a moment, she wanted to question him, possibly to comfort him, but she pushed the foolish notion out of her head.

He moved past her and grabbed the small broom near the wood stack then swept the ash that had blown out of the stove.

"Oh, sorry," Lydia said. The ash had made a mess, and she hadn't even noticed.

Mr. Dawson nodded and continued to sweep. Lydia took this as a sign for her to get to work. She went to her desk and sorted through the mail stack that had been delivered on Saturday. Her job was straightforward, requiring little interaction from her boss. She was to answer correspondence, pay bills, and review the accounting ledgers. Mr. Dawson spent time in the office on Saturdays, although she wasn't required to. The mine was closed only on Sundays.

She sorted bill statements. Mr. Dawson had given her leave to write out bank drafts for his signature.

"Miss Stone," he said, crossing to her desk, broom still in hand.

Her heart thudded at the sound of her name. His tone sounded serious. She looked up to see that his gaze matched the solemnity of his voice. They were in the office alone together quite often, but this morning felt different somehow.

"I need to explain about last night—"

A thud sounded on the outside porch; one of the miners was coming in.

Lydia held up a hand and quickly said, "You don't owe me any explanation, Mr. Dawson."

"Hello there," a deep voice sounded.

Lydia looked toward the opening door as Mr. Janson stepped inside, his gaze directed at her. She swallowed against a sudden thickness in her throat.

"I've come to apologize, Miss Stone," Mr. Janson said, moving fully into the room. His height made the office space seem to shrink.

Lydia's stomach twisted. Did he want to make their dispute known in front of their boss?

Mr. Dawson had stepped back, allowing Mr. Janson to approach the desk.

"No need," Lydia said, rising from her chair and glancing at Mr. Dawson. He'd turned away out of politeness.

Mr. Janson took off his hat and barreled on. "The woman by the saloon was only asking a question. I swear to you that I don't know her at all, and when I tried to catch up with you, it was clear you were upset with me."

Yes. Very clear. I told you not to call on me again.

He brought his hand out from behind his back and handed her a bunch of wildflowers.

Lydia's neck heated, and she steeled her emotions. Mr. Janson was being very forward, and her boss could hear every word. She took the flowers and laid them on her desk. "Thank you for the flowers, but I must return to my work." She met his gaze, keeping hers steady.

"Would you join me for supper tonight?" he asked. "The place run by Lizzy Maughan is quite good."

Lydia let out a breath. "I'm not available tonight, Mr. Janson. If you'd be so kind as to let me return to my work, I'd be most appreciative."

"Do you have plans with Mr. Parker? He said he wanted to take you somewhere, so I thought I'd better beat him to it." He winked. "Even though last night didn't go so well."

Her mouth fell open, but she quickly closed it again. Mr. Parker and Mr. Janson had been discussing *her*?

"Tomorrow, then?" Mr. Janson continued, his expression taking a pleading look.

Lydia's mind hadn't yet caught up to the fact that Mr. Janson was looking at courting her as some sort of competition. Not that she was entirely innocent in having her own competition by creating a list of eligible bachelors . . .

"I—" She cleared her throat, her gaze landing on the flowers. She thought she'd sent him a firm message the night before. Only one thing left to do. Picking up the flower bunch, she handed it back to Mr. Janson. "I'm sorry. I can't accept these. I won't be available to go to dinner with you or any other gentleman. You may let Mr. Parker know as well." She held the flowers out until Mr. Janson took them.

"Miss Stone," Mr. Janson said, his voice growing louder, "I can give you a few days to decide. Perhaps—"

"She's asked you twice to leave," Mr. Dawson interrupted. He'd turned around and was now walking toward Lydia's desk. He stopped inches from Mr. Janson, saying nothing further, just staring at him.

Mr. Janson took a couple of steps back, then shoved his hat on his head, turned, and left.

Lydia stared after him, her heart hammering. Mr. Janson was not the man she'd thought he was, and neither was Mr. Parker—another name she'd cross off when she had the chance. At least Mr. Dawson had come to her aid.

"Are you all right?" he asked.

"I am, thank you," Lydia said, her voice barely above a whisper. She couldn't look at him, because, in truth, she felt like crying. Not because she had to turn down Mr. Janson, but because it appeared that no man was as he seemed in the town of Leadville.

She felt Mr. Dawson's searching look, but then he moved away and went about working on his ledgers at his own desk. Another miner came into the office, making Lydia's heart jump. But it wasn't Mr. Janson or anyone else on her eligible list. The miner went straight to Mr. Dawson's desk and talked to him about taking days off for his wife's illness. She was in bed, expecting a child at any time.

Lydia never tried to listen in on conversations, but it was hard not to overhear.

"I can give you two days' paid leave," Mr. Dawson said. "If you need more time, then you won't be compensated."

"My wife's cousin is coming to help, but we don't know when."

Lydia glanced up to see Mr. Dawson's elbows propped on his desk, fingers steepled together.

"Then hope she arrives soon," Mr. Dawson said, "because I can't give you more than what's in the company policy."

The miner lowered his head and scratched the back of his neck. "All right," he said, although his tone sounded begrudging.

"You're a brave man to start a family up here," Mr. Dawson continued.

The miner laughed. "It wasn't exactly planned, and she's not exactly my wife."

Mr. Dawson chuckled.

Lydia flushed at the comment and tried to focus on the letter she was composing to tune out the conversation. Mr.

Dawson's laughter told her that he wasn't a family man either. Good thing she'd crossed him off her list.

The office continued to be busy throughout the morning, with the foreman coming in to report that another mine in Leadville had gone on strike. Mr. Dawson left with him for a while, and just when Lydia was about ready to leave for the day, he returned.

His expression was tight and worried. "May I walk you home today, Miss Stone?"

Lydia nearly dropped her satchel. She didn't have time to collect her thoughts before she responded, "Yes."

He put his hat back on and opened the door, waiting for her to gather her things and pass through. He locked the door and stepped next to her on the porch. "You live above the Smith Bakery?"

"Yes," Lydia said again, apparently unable to speak a decent sentence.

He gave a small nod, and they started walking. For several moments, neither spoke. The sun had disappeared behind the mountain range, but the purple twilight gave them plenty of light.

"Miss Stone." Mr. Dawson's voice broke through the silence between them. "About last night—"

Lydia laid her hand on Mr. Dawson's arm for a moment. "Please, you don't need to explain anything to me. It's none of my business." She moved her hand, feeling chagrined at her forwardness. Yet, she admitted to herself, she was grateful to her boss. Not only for her job, but for how he effectively ran Mr. Janson out that morning. And now he'd offered to walk her home. She hadn't realized until now that she'd stored up plenty of worry over who she might run into on the way home. Mr. Janson and Mr. Parker sounded far from appealing right now.

Mr. Dawson gave a brief nod. "I appreciate your honoring my privacy, though I would like to say that it wasn't what you may think."

Lydia let the information sink in, but since Mr. Dawson was already off her list, she didn't care to hear anything personal.

"If any of the miners bother you again, I want you to let me know," Mr. Dawson continued.

She glanced over at him in the dwindling light. "I haven't had any trouble until last night. I think Mr. Janson felt remorseful."

"Remorseful over what?"

Lydia told the story, leaving out the part where she saw Mr. Dawson coming out of the brothel, of course.

He nodded as he listened, then said, "I think you made the right choice. About Mr. Janson *and* Mr. Parker."

A bit of panic jolted through her at his words. *He can't possibly know about my list.* She forced herself to relax. "I've only spoken to Mr. Parker a handful of times. He's never asked me to supper."

"Good." Mr. Dawson said, coming to a stop and facing her, so Lydia stopped and faced him as well. They were just outside Main Street. In a few moments, they'd be surrounded by the evening crowd. "As your employer, I feel responsible for you. Mr. Parker is not who he may seem, and Mr. Janson has a wife back in California."

Lydia was stunned. Mr. Janson—soft-spoken, yet a bit misguided Mr. Janson—had a *wife*? She stared into the green eyes of Mr. Dawson, too dumbfounded to speak. Her pulse increased. Now she was beyond angry. She might as well cross every eligible man off her list and be done with it.

Forget about marriage.

She took a shaky breath. "I had no idea."

"Word is that Mr. Janson's wife kicked him out." Mr. Dawson looked past her. "Of course, that's not an excuse to be courting other women." When his gaze moved back to Lydia's, she was struck by the intensity in his gaze. "I plan to walk you home each evening, if you don't mind. I don't want any man to get ideas into his head that you're vulnerable."

Her breath caught as warmth flooded through her. She wouldn't let herself analyze the polite offer. Of course he would want to make sure she was safe—she was his employee, after all.

Besides, it would be nice to not have to walk home alone now that the days were getting shorter.

SIX

Mr. Dawson left home earlier than usual to visit Margaret. After walking Lydia Stone home the night before, he had a renewed determination to make his sister see reason. He didn't know why he cared so much how Miss Stone viewed him, but he dreaded her finding out that he wasn't able to protect and care for his own blood especially when nothing should be standing in his way, save for his sister's stubbornness.

It seemed stubbornness was a family trait, Erik figured, as he trudged along in the early light of the morning. What if his sister refused to see the reverend and died before she could confess? What did that say about him as a brother?

He was the only family that Margaret had left. He simply couldn't fail her. Knowing it was early, when he arrived at the side door of the brothel, he checked to see if the door was locked. He was both relieved and disappointed that it was. Relieved because it meant someone had been sober enough to lock it, and disappointed because he'd now have to knock, and who knew who he'd wake up.

He knocked softly at first, waited a few moments, then knocked again.

Beverly answered—the youngest of the women. When Erik had first met Beverly, he'd felt sorry for her, until she opened her mouth. He'd never heard such foul words coming from any man before, let alone a woman.

"Hello, sugar," Beverly said, her smile wide even though her eyes were barely open.

He gave her a brief smile so as not to be rude. Like a gentleman would, he kept his gaze trained on her face. Traces of lipstick still stained her mouth, and she had a vulnerable look about her with her sleepy blue eyes and blonde, tousled hair. It was difficult not to notice that she was barely dressed. She wore a red satin robe, sloppily pulled on and showing enough skin that he knew he was blushing.

"I bet I know what you've come for," she said in a low voice before he could ask about his sister. Beverly's painted fingernails trailed down his chest, stopping at his waist.

He swallowed hard. He definitely wasn't interested in any liaison, but he was still a man. With a gentle push, he moved her hand. "Is Margaret awake?"

Beverly fluttered her eyelashes and pulled him inside the parlor, then shut the door, plunging them into near darkness. A couple of parlor lamps had been lit, casting a glow over the plush furniture and velvety wall hangings. He averted his eyes from the nude figures depicted in the latter.

"I can keep you busy until she wakes up," Beverly purred.

"I'm on my way to the mine, so I need to speak to Margaret right now," Erik said, practically choking out the words. "She can go back to sleep after."

Beverly's hands were at his waist again, and she pressed against him. "You need to loosen up, Erik Dawson." One hand slid around to his back.

Erik grabbed both of her arms and moved them to her side. "You know I'm a churchgoing man."

Beverly threw back her head and laughed in a throaty voice. "I've heard that one before, sugar."

"Bev, who's there?" Margaret's voice came from the corridor leading off the parlor. She shuffled into the room, her green eyes wide. Margaret had once been a beautiful woman, but her cheeks were sunken, and her arms were frail. Her dark-brown hair had started to gray and thin. She wore it braided over one shoulder.

"Erik," she breathed, and her body seemed to sag.

He hurried to her and grasped her arm. He hadn't seen her walking for days. Hope surged through him—she must be getting better. "You're walking. How are you feeling?"

"Better than usual." She blinked up at him. "Why are you here so early? Come to try to cart me off again?" She had a small smile on her face, but her eyes were steely.

Erik couldn't stop staring at her. "No, I—I can't believe you're up."

Margaret pulled her shawl tightly over her shoulders. She was dressed more modestly than usual, probably due to the fact that her illness made her cold all of the time. She'd grown extremely thin over the past few months, and her beauty had faded to the merest wisp of its former glory.

"The doctor man is coming. I thought I'd show him what's what," Margaret said, walking to one of the parlor chairs. She sat on the plush fabric. "Bev, will you get us some tea?"

"I'd love to." Beverly smiled and sashayed past Erik, brushing her hand along his arm as she moved by.

Erik ignored the gesture and sat on the small sofa opposite his sister. He couldn't stop staring at her. Was she really getting better? She brought a handkerchief to her mouth and quietly coughed. Even that didn't sound so deep as it had.

"Now that I'm feeling better, Erik, I want to tell you something," Margaret said.

Erik knew better than to think she was about to thank him for being a caring brother. He glanced away, his gaze landing on a nearby table filled with silver and crystal trinkets—likely gifts from clients. His sister prided herself in entertaining only gentlemen—if such a feat could be respected above servicing anyone who knocked on one's door.

"I don't appreciate your trying to get me to see some preacher," she continued, her voice soft but firm. "You know I won't step foot in any church. Why do you bother?"

Erik rubbed the back of his neck and met his sister's gaze. The fire in Margaret's eyes told him to proceed with caution. "It's not about going to church. It's about—"

"Would you like some sugar?" Beverly's voice cut in. She entered the room, carrying a silver tray with three china cups of steaming tea. "Margaret likes it sweet—three scoops." She fluttered her eyelashes at Erik; none of the insinuation was lost on him.

"No sugar, thanks." He took the offered tea cup and sipped the hot liquid.

"What did I miss?" Beverly asked, looking between brother and sister as she lit a couple of lamps.

Sometimes Erik couldn't believe that his sister put up with Beverly, but he supposed Margaret couldn't be all that picky about her employees.

"My brother was just trying to tell me how to save my soul."

Beverly barked a laugh and settled her hands on her curvy hips. "That's what I like about him. You don't find many dreamers nowadays." She reached for his tea cup and placed it back on the tray.

Erik opened his mouth to protest, but before he could, Beverly sat on his lap, curling her arms around his neck. "You know, sugar, I'd become an honest woman if you'd have me."

Margaret chuckled. "Don't let her fool you, Erik. She says that a dozen times a day."

Beverly pulled away, much to his relief. "I do not!" she shot at Margaret. Then her pleading eyes were back on Erik. "What do you think, sugar?"

"I think I'd better go to work," Erik said, setting Beverly aside so he could stand. "Thanks for the tea, Margaret. I'm glad you're feeling better."

Despite Beverly's advances, his heart felt lighter. If his sister recovered, he would find a way to convince her to leave her ladies and settle into a respectable life, even if it meant selling his mine shares and going to a place where they could both make a fresh start.

But as he left the brothel and walked along Main Street, the doubts came back. Any new place in the west would also have saloons, brothels, and harsh frontier living.

SEVEN

Lydia stepped onto the boardwalk the next morning, looking first right, then left. Main Street was just coming to life, and there was no sign of Mr. Dawson.

Of course he wouldn't be here to meet me. She had no reason to expect him to walk her to the office, but she felt disappointed all the same.

Her heart needed a stern talking to. The man had been off her list now for two days, and come Sunday, she'd need to be more proactive in getting to know the other men still on it.

She passed the town doctor, Mr. Andrus. He was a tall, sturdy man, said to be recently widowed. When he tipped his hat and nodded, she wondered exactly how old he was. Possibly in his early 50s.

Stop, she commanded herself. *You can't be so desperate as to want to marry a widowed doctor. He's old enough to be your father. Besides, he's never been to church.* She continued to argue with herself, debating how often any doctor could attend church. He was always on notice, night and day.

She patted her bodice where she kept her list—she would *not* be adding a non-churchgoing man's name. She didn't feel the paper, so she touched her bodice again. She must have left the list in her room. Since she was more than halfway to the office, she'd have to be parted from it for the day. It wasn't as if she didn't know it by heart.

By the time she reached the office, her head hurt. She needed a break from thinking about men. It was good that she'd left the list at home; she wouldn't be able to take peeks at it several times today. Maybe she should take up crocheting again. She hadn't touched her hooks since arriving in Leadville. Before going home tonight, she'd stop at the general store for yarn.

Her mind made up, she stepped into the office. Mr. Dawson looked up from his desk and smiled.

Right then and there, Lydia knew it would take more than crocheting to get him out of her thoughts. "Good morning," she said and was surprised when Mr. Dawson stood and walked over. She took off her shawl and hat, hanging them near the door.

"Did you make that shawl?" he asked, stopping a couple of feet away, his gaze on the shawl.

"I did." From this distance, she could smell his clean scent, something that she realized she'd become familiar with.

He reached out and inspected the shawl. "If I paid you for the material and your time, would you make one for my sister?"

Mr. Dawson had a sister? "I suppose I could." She was planning on picking up crocheting again anyway. It wouldn't hurt to do it for hire.

"How long would it take?" He was still standing quite close to her, and she found herself gazing into his green eyes a bit too long.

She looked away and gave a little shrug. "Maybe a week, if I work on it every night."

"You don't have any pressing engagements?"

Lydia felt a bit embarrassed to admit that no, she hadn't any commitments or social life beyond her job. "Not in the near future. Not after Mr. Janson and Mr. Parker's antics."

Now why had she gone and told him that?

Another smile touched his face, and Lydia had to admit it almost made her want to put him back on her list. Almost.

"You know, not all of the men in town are horrible." His eyes filled with amusement. "Perhaps I made it sound that way when I offered to walk you home each night."

Lydia couldn't help but smile back. "Oh? And who are the men who aren't quite horrible?"

Mr. Dawson leaned against her desk so he wasn't as close to her, but his pose made their proximity seem more intimate. "Are you interested in knowing, then?"

Her face grew warm. "I suppose I am."

He folded his arms, and Lydia tried not to notice how solid and sturdy, and, well, *strong* they looked. "And you are willing to accept my help?" he asked.

She stared at him. How could he be so brazen? "Mr. Dawson," she said, "I can manage my own affairs."

But he wasn't looking at her anymore. He'd pulled out a folded piece of paper from his pocket, and it took only seconds for the horror of understanding to dawn on her.

"You must have dropped this before we left last night. I wouldn't have opened it if I'd realized what it was." He handed over her list. The one with ten names, three crossed off—one being Mr. Dawson's.

She took the paper, mortified. Had he read it? Of course he had. "I . . . I don't know what to say." She couldn't even look at him.

"Miss Stone," he said in a quiet voice. "I couldn't help but read it after seeing my name at the bottom. If I understand correctly, you've made a list of men you're interested in getting better acquainted with?"

"It's a list of eligible men who go to church," she whispered.

He was standing next to her now. "What makes them eligible for consideration?"

She couldn't speak, shouldn't speak.

"I can help you with your list if you'd like," he said, and she felt his warm breath on her cheek as he leaned over to look at it in her hand. He was so close. "I think you did right by crossing my name off, along with Mr. Janson's and Mr. Parker's."

"It's not what you think."

He chuckled. "I'm not offended. In fact, I think I can help you narrow it down further."

Lydia's eyes started to blur as she stared at the list. Mr. Dawson wasn't offended that she'd crossed his name off? That was a relief. Or maybe not. She pushed the thought away. But he could be a valuable resource to her, seeing as he knew all of the men.

"All right," she breathed, suddenly feeling exhausted. "Tell me about them."

I said I wasn't offended, but I am damn curious. Erik would have been lying to himself if he didn't admit that he was pleased that he'd been on the list. Granted, at number ten, but maybe there wasn't a specific order.

He was glad she was willing to at least talk to him about it, so he didn't have to pry to learn of her requirements.

She sat on her chair while he leaned against the desk. He pointed to Mr. Brown's name. "You'll have a brood of redheaded children with him." He smiled when Lydia laughed.

"I know. Don't think I haven't thought about that," she said, blinking her gray eyes up at him. "Although, I don't have anything against red hair."

"His hair is *very* red, though."

She gave another laugh. "Very."

With some effort, he pulled his eyes away from her and looked at the list again. "Ah. Mr. Roberts. A fairly decent fellow. Last year, he was engaged to a girl who died."

"Sad," Miss Stone murmured. "What happened?"

"Stagecoach accident," Erik said. "But he's a hard worker, and he sings."

She nodded. "My father sang—I think he knew every hymn."

That was about as much information as she'd ever volunteered, and it intrigued him. "Do you sing as well?"

Miss Stone fell silent for a moment. "Not anymore."

He sensed her reluctance, so he turned back to the list. "Now, you may want to reconsider having Mr. Bartholomew on your list. He's not known for staying sober for long. I've kept him on because he's done better lately, but old habits die hard."

She leaned her cheek on one propped-up hand. "Is there anyone on this list you can wholeheartedly endorse?"

So she wanted to cut to the chase, did she? "Definitely cross off Mr. Amos. He enjoys the gambling tables, and I've caught him in a lie more than once. You wouldn't do well with Mr. Richards, either. He's not the marrying kind."

Miss Stone gave him a sharp look.

"Since you've already crossed *my* name off, I'd have to say it's a tie between Mr. Christensen and Mr. Kirkpatrick. Both are hard workers and seem to keep their noses clean."

Mr. Christensen was a burly man who had a loud laugh. Mr. Kirkpatrick wore spectacles and was as thin as a spring branch. Nothing was inherently wrong with either man that Erik could think of.

She seemed to consider for a moment. She'd said nothing about his comment of her crossing off his name, which was just as well. He had to put Margaret first, before anything or anyone else.

Picking up a pencil, Miss Stone put a star by each of their names. Erik's heart fell a notch.

"I could introduce you at the Saturday social," he offered.

She looked at him, her eyes filled with gratitude. "Would you?"

There was only one thing to do: say yes.

EIGHT

Once a month, the congregation held a social on a Saturday night. According to Mrs. Smith, who worked the bakery below Lydia's room, everyone brought a dish to share.

"There you are." Mrs. Smith's energetic voice rang from the bottom of the stairs as Lydia descended. Mrs. Smith was a widow who rented out her two spare rooms, one to Miss Delany—a schoolteacher—and the other to Lydia. "I've got rolls for you to take to the social. I'd go myself, but my ankles are swollen today."

Lydia tried not to smile at the comment. Mrs. Smith complained about her ankles every Saturday, effectively allowing her to stay home from church on Sundays. The first time it happened, Lydia had suggested they take the bakery cart to church, but Mrs. Smith seemed appalled at the idea.

As Lydia reached the bottom of the stairs, she accepted the sack of rolls from Mrs. Smith. "Thank you so much." Included in her rent was two meals a day. The morning meal was usually nothing more than tea and a day-old cross bun, and the evening meal consisted of either a stew or casserole with Mrs. Smith's specialty—giant rolls—of which Lydia now had a full sack.

Mrs. Smith beamed, displaying a pair of dimples on her rosy cheeks. Whether she was baking or not, she always had a flushed look about her. "Miss Delany is not feeling well this evening," Mrs. Smith added. "I'm afraid you're on your own."

"That's all right. Mr. Dawson has agreed to escort me."

The woman's eyes darkened, and Lydia regretted mentioning it.

"He may be your employer, but I wouldn't advise spending any time outside of the office with him. Even if he does go to church."

Lydia knew and understood Mrs. Smith's warning—she'd given it to herself. Why did it bother her so much to have Mrs. Smith criticizing Erik Dawson? "He's been nothing but a gentleman toward me. Besides, he offered to introduce me around."

Mrs. Smith gave a nod, but her mouth was pinched.

Lydia walked to the front windows of the bakery and waited for Mr. Dawson. He couldn't come soon enough. She didn't want to engage in further conversation with Mrs. Smith.

He showed up moments later, on time, and Lydia pushed through the door, intent on meeting him outside. Her step faltered over the stoop, and Mr. Dawson caught her elbow.

"Thank you," she said, feeling out of breath for no particular reason.

He smiled. "You look beautiful."

It was the first compliment Lydia could remember him giving her. She gripped the sack with both hands, wishing she could fight off her rising blush. She might have said thank you again, but she wasn't sure.

A wagon hitched to a couple of horses rattled past, and Mr. Dawson stepped onto the boardwalk.

"Didn't you bring a dish to share?" she said, trying to start some sort of conversation.

He chuckled. "I'm not much of a cook, Miss Stone. And I think the miners have had enough of scrambled eggs and gruel that they don't need to try mine." He was looking at her with a smile. "Did you bake something for the potluck?"

"Not quite," Lydia said. "Mrs. Smith gave me a couple dozen of her famous rolls."

Mr. Dawson stopped and faced her. "We should go back and eat them ourselves. I'm sure nothing else will compare." He raised an eyebrow, his green eyes intent on hers.

"Do as you will, Mr. Dawson. But I'll be taking these to the social—with or without you."

He nodded, a smile tugging at his mouth. "Very well, I'll accompany you there, if only to get my fair share. But I should carry that sack to keep it out of harm's way."

Lydia laughed and handed it over. They continued walking and chatting about trivial things. It was refreshing, actually, but it also worried Lydia a bit. She found herself enjoying her employer's company more and more. By the time they arrived at the church, the sun had set and twilight had descended. A couple of tables sat outside with lanterns on them. A man was tuning his fiddle, and another had a ukulele.

"Music? That will be nice," Lydia said, slowing to take in the scene. About twenty men and women were in attendance, as well as a few children.

"Do you like to dance?" Mr. Dawson said.

Lydia hadn't danced since the night of her engagement to Roger. By the next morning, she'd realized she'd made a mistake and called it off before anyone other than her mother knew about it.

Mr. Dawson was watching her with curiosity, and she

209

realized she hadn't answered the question. "I don't mind dancing." The truth was, her heart fluttered at the thought of it, because she imagined what it might be like to feel Mr. Dawson's arms about her.

"I'll just set this on the table, and then we can start your introductions," he said.

As Mr. Dawson walked to one of the tables loaded with dishes of all sorts of food, she scanned the gathering. More people were arriving—some of whom she didn't remember seeing at church. Reverend Stanley was in a jovial conversation with a young woman. The music struck up, and a few couples began dancing. Lydia couldn't help but look again at Mr. Dawson, who happened to be walking right toward her after dropping off the rolls.

"Ready?" he asked when he reached her. "Mr. Christensen is over by that tree."

Mr. Christensen's large form was unmistakable. His longish brown hair was slicked back, and he held a cup, watching the gathering as if perfectly interested.

Lydia and Mr. Dawson walked to the tree, where he introduced her to Mr. Christensen. Despite his size, the man moved with ease and lifted her hand in greeting, pressing it to his lips. His brown eyes were nice. "Welcome to Leadville," he said in a low, appreciative tone. "Mr. Dawson here needed some good help. Everyone at the mine was glad to see you arrive."

"Thank you," Lydia said.

"How are you adjusting?" Mr. Christensen asked, his conversation coming smoothly, which put Lydia at ease.

Mr. Dawson left her and Mr. Christensen standing beneath a tree. Lydia tried not to notice Mr. Dawson's absence. She smiled at Mr. Christensen. "I've adjusted quite well, thank you."

"I have a buckboard and a sturdy horse if you ever need a ride, especially with the weather coming." He hooked one thumb over his thick belt. "I don't want a young lady to be out walking alone."

He sounded a bit like Mr. Dawson, and the thought made Lydia want to laugh. "I'll keep that in mind. Thank you for the offer."

Another woman joined them. "We haven't met," the woman said, her narrow eyes peering at Lydia.

"I'm Lydia Stone, recently hired to work at the Dawson mine."

"Rachel Best," the woman said, then turned to Mr. Christensen. "You must try some of my pie."

He grinned and followed Rachel to the table without so much as saying goodbye to Lydia. She stared after him, a bit stunned. Perhaps she should bring a pie next time.

"I brought you a plate," someone said behind her.

She turned to see Mr. Dawson. He motioned toward a nearby bench that had been brought out from the church. She sat gratefully, even though her stomach felt a bit too tight to eat. "You got some of the rolls."

He laughed. "Of course. What do you think of Mr. Christensen?"

Lydia glanced up from the casserole on her plate. "He's . . ." She spotted Mr. Christensen in the crowd. He stood with Rachel, plate of pie in hand, smiling at her. ". . . in love with Rachel's pie."

Mr. Dawson squinted at the couple. "It did look quite good. I may try some myself."

Lydia elbowed him.

"I can get some for you as well," he said.

She elbowed him again, and he laughed.

"Erik! Erik Dawson!" a woman's voice cried out. The crowd hushed as a woman pushed through.

Lydia couldn't take her eyes off of the blonde woman whose dress left little of her bosom to the imagination. She was beautiful but unquestionably from a house of ill repute.

Mr. Dawson stood. "Beverly?"

The woman rushed toward him as the crowd parted to give her room. Tears streaked her face, making a mess of what must have once been artful makeup. "Your sister—she's—" The woman fell against him and sobbed.

He had to practically hold the woman up. "Take me to her." She took a shuddering breath and let him steer her through the crowd.

Lydia stared after them. Mr. Dawson had a sister who was somehow associated with that Beverly woman? Lydia wasn't sure what to think, but it sounded like his sister was very ill.

Reverend Stanley rushed to Mr. Dawson's side, and after a few hushed words, he left as well, headed into the church.

Lydia's heart pounded as she hurried after the reverend. She reached the porch just as he came back out.

"Is there anything I can do to help?" she asked.

"I don't think there's anything anyone can do. It sounds like it's too late to save his sister's soul." He moved past her and strode into the darkness toward Main Street.

Lydia's mind turned as things fell into place. Was Mr. Dawson's sister a prostitute? Is *that* why he visited the brothel? And now, was she . . .?

Her eyes burned as she thought about what Mr. Dawson must be experiencing right now. She couldn't say she was the right person to offer help, or that he'd want it, but she couldn't stay here either—where the social was back in full force with dancing, eating, and merriment.

It seemed that everyone had forgotten about Erik Dawson and the fact that his sister might be on her deathbed this very moment.

Lydia fetched her shawl from the bench where she'd been sitting, barely acknowledged Mr. Parker's friendly greeting, and hurried off after the reverend.

She wouldn't be able to reach him before he got to Main Street, but at least he could lead her to the right place. Sure enough, he turned down the alley by the same brothel she'd seen Mr. Dawson leave.

The closer she drew, the more her stomach twisted. She'd never set foot inside such a vile place, but she had to see if there was something she could do. As she reached the door, she heard a sob from the other side, and then the door burst open.

A man in a long, dark coat stumbled out, with Beverly right behind him. "You're a quack, that's what you are! I won't pay you one coin for all your lying! She was walking yesterday, and now—" Beverly burst into sobs and sank against the doorframe.

The man, whom Lydia now recognized as the town doctor, walked away, adjusting his hat and mumbling.

"What do you want?" Beverly spat at Lydia. Her tear-filled eyes narrowed. "Are you Erik's girl?" She seemed to collect herself. "I suppose you should come in. He'll not be too happy with how the doctor has mistreated his sister."

"What happened?" Lydia croaked as Beverly grasped her arm and tugged her into an extravagant parlor.

Beverly barked a half-laugh, half-sob. "He bled her so much he killed her, he did. Now I don't know what I'll do." Her wails started up again.

Cold knifed through Lydia. Mr. Dawson's sister was *dead*? Lydia felt sick. She didn't belong here. Looking around, at the opulent furniture and thick wall hangings of nude men and women, she didn't want to spend one more moment in a place like this. But her heart tugged for Mr. Dawson and what he must be facing.

"I should go," she choked out. "Let him know that—" She couldn't finish, so she simply turned away and opened the door.

"Lydia?"

Mr. Dawson's voice stopped her, and she turned back, mortified that she'd come all this way only to intrude on something so personal and horrible. But what she saw on his face was not anger.

"You came," he simply said. Grief was plain on his face, his eyes haunted with the look of a man who had lost someone dear.

Before she could think twice, she was across the room, pulling him into her arms. She didn't know how he'd react, but when his arms went around her, she was glad for it.

"I'm so sorry," she said. Lydia stayed where she was, eyes closed, in Mr. Dawson's embrace, for several moments.

At some point, Beverly moved past them and walked down a hallway, sobbing.

Lydia could only hold onto Mr. Dawson. When she finally pulled away, he seemed reluctant to release her. "What can I do?" she whispered.

The tears in his eyes tore at her heart.

"The reverend read Margaret her last rites," he said, his voice trembling. "But I think it was too late."

Lydia felt tears start in her eyes, even though she'd never met his sister. "It's not too late. We can still pray for her soul."

Mr. Dawson nodded, and Lydia realized that he was gripping her hand. She gripped it right back.

"Would you like to see her?" he asked.

If Lydia would have had time to think about the request, it might have felt strange. But the sorrow in Mr. Dawson's eyes made her want to do anything to help ease his pain. "Yes."

His hand still holding hers, he led her along the corridor. Beverly's crying had subsided, and they stepped into a small but opulent room. The sour smell made it plain that it had been a sick room for quite some time. Reverend Stanley was kneeling by the bed, his head bowed, his lips moving in prayer.

The woman on the bed was pale and thin, her eyes closed, her mouth partly open. The sight should have given Lydia a creepy feeling, but with Mr. Dawson's hand in hers and the reverend praying, the atmosphere was reverent.

The woman's nightdress was askew, her covers pulled down. Lydia released Mr. Dawson's hand and stepped forward. She straightened the woman's nightdress and smoothed the covers. Then she removed her shawl and draped it over the still body. Tears started as she thought about this woman's lost life.

Lydia stepped back, and the reverend rose. He spoke to Mr. Dawson about funeral arrangements, which would take place first thing the next morning, and then he was gone. Beverly sniffled in the corner, and after a few moments, she, too, left. Lydia heard her talking to another woman somewhere else in the house.

When she and Mr. Dawson were alone, he turned his red-rimmed eyes toward her. "I'll walk you home."

"No," Lydia said, placing a hand on his arm. "I'll be fine. You stay here and do whatever you need to." She rose up on her toes and kissed his cheek. "Take care, Erik. I'll see you tomorrow."

NINE

It wasn't until she was ready to fall asleep that Lydia realized she'd called Mr. Dawson *Erik*.

And that he'd called her *Lydia* when he'd first seen her at his sister's place.

A small bit of comfort that allowed her to fall asleep at last, even though it was well past midnight.

Morning came hard and fast. Lydia woke feeling exhausted, and it hadn't even been her loved one who had died the night before. She dressed quickly and went downstairs before Mrs. Smith awakened. After writing a brief note saying that she had had to leave before breakfast, Lydia headed out.

The day was overcast and windy as Lydia made her way along Main Street. It felt like a day for a funeral. When she arrived at the churchyard, she was surprised to see quite a few people already gathered there, although it was plain that the women were from the brothel or similar establishments. Several men were in attendance as well, and Lydia could guess what some of their relationships had been with Margaret Dawson.

Eric Dawson stood near Reverend Stanley alongside a wooden casket. Lydia's heart went out again at the loss Erik must feel. She had all kinds of questions about his sister, but they could wait. For now, she was there to support him in any way she could.

Reverend Stanley began the service with a prayer, remaining by the casket as he spoke, and for a moment Lydia wondered why the service wasn't held inside the church. But looking around at the eclectic group, she realized it made more sense to have it outside, where everyone would feel comfortable.

At the conclusion of the reverend's words, Eric placed a bouquet of flowers on the casket. Sobbing broke out from one of the women, and it wasn't hard to recognize Beverly. The other women started crying and hugging one another.

The wind picked up, tugging at Lydia's hair and clothing. She watched the mourners, feeling apart from them but also grateful she'd come. Soon the rain started, and she wandered into the empty church while the funeral goers talked and consoled one another outside. She didn't know how long she sat on a pew there, feeling numb with lack of sleep, but the rain had let up by the time she realized she should probably go back outside.

As she stood, Mr. Dawson walked into the church. His jacket was rain specked, and he'd taken off his hat. His hair looked like he'd run his fingers through it several times. "You're still here."

"Yes," Lydia said.

"Thank you for coming." His voice sounded hollow, barely there.

"You should get some rest," Lydia said. "Did you sleep at all last night?"

His eyes seemed to finally focus on her. "I'm not sure."

"Come on," she said, crossing to him and linking her arm in his. "I'll take you home."

He followed her lead like he was grateful for someone else to take charge. Out on the porch, she said, "Which direction, Mr. Dawson?"

"Erik," he said.

Lydia's heart lifted.

He nodded south, the direction leading away from Main Street. They set off down the steps and walked toward the road. The rain had let up, and only a few random drops made their way to the ground. Lydia and Eric passed the churchyard, where two men shoveled dirt into the open grave.

Lydia looked away from the lonely scene.

"I'm sorry I didn't get to introduce you to Mr. Kirkpatrick," Erik said.

Lydia glanced up with surprise. He was thinking about *that*? After all that had happened since then? "Meeting Mr. Christensen was enough."

Erik nodded, seeming to take her reply very seriously.

They walked in silence the rest of the way to his place. A clapboard house sat on about an acre of land, surrounded by tall aspens. "This is your house?"

"I'm renting it," he said. "With Margaret gone, I'll probably sell the mine and move on."

She didn't know if it was his despondency talking or if he was really planning on leaving Leadville. But she did know that she didn't plan on letting him out of her life that easily. She should have said goodbye at the porch, but she couldn't leave him in this state. Inside, the kitchen was surprisingly clean, and she found a bowl of apples and a half loaf of bread wrapped in a cloth.

"Sit and eat something," she said and was pleased when he obeyed her.

She found a knife and a crock of butter, then cut him a slice of bread and buttered it. Next she cut up the apple. He ate a few bites of each, and after the second yawn from him, she said, "Why don't you try to sleep? I can clean this up."

"Thank you." He rose from the table and disappeared into what must have been the bedroom.

She stared after him for a moment. Was she the only one whose heart pounded when they were together? He'd been friendly and polite to her, but that was all. And all too willing to introduce her to other men.

It took only a few minutes to put the kitchen in order. She found a broom and swept the floor, then straightened the two chairs at the table. She walked to the window and watched the streaking rain. Beyond the front yard sat a barn and a fenced lot with two horses.

She'd go home when the rain stopped. In the meantime, she'd sit on the sofa and wait.

After all, what if Erik awoke and needed something?

TEN

Erik rubbed his eyes, but Lydia Stone was still there—asleep on his sofa. She wasn't an apparition. The sky had cleared, and the sun was already setting, which meant he'd slept most of the day. He felt as if he were in a dream, probably because he'd slept so deeply, the opposite of the past months. And now he felt completely restored. Except for the grief in his heart over losing his sister, he was glad that the pain from her illness had passed.

He still couldn't believe she was truly gone. He supposed it would take weeks and months to get used to. Sitting on the only chair in the room, he watched Lydia. He could only think of her as his dear Lydia now. After the past night and day and how she'd been there for him. He thought of the tender way she'd used her own shawl to cover his sister.

One of Lydia's hands supported her cheek like a pillow, and the other was curled around her waist. She looked so peaceful and delicate. When she was awake, she was a strong woman, but now she looked vulnerable.

He blinked and looked away. It wouldn't do to fall in love with this woman. With Margaret's death, there was nothing holding him in this town now. Lydia could work for a new manager, and that would create a smooth transition between owners. He would move on, and so could she. That was the way of places like Leadville. Always changing.

Erik let out a sigh, louder than he intended, and Lydia's eyes fluttered open.

"Oh." She rose to a sitting position. Her hair had come out of its pins and tumbled around her shoulders.

Erik had a sudden urge to sit by her and run his fingers through her hair. "I think we both needed some sleep," he said.

Lydia blinked a few times. "I didn't mean to fall asleep. It was raining, and—" She stopped talking and looked past him.

Erik turned to see what she was looking at. He'd forgotten about his sister's portrait, one that had been painted of her at the age of sixteen . . . before all of the changes.

"Is that Margaret?"

"Yes," Erik said, having trouble keeping emotion from his voice.

She stood and crossed the room to get a closer look. "She was beautiful." She looked over at him. "Tell me about your family, Erik."

He rose and faced the portrait. It took him a moment to speak. "When my mother left, my father never recovered. He drank himself to death. After that, everything in our lives was different. We were barely able to survive. I never really appreciated all that my sister must have gone through."

Lydia turned her gaze to him, and the calm peace he saw there gave him courage to continue. "Margaret had a lot of pride. I see that now. She didn't want her little brother to go without. In fact, she wanted more for him, as sort of a revenge on our parents' neglect. She was going to show them how she'd gotten control of her life and provided for her brother."

"She sounds like a remarkable person."

A lump stuck in Erik's throat. *Had* his sister been a remarkable person? He'd been angry and embarrassed about her for so long. Had he completely misjudged her all of this time? "When I found out how she was paying for my education, I was furious. I quit school."

"Oh, Erik," Lydia said in a soft voice.

"I know." He couldn't meet her eyes. Guilt was filling him up faster than a broken dam flooding a valley. "I couldn't accept where the money was coming from. My heart was too hard." He fell silent; the battling emotions inside of him were too fierce to express.

"Your sister loved you," Lydia said. "And you were a good brother to her."

His eyes burned. "How can you know that? All I did was follow her around and criticize her. Hell, I even bribed a reverend to try to guilt her into coming to church."

Lydia's arm slid into the crook of his arm, and she leaned her head against his shoulder. "Because you cared. You cared for her, and I believe she knew it. I believe she was proud of you. Even though she wouldn't, or possibly couldn't, change her life, she appreciated your concern."

Erik exhaled, closing his eyes. How could this woman he had known for only a few weeks see his entire life so clearly? He let her words sink in and soften the hard knot of guilt. Maybe he hadn't completely failed his sister. Maybe he'd somehow taken care of her after all.

Next to him, Lydia straightened, releasing his arm. "I have been so wrong about you, Erik Dawson, and I must apologize about that."

He looked down at her. "You have nothing to apologize for. I should have let you know it was my sister living in that brothel instead of letting you think otherwise."

Her gaze held his, and his heart expanded.

"I should have never thought otherwise," she said, touching his cheek. "You're a good man. Many people care for you and respect you."

"Some might, but I haven't had much luck with the women in my life. First my mother left, and now my sister is gone." He couldn't meet her gaze anymore. Surely there was pity in her eyes, pity he didn't want to see.

Her hand brushed his, sending fire into his veins, but he didn't move, didn't dare touch her in return. It was better that he keep his heart protected. He didn't want to feel any of the pain and rejection he'd lived with since the age of nine.

"Erik, look at me," she said in a soft yet commanding voice.

He didn't know how she managed that—causing a man's knees to quiver.

He obeyed. Her eyes were a deep gray, matching the twilight of the sky beyond the window.

"I'm not your mother," she said.

"I know." He tried to smile, but it wouldn't come. "You don't look a thing like her."

Her hands slid into his, her fingers curling around his fingers. His heart thumped as warmth spread up his arm. "That's not what I meant," she said. "I'm not going to leave you like she did."

He exhaled, letting the information sink in. Was it possible that Lydia would stay with him? That somehow he wouldn't drive her away? "You won't?" he whispered, his voice hoarse now.

Lydia shook her head, her gaze intent on his. "And I'm not your sister, either."

He could only stare at her.

She moved closer, so that their bodies were nearly touching. She pressed one finger against his chest. "I should have never crossed you off my list. You are the only man I want."

Fire pulsed through his veins. It was more than he could have ever hoped for—that a woman like Lydia, a woman he realized he loved, could desire him in return. Truly love everything about him. She wasn't leaving. She wasn't turning him away. She wasn't rejecting him.

"I'm not number ten anymore?"

"No," she said with a small laugh. Her hand released his and moved up to his shoulder. Her fingers brushed the skin of his neck, and he inhaled sharply, knowing he couldn't *not* touch her much longer.

"I think you were always the only one on my list." Her fingers caressed his neck, then threaded into his hair. "And I think you should kiss me now, Mr. Dawson. I've confessed an awful lot, you know."

Erik knew it would take only one small move, and she'd be in his arms. She'd be his. He closed his eyes, breathing her in, feeling her warm touch against his skin—the warmth moving through him until it cocooned his heart.

He opened his eyes to find that she was gazing at him. Those calm, gray eyes so wise and sure. Those eyes that said she loved him and that she wouldn't leave.

His hands trembled as he lifted them and cradled her face. The edges of her mouth curved into a smile, and her eyelids fluttered shut. Finally he let his heart take over, and he kissed her, finding her lips soft and warm and eager to receive his.

His pulse raced as she wrapped both of her arms around his neck and tugged him closer, kissing him in return. He moved his hands down her back, and her body molded to his, taking his breath away. Every worry and barrier seemed to fade. The miners, his mother, his father, his sister, twenty years of pain and loss. Lydia's kisses filled his soul and pushed away his loneliness.

Wrapped in her arms, he felt like he'd come home after years of following his sister and trying to give her a home. And now, with Lydia . . . he knew a true home wasn't found in a wooden or brick house. It was in the heart.

Their kissing slowed, and Lydia nestled against him, her face pressed against his neck so he could feel her warm breath on his skin. It was like heaven had come to Leadville, Colorado.

"I hope you're planning on courting me, Erik," she whispered.

He loved hearing her say his name. He tightened his arms about her. "I don't think I could let you get away now."

"Good," she said. "Because after that, I don't think I could ever kiss another man ever again. You've ruined it for me."

He chuckled. "Thinking of kissing another man, are you?"

She drew away from him, and he hated the distance. But her gaze was soft, welcoming. "Never."

"Then let me see that list of yours."

She smiled as she reached into her bodice.

"You keep it in your . . ."

"In case I need to make immediate alterations. Which I do." She unfolded the paper.

He laughed and took it from her. "May I?"

She nodded, and he proceeded to rip it in half, then in half again. Before he could rip it a third time, her arms were around his neck again. The pieces of paper fell to the floor as they kissed, because out of all the names, only one mattered.

ABOUT HEATHER B. MOORE

Heather B. Moore is a *USA Today* bestselling author. She writes historical thrillers under the pen name H.B. Moore; her latest is *Finding Sheba*. Under Heather B. Moore she writes romance and women's fiction. She's a coauthor of The Newport Ladies Book Club series. Other works include *Heart of the Ocean, The Fortune Café,* the Aliso Creek series, and the Amazon bestselling Timeless Romance Anthology series.

For book updates, sign up for Heather's email list: hbmoore.com/contact

Website: www.hbmoore.com

Blog: MyWritersLair.blogspot.com

THE SWEETEST TASTE

by Annette Lyon

Other Works by Annette Lyon

Band of Sisters

Coming Home

The Newport Ladies Book Club series

A Portrait for Toni

At the Water's Edge

Lost Without You

Done & Done

There, Their, They're: A No-Tears Guide to Grammar from the Word Nerd

ONE

Shelley, Idaho—1905

Della stood at the back door, staring with dread at the chicken coop. Cleaning it out had to be one of the smelliest, most disgusting jobs in the world. And it was all hers for the foreseeable future, now that her older brother, Andrew, had gone off to work on the railroad. He wouldn't back soon, if ever. The moment he had enough money saved up to buy his own land, he'd settle down with Susan Hyde.

Why cleaning the chicken coop today in particular put a bee in her bonnet, she didn't know. She clomped over to the coop wearing big ugly boots so she wouldn't spoil her regular shoes. And she wore an ugly apron to protect her dress.

As she unlatched the coop and shooed the birds out, she knew that the object of her disdain changed by the day. Today it was the coop, but tomorrow it could well be milking the cows. Or the eternal laundry days, during which her fingers cracked from all the scrubbing and water. The bluing alone was reason enough to despise the laundry, considering that time it spilled on her favorite white blouse and ruined it. Or the weeks on end every summer, spent canning all manner of fruits and vegetables in the heat, sweating nigh unto death, so they'd have enough food to eat in the winter.

With a wet slurping sound, her boot sank into a mud puddle. Della yanked it out, but mud splattered everywhere; surely her dress was soiled too.

She shook off the mud as best she could. After cleaning the coop, she'd make some lemonade and sit down for a break. *See, farm life? You can't get the better of me.*

Yet it did. Farm life controlled every aspect of Della Stafford's life, and she hated that fact more and more each day.

A shovel rested outside the coop, waiting for her. She lifted it, nose crinkling in anticipation of the smell. Surely the women in catalog pictures never had to scoop the messes from chickens. Or kill chickens with an ax—and pluck them. Or a thousand other things that made up the life Della had grown up on.

I'll leave. I'll get away from all of this someday. Somehow.

A thousand times she'd imagined what life would be like in a big city, with trolleys and electric lights and busy people everywhere—and no farm chores to worry about. In the city she'd see some of those moving pictures people talked about. Visit the theater. See many of the grand sights of America and experience different foods. It would all be tremendously exciting, of course, and in the middle of it all, she'd find the man of her dreams. He'd sweep her away, and her life would be entirely different. Her hands would be soft because they no longer had to work themselves to the bone. She'd have fashionable dresses and hats and shiny new boots. And she'd never, ever have to mend the same dress for the fifth year in a row.

Her parents still held out hope that she'd pick a local boy and settle down to raise a family right there in Shelley.

There was plenty of land yet to develop, and Della was plenty old enough for such things—at twenty-two, she certainly felt the pressure to marry and be in charge of her own house and chores and chickens.

No, thank you. She'd find a way to leave this place and do something else. Maybe she could be a seamstress in the big city. Or one of the women who modeled dresses and hats for the artists who drew the pictures on the fashion pages of the paper. She could find some way to get by, surely, and whatever it was, it had to be better than this sorry place of too much heat and dust in the summer, too much cold and ice in the winter, and too much work all the year round. Perhaps she would have been content if she hadn't had a glimpse through books, newspapers, and the occasional visitor from far away, of what life was like in the big cities. She remembered all too well a woman from Seattle who came through on her way to teach in a school in Colorado. How elegant she looked. How refined.

She'd spent one night with Della's family, during which time she regaled them with stories of her life back home, one so different from anything Della had ever imagined. She yearned to experience even a portion of what she'd heard about.

Standing before the chicken coop, thinking of the teacher from Seattle, she shook her head. Surely that woman had never cleaned a chicken coop. With one hand on the coop latch, Della inhaled deeply—her last breath of fresh air for now—and plunged inside. She held one sleeve over her nose but knew that couldn't last, so she quickly went to work, scooping the droppings from the floor and roosts and, it seemed, virtually every other surface. How the chickens managed to mess up everything boggled the mind.

The shovel slipped, and the slime of chicken droppings flew through the air. A blob landed on her cheek. Della tried to not gag entirely and refused to touch it. She knew from painful experience that the droppings would only smear all over her hand if she tried wiping it off now. She'd need a rag, and she wouldn't have one of those until she got back to the house.

Eventually she emerged from the coop, feeling covered in muck, even though it was mostly the apron's hem, the boots, and the blob on her cheek. Some pieces of hair had escaped her bun and flew about her face in twenty directions. And she had to smell . . .

Wearing what she knew must be a look of disgust, she shook her head, walked out of the coop, and marched back to the barn wall, where she'd return the shovel. She had just placed it against the wall when a deep voice spoke to her from the fence.

"Why, Della Stafford, is that you under there?" Joseph Cartwright said with a laugh.

For a moment she froze, mortified, until she realized the voice belonged to Joseph, whom she'd known most of her life. He was one of her dearest friends in the world, so she could laugh at herself along with him.

He was also one of the town's few eligible bachelors, and one plenty of people hinted that she should bat her eyelashes at. Had he not just bought his own land with plans to start a cattle farm of his own, she might well have given the idea some thought. After all, he *was* handsome and tall and kind and funny.

"Why, hello, Joseph Cartwright," she said, mimicking his formal tone but grinning ear to ear. She held out her arms, revealing the disgusting mess of her dress. "Care to dance?" she asked, taking a few steps toward him.

Joseph held out one arm and took several steps back, holding out one arm. "Whoa," he said, backing away from the fence. "Not like that, I don't."

"Oh, come now, Mr. Cartwright. You aren't afraid of a little dirt, are you?" She took another two steps toward him, laughing.

"Dirt? Never." He swept his cowboy hat off his head, wiped his brow with one sleeve, and replaced the hat on his head with a determined plop. "That's not *dirt*. Some may call me finicky, but I prefer my women to smell of lavender, not eau de chicken coop."

Della reached the fence, but instead of following through on her threat, she set to wiping the mud and muck from her boots onto one of the posts. "If I never see a chicken or an egg again in my entire life, it will be too soon."

Joseph leaned against the fence, relaxing into their old friendly banter. "You'd likely change your mind next time you ate a cake made with no eggs or had a roasted chicken supper without the chicken."

She looked up and considered his point. "Very well. Someone else can handle the chickens. I'm happy to enjoy the fruits of their labors, but I hope to one day be permanently far from any chicken coop."

With the worst of the mess off her boots, she gave one heel a final swipe on some tall grass, then studied her appearance. "Oh, I do hope Mother doesn't expect me to do much else today; I'll barely have time to clean up for the dance as it is."

"That's what I came over for," Joseph said. "To see if you were planning on going to the dance."

"Oh, yes. I'll be there," Della said. "That is, assuming Mother doesn't saddle me with a hundred other chores to complete before then."

"Feeling a bit like Cinderella, are we?"

"So what if I do?" Della folded her arms and leaned against the fence too, happy to forget about her smell and appearance for the moment.

"So long as you aren't expecting a prince to come rescue you and give you a different life." Joseph chuckled, but when Della didn't laugh back, his brow furrowed. "You don't expect that, do you?"

How could she answer such a question? Of course life wasn't a fairy tale existence. No prince would sweep her away and take her to a life of bliss and rest. But yes, she did plan to leave this place and leave it behind for good.

Their eyes met for several seconds as Della tried to come up with a response. Joseph looked genuinely concerned. She wanted to reach up and smooth the worried crease between his eyebrows.

Instead of answering his question, she returned to an earlier topic. She smiled broadly and tilted her head. "I'll be expecting to have you as my partner for several dances tonight."

Joseph blinked twice and lowered his head for just a second. Della couldn't see his face, only the top of his hat. He stayed that way for a moment, as if he needed the time to change directions. As she waited for him to speak, Della's heart sped up. He needed to play along, to say that of course he'd be her dance partner tonight, as he often was. And to not ask about her hopes of leaving town.

She couldn't tell him about that, in part because he wouldn't understand. He loved Shelley and the Idaho frontier like a child adored a parent; he wouldn't understand why she'd want to leave.

Another reason was that when she did finally leave, she'd miss Joseph, and she didn't want to think about that farewell any sooner than she had to. Aside from her family, he was the only part of Shelley she'd miss terribly. Whenever she came home to visit her family, she'd certainly bump into him in town, but the time would come, likely sooner than later, when he'd find a wife. That's when the friendly banter they'd shared for years would be a thing of the past. She hoped to find a friend in the city who could fill that spot in her heart.

Though she denied the truth even to herself, a little voice whispered in her mind that no one would ever be this dear to her again. Certainly another girl could never be the friend Joseph had been to her, especially over the last couple of years. And she most certainly couldn't imagine another man ever being so kind and funny and attentive . . . and handsome. Yes, she had to admit the facts. Joseph Cartwright was a fine-looking man.

Her dreams of a different life remained, however. Apollo himself couldn't convince her to stay here and muck out chicken coops for the rest of her life. Yet the idea of leaving Joseph behind made her throat go dry. The silence between them seemed to stretch thinner than taffy pulled into threads.

"You will be there, Joseph, won't you?" She put on a smile and tilted her head at a flirty angle. "You didn't come to see if I was going to the dance, only to stay home tonight yourself, did you?"

He finally raised his face and met her gaze. "I'll be there tonight, Della," he said. "I always am."

His warm voice had something more in it, an emotion she couldn't quite name. Something intent and serious. Something that sent a warm, tingly feeling up and down her spine.

"See you tonight." With that, Joseph's mouth curved into a slight smile. He tipped his hat, then turned on his heel and walked away down the lane, turning toward State Street.

Della watched his every step until he was out of sight. Too bad Joseph had no aspirations for a grander life, which was really a shame, because if he did . . .

She shook her head quickly to chase away the thought. No more of that. She had chores to do—detestable chores— before the dance tonight. And she was bound and determined to bathe before she dressed up. No one would know she'd spent her afternoon covered in chicken waste. Not if she had any say about it.

TWO

Della hurried through the rest of her chores so she could spend extra time getting ready for the dance. She ironed her dress within an inch of its life, determined to eradicate every wrinkle. She used the curling wand on her hair and reheated it on the stove every time it cooled off, which was several. Every hair needed to be just so.

As she gathered her gloves and hat, her mother met her at the door and handed her a sprig of tiny white flowers. "For your hair, if you'd like, now that spring is here."

Della smiled and nodded, tilting her head so her mother could tuck the sprig behind her ear and secure it with a pin. Her mother pulled back and looked her over, holding her by the arms.

"You'll be the most beautiful girl at the dance."

"Thank you, Mama," Della said, giving her mother a hug. "No doubt if I were in New York City or Seattle no one would so much as notice me."

Considering how small the dance would be, she didn't have much competition, but Della appreciated the thought.

It wasn't that she was so vain as to believe she'd been born with some great innate beauty; she simply worked harder at her appearance than most young women in the tiny town of Shelley. She wore brighter colors, arranged her hair more elaborately. In short, she *worked* at looking like the beautiful, stylish women in the newspapers and catalogs.

Her mother sighed. "Oh, sweetheart. I hope you can find a way to be happy where the good Lord planted you."

They'd had this discussion many times, yet Della felt compelled to try to explain again. She needed *someone* to understand. "I want to choose my path," she said. "Shelley is just too small for me. It didn't have a name until just last year."

"I suppose it is small," her mother began. "But—"

"I feel cramped, like I have wings that have been clipped, so I'm stuck here in the wilderness when I was meant to fly into bigger places and do great things."

As if on cue, a group of black birds took flight from the family's cherry tree. Both women watched them squawk and chirp as they flew en masse to another tree farther away and settled on its branches.

Her mother kept her eyes on the birds as she spoke next in a quiet voice. "Birds usually return home after flying away."

"Yes," Della said carefully. "Some do."

She left the idea hanging in the air, allowing her mother to believe that perhaps, after visiting a big city for a season, Della would be content to return home.

And voluntarily clip my wings for the rest of my life? What kind of existence would that be?

Voices carried on the wind through the door, which was open a crack. Della pushed it all the way open and looked out. Estelle and Betty were coming up the lane from the road, on their way to pick her up for the dance.

"I'd—I'd better go," Della said quietly. "Thank you for

the flowers, Mama." She leaned in for a quick peck on her mother's cheek and a final hug before heading down the lane toward her friends.

Tonight's dance would be held at the Parker home, a good half mile away. With any luck, the young women would arrive without kicking up much dust to soil their dresses.

When Della reached her friends, Betty held up a basket of fresh peas. "First pea harvest of the year was this morning. I convinced Mama to let me take some, in case we can convince Old Sam to play a *slow* waltz." She grinned mischievously.

They laughed. Rumors had it that when their own mothers were young, the waltz had been a bit on the edge of propriety, what with how partners danced in a closed position, looking at each other the whole time, their bodies often *touching*. Estelle's grandparents still considered it vulgar. Fortunately for Della's generation, it was only the slow waltzes some people raised an eyebrow at, believing it to be too conducive to youth losing their heads and falling for each other.

Perhaps they had a point, Della thought. The thrill of dancing that close to a handsome young man was part of the reason they liked it so much. Fortunately, Old Sam, the leader of the band who played at virtually every dance and was the best fiddler around, found nothing shocking about the waltz at any speed. Better yet, he was easily persuaded to play extra slow waltzes if given the right incentive.

Estelle nodded excitedly. "You *know* how much he loves fresh peas."

Della's eyes lit up. "Wait one moment. I'll be right back." She picked up her skirts and hurried back to the house, where her mother still waited on the stoop.

"Everything all right?" she asked when Della came close.

"May I bring a jar of your raspberry jam as a gift to the

band?" *Bribe, more like.* But she wasn't about so say so.

Her mother smiled as if she knew what Della was really up to. "There's an unopened jar in the pantry."

"Thank you, Mama!" She hurried inside and found the jar, then gave her mother a quick wave before heading back out to join her friends.

Her mother had talked about waltzing in her own youth, so while she might not have strictly approved of bribing Old Sam, she wouldn't mind Della waltzing. However, Della most certainly didn't want her family watching her waltz; that would be a mite embarrassing. Good thing she was the only one from the household going tonight.

As Della reached her friends, she raised one hand to block the sun, which was about to set, sending its rays right into her eyes. In her other hand, she held up her spoils. "Raspberry jam," she declared triumphantly.

"Your mother's jam is *famous*," Estelle said.

Betty's eyes went wide and dreamy. "Oh, I'd love to waltz twice with Arnold Francom."

They walked along quickly, eager to arrive. Estelle and Betty did most of the talking, however, as Della's mind was more preoccupied than usual with thoughts of life in a big city, especially as they crossed State Street near the spot where, a few years ago, a fire had destroyed seven buildings—largely what had amounted to their downtown area, such as it had been.

The buildings destroyed by the fire had been razed, and several new buildings stood in their stead. But a few scars from the fire remained, and even from a hundred yards away, they practically yelled at Della to leave, and soon.

She tossed her head, not wanting to look at the burned area, and focused squarely on the evening ahead of her. She held the jar of jam close so it wouldn't fall and so the young women at the dance would get their second slow waltz.

Surely that dance didn't raise any eyebrows in San Francisco or Chicago. And big-city dances were surely in large halls, not in someone's home, where the furniture had been taken out or pushed to the edges to make room.

Betty and Estelle's chattering floated about Della's head as she walked, scarcely aware of their words as she imagined wearing a satin gown as she entered an elegant ballroom with electric chandeliers.

Della's attention returned with a start when she heard Betty say, "Los Angeles."

"Wait, what did you say about Los Angeles?"

Her friend smiled curiously. "Just that my aunt Eleanor is visiting. She hasn't been back to Idaho since she moved out there to marry her husband fifteen years ago." Betty shrugged. "Apparently she left when I was two years old; I don't remember her from then at all. She'll be at the dance. I'm sure she'd love to meet you."

Los Angeles. After a couple of fast thuds of Della's heart, she asked, "You think she'd talk to me about what it's like in a big city? I'd hate for her to think I'm some backward farm girl." In spite of the fact that that was exactly what Della was, if one ignored how many books and magazines she'd read.

"Of course," Betty said, tossing her hand dismissively. "She's here to talk with as many local girls as she can. She's looking for a new housekeeper. Or was it a cook? Or laundress? I forget."

Della had to force herself to *not* squeal. "Has she—has she found anyone yet?"

"No, more's the rub. I said I'd go, but of course, neither of my parents will allow it. They insist I'll be exposed to devilish things in the city." She said it with a grin and sparkling eyes, as if she would be perfectly happy to discover and experience a few "devilish" things.

Della's fingers gripped the jar of raspberry jam so tightly it could have slipped out of her hands entirely, but she couldn't help it. Her insides were going all twisty in a delightful and nerve-wracking way.

Betty went on, clearly not noticing Della's reaction. "That's why she's coming to the dance—to see if there's anyone she missed talking to who would make a good worker and be able to go with her. They leave tomorrow after the train comes for a supply delivery along the Shelley spur line."

This was Della's chance, dropped right into her lap. She would go to California with Betty's aunt, work for her in whatever capacity was needed, and at last experience time away from the doldrums of a tiny farm community. She'd finally experience *life*.

THREE

Joseph arrived at the dance five minutes early, but he was one of only four guests. If it hadn't been for the large parlor being emptied of furniture, he would have thought he'd come at the wrong time. He greeted Mr. Parker and his wife, then tried to find something to say to the others standing in one corner in an effort to pass the time.

To his relief, Ruby Schofield chattered on about something to do with a near-tragedy regarding her dress and hair, freeing Joseph from feeling any obligation to invent a topic of conversation.

Good thing, too, as he couldn't have managed more than one coherent sentence, and he'd already spent that in his greeting to the Parkers.

Silly to be so nervous, he thought. *It's not as if I'm proposing marriage.*

Yet in a sense, what he would be doing tonight wasn't far off from asking for Della's hand, and the results of tonight's actions could well lead to her one day becoming his wife. God willing.

Joseph's hand patted his vest pocket to check for the necklace he'd bought at the general store. It wasn't fancy or expensive—neither of which he could afford even if the local store had stocked such things. The pale-blue stone—a piece of glass cut to look like aquamarine—reminded him of Della's eyes, which looked even bluer when she wore her blue dress. He hoped she'd wear it tonight. He'd slip the pendant and chain around her neck, and it would be a symbol of the official beginning to their courtship.

He could hardly stand the wait. The necklace seemed to burn a hole in his vest, and his palms were growing sweaty. *She's not even here yet.*

At long last, more and more guests arrived, including Della, with Betty and Estelle in tow. He caught Della's eye, and she smiled significantly, lifting a canning jar as she headed toward the four-piece band setting up in the corner. A bribe. A bribe for a waltz.

He smiled with satisfaction, picturing the two of them waltzing. This evening would turn out perfectly. He'd pictured it all a thousand times if once.

As the band got ready, Della chatted in a circle of other young women. The fiddler finally got his instrument tuned, then nodded to Old Sam. The dance was about to start. The upright piano at the back held a pile of booty stacked on one side. Judging by the size of the stack, tonight might well promise three or four waltzes, provided the older folk didn't protest.

Old Sam clapped three times to get everyone's attention, and the conversation in the parlor and the adjoining room quieted, with people poking their heads in through the door. Enough guests had come that the dance had spilled into the other room and, by the looks of it, had filled it as well.

"Welcome to tonight's dance," Old Sam said. "We'll begin with a cakewalk. Gentlemen, find your partners."

He turned his back to the guests and spoke to his players. Joseph hurried to secure Della as his partner, but by the time he navigated around and through everyone, she was gone. He whirled about, only to see her already standing in the circle with Willy Millward. Not a problem. The dance had hours to go, and surely he'd be able to dance with Della several times. He asked Margaret Bell to join him, and she readily agreed.

After the cakewalk came a *galop*, a faster dance, and one in closed dance position, which he, of course, preferred to the hand-holding quadrilles. Margaret seemed to assume he'd dance with her a second time, and as Willy seemed to be doing the same with Della, Joseph complied.

Dance after dance, he lost the opportunity to dance with Della, until two hours had passed and the moon was already rising. Another dance ended—the first waltz of the night—and yet again someone else reached Della before he did. Joseph opted not to dance this number, in favor of watching and admiring Della—and being able to reach her quickly after the song ended.

When it finally did, Della thanked her partner and walked off the floor, breathing quickly from the exertion of the dance. She headed straight for Joseph, as if she'd known he was waiting for her. She wore the smile that always made his knees weak. His fingers instinctively moved toward his vest pocket and felt for the shape of the necklace inside.

Della reached him and took his hands in hers. "Isn't it delightful?" she said. "And see the gifts Old Sam was given."

Joseph's smile broadened. "I'd say we're in for many slow dances tonight."

"Oh, I hope so," she said, then fanned her hand before her face. "But first, I need a break. I'm out of breath, and it's so hot in here."

He'd been about to ask for her hand in the next dance, but a rest would be fine; they could talk, just the two of them, before dancing. And he'd make sure the topic was *not* chicken droppings.

They threaded their way through the crowded room until they reached a table set up outside the kitchen, with apple juice and cookies.

"That looks divine," Della said, eyeing the table.

"I'll get you a drink," Joseph told her. He filled a cup with apple juice and selected two cookies—one for her, one for himself. Mr. Parker came out of the kitchen, lugging a barrel apparently full of apple juice.

Joseph set the cup and cookies onto the table. "Would you like some help?" he asked, moving over to steady the barrel.

"Yes, please," Mr. Parker grunted. "Either apple juice is getting heavier, or I'm getting older."

Together, they got the barrel arranged, after which Joseph helped carry some chairs back into the room for two elderly ladies to sit on in the corner. "Anything else I can help you with?" Joseph asked.

"I don't think so," Mr. Parker said. "Thank you for stepping in. Now go enjoy the dance." He patted Joseph on the side of the arm and nodded toward Della as if he knew Joseph had eyes for her. Perhaps he did know.

Is it so obvious?

By the time he returned to Della, she was occupied in conversation with a woman he didn't recognize. Della's face was flushed with excitement over whatever it was they were discussing. Curious, Joseph walked up to them and offered the cup and cookie, hoping for an introduction.

"Oh, thank you, Joseph," Della said, reaching for them. She took a sip of the juice and nodded. "Mmm. Tasty and cold, too. Just what I needed." She gestured toward the woman she'd been speaking to. "I should introduce you."

"This is Joseph Cartwright," Della said, gesturing to him.

He turned to the woman. Now that he was closer, she looked to be in her forties or perhaps her early fifties.

"Pleased to make your acquaintance." He bent slightly at the waist and nodded.

"And this"—Della gestured to the woman—"is Betty's aunt, Mrs. Eleanor Baker."

Mrs. Baker nodded slightly. "A pleasure."

"She's from Los Angeles," Della said in a tone clearly meant to awe Joseph. Instead, his stomach felt a little sour. No wonder she seemed so excited to meet this woman. Surely Della would stay close to Eleanor for the remainder of the evening, like a puppy trailing its master, as she tried to learn all she could about the city.

"How long are you visiting?" Joseph asked, speaking above the music playing in the other room—a fast waltz. At least he hadn't missed a slow one.

"I leave tomorrow, actually," Mrs. Baker said. "I'm still hoping I'll find a suitable girl to come with me. I'm in need of more help at home—just a maid to help with the cleaning and cooking and odds and ends. My last girl didn't know how to work hard, so I came back home to look for someone new. After all, Idaho farm girls tend to be wiry and tough—hard workers."

Della's smile dulled a bit at the half compliment, half insult.

Mrs. Baker went on. "But I may have found my maid, right, Della?" The two smiled at each other knowingly.

"Wait, what?" Joseph's mind tried to catch up. Did Mrs. Baker mean . . . Surely not. He turned to Della. "You aren't going—"

"Old Sam just announced a *lancier*. Come, Joseph. Do be my partner." Della took his hand and pulled him gently in the direction of the parlor.

He looked from Della to Mrs. Baker and back. He'd wanted to dance with Della from the moment he'd walked in. Of course he should go. Yet the simple pronouncement that Della would be leaving in the morning for California left him reeling, as if he'd been kicked in the stomach by a horse.

He nodded toward Mrs. Baker and followed Della. They took their positions across from each other, and when the dance began and they took hands, he tried to find out what was really happening.

"Della, do you mean—"

But a turn separated them. He tried again as they sashayed, hand in hand, down the lane of dancers. "You aren't leaving tomorrow, are you?"

Before she could answer, they'd reached the moment of briefly changing partners. He tried once or twice more, but Della either didn't hear or didn't want to discuss her plans in front of everyone. So they danced in silence, Della still grinning ear to ear, while a sickening feeling of dread overtook Joseph. When Old Sam finally cut the music, Joseph wiped his brow, relieved. He'd never endured a more miserable time on the dance floor.

Della drew close and said, "I promised Harry I'd dance with him tonight, and he's standing by the piano looking rather forlorn. Old Sam promised a polka next, and that's Harry's favorite." She turned as if to move toward Harry, but Joseph held onto her hand. She turned around, a question in her expression.

So much Joseph wanted to say, but he struggled to speak at first. "After the polka . . ."

"Yes?" she asked expectantly.

Joseph took in the shape of her face, her peaches-and-cream skin, her long lashes, and tried to memorize it all, in case his worst fears were about to come true.

"Joseph?" she prompted.

"After the polka," he repeated, "walk with me outside?" He swallowed and put on a smile. "It's a bit hot and stuffy in here."

"Sure thing." She squeezed his hand before walking away. Joseph watched every step. Of course Della would go out of her way to be Harry's partner for his favorite dance. It was part of her nature to remember what other people cared about and then to act on that knowledge. In this case, it was making sure Harry had at least one partner tonight and ensuring it was for the polka.

Joseph slipped into a shadowy corner to watch Della fly about the room in rhythm to the fiddle. The grin on Harry's face was proof enough that Della's kindness had done its work.

At last the polka was over. Della walked off the floor with Harry, her arm through his. They chatted a few minutes, which Joseph didn't begrudge Harry at all, not now that he knew why Della had given him her attention. Some people might look at her and think she was nothing more than a silly girl who liked to dance, but he knew better.

She wasn't a silly thing at all, in spite of her occasional nonsense about leaving Shelley to explore the world. Mrs. Baker couldn't possibly take Della away tomorrow. Even if she wanted to, and even if Della thought that's what she wanted—and Joseph couldn't imagine she did—Della's parents wouldn't allow it.

He lost sight of her for a moment, and when he spotted her again, he could tell that somehow she'd managed to find Harry another partner. He was back on the floor getting into position with Sarah Jones, a shy little thing who probably hadn't danced much yet tonight either, and Della was just leaving their side.

Joseph shook his head with admiration as Della reached him. "Ready for a walk?" she asked.

"Definitely." Joseph put out his arm for her to take, and she slipped her hand through it. Together they walked out the back door of the Parker house, past their barn, and into their apple orchard.

Joseph had pictured this part many times. He'd even picked out which tree he'd stop at. The night was still save for the muted sound of the music and dancing in the house, their footsteps and Della's dress swishing as she walked, and a small chorus of crickets chirping.

A last they reached the spot he'd picked before, by a bench Mr. Parker had made. It stood below a tree he and the Parker girls used to play in when they were young. Now the bench was weathered, its white paint so peeled as to be almost gone, but by the light of the moon it looked nothing short of the most romantic spot in the world. The bright moon lit up the tree and bench, casting slanted shadows all around.

He gently handed Della toward the bench. She took the hint, sitting, and he sat beside her. "Beautiful night, isn't it?" he said.

"It is," she agreed, craning her neck. "The stars are so bright."

Moonlight seemed to spill over her face, making her look like an angel. Joseph had to remind himself to breathe. He reached for his vest pocket. Even though he'd felt for the necklace all night, now his hand trembled so much he had to try three times to find it this go 'round. He finally had success, however, and placed the necklace into his palm, then closed his fingers.

"Della?" Now his voice trembled as well as his hands.

"Yes?" Her voice was light and detached, as if her mind was lost in some dream in the stars.

"We've known each other for a very long time . . ."

"Ever so long," she said, nodding slightly and still gazing at the sky.

A smile touched her lips, her pink lips, ones he was quite sure were soft. He wanted to find out how soft. Somehow, Joseph went on but didn't quite get to the point yet. "When we were in school, I used to tease you something awful. Remember the jar of spiders?"

She laughed lightly and leaned her head against his

shoulder. He wrapped his arm about her shoulders and leaned his cheek against her hair. Sitting this way felt right.

"Of course I remember," she said. "Those spiders gave me nightmares for two solid weeks. But you weren't all bad. Remember how you helped me bury Bo?"

Bo had been her dog. Six years ago, the poor mutt had gotten caught in some barbed-wire fencing and wasn't found for two days. By then, his wounds were infected, and he was near death without food or water for so long. Joseph and Della had cared for him as best they could, and when he died, they dug his grave together and held a funeral for him. A sandstone rock they'd found in the foothills still marked his grave. Joseph remembered all too well how she'd cried in his arms after that, off and on for several days.

"Bo was a good dog," he said.

"I never did thank you for helping me with him. For letting me cry so much."

"That's what friends do." Joseph's hand slowly reached up and stroked her hair. She closed her eyes as if the sensation soothed her. "I did those things because I liked you so much and cared so much. I—I still care about you. You know that, right? More than for any other girl." He felt her stiffen slightly, which made his chest tighten. When she didn't speak, he did. "Della, we're getting older now, and I reckon it's time to start planning our futures. I've been thinking. I'd like—" His throat seemed to constrict; he had to clear it twice to get out another word. "I'd like to ask if you'd consider allowing me to . . . to court you officially."

She slowly lifted her head from his shoulder to sit straight again. Her mouth was a round O. Joseph opened his palm and held out the necklace. The words rushed out then; he simply jumped off the cliff. "This is for you, if you'll consent to my being your beau. A sort of token, I suppose. It's blue, like your eyes. It's not real, of course, but I hope that one day I can buy you a real gemstone, and . . ." He let his voice trail off, which at this point was the only way for him to stop blabbering like an idiot. Heart pounding, he lifted his palm another inch toward her and finally looked into her eyes.

Their gaze held for several moments. She'd never looked at him like this before, with such emotion and intensity. Her eyes seemed to shine, and his heart near beat out of his chest as he waited for her to say yes and take the necklace.

At last she made a movement. She closed her eyes, sending plump tears down each cheek, and she lowered her chin. She was crying. Tears explained her shining eyes, but . . .

"Dell?" he asked warily.

"I'm going to California, remember?"

"You don't have to go," Joseph said. "I'm sure she'll find other help. No need to feel obligated."

"But—but I *want* to go."

Joseph's mind went blank for a moment. He repeated her words in his mind; they didn't make sense. "You *what*?"

Della's shoulder sagged. "You know that this life isn't for me. I don't want to settle down here, with hot, dusty summers and freezing winters with ice and snow. I don't want to barely eke out a living, hoping that this year's crop will be enough to feed the family for the winter. I don't *want* this life. You *know* that."

"I . . . I didn't think you were serious." Joseph's hand closed over the necklace again. Of course she hated parts of life on the land. No one in their right mind looked forward to cleaning a chicken coop. But leaving home? Never. "But we'd be perfect together."

Della slowly, reluctantly, shook her head. "No, we wouldn't. We're too different. You belong here. You feel most at home when you're in the saddle, herding cattle or fixing a fence. But I . . ." She shook her head and looked down, avoiding his gaze. "I feel as if I was born in the wrong place. I don't belong here, Joseph. We have different ideas of what happiness looks like."

Joseph's voice was a mere whisper now. "And your vision of happiness doesn't include chicken coops."

She nodded grudging agreement. "And a lot more than that. It also doesn't include saddles or fences or stupid cows that run off or mosquitos or dust or—"

"I understand." Joseph felt like he needed to leave, but he didn't want to.

"Do you understand?" Della said, leaning forward now as if it were imperative that he understand her point. "There's much more to life than just . . ." Her voice trailed off, but he filled in the gap.

"Than life with a cowboy."

She reached for him, but he instinctively pulled away. She clasped her hands in her lap and sniffed. "I'm so sorry."

Joseph tried to fully comprehend what all of this meant, what was happening . . . and what *wasn't* happening. Della, the woman who would always have his heart, was going away tomorrow with Mrs. Baker. He might not see her for years to come, if ever again.

He'd end up an old bachelor; the look in her eyes said quite clearly that there would be no changing her mind.

Reluctantly, he adjusted his hat, then held out his other hand, opening his fingers to reveal the necklace again. "Take this anyway."

"But—"

"To remember me by." She seemed about to protest, but he insisted. "For my sake. Please."

After a moment, she dabbed the back of a finger to wipe her tears, then nodded. "Would you put it on me?" Della turned on the bench, putting her back to him. He silently unlatched the necklace and secured it about her neck. He tried not to breathe in her perfume. When he was done, she turned to face him again and lowered her eyes to the pendant. "It's beautiful."

It was. And the blue matched her eyes perfectly.

"When you see it, think of me." His voice sounded hoarse to his ears.

"I will," she said, still looking at the necklace.

"And maybe one day when you look at it, you'll see that we aren't so different. I don't mean just that we were both born here and that we both grew up on farms."

"Then . . . what?" She, too, spoke in a whisper, but now her eyes were raised to his.

His jaw worked for a moment as he tried to put his thoughts into words. "We both see pictures in clouds." It was a small thing, but it was true. When they were younger, they'd spent many a summer afternoon lying under a tree and pointing out pictures in the sky above them. No one else could ever see the pictures in the clouds that they did.

Joseph went on. "We both laugh reading Mark Twain." He didn't have to remind her of the winter they'd spent by the stoves in each other's houses, reading from a book of Mark Twain's work, laughing so hard they could hardly breathe. He could tell by the way she pressed her lips together, as if she was trying not to cry, that she remembered.

Encouraged, he tried again, this time thinking of the weak foal born only a few months ago, which he and Della had nursed to health.

"Neither of us can stand to see an animal suffer. We both love the taste of strawberries just picked. And we both want to be happy."

Della didn't answer, but her entire body seemed to tremble with emotion. She pressed her eyelids shut, and tears spilled down her cheeks. He'd made her cry. Feeling a stab of guilt, Joseph leaned forward and pressed his lips to her forehead. He'd dreamed of pressing them to her lips, but that was not to be tonight, or likely ever.

"Most importantly, I want *you* to be happy. So, go. I hope you really do find what you're looking for out there."

She nodded and whispered something that may have been *Thank you* before he couldn't bear to stay any longer. She reached forward to hug him, and he held her back. Finally, he kissed her hair, pulled away, stood.

"Just remember me," he said quietly. Then strode out of the garden without looking back.

FOUR

When the train pulled into the station in Los Angeles at last, Della breathed a sigh of relief. The hours since Joseph had left her in the orchard had dragged by, but now she was in the city. She could put away that part of her life and let herself get all excited and jittery over the sights she would finally get to see, the things she would experience that until now had only been part of her dreams.

"Come along now, Della," Mrs. Baker said, standing and walking toward the train door.

Della followed obediently, brushing off the whisper of a thought that she didn't like being spoken to like the family dog.

But she was finally out of tiny little Shelley, she reminded herself yet again. She was away from farms and all of the work and smells they brought with them. Away from the boring, humdrum, predictable life she'd always known and hated. She lugged her own carpetbag plus Mrs. Baker's suitcase behind her, hurrying to keep up as she walked awkwardly along, bumping the seats and other passengers as she went.

"Sorry. Oh, I'm so sorry. Excuse me." And so it went all along the train car until she reached the exit and stepped out of the train. Mrs. Baker helped her keep her balance as she went down the metal steps and alighted on the platform.

I'm here. I'm really here. Della stood tall, looked about at the bustling crowd of people all around her, which moved like the busy insects in an anthill. She'd never seen so many people in one place in her life. She tried to look about her but was quickly jostled by other passengers disembarking.

"Don't just stand there, silly goose," Mrs. Baker said with a high laugh. "Come along. We'll find a cab out front, and I'll send Charles back for our trunks."

Della stopped gawking, realizing that doing so made her look like some backward farm girl. If she wanted to fit in here, she needed to look like she belonged. Yet as she lugged the suitcase and stumbled along behind Mrs. Baker, she couldn't help but look around her in awe.

I'm allowed to gawk today. After all, I've never seen a city this size. Tomorrow this will all be old hat, and I will act refined and cultured.

They reached the street, where the buildings stood many stories high, climbing toward the sky. As Mrs. Baker went to find a carriage for hire, Della counted how many levels the tallest ones had—five on that one. *Six* on another. Goodness. These buildings were three times as tall as the tallest structure in Shelley. And they were all tucked side by side in rows as far as she could see. Could they really go on like this for miles and miles? The idea seemed impossible, yet she was staring at the reality.

Mrs. Baker waved Della over to a cab waiting at the side of the street. "Here we go."

Della picked up the suitcase again, suddenly aware of her boots clicking on the pavement. Pavement!

She increased her pace and finally reached the carriage, where the driver relieved her of the luggage and handed her up as she climbed in, as if she were a lady or something.

What would Joseph say? The thought crossed her mind before she could stop it. Her eyes pricked for a moment, but she shook away the emotion and took in the sights, settling into the open-air carriage beside Mrs. Baker. The horse clip-clopped along the road and navigated through traffic.

How many carriages, buggies, and other forms of transportation snaked along the street right at this moment? She could hardly fathom it. She heard a clanging bell and turned to see a trolley moving along a track, filled with passengers—men, women, and children from many walks of life, mostly those not wealthy enough to hire a carriage. Della imagined herself riding a trolley to visit different parts of the city. It would be such a thrill—much like an old buckboard pulled by a horse, but without the dust cloud, and with padded seats instead of a hard, wooden bench.

Between the carriages, buggies, and the trolleys—a second now approached from the opposite direction—she gaped at the amount of traffic and what that said about how many people lived here. Shelley's biggest road, State Street, never saw this much traffic even during Independence Day parades.

Shelley's population could be counted in the hundreds and its environs in the low thousands. But a single Los Angeles street block could easily hold everyone who lived there.

She leaned toward Mrs. Baker. "How many people live in Los Angeles?"

"I think the population is close to two hundred thousand now," Mrs. Baker said offhand. "It's always growing, of course. Some say that in another five years, it'll be well over *three* hundred thousand."

"Goodness," Della whispered, sitting back against the bench. She tried to picture that many people but failed miserably.

They passed block after block of city streets. Della looked down each cross street for the brief moment it was visible, trying to commit every detail to memory. The city really did seem to go on forever. Businesses large and small lined the streets—a cobbler, a drug store, a newspaper office. She gazed longingly at the newspaper office, feeling sure she'd held a paper created in that very building, and now here she was, yards away from where it had been printed.

They passed several restaurants and diners as well as entertainment venues. Theaters of various kinds: a vaudeville stage and another that showed moving pictures—she simply *must* see a moving picture soon. Then she spotted a fancy-looking theater advertising a production of *Julius Caesar*. She searched her mind for the reference and finally remembered—Shakespeare.

For one of Joseph's oratory assignments during their school days, he had recited Marc Antony's speech. She could hear it even now: *Friends, Romans, countrymen, lend me your ears.*

Joseph hadn't enjoyed much about school, preferring to spend a day riding his horse over studying sums and memorizing maps. But he had enjoyed learning about history, and *Julius Caesar* had struck a chord, making him a sudden bookworm for about a year. He'd love to see such a magnificent production of the play.

He'd be as awed with the city as she was. She'd have to write to him, and soon, to tell him all about it.

Again, thinking of Joseph brought back the memory of the last time she'd seen him, and it returned in sharp, painful relief. Her fingers instinctively reached for the necklace still about her neck. She'd been away from home for only a couple of days. While she hadn't given Shelley much thought at all, somehow Joseph always returned to her mind.

And now that she was here in Los Angeles, she yearned to be back in Shelley, going on a long horse ride with Joseph.

He would ride his chestnut mare, and Della would ride a smaller, gentler pony.

Her throat restricted with emotion, but she drew a deep breath and forced herself to be rational. Such nonsense to be feeling two strong, conflicting emotions at the same time. How could she possibly be so happy and excited about where she was right that moment, yet at the very same time miss Joseph just as intensely? It made no sense.

Perhaps I can convince him to visit. The thought brought a smile to her face. Yes. That would be the solution. She could enjoy everything about the city and plan how to show it all to Joseph. She'd show him the city and all its splendor. Maybe he'd even want to stay. Her heart warmed at the thought, but she forcefully extinguished the hope as soon as it appeared. She could *not* hang her hopes on something as likely to happen as the moon falling from the sky.

Quite simply, she had already faced a difficult decision, and she'd made it. Hard choices always required sacrifice. In her case, seeking happiness in her dreams meant leaving dear Joseph behind.

It's for the best, she reminded herself—again. She would be miserable staying in Shelley. And he most certainly would *not* care a whit about Los Angeles. Perhaps he'd enjoy the theater, but by the time the curtain fell, he'd be hankering to get back home to groom his horses and ride the fence.

She glanced at Mrs. Baker, wishing the woman were closer to her own age, someone a young woman could confide in, laugh with, and go on outings with. But her new employer sat ramrod straight, her hat perfectly perched on her head and her hands resting primly in her lap.

Della turned her gaze forward again. Suddenly the glorious sights of the city faded and blurred. Instead of discovering a new and exciting world, she felt as if she'd been dropped into a giant ocean where she was only a speck floating in the vast expanse of water. She felt alone. So horribly alone.

She focused on the horses and found an unexpected comfort there. They were a small reminder of home in the middle of this sea where she was completely insignificant.

Everything will be better when I'm settled and into a routine. She clasped her hands in her lap just as Mrs. Baker did. Della put her shoulders back and her chin up. Change was never easy; she'd known that when she'd made the choice to come here.

But she was convinced that she'd made the right choice.

And I will be happy here.

FIVE

For a full week, Della had spent every waking hour working her fingers to the bone. Seven days doing some chores she was familiar with and others that were entirely new to her. Electricity completely baffled her—and at first, it scared her. As did the sewing machine, which Maria, the head housekeeper, tried to explain to her.

"May I just use a needle and thread tonight?" Della asked, eyeing the needle darting up and down with wary eyes. Maria rolled her eyes, so Della quickly added, "I'll learn soon. Just not right away when so many other things are new."

Like the telephone and the gas stove.

"Very well," Maria said with a tone that indicated she didn't have the energy to argue. "Did you get your supper?"

Della nodded. "I did, thank you."

"I'm turning in," Maria said. "I expect that pile to be gone in the morning, before you leave."

"It will be. I promise," Della said with a bob of her head. Tomorrow was her day off. So long as the mending was done, she was free to spend the day as she pleased. The idea gave her butterflies in her stomach.

Maria grunted and left, closing the sewing room door behind her.

Della turned to the pile of mending, feeling a bit hopeless and wishing she'd had the nerve to learn how to use the sewing machine, because the pile would take her an hour or two with only a needle and thread—a pile that, when she'd first sat down to it, had seemed almost as tall as the Blackfoot Mountains.

As she stitched, her stomach growled, making her think of the meal that masqueraded as her supper—and made a face. The truth was, she hadn't been able to eat much of it.

The meat had been tough, the mashed potatoes tasteless, and the strawberries pale and bland. She'd tried the whipped cream with them, but even the cream tasted weak. Perhaps she was just used to fresh milk from the family's own cow. Della was certain she could make the meat more tender and tasty if given the chance; perhaps the cut was poor, or Maria should purchase meat from a different butcher.

Yet how did one ruin a dish as simple as mashed potatoes?

She almost heard Joseph's voice in her head saying how Idaho potatoes were second to none, that they simply didn't taste as good elsewhere.

At the thought of dear Joseph, the needle pricked her finger; Della winced and sucked on the tip, then examined the cloth to be sure she hadn't bled on it. Fortunately, she hadn't. When the bleeding had stopped, she continued sewing tiny stitches to repair a hole in a pair of Mr. Baker's trousers. When they were finished, she reached for the next item, a men's shirt missing a button. At least that mend would be easy.

Tomorrow. Think of tomorrow. She could hardly wait to

leave the townhouse and enjoy every moment of her free day, exploring the city and soaking it all in. She spent the rest of her time mending in her daydreams, imagining the wonders that awaited her tomorrow.

Finally, when her fingers and mind felt equally numb, Della snipped the final piece of thread from fixing the hem of one of Mrs. Baker's dresses. She set the dress aside and stood, stretching her back and yawning. Time for bed.

At last. Instinctively, she looked about for a candle to bring along, only to be reminded yet again that she had no candle; that she'd turn off the light with the switch by the door.

She did so, yawning again, and made her way to her room, where she got ready for bed, clicked off the light in her tiny room, and dropped onto her small mattress. Every day, it was the same. If anything, she felt as if she woke earlier here than on the farm. The clock disagreed, but her exhaustion said otherwise.

She lay in the dark, starkly feeling the absence of the familiar glow of a candle to ease her into bedtime, the scent of smoke swirling to the ceiling after she'd blown it out. Instead, one moment the room was bright as day, and the next, it was dark as pitch.

After rolling to the side, she punched her pillow and pulled her covers tight then closed her eyes and wished for sleep. Every night, she lay here, trying to get to sleep—and to *not* cry. She'd *wanted* this, right?

Well, not *this* exactly. She had yet to step outside Mrs. Baker's townhome since crossing the threshold, and she itched to do so.

In the morning, she would get her first taste of the city since her ride from the train station. She'd be sure to take in every detail so that when she'd saved enough money, and perhaps found different work, she would at last have the life she'd always dreamed of. She was one step closer here.

Some nights, she managed to drift off to sleep in spite of her chapped hands, with images of what her future work might look like. Perhaps she'd be a seamstress. Or a secretary. Maybe a teacher. Or a nurse. Although the latter would likely require extra money and time for schooling, so she set that idea aside in favor of something that would give her a new apartment all to herself. Or a boarding house, or a room she let out. She wouldn't mind sharing a room with another girl.

Whatever it would be had to be easier on a body than being Mrs. Baker's house help, where she was required to clean and launder and cook all the day long.

Someday. Someday soon.

Yet her last conscious thought was of how Joseph's strawberry path grew the sweetest, juiciest fruit, and how much she would enjoy a picnic eating them, gazing at the clouds above them.

SIX

In the morning, Della awoke with a start, even though she hadn't gotten more than five hours of sleep. She washed and dressed quickly, then left the townhouse before anyone could speak to her—she wasn't about to tempt fate by even stopping in the kitchen for a bite of bread. Maria might be all too willing to give Della just one more chore to do before she left.

She closed the townhouse door behind her, adjusted the gloves she hadn't worn since the day she'd arrived by train, and cocked her head to make the most out of her pretty new hat, which her mother had bought for her grand adventure.

Della walked along the street, smiling at everyone she passed and breathing in the air, which smelled so different from the air at home—but in a good way, she assured herself.

After walking for an hour, her feet ached inside her boots, so she retreated to a soda shop, where she treated herself to ice cream with caramel sauce. She enjoyed every single bite.

With her feet rested, she browsed the shops lining the

streets and even went inside several stores to look at the wares, although she didn't have enough money yet to buy any of the dresses or shoes and hats. She imagined herself wearing plenty of them, though. Or at least, she did until she held up a necklace and admired her reflection in a mirror on the wall. That's when a worker about her own age approached quickly and reached for the necklace.

"Need help finding something?" she asked as Della surrendered the necklace. The girl wore an expression that confused Della at first—patronizing and distrusting in spite of the toothy smile.

"Just looking," Della said and made to move around the worker, who stepped to the side and blocked her way.

"Visiting town?" The girl's eyes sketched to Della's hat, then back to her eyes, but her face now read amusement as well as disdain.

"I—yes. I mean, no, I'm not visiting. I recently moved here."

The girl tilted her head and took Della in from hat to boot. Her smile went a bit broader, if that was possible. "I can tell. Farm girl for sure." She turned about and replaced the necklace on the shelf, then moved away and chuckled.

Heat climbed Della's neck and reached her cheeks. She suddenly felt as small as the day in school when she'd been only six and the teacher had made her stand in the corner, wearing the dunce cap for three hours because Maggie Pye had lied to the teacher, saying Della had copied sums from her slate.

With equal parts humiliation and indignation, Della strode out the door and headed down the street. Was she so obviously a farm girl, then? Were her pretty dress and new hat out of fashion? Silly, even?

After marching two full blocks, she stopped before a wide window and took in her reflection. She tried to judge her appearance with objectivity. Was she plain? Old-fashioned? She certainly wasn't as stylish as most of the women around her; she had to admit that much. They wore styles she'd never seen anyone wear in Shelley.

For several more hours, Della was painfully aware of every eye that took her in; she was suspicious of every smile. Maybe she wasn't meant to be here. She didn't fit in.

No, she said to herself. *Stand tall. You can buy new clothes and fit right in.*

She straightened her shoulders and lifted her chin and walked on. Almost immediately, she caught the eye of a tall young man in a suit coming toward her. He grinned at her, and once again, the butterflies were back. He slowed, then stepped to the side, gesturing for her to do the same—so other passersby wouldn't be impeded by them.

He held out a hand. "Maxwell Walker," he said. "But you can call me Max."

She put out her hand and shook his. "Della Stafford," she said, smiling shyly.

Max folded his arms and leaned against the brick wall. "New in town?"

Della flushed again and looked about, uncomfortable. Was it so obvious? She was in no mood to be mocked a second time. "Excuse me, but—"

He held up a hand, which made her stop. "I just haven't seen you around. I think I'd remember a pretty thing like you." His smile widened, and Della couldn't help but feel flattered.

"Thank you," she said, taking a step backward to her original spot. "I am new. Just getting to know the city on my day off."

"How about that? I have the day off too. Could I show you around?" He turned so they were facing the same direction and held out his arm for her to take.

Della eyed it, then looked up at him. His dark eyes sparkled playfully, daring her. That's what made up her mind; Della Stafford would *not* be made to look a sissy. And if looking like a lady of Los Angeles meant walking with a devastatingly handsome gentleman, so be it.

"I'd like that," she said and looped her arm through his.

"I knew you would." Max tipped his hat in her direction, and they were off.

He showed her a park, where they had a pleasant walk, and then they went to a café, where he bought her a meal of fish—a kind she'd never tasted before. She was used to trout, but this had an entirely different flavor—one she loved. And the rolls were nothing short of divine; they practically melted in her mouth.

I could eat these forever and never make my own rolls again, she thought as she broke another one apart.

She found herself flirting back as Max joked and flattered her, and soon she felt as if she'd belonged to Los Angeles for years and had known Max forever. At some point in the afternoon, he bought her a flower from a street vendor—a single red rose.

"A beauty for a beauty," he said, leaning in closer as he handed it to her.

She didn't pull away, instead admiring his jawline and deep penetrating eyes. The butterflies swarmed so much they felt ready to burst through her ribcage and fly away. Della stepped forward, and they were walking again. She brought the flower to her nose and breathed in the scent, then lowered the petals and noticed a fruit stand on the corner ahead.

"You'll have to educate me," she said, nodding toward the colorful stand, which had stacks of fruits she'd heard of but never tasted. One row had large, yellowish fruits with big green stems coming off the top, almost like disheveled hair.

"This," Max said, hefting one, "is a pineapple."

It looked nothing like a pine tree or an apple. Della nodded and pointed to the small green ones. "And these?"

"Limes. Sort of like lemons, but not quite so tart."

"And I know those are oranges," she said quickly, pointing. She wasn't completely ignorant. "I've had some before."

"Ah, but I doubt you've had one like this, fresh from the tree today." He looked at the fruit vendor with a question in his eyes.

The man nodded. "Picked this morning. You'll never taste a sweeter orange than these here, straight from my own trees."

Max handed over some coins, and they left with a small paper sack holding two oranges. He proceeded to peel one, then handed her a wedge. "Try it."

She did, biting into it, and at the juicy sweetness, her eyes widened. "Delicious," she said, then snapped her mouth shut, embarrassed to have spoken with food in her mouth.

"Told you," Max said. "Nothing is quite like a California orange. And that's not even a fresh one. It was probably harvested at the first of the year."

"But it's so sweet . . ." She took another bite and enjoyed every moment before she swallowed.

They walked along in relative silence as she ate more of the orange. A stray puppy, mangy and bedraggled, started following them, whimpering. Della glanced over, ready to share her orange with the pup. It was surely hungry.

Max glanced over his shoulder and grunted. "Too many strays . . ." He quickly swooped one foot out, knocking the dog into the gutter, and shook his head. "You can't give them food, or they'll keep begging for more, and next thing you know, they'll follow you and adopt your home as theirs."

Perhaps, Della thought. But couldn't one find another way to behave besides kicking a dog in the ribs?

Maybe, after more time in the city, she would understand. She finished her orange and tried to think of something else. Someone would probably see her cutting off chicken heads as every bit as cruel as she thought kicking a dog was. It was all in the perspective, and she didn't yet have the eyes of a Californian.

In time, she assured herself.

After walking another block, she looked up at the sky above the buildings in the distance and admired the clouds drifting by. Something about them looked different from the ones at home, but she couldn't quite put her finger on what. Even so her old habit returned, so soon she was looking for images.

"Look at that cloud," she said, pausing on the sidewalk and pointing. "It looks just like a chicken."

Max eyed the sky, then looked at her with one eyebrow raised. "A chicken?"

At the look of disbelief in his eyes, she cringed. *I'm doing it again. Stop acting like a backward farm girl.*

"A bird. It's—it's just a bird," she said quickly, then pointed. "Never mind."

"You're adorable," Max said. He unlocked their arms, and he slipped one around her waist.

The action nearly stole Della's breath entirely, and she took several steps more before she could think enough to react. Only when she *could* think, she didn't know what to do or if she wanted him to remove his hand at all.

Mother would be appalled at how forward he's acting. We only just met. But that thought only encouraged the situation. And the truth was, she'd spent more time already with Max in one day than she'd ever spent in the company of several young men her mother would be more than happy to see her married off to.

But Joseph would be disappointed. That thought made her stomach feel like lead.

What to do? Dread and an uneasy, anxious feeling overcame her until she spotted a book shop.

"Oh, Max," she said, putting a hand on his arm. "Look!"

She hurried ahead of him, only vaguely aware that running off was a way to remove his arm from her waist. She stood before the window, admiring the volumes on display and the shelves and shelves of books deeper inside. She didn't recognize most of the authors' names, and she felt entirely ignorant and uncultured at that fact. L. Frank Baum? Joseph Conrad? And then there it was—Mark Twain's *A Connecticut Yankee in King Arthur's Court.*

"Do you like Mark Twain?" she asked. "I haven't read this one, but I thoroughly enjoyed his book about Huckleberry Finn, and his short stories are the funniest thing you'll ever hear. I could read 'The Man That Corrupted Hadleyburg' every day of my life and never tire of it."

Max gave a one-shouldered shrug. "I prefer reading newspapers and magazines." She must have looked crestfallen, because he quickly followed that up with, "But a story about man corrupting a town?" He nodded as if he was impressed. "I'm sure I'd enjoy such a story very much if you do. Here, I'll buy it for you."

Della's eyes widened, and the butterflies came to life again. "Would you?" she said, a hand going to her chest.

He nodded. "I'm happy to." Max led her inside by one hand. Her other one still rested on her chest, beside her necklace from Joseph. She couldn't help but look at Max and wish he'd read at least a bit of *Tom Sawyer.*

A few minutes later, she patted the necklace to push it out of her thoughts as Max handed her the book, newly wrapped in paper with string.

"Now," he said, holding the door for her as they went back outside. "I have a wonderful thought. That story you mentioned gave me the idea."

"Oh?" Della clutched the book, eager now to get back to her room to read it—or at least, she would tonight, even if it meant staying up late and losing some sleep on her last hours of freedom before she had to work again. She could stay up late now that the worry of using up candles wasn't a concern. She wasn't entirely sure what electricity cost, but Mrs. Baker hadn't said a word about conserving it, so Della didn't intend to, at least not tonight.

"There's a delightful little vaudeville show around the corner that is just up your alley; I'm sure of it." He looked over and winked, then wrapped her hand around his arm again. "Care to?"

"I'd be delighted," Della said, and they were off. She would attend a theater her first day off. Perfect!

At the ticket office, a sign was posted in the window. Della pointed to it. "What is a blue show?"

"You'll see," Max said with a mischievous grin. He took their tickets and led her inside.

Most of those in attendance were men, which made Della a little uneasy. She took her seat beside Max and looked about for friendly faces of other women. Few would acknowledge her. Perhaps some of that was because she was still quite obviously a newcomer. But some of the women were simply preoccupied with the men they were with, snuggling close and even kissing—something Della looked away from in shock more than once. She tried to keep the images of the women out of her mind—their low-cut dresses and painted faces, which looked nothing short of garish. But perhaps the electric lights made them look so.

She still decided to keep her gaze on the stage, even though the show had yet to begin. Max took her hand in his, looked over, and winked, which put her more at ease. She took a deep breath and settled in as a man appeared from behind the curtain and introduced the show with a booming bass voice and broad hand gestures. The crowd applauded, and Della sat straighter, eager to see her first real vaudeville show.

Over the next twenty minutes, Della's jaw went slack again and again at the off-color jokes and disgusting lyrics.

Every time one act ended, she breathed a sigh of relief, certain that the next one couldn't be as bad, that surely the crudeness would be over and she'd feel comfortable again.

But the next act was even worse—bawdy and vulgar and oh, so awful.

Della's eyes burned, but she refused to cry. When two women came on stage wearing practically nothing, it was the final straw. She could not bear sitting there, viewing and hearing such filth.

She leaned toward Max and said, "I have to go."

Then, before he could respond, she hopped out of her seat and raced up the aisle toward the back of the theater. She ran as fast as she could, caring nothing for stares and snickers aimed her way. She simply had to get out, now.

Finally outside the theater, she walked to a corner and crossed the street, needing distance from the horrid affair she'd just escaped. She found a bench and sat on it, trying to calm her unsteady heart.

What a fool she'd been! She'd trusted a total stranger with her day. Let him guide her around the city. She'd let him put his arm around her waist. She shuddered at the latter, her lower back now feeling as if a snake had been wrapped there instead.

When she'd managed to calm down, she looked about and realized she had no idea where she was. She asked a pleasant-looking woman for help, not caring the least bit if she looked like a backwater girl anymore.

She took a trolley most of the way back, but the ride held none of the romance or fascination she'd anticipated. She overheard two women across the aisle talking about how something needed to be done about the expansion of shows with blue content.

Blue? She listened, even though she'd been taught that eavesdropping was wicked. When the women didn't define the term, Della steeled herself and asked. She *had* to know.

"Excuse me," she said, her voice sounding timid. "I heard you talking about *blue* shows. What does that mean?"

One of the women huffed and shook her head in disgust. The other answered Della's question. "There was a time when theater owners gave notes to actors in blue envelopes giving them firm orders to take out unseemly parts of their acts, or they'd be fired."

The first woman filled in the rest. "But in recent years, the term has become a marketing ploy. Some theater-goers *look* for shows advertised as being so atrocious they would have gotten plenty of blue envelopes." She tsked and shook her head. "And by the looks of things, the advertising works. Those shows are always full, it seems. Disgraceful."

"I see," Della said. "Thank you."

She rode the rest of the way in silence, thinking through her time in Los Angeles. Thinking of how miserable she'd been. Part of it was due to being a stranger, and those things—even things like walking into a blue vaudeville act without knowing any better—would change over time, as she gained experience.

She could find someone else to court her who wasn't like Max at all. He'd been handsome, sure, and charming, in his way. But as she remembered her day, small moments stood out, things she'd brushed off at the time but that now seemed to be all her day had consisted of.

Joseph would have looked for the chicken in the cloud. He would have laughed and laughed over Twain and "Hadleyburg." And he most certainly wouldn't have kicked a poor stray dog.

The trolley reached her stop, and she got off, walking the rest of the way to the townhouse. With every step, the feeling of utter wretchedness only increased. Everything was different here. She would have given much for proper mashed potatoes or an apple from her father's tree.

But her feelings were from more than homesickness,

too. Somehow, even if she met a good man here, it wouldn't matter. He wouldn't be Joseph.

As she put her hand on the front doorknob, the realization washed over her. Everything always returned to Joseph. Every experience she had here, every hope and dream. Always Joseph. She stepped inside and walked to her room, where she sat on her bed and thought some more.

She pictured her life in five years' time there in California. Saw herself wearing stylish clothing, knowing exactly where she was headed and how to get there. She would have a new job and a new place to live. But somehow, her mind always included details from Shelley.

And more, *Joseph* kept appearing at her side.

No matter how hard she tried, she simply couldn't imagine her life anywhere but in Idaho. And she simply had no future worth living if it wasn't shared with Joseph.

Even if that meant living with chickens and cows and horses and all of the work they entailed. She *wanted* to live with those things if it meant being *home*.

And home means Joseph.

With new determination, she stood and strode out of her room to find Mrs. Baker. The girl she'd once been would have quaked at the prospect, but no longer. She found her employer writing a letter in the parlor.

Della straightened, lifted her chin, and stepped inside. "Mrs. Baker, may I speak to you for a moment?"

The woman raised her face and removed her reading glasses. "Della? Is something wrong?"

Everything was so very wrong. But all could be made right. All she had to do was speak, yet her knees trembled.

Joseph. Think of Joseph. His image came to mind: his warm eyes, his playful smile, his tender embrace. Once more, Della was strong. She squared her shoulders and began.

"Mrs. Baker, I am very grateful for all you have done for me, so I regret that I must tender my resignation, effective immediately."

SEVEN

Somehow Della survived the trip back to Idaho. She knew how to buy a ticket and which line to take to go home. She didn't need Mrs. Baker to do those things for her anymore.

She arrived at the rail spur in Shelley just as the sun was dipping into the horizon. She left her trunk on the platform, knowing one of her brothers or her father could pick it up tomorrow. No one knew she was coming back yet.

Not even Joseph.

From the spur station, she walked to Joseph's farm, a full mile away. The violet gray of twilight had fallen by the time she'd reached the lane leading to his small house. The house he wanted her to be mistress of. The house she now wanted to live in, with her dear Joseph, if he'd still have her.

As she stood there, worry gripped her heart. What if one of the other girls in town had swooped in to win her Joseph? He'd need a wife, surely. He could have moved on already. It had been only two weeks, but she couldn't expect him to light a candle for her indefinitely.

There was only one way to find out—and that was why she was here.

Della reached up to touch the pendant again to make sure it was visible and to feel a connection to Joseph before she saw him again. The cool metal against her fingers gave her a renewed sense of courage.

She stepped onto the lane and hurried up it, her boots crunching gravel as she went. At last she reached his door. Her hand hesitated only a moment before she knocked three times in succession—and then had to wait.

No sounds came from inside. Perhaps he wasn't home after all. But no, the upstairs bedroom window was lit up by the glow of a candle. Della knocked again and waited some more.

At long last, the door opened to reveal Joseph, tired and weary, his suspenders hanging at his sides, his hair mussed up. When he realized who stood on his front stoop, he startled. "Della, what are you—how—" His voice cut off, and he lapsed into silence.

They gazed into each other's eyes for several moments as Della called on her last shred of courage. What she was about to do didn't fit the label of being ladylike, but it had to be done. And if the look in his eyes was any indication, he still cared.

Della swallowed, took a deep breath, and then she managed to speak.

"We both see pictures in clouds," she said.

Joseph's eyes narrowed as if she didn't know what she meant. He would understand. He had to.

Not dissuaded, she continued. "We both laugh reading Mark Twain."

The corners of Joseph's lips twitched as if he was ready to smile. She took that as encouragement.

"We both love strawberries just picked. And neither of us can stand to see an animal suffer. And we both want to be

277

happy." She licked her lips and finished. "So you see, we're not so different after all. And I know I'd be happiest with you, right here in Shelley. For the rest of my life."

Her speech completed, she pressed her lips together and hoped for the best. He didn't reply right away, and although it might have taken only two or three seconds, the wait felt like a lifetime.

Joseph finally spoke, just a single word. "Really?"

She nodded. "I'm back. For good. This is where I belong. I just didn't know it before."

His eyes were soft and warm as he reached for her hands. At his warm touch, Della's heart pounded out of her chest. His hands weren't enough. She stepped in and threw her arms around his neck, holding him tight.

He held her in return, and she could feel his heart pounding in his chest. "Della, I've always loved you."

"And I, you," she said. "But I didn't see it before."

Joseph pulled back and looked into her eyes. Then, with his thumb, he gently stroked her jawline. He slowly moved closer and pressed his lips against hers.

His kiss was far better than any California orange, or even a Shelley strawberry. She was in his arms. She was home. And she'd never leave again.

ABOUT ANNETTE LYON

Annette Lyon is a Whitney Award winner, a two-time recipient of Utah's Best in State medal for fiction, plus the author of ten novels, a cookbook, and a grammar guide as well as over a hundred magazine articles. She's a senior editor at Precision Editing Group and a cum laude graduate from BYU with a degree in English. When she's not writing, editing, knitting, or eating chocolate, she can be found mothering and avoiding the spots on the kitchen floor.

Find her online:

Website: http://annettelyon.com

Blog: http://blog.annettelyon.com

Twitter: @AnnetteLyon

FAITH AND THE FOREMAN

by Marsha Ward

Other Works by Marsha Ward

The Owen Family Saga:
The Man from Shenandoah

Ride to Raton

Trail of Storms

Spinster's Folly

ONE

A bell jangled on the horse-drawn streetcar outside as Faith Bannister folded the letter she'd been reading and rose to pace the room. After two circuits, she stopped before her cousin. "I am ruined."

Clarissa Pembroke looked up from the bandage she was knitting and shook her head. "The news can't be all that bad, dear. We've managed to survive the bank crisis fairly well thus far."

Faith waved the letter. "The interest on my stocks is practically zero."

"You should have told me. I must try harder to find employment." Clarissa breathed heavily. "I can't believe my usefulness as a nurse is over because of a few gray hairs." She straightened her back as though in denial of her age. "I'm going to Doctor Harley's lecture tonight on treating poisons. It could be useful to learn about medical advances."

"You shouldn't have to support me," Faith said. "I'll sell the house to that fat banker who lusts after it."

"Faith! Mind your language."

"Mr. Spencer has wanted it ever since Poppa and Mama got killed." She bit a fingernail, then, at Clarissa's continuing reproachful look, removed her finger from her teeth. "I know. Mama tried so hard to break me of that." She brushed a blonde curl out of her misty eye and whispered, "Stocks and bonds are no replacement for one's family. I'm most grateful for your companionship."

Clarissa wiped her own tearing eyes.

Faith turned away. "Perhaps I can enter the nursing school at Bellevue Hospital. Mr. Spencer offered a price sufficient for me to pay tuition and rent us an apartment." She shrugged. "I'll have to let the servants go. If it appears I don't have time to train as a nurse before we're destitute, I'll become a governess or a shop clerk."

Clarissa shook herself as though to restore a cheerful outlook. "Let's not fret about finances now, dear. Come with me tonight and enjoy the lecture." She held up her knitting. "This bandage will be finished by then, and I have another eleven for the good doctor."

"Slim! Slim McHenry!"

When Amos Ramsey bellowed his name, Slim changed direction from going toward the bunkhouse to heading for the boss. What had he done to make Mr. Ramsey so angry? He couldn't recall any slip-up today. "Yes, sir?" he said, hoping he still had a job.

"Dan Crowley is leaving. After ten years!" Amos glowered at Slim. "His wife claims he's too busted up to cowboy anymore. She's taking him off to Tucson."

"That's bad news, boss. He's a good foreman."

"You're takin' his place. Ask Dan what to do."

Mr. Ramsey walked off, leaving Slim with his jaw hanging open. *Foreman! He wants me to be foreman?* He whistled in surprise, struck by the man's abrupt manner. Usually Ol' Amos enjoyed conversing with his cowhands, but not tonight. *Could be he's upset about Dan quitting, but he could've been more forthcoming with the details of the job.* He hoped Hoosier Dan was of a mind to enlighten him.

Slim started toward the foreman's little bungalow in back of the main house. If Dan wasn't at supper, Mrs. Crowley would know where he was. Dan was sitting down to eat, but he took time to shake Slim's hand and give him a rundown on his new responsibilities.

Half an hour later, Slim left, his head swimming and his hand sore from Dan's enthusiastic congratulations. *Each night I check with Ol' Amos about the next day's work, then parcel out the tasks in the morning. I fancy I'm up to the job. Maybe.* Before trepidation took over, he went to eat his own supper, wondering how the cowhands would receive the news.

He supposed he could count on Curly Price to offer congratulations. He and Curly had ridden together for several years and were good friends. Baldy Babbitt would most likely put on a pout, but he wouldn't want the job either. Too much responsibility.

Slim decided none of the other hands would give him more than occasional grief and sass, except Rance Hunter. He snorted. Hunter was a difficult case, prickly as could be. He was the boss's stepson, but there was no love lost between them.

Slim paused to slap the horseshoe hung over the bunkhouse door before he entered to eat. He would need all the luck he could get.

A day later, Faith gasped, tightening her fingers on the day's newspaper. She looked toward Clarissa, her anxiety seeping away.

"I like that bright light in your eye," Clarissa said.

"I have a better plan than nursing school." Faith rose and took the *Times* to Clarissa.

Her cousin looked up from her needles. Three new white bandages lay rolled beside her on the sofa.

"Look." Faith showed her the newspaper page. "Here's an advertisement seeking a schoolteacher in the West for ten months. The school board will pay transportation costs, provide a living space, groceries, firewood, and they'll pay a salary besides. I can teach mathematics and reading and writing and . . . even stitchery! Once I sell the house, the proceeds and a teaching post will provide income sufficient for us both."

"Hmm. Teaching will suit you better than nursing." Clarissa resumed her knitting. "How do you win the position?"

Faith crimped the newspaper between her hands. "I must send a telegram immediately to the president of the school board in this town of—" She looked at the advertisement again. "Bitter Springs, Arizona Territory. This will solve our difficulties."

"You must hurry so your answer to the advertisement arrives ahead of any others."

"Yes." Faith hurried to compose a brief message with a list of her academic accomplishments and prepared to go to the telegraph office. "That should serve. Let's pray I'm the most worthy applicant."

"McHenry!"

Slim grunted. *Rance Hunter sounds feisty this morning.* He turned from saddling his horse to watch Hunter walk toward him. The wiry man at Hunter's side had spent the weekend in the bunkhouse with the other hands. He wore a gun belt that had seen much use, and he had pulled his hat low over his eyes.

When the men drew near, Slim nodded to them.

"We need another man for the roundup," Hunter said. "This here's Nick Bray. Hire him on."

Surprised at the demand, Slim slipped around the horse to hide his face. He took time to adjust the length of his stirrup, then looked back toward the men.

He appraised Bray, who inched his hat back with one finger under the brim. The man's inky black eyes gave Slim a moment of pause. What kind of man was this Nick Bray?

Slim finally broke the silence. "Where'd you last work, Bray?"

"New Mexico." He crooked his head toward the east. "A man name of Peterson."

"You handle cattle for him?"

"Steers, mostly. He was shipping."

"What've you done this summer?"

"Rode fence, mostly."

Slim looked at the man for a while longer. Then he asked, "Why'd he let you go?"

"No work." Bray nursed tight black gloves onto his hands.

Slim made a decision. "We can use you for a time. Ride with Hunter. He has no partner right now." He turned to Hunter. "You two take the buckboard and load up the barbed wire from the shed. I sent a crew to fix that break on the Diamond Point fence."

Bray nodded assent. Slim was satisfied, seeing the man was ready to tackle the job.

Apparently Hunter wasn't ready. "My horse needs to be worked," he said.

"Not this morning. We've lost cattle through that break, and your—" Slim stopped short before he said *father.* "Mr. Ramsey wants the job done today."

Hunter's face flamed, but he spun on his heel and

stomped over to the wagon yard. Bray kept pace with the angry man. Slim watched for a moment before he bent to pull the cinch tight.

As they approached the equipment shed, Bray glanced at Rance. "You got me hired on. What's the plan?"

Rance slowed his pace. "I want the old skinflint out of the picture. If he gets sick and dies, I'll end up with the whole outfit and be a rich man." He opened the shed door and grabbed a pair of leather gloves. "Put these on. They're thicker than those you got. That blasted wire cuts your hands ragged, and I don't want you bleeding on me."

Bray put the gloves on over his own.

"Pull out about six of them rolls, and I'll go get the buckboard," Rance said.

Bray turned and did as he was told while Rance hitched a team to the buckboard and led the horses to the shed. The men loaded the barbed wire rolls and various tools onto the vehicle, and then Rance grabbed the brake handle and swung himself up onto the seat. He looked down at Bray.

"You coming?"

Bray nodded and climbed into the buckboard. As he sat on the seat he asked, "How do you plan to get rid of your . . . the old man?"

Rance took the lines. "You know the locoweed plant? I gathered some of them prickly pods and powdered the seeds. That poison will drive a cow mad and kill it. It'll do the same to a man."

"You're going to poison him?"

Rance slapped the lines on the rumps of the team. "Hi! Get up there!" He turned to Bray, grinning. "I already am."

"I think shooting him is better," Bray grunted. "It's quick."

"Nah. All the fingers would point at me. Folks know we

argue. Poison's slow, but it's sure."

Once they arrived at the broken section of fence, they unloaded the barbed wire rolls and tools for the cowhands who were there doing the repair. Rance dropped a shovel, then ran to the front of the buckboard, climbed up, grabbed the lines, and started the team. Bray vaulted onto the back of the vehicle to avoid being left behind.

"Hey," he yelled. "What's your hurry?"

Rance muttered over his shoulder, "I don't want them getting the idea I was sent down to mend fence."

Bray climbed over the back of the seat and settled himself. "You could've warned me."

"What's it matter? You made it aboard."

"You're crazy, Hunter," Bray said. Soon they were out of sight of the work crew, and he asked, "How do you get him to take the poison?"

"He drinks a glass of whiskey every night before bed. I put a pinch of powder in the bottle every day or so. He doesn't know why he's getting sick, nor does anyone else."

Bray gave a grudging smile. "So it's working?"

"Oh, yes. You'll see how he acts. Soon I can quit selling off cows." He clucked to the team and slapped them into a run toward the ranch headquarters.

A week after sending the telegram to Bitter Springs, Faith stopped by the telegraph office, as she had been doing the last three days, and found a message addressed to her from Mr. Ralph Perkins, school board president. She hurried to the new apartment to show Clarissa the telegram.

"Cousin, they've hired me. I'm to be a school teacher. He's wiring money for my expenses."

"That's good news, dear."

Faith embraced Clarissa. "Thank you for bearing with me through my financial difficulties. I couldn't have gone on without your kind heart."

A week later, Faith and Clarissa stood on the stoop with a valise and trunk at Faith's feet. Clarissa turned from gazing down the street and took both of Faith's hands in hers. "The cab is coming, dear. I'll worry for you, crossing the country all alone."

Faith squeezed her hands. "You needn't do so, cousin. I'm sure I'll find my way on the trains. Think of it as a great adventure, a breakthrough for womankind." She extracted her hands and retied the ribbons holding down her hat as the cab drew up before them.

"You will be careful?" Clarissa asked. "Don't let strangers near your luggage. And don't talk to anyone suspicious."

"I have my pistol," Faith said, patting the pocket of her duster. "I'll take care; really, I shall." Holding back tears, she patted Clarissa on the shoulder and turned to the waiting cab.

The driver had already placed her trunk and valise in the rear storage area. He handed her up to the seat, then took his position and started the horse off with a click of his tongue and a flip of the lines. Faith looked through the back window at Clarissa, who got smaller and smaller in the distance.

At last Faith turned forward on the seat, biting her nail. Would anyone be at her destination to meet her? She'd wired Mr. Perkins the expected date of her arrival, but what if she arrived late? Or early?

I do hope I am not making a mistake.

TWO

Faith took the train conductor's hand, stepped down from the passenger car, and stood at last on the platform of the rustic railroad depot in Winslow, Arizona Territory.

Gripping her valise in one hand and a newspaper she'd purchased at the last stop in the other, she looked around, inhaling deeply to calm her nerves. She immediately choked on unfamiliar scents and the residual smoke from the steam engine. She coughed several times, embarrassed to make such an entrance. If her employer could see her now, he might change his mind at the sight. She straightened her shoulders. Being again on terra firma was a welcome change after the constant motion of the railway cars.

Faith moved away from the train. She turned and saw—with great relief—her trunk being manhandled down the gangplank from the baggage car. She could put to rest her worry that it would remain on the train and travel to San Francisco without her. Now she directed her concern to finding who had been sent to meet her, restraining a wild impulse to clutch her duster close about her body and flee back into the familiar train car.

Calm yourself, Faith. You have been well schooled. You are capable of teaching children, though that was never Father's intent in educating you.

She took a breath, a shallow one this time, and looked around. Several people stood on the platform but gradually departed as they met their relatives and friends. Soon the area was cleared of all except a large-boned man whose slouch hat was shoved to the back of his head. He stood a ways off, looking in her direction.

That must be the person sent to meet me, she thought and took a step toward him. The big man must have arrived at the same conclusion, as he began walking toward her.

"'Lo," he called, snatching the hat off his head. "Are you Miss Bannister? Miss Faith Bannister?"

"I am she," Faith replied. *What a large man! Are all Westerners of his size?*

"I'm Clint Dobbs. Mr. Perkins sent me to take you down to Bitter Springs. Let's go." He clapped his hat on his head and turned toward the end of the platform.

"Excuse me," Faith called to his back. "I have a trunk. It's sitting over there." As he turned around, she gestured toward her luggage.

"Oh. Well, I guess you want me to get that." He walked over, easily picked it up, and slung it across his shoulders, then marched off. Faith followed.

Mr. Dobbs led the way to a two-seater buggy, where he shrugged the trunk into the rear seat beside other items covered by a piece of canvas. He took Faith's valise and put it next to the trunk. Then he turned to Faith and picked her up by the waist. The movement surprised her; she gasped as she left the ground. He didn't seem to notice and set her on the front seat. He went around the buggy, got onto the seat, clucked to the horse, and they were underway at a slow trot, passing through the town in under five minutes.

The next day, Mr. Dobbs brought them into town a half

hour after noon. They stopped before a building that had to contain a store. Barrels, stacked galvanized buckets, and baskets of produce competed for space under an overhang covering a board walkway.

Mr. Dobbs came around the buggy, lifted Faith down in his accustomed manner, and nodded toward the building. "Mr. Perkins keeps store here, miss. He's the head of the school board."

"Mr. Perkins. Yes, the gentleman with whom I corresponded."

"He'll be pleased to see you're here safe."

"Thank you, Mr. Dobbs. You've been a kind companion."

"Let's get you inside, miss."

Townspeople began to gather around the building, surely to get a glimpse of the new school teacher. Some cast suspicious eyes her way. Faith shuddered but nodded and smiled to those who wished her well and followed Mr. Dobbs into the store, her stomach roiling.

The dark interior blinded her for a moment, but her eyes soon adjusted to the dimness. Before her stood a slight, balding man, wearing an enveloping apron, and a woman whose hands fluttered about her face as though she would burst with nervous excitement.

The man took her hand and wrung it. "Here you are at last. I'm Ralph Perkins." He put out his hand to indicate the fidgeting woman. "Faith Bannister, I want to introduce my wife, Edith."

Mrs. Perkins gave a slight curtsy, bobbing her head. "I'm pleased to meet you, Miss Faith. My Curtis and Joey are excited to begin school."

"You'll start teaching next Monday," Mr. Perkins said. "Now that you've arrived, the ladies of our fair town will arrange a dance social at the schoolhouse so everyone can make your acquaintance. Edith, will the dance be a week from Saturday night?"

"Yes. I look forward to it," Mrs. Perkins said.

"How lovely," Faith murmured. *Oh my land!* she thought.

Her driver grinned and said, "The town boys are near crazed waiting to see you. Between them and the cowboys, all your dances will be taken."

Faith smiled back. "I'm sure the social will be a great success." Her throat felt dry as parchment.

"That is our hope, miss," Mr. Dobb said, then turned to Mr. Perkins. "Is your rig out back?" When the storekeeper nodded, Mr. Dobbs said to Faith, "I'll put your things into his buggy and be off to my work."

"Thank you for a pleasant journey, Mr. Dobbs."

As the big man grinned, nodded, and left the store, Mr. Perkins dithered around, seeming to look for something. Finally, he asked, "Where's my hat, Edith? I need to drive Miss Bannister over to the schoolhouse."

Mrs. Perkins fetched the article. "I'll be over to call on you later this afternoon, Miss Faith. I'll bring a box of groceries to start you out."

"You've very kind. Thank you."

Faith climbed into the buggy for the final leg of her journey. Mr. Perkins got in the driver's seat and turned the horse onto the street.

"We built a little house behind the school, Miss Bannister. You'll set up housekeeping there. The townspeople will bring you wood and groceries. That's part of the fee they pay you for schoolin' their youngsters."

A short time later, Mr. Perkins put Faith's luggage in the little house, said goodbye, and left her.

Faith stood still, eyes closed, taking shallow breaths until she felt her nerves settling. *You will do fine*, she told herself. *You have come this far, and you will not fail.* She slowly opened her eyes, looked around, and set about exploring her world.

Two tiny rooms made up the house, one a kitchen and sitting room and the other the bedroom. She supposed she was to use the school's privy for sanitary purposes. A pair of shelves hung in the living area, ready for her books. Pans and dishes filled one cupboard, while a second held food staples. The bedroom was just large enough to hold a bed and wardrobe. Faith relaxed her shoulders and began to unpack her trunk.

Slim had kept the hands as busy as he could, hoping to stay ahead of bad weather, when a storm blustered up, full of thunder and lightning, and everyone had to stay indoors, mending tack and doing similar chores until it blew over.

While Slim patched a harness, he worried about the boss. Due to blurred vision and dizziness, Mr. Ramsey couldn't ride a horse now. Worse, his manner had changed. For instance, he'd been pretty abrupt that day he'd made Slim the foreman.

When the storm quit, Slim and the hands went outdoors to find that a large lightning-blasted cottonwood tree had fallen and smashed a section of corral fence. Slim assigned a few hands to cut up the tree and mend the fence, but Mr. Ramsey showed up, ranting and raving that they had to leave the tree alone.

"Boss, we got to fix that fence, or the horses will break out and be down the country in no time," Slim said.

"No! Leave it be." Mr. Ramsey raised his arm up in a jerky movement, and Slim feared his boss was set to strike him.

"All right," he said. "You're the boss. We'll deal with it another way."

"You see that angel settin' on the tree?"

Slim looked, but there wasn't any holy vision anywhere.

"I guess the light's in my eyes, boss," he said.

"You just leave the angel alone, you hear?"

"I hear." Slim swore silently and had the crew pile brush against the break in the fence. Every day, he asked Mr. Ramsey if they could tackle the cottonwood, but every morning, the boss saw something new sitting on the tree. Slim had to go about his work, worrying even more about Ol' Amos.

"I am Miss Bannister," Faith announced to the gathering of pupils early Monday morning. "Let's get acquainted. We'll go one by one around the room. Tell me your names and ages."

Eleven heads nodded. The smallest pupil needed a poke or two from an older girl seated behind her, but she finally began and said her name was Lovinia Evans. Then she ducked her head, hid her face, and refused to say anything else, despite repeated pokes from the other girl. Lovinia shook her head until her blonde braids whipped back and forth.

"That's fine," Faith said, and then to the older girl, "Your name, please?"

The girl sat up straight and said, "I am Prudence Evans. My father is the telegraph operator. My sister is six years old. I am nine years old. My brother is thirteen—" The oldest pupil, a boy, had jerked one of Prudence's braids. She swung around and slapped him. "Charley, leave me be. That hurts!"

The big-boned young man rubbed his cheek. "You didn't have to do that in front of the schoolmarm, sis."

"Leave my hair alone."

"Children!" Faith indicated a boy on the end of the front row. "And you are . . . ?"

"Joey. Joey Perkins. My pop is the grocer. I'm seven."

Joey had a bit of a lisp. He turned and pointed to a chubby boy a row back. "That's my brother, Curtis. He's ten."

Curtis scowled at Joey. "I can say that for myself."

"Thank you, Joey. Curtis, have you anything to add?"

"Yes, miss. I do sums best."

Faith smiled. "Then you must help me with the younger pupils. Next?"

The other children each took a turn. Charley, Hortense, Mary, Thomas, Paul, Christine, and Martha. Faith tried to keep their names in her head until she had a chance to write them down.

"Now that I know who you are, I will tell you a little about myself," Faith said. "I come from New York City, far away in the east. New York is located principally on an island between the East River and the Hudson River. Can anyone tell me the name of the island where I live?"

Several pupils raised their hands. Martha knew the correct answer. After giving a lesson on geography and wishing she had a better map, Faith moved on to arithmetic. She allowed Curtis to tutor the four youngest pupils while she taught the older ones a lesson she hoped he could catch up with later. Recess followed. Faith caught her breath, made note of the pupils' names in a seating chart, ate her lunch, and straightened the room a bit. Then she rang the bell to call the children back into the schoolroom.

The rest of the day went swiftly, and when four o'clock came, it took her by surprise. She released the pupils. They went to the back of the room, where they found their belongings and left, running as soon as they hit the ground.

The next day was much the same as the first, although Faith also made assignments for cleaning the blackboards and carrying in stove wood.

"You've done well today, children," she said as four o'clock approached. "Thomas, it's your turn to clean the blackboards. The rest of you may go, but remember to clean your slates tonight."

The pupils hurried out of the room, laughing and chatting with their friends. Thomas asked if Miss Bannister wanted him to lay a fire for the next day.

"I don't think we'll need it yet, Thomas. The weather is still quite warm. Perhaps tomorrow?"

As Thomas started his task at the blackboard, a masculine voice spoke from the doorway. "The weather can turn bad in fifteen minutes, miss."

Faith turned to see a handsome man standing at the back of the classroom. He removed his hat and held it in one hand while, with the other, he smoothed his black hair carefully to each side of his head from a center parting.

"Rance Hunter at your service, miss." He made a slight bow. "You'd best have wood laid up in case of a storm," he added, his black eyes snapping with deviltry.

Faith admired the man's thick, full-bodied hair. Then her eyes returned to his face, and she noted that his Roman nose was perfectly symmetrical beneath black brows. She began to smooth wrinkles from the front of her skirt.

"I'll put a few sticks in the stove for you, if you'd like," Mr. Hunter said.

She nodded. Realizing how easily the man had entered the schoolroom without her hearing him, she glanced at Thomas. He had nearly finished with his job, as he was cleaning the erasers. She got his attention with a hand on his shoulder. "Thank you, Thomas. You've helped a great deal."

The boy looked up at her, then at the man. "Is it okay if I leave now, if you don't need anything else?"

She meant to say, "Please stay here with me." She couldn't think of another task to set for him, however, so she replied, "That will be fine. Thank you."

As the boy left, Mr. Hunter backed away from the stove, brushing his hands together after laying the fire. "That bundle of sticks should be easy to light if a storm blows up."

His gaze went on too long and became a stare; she repressed the desire to squirm.

At length, he asked, "Have you made plans for supper? It'd please me to take you to the restaurant and buy your meal."

Faith's eyes went a bit wide. *He has a high opinion of himself.* After recovering from her surprise, she said, "I must decline your kind offer, Mr. Hunter. I have several matters to attend to this evening."

The man frowned, said, "Have it your way," and left the schoolhouse.

Faith watched his departure, slowly relaxing. *I suppose I haven't seen the last of Mr. Hunter.*

To Slim's consternation, the cottonwood lay across the corral fence all week long, and Mr. Ramsey hemmed and hawed every day about it, still seeing visions in the branches. More than once, Slim had to send a cowhand to round up escaped horses.

On Saturday morning, the boss's head seemed to have cleared enough to give Slim orders. "McHenry, today is a half-work day because of the social. Get that damn cottonwood cut up and stack the wood in the back lot where it won't burn anything down when we light it up."

"That'll make a fine bonfire, boss."

Slim couldn't get anybody to do the job. Every cowhand had a reason why he couldn't use the old two-man saw on the tree. Seeing the excuses stacked against him, he shrugged and assigned himself and Curly to the job.

Curly wasn't much pleased with the hot, sweaty chore, but he dug in after a little persuasion from Slim's cash hoard.

The day was hot for September. By midmorning, both Curly and Slim were puffing and blowing with the heat of the exercise and the slowness of the chore.

At this rate I won't get to the dance social before the last set's over, Slim thought. Another trickle of sweat ran down past his ear. *It must be eighty degrees in the shade.*

Curly frowned at him. "Slim, you pulling on your side, or am I doing all the doggone work over here?"

"I was thinking the same thing about you." Slim eyed Baldy Babbitt going by with a couple of buckets of wash water. *Dang that lazy Babbitt! He's headed for the bunkhouse to slick up for the party.* Slim pushed harder on the saw and hoped the man would stumble over the black dog lying in the shade by the door and spill his water. No such luck. He stepped over the dog and through the door. *Maybe on his way out . . .*

Disgusted with the man, Slim jerked on the handle.

Curly grunted with exertion. "This old saw must be duller than a butter knife," he wheezed.

Slim checked the time by the sun. "You thinking what I'm thinking?" He put more muscle into the effort.

"We ain't gonna get this done before quittin' time?" Curly did more work on the next pass.

"Yup."

They sped up, and the stringy trunk finally separated. Both of them took a quick breather, then started on the next cut.

At least the horses get to rest for a while, Slim thought. The team was tied to the fence in the shade until he and Curly cut more sections of wood to haul away. One horse moved in the traces, switching his tail to keep off flies. The other nickered and shook his head.

About eleven o'clock, they commenced dragging wood again, one or two sections of trunk at a time, whatever the chain would fit around. When they'd hauled all of the sections they'd cut, Curly sat down, taking a breather and letting the horses do the same, while Slim freed up the logs. He unwrapped the last turn and tossed the chain behind the team.

Morning and the best part of the afternoon evaporated before they finished, and when they'd put up the team and were washing themselves, it was so late that Curly said he maybe was too exhausted to go into town.

Slim shook his head in disbelief, water droplets flying off his hair. "Aw, you won't miss that dance social for nothing. You always have too much fun at them."

"What's the use of going to a dance if I can't move my aching body enough to do the hoedown?" Curly whined.

"You're just bellyaching. Stay here if you've the notion. Nothing's keeping me home tonight."

In the end, Curly found enough strength to fork his horse and accompany Slim after all.

That's too tight, Faith thought, and re-tied the sash of her dress. It wouldn't do for the school teacher to faint at her first outing.

She fluffed out the bow and looked back toward the glass hanging on the wall of her bedroom, wondering if she fit the picture of—what had Charley called it?—a schoolmarm.

I know I can do the job well enough, she thought, smoothing the front of her dress. She checked the slight tilt of her hat and pinched her cheeks, just a little. A faint rosy glow responded, and she breathed a sigh of relief.

"A perfect schoolmarm," she said, and nodded. She turned to the door, picking up her drawstring reticule. Then she cast another glance in the direction of the glass. "Bitter Springs, here I come," she whispered, and blew out the lamp.

Slim and Curly arrived late to the dance and spent most of the first fifteen minutes leaning against the wall, watching the girls as they danced by in their best clothes.

Slim saw one gal he'd almost decided to court, Edith Longstreth. The man dancing with her now had laid a claim on her before Slim got up the nerve to ride to her poppa's house and ask if he could come calling. That was too bad, 'cause she was the best-looking of all the girls around. A doleful regret settled on him for letting her get away, and he vowed that wouldn't happen to him again.

He was just peeling himself off the wall, aiming to see what the town ladies had provided for refreshments, when Ralph Perkins banged on a pie tin to get everyone's attention, then said he had an announcement. He beckoned for someone to come forward out of the crowd, smiled expansively and said, "This little lady coming up here is our new school teacher, Miss Faith Bannister. She comes to us from New York City and has a wonderful knowledge of the arts and sciences, as well as mathematics and grammar. Let's make her feel welcome."

Mr. Perkins proceeded to clap, and several other people around him joined in. By this time, the lady in question had made her way through the throng and turned to face in Slim's direction. His jaw went slack.

Miss Faith Bannister was quite a sight for a country boy to take in. She wore a white dress with those large, puffed, leg-o-mutton sleeves. She sported a light-blue ribbon tied around her little waist and had a sort of hat on her head. It wasn't big enough to hide the fact that her hair was the color of goldenrod in a meadow. A little bag hung from her wrist by a pair of strings. Slim stared, shifted his feet, and forgot Edith Longstreth. The only woman on earth stood before him across the room.

Curly came up behind Slim and gave him a nudge with his shoulder. "Close your mouth. You're droolin' all over the floor."

Slim obeyed and swallowed hard. He couldn't be

drooling, 'cause his mouth was dry as sand. He couldn't even raise enough spit to bicker with Curly. He only shook his head and adjusted his hat low over his eyes.

A voice called from the crowd. "How much 'perience does she have?"

A flush crept over the lady's face. Slim bristled, wanting to offer a challenge to the man who had besmirched her reputation by asking such a question, but he couldn't tell who had spoken. He heard grumbling in front of him. Others had the same question in mind.

"Miss Bannister is well educated," Mr. Perkins avowed, somewhat heatedly. "You won't be disappointed in my selection."

"I will do my best for your children," Miss Bannister said in a clear, soft voice. She moved through the crowd, coming in Slim's direction as she greeted folks. In a moment, a milky-white hand extended into his eyesight. "I'm Faith Bannister," said the soft voice. "Have you children in the school?"

Slim raised his head and looked into misty-blue eyes surrounded by a fair face on which the flush had not totally abated. He pulled off his hat and shifted it from hand to hand before deciding which mitt to put forward to meet hers. "Howdy, miss. No, miss. I'm Slim McHenry of the Four Rivers Ranch. Pleased to meet you." After giving her hand one pump, he let it go.

"It's a pleasure indeed, Mr. McHenry." Her voice was so soft that he strained to hear it over the hubbub.

"Ah, I'm—I'm just Slim, miss."

Miss Bannister raised one hand to cover her mouth. He could tell she was smiling. *Did I make a joke?*

"Why, yes, that's quite correct." She lowered her fingers to chin level. Sure enough, she was smiling at him. "I've no doubt you're very nice, also."

Slim's face burned as though he squatted next to a

branding fire. He gulped, said something nonsensical, and hoped Miss Bannister would walk on by.

Instead, Curly elbowed him in the ribs and chuckled. "You'll have to cut him some slack, miss," he said to the lady. "He's working with only half a brain. Our boss made him foreman a couple weeks ago, and he's still finding his way." Curly winked at the schoolmarm. "Now take me, miss. My name is Curly Price. I have all my brains in place, and I'm the best rider and cowhand in the whole valley."

Slim glared at Curly. Bragging like that was underhanded and self-serving, and besides, he was dead wrong. *Slim* was the best cowhand in three counties, and Curly darn well knew it. Slim had to get the lady away from that rascal.

Just then, the musicians played a chord.

"Would you care to dance, Miss Bannister?" Slim crammed his hat on his head and held out his hand.

"Why, yes. That would be lovely," she replied, putting her smooth little hand into his rough one. "I would be honored."

Slim did his best to bow gracefully over it, then led her onto the sawdust-covered floor.

What a wonder that dance was. Slim swore that a higher power led his legs around the room, for he hardly stumbled at all. Miss Bannister smiled and waltzed and seemed happy to follow his lead.

At one point, she gazed into his eyes and asked, "Did I understand your friend correctly? You're the foreman of the Four Rivers Ranch?"

"I am." He missed a step and almost trod on her toes. "I'm still learning the job." How long would the dance last? He was torn between running off in shame at his stumble and holding the lady in his arms forever.

"Perhaps someday soon you could show me around the ranch, Mr. McHenry."

"That would be my great pleasure, miss." Slim smiled at her, and something warm welled up in his chest. "I can show you around the whole area, if you'd like."

She smiled. "Let's start with your ranch first."

"How about next Saturday? I'll bring a wagon and pick you up about eight in the morning."

"That sounds delightful indeed," she said, looking thoughtful. "Do you mind if I ask Mrs. Perkins to come, as well?"

"Sounds good to me. I'll meet you in front of the general store, then. Eight o'clock."

She smiled again, and then the dance came to an end, and he released her from his arms.

"I will be waiting," she murmured. Then she was gone, and his arms felt empty, robbed of her warmth and grace.

Shortly thereafter, Slim was drinking punch from a little glass cup when he looked up to see Rance Hunter making an entrance. Slim couldn't miss him. Hunter guffawed at something Nick Bray said, then made a protest that there was no liquor bar set up. He weaved a bit as he walked.

I reckon he's already had a snoot full of strong drink.

The problem was, he walked right up to Miss Bannister. He asked her to dance, but she looked reluctant. Then Hunter loudly bragged on his close kinship to Amos Ramsey, owner of the largest ranch in the valley. The schoolmarm finally agreed to dance with him.

Hunter spun his way around the room with the lady in his embrace. She was trying to make conversation, and he smiled down at her with a smooth look that made Slim's stomach queasy. He didn't know what it was about Amos Ramsey's stepson that set his teeth on edge, but the fact was, Slim detested the man.

Slim disposed of his cup so that as soon as the musicians stopped playing, he was on hand to rescue Miss Bannister. "Would you like refreshments, miss?" he asked, taking her by the elbow.

"Yes," she said, looking a bit confused, for Hunter still held tight to her other hand. "That would be lovely." She turned to Hunter. "Thank you for the dance, Mr. Hunter. I'm sure it was delightful." She got her hand free and turned her attention to Slim. "Where is the refreshment table, Mr. McHenry?"

"In the schoolyard, miss." He put pressure on her elbow to steer her away from Hunter, who looked at Slim as though he wished him dead. Slim hustled the girl toward the door.

They stepped outside, and Miss Bannister looked at Slim's fingers gripping her elbow. He let go, feeling abashed that he'd been clutching at her so tight.

"I like this better," she said, slipping her hand onto the crook of his elbow. His mood changed some as they strolled into the glare of the torches set around the yard. With her on his arm, he felt ten feet tall. She pointed out what she fancied among the array of tasty tidbits the ladies of the town had provided, and Slim juggled two plates and served up the food.

They sat on a bench built for the youngsters under a stand of cottonwoods alongside the schoolyard fence. Slim made certain Miss Bannister was settled before he went back to the line for liquid refreshment.

He returned carrying two cups of fruit punch. Miss Bannister picked at the food on her plate. He presented her the cup with a slight bow.

She smiled and took a sip. "That's very tasty. Thank you. I was becoming a bit parched."

Slim thought he grew another foot taller.

He sat beside her. Miss Bannister asked about the work he did as foreman. Her interest made him feel special. Soon he forgot his sweaty hands and gawky feet and talked his fool head off. He scarcely touched his food, and when the musicians signaled the commencement of the second half of the dance, he had nearly an entire plate left to eat.

When Miss Bannister said she didn't have a partner for the next dance and asked if he would kindly oblige her by whirling her around the floor—or words of the same meaning—he gladly abandoned the plate.

Once they'd entered the building, Slim took her in his arms for the dance, and believe it or else, he floated her around that floor like he'd been born to the ballroom.

I feel like a gentleman. Me, a rude cowman, ill schooled and all rough around the edges, he thought. *I swear it's her doing, smiling at me like that.*

Slim felt a turning inside his chest and realized he'd just fallen in love with Miss Faith Bannister.

THREE

"It is *not* my turn," Baldy Babbitt insisted, punctuating his point with a finger jabbed into Slim's chest.

"Hold your horses," Slim rejoined. "Which of you fellows mended fence last week?" He looked around at a circle of antagonistic faces staring at him.

Baldy didn't yield his place in front of Slim. "It was me 'n' Banjo. We was the ones who done the work. It ain't right you want us to dig post holes this week too."

Slim searched his love-befuddled memory. After a moment he said, "You're right, Baldy. I was wrong. Get back to the herd. Banjo, you're off the hook too." He gestured with his head.

"See now," Baldy said. "You should've said that right off when I brung the sitchiation to your notice. You're larning, McHenry." He caught Banjo's eye, and they moved away.

As the two men left the circle, Slim swung his gaze over the other cowhands. "Hunter, you and Bray are up for the post hole digging. Get a move on."

Hunter mumbled something foul in a low voice, gave

Slim a hard look, and marched off. Bray followed, looking over his shoulder at Slim.

Slim endeavored to hide his shudder. Those two together spelled trouble. He could feel it to his toes as he assigned out the other work for the day.

A few days later, finding his stock tally short, Slim tapped Curly to accompany him into town for supplies for a pursuit.

"Fifteen head," Slim said, a grim set to his mouth. "This rustling has to stop."

Faith listened as Charley recited a poem she'd taught the class last week. His resigned face sagged in surprise when Mary began to scream.

Her piercing shrieks continued as Faith jumped to her feet and rushed around her desk to offer aid and comfort. By then, Mary had climbed atop her desk, hauling Hortense along with her. Her cries turned to sobs, and she clung to Hortense with all her might.

Faith stopped short and slowly motioned Charley back toward the corner. A rattlesnake slithered under a desk, then veered into the aisle near the stove and began to contort itself into a coil. "Children, get up on your desks," she managed to say through a constricted throat.

Puzzled but obedient, they scrambled up, then looked around the floor for danger. The older girls cried out in alarm.

"Charley, there's a pistol in my desk drawer. Please hand it to me," Faith said.

He found it, making snuffling noises.

Faith put her hand backward to receive the gun, as she

dared not take her eyes off the reptile. She adjusted her grip as she said in a low voice, "Paul, please tell the class what manner of snake that is."

"Wa-wa-western duh-duh-diamondbuh-back rah-rah-rattlesnake, miss," Paul stuttered while Faith took a step forward. The girls all sucked in their breath in unison.

"No, miss!" wailed Mary's sister, Christine.

Faith took another step, fighting her panic. She had to be close enough for her shots to count. She hoped Father would be vindicated in his decision to educate and train his daughter as well as if she'd been a son.

From the corner, Charley sniffed. Faith placed her left hand on Joey's desktop and leaned forward as the snake began to shake its rattle.

God, please guide my aim, she prayed and grasped the gun with both hands. She extended her arms, slowed her breathing, and sighted on the head. Then she held her breath and squeezed the trigger once, then twice more for good measure.

Bang! Bang! Bang!

She dimly heard an uproar over the ringing in her ears; remembered the children. She let out her breath, took another, and said, "Go! Out the door."

Feet clumped on the floorboards as the children escaped. Faith heard her heart thumping in the dense silence that followed. Then heavier footfalls pounded into the schoolhouse, and she looked up. Slim McHenry hesitated inside the door, staring at the headless snake. He rushed down the aisle.

Faith began to shake.

Slim kicked the dead snake aside, took the pistol from Faith's hand, and laid it on a desk. Then he grasped both her hands in his and asked, "You killed it?"

She couldn't stop shaking, but nodded.

"Holy Hannah," Slim murmured.

She wished he would embrace her like Father would have done. She looked into his eyes, saw something approaching awe. His gaze softened, he enveloped her in strong arms, and she gave in to sobs, just as Mary had done.

"There, there, miss," he whispered. "What a grand woman you are."

As he left the schoolhouse, Slim thought how lucky he and Miss Faith had been that she was able to compose herself before anyone else had arrived to investigate the gunfire. Just after she'd left his arms, quite a crowd had gathered to comment on the lady's bravery and to examine the snake.

He mentally shook himself, picked up Curly and the supplies, and got on the trail of another kind of snake, a human who stole cattle.

They didn't know much. Was the rustler armed? Would the chase take them into Pleasant Valley, where the feud was winding down but a stranger was still a stranger? Intruding into his assessment of the dangers he and Curly might face was the hum in his nerve endings lingering from his embrace with Miss Faith. He'd only offered her needed comfort, but Great Nellie! It had felt mighty good to hold her for a moment, to indulge in a dream.

Unfortunately, they lost the tracks of the cattle on an area covered with splintered malapai rock. Although they cast around for any sign of the herd, they came up unsuccessful.

"Who drives cows into this loose stuff?" Curly complained.

Slim pressed his lips together tightly before he spoke. "Some varmint who knows we're coming after him." There was nothing to do but return to the ranch empty handed.

After breakfast the next morning, Slim asked the cook,

"Has anybody been missing meals the last few days?"

"Only you and Mr. Price," Mrs. Marks said. She thought for a moment. "Mr. Hunter did ask me to pack extra victuals for him and Mr. Bray while they worked on the fence line. He said it was a waste of time to come in for meals if they could stay out and finish the job."

That made sense. It didn't sound like Hunter's usual attitude about work, but Slim had emphasized the importance of fixing the rest of the fence. Perhaps the man wanted to get the chore over and done with. He thanked Mrs. Marks and turned away.

Although Slim hadn't caught the cattle thieves, he had work to do before he took Saturday off, when Miss Faith would be visiting the ranch. Warmth flooded his soul at the memory of the embrace he had shared with her. Pleasant as the occurrence had been, he would not dare mention it to anyone. Miss Faith had been under duress. He wouldn't cause her embarrassment.

Stifling his yearning to further his acquaintance with the school teacher, Slim went to work.

Saturday came. Faith stood on the walk in front of Perkins' store, brushing imaginary specks of lint off her dress and waiting for Slim McHenry to come with his wagon. Mrs. Perkins came out of the store, waving goodbye to her husband.

"I declare, it's mighty kind of you to invite me to accompany you, Miss Faith. I appreciate the time off."

Faith leaned into the street to look down the road. "I don't see Mr. McHenry. Is he late?"

"He'll be along. Slim's a punctual young man."

Faith tried to gather her wits enough to make small talk. "Have you lived here long, Mrs. Perkins?"

"Call me Edith, dearie. Mr. Perkins and I have been here nigh on to six years, now. It seems like we come just yesterday." She also looked down the street.

Faith brushed her dress again. "What could be delaying him?"

"Don't worry. He's not late. It isn't eight o'clock yet."

"It's not? I thought I arrived late." Faith pulled a tiny watch out of her bag and shook it, then held it to her ear. "It's not running."

Mrs. Perkins laid her hand on Faith's arm. "You're nervous waiting for that good-looking cowboy to show up and meeting Mr. Ramsey and all. It wouldn't surprise me none if he's taken a shine to you."

"Mr. Ramsey? We haven't met."

"Why no. I mean that lanky foreman, Slim McHenry." Mrs. Perkins leaned her head to one side and winked.

Faith drew herself up in righteous indignation. "Mrs. Perkins, I am the school teacher. I didn't come here to find a man or carry on with a cowboy. You know that's forbidden in my contract."

"I meant no harm, gal."

Faith nodded. She wanted to say, "Just leave it be," but restrained herself. In truth, the foreman intrigued her with his blend of rough and tender attributes. She recalled the strength in his arms around her. Her skin tingled.

A cloud of dust caught her eye as a wagon drawn by two horses approached. Slim soon brought the team to a halt in front of the store.

"Good day, ladies!" he shouted, grinning, and dropped to the ground from the seat. "It's a fine day, and there's a breeze curling the tips of the pines. Come take a ride."

"Indeed," Faith said, lowering her tight shoulders. She felt a smile on her lips.

Slim helped Faith onto the seat, then boosted Mrs. Perkins up. He got in beside Faith and turned the horses to retrace his route. "Have you driven through the country before, Miss Faith?" he asked as they pulled into a stand of tall, whispering pines blown by a soft breeze.

"Not since Mr. Dobbs drove me down from the depot."

"I'll bet you were tired then, after the long trip on the train cars. Sit back and relax yourself. Take in the view."

Faith breathed in the sharply sweet scent of pitch, remembering the pine gum one of the pupils had brought her this week. Now here she was on her way to a real ranch. She clasped her fingers together and tried to concentrate on Mr. McHenry's descriptions of ranch life.

". . . during the roundup next spring, then we ship the cattle to Chicago for processing. That's a fancy word for slaughter. I hope that don't offend you, Miss Faith." He slapped the horses' rumps with the lines.

Faith swallowed as Slim's arm brushed hers. "Why, no. It's all so interesting."

Mrs. Perkins said, "Don't you scare off our schoolmarm. We want to keep her."

"I must earn my own way in the world. I hope to stay as long as possible, if my work is agreeable to the school board."

"I'm sure there's no problem there, as Ralph—Mr. Perkins—thinks you're a great asset to the community," Mrs. Perkins patted Faith's hand. "My boys love having you as schoolmarm. All they can talk about is how brave you are, killing that snake and all."

Faith bit her lip without replying. She wished to forget the snake.

"You're not worried about what that drunk said at the dance, are you? He don't know the broad side of a barn from his backside."

Faith colored. "Thank you, Mrs. Perkins. I appreciate your support."

"Not at all, child. You'll teach for a term or two, then retire to marry one of our eligible men. We have a bunch of them, and some of them are looking for a wife." Mrs. Perkins chuckled. "Some of 'em don't know they're looking."

Faith felt her face flush. A sidelong glance told her that Slim's face matched her own.

"Ladies," he said in a strangled voice, "watch for the view ahead. Sets my heart a-bumping every time I see it."

They emerged from the pine forest, and the decided nip in the morning air abated with the warmth of the sun. Slim stopped the wagon. Before them, an immense meadow full of dry grass stretched to the up thrust of the Mogollon Rim. Patches of cloud fluffed in the sky. Nestled amidst a stand of cottonwoods, a two-story house gleamed white, surrounded by outbuildings. The perpendicular ridge of the Rim, red and brown and topped with majestic pines, stood guardian. The sight took Faith's breath away.

"It's magnificent!" she cried.

"I'm glad you like it. It's a pride to us all," Slim said, twitching the lines to get the horses started again. "Mr. Ramsey spent a good long stretch of years building it up."

Mrs. Perkins chattered away at Faith's side. "It's lovely, just lovely. Imagine me getting the guided tour. I've never seen the place before."

Slim halted the horses in front of the house and got down from the wagon to assist the ladies. Soon they stood on the porch under the slope of the veranda roof, dusting their dresses.

"I got the cook's permission to show you around the house," Slim said. "Come in and look at the fancy gee-gaws."

As they went inside, Faith looked at the glass fan window above the door. A ceiling of stamped tin arched high above them, and a design of yellow roses and thin, gray stripes marched down the papered walls. Dark patches on the wallpaper showed where pictures had been removed. This was a lone man's house now.

Faith turned and looked around her. A door stood open

to her left, through which she saw a room decorated with mounted animal heads. She felt a pang at the familiar sight, remembering the security she'd always felt in her father's study. She turned away and look about. An attached staircase led to the upper floor. Another door led to a room on the right. Along a passage, she saw a third door, which she guessed was the kitchen.

"It's very lovely, Mr. McHenry," Faith said. "Is your employer out on the grounds?"

Slim's mouth twitched. "Ah, he's not feeling well. Hasn't been for weeks. We finally had to put him to bed."

"The poor man!" exclaimed Mrs. Perkins. "What ails him?"

"Not sure, ma'am. His sight is getting bad, but worse than that, he's, ah, not keeping food down, and he sees things that ain't there."

"Has the doctor been to see him?" Faith asked.

"Well, no. Ol' Amos refuses any caretaking."

"That's nonsense!" Mrs. Perkins said. "Men can be so impossible."

Faith laid her hand on Slim's arm. "We should look in on him."

Mrs. Perkins agreed.

"He won't like it."

"I insist. He may be very ill."

Slim made a face. "I'll take you to him, but I hope he don't yell at you ladies." He started up the stairs, and Faith and Mrs. Perkins hurried to keep up.

"McHenry!" a voice roared from above their heads. "Why did you get rid of that angel?"

"Oh, he's having a bad spell," Slim moaned. "He's carryin' on about that angel again."

Faith caught up to him. "What angel is that?"

"For the last little while, he's been talkin' about seeing an angel. A week or two."

"He must have the doctor to see him," Mrs. Perkins puffed as she joined them on the landing.

Slim shook his head. "He won't do it, ma'am." He cringed as foul language poured over the transom from a room ahead. "Begging your pardon, ladies. He's getting mighty rank in his language. Maybe you'd prefer to take that tour of the grounds."

"Definitely not!" Faith exclaimed. "The man's clearly in distress. Mrs. Perkins and I can forgive his language. Isn't that so?"

"Certainly, dearie. He's not in his right mind."

"He don't appear to be," Slim agreed, halting before the door and biting his lip. "Ladies, you can still change your minds . . ."

"Lead the way, Mr. McHenry," Faith said. "The man needs assistance, not censure."

"Thank you for your Christian attitude, miss," Slim said and opened the door.

Faith hesitated before stepping into the room, steeling herself for any verbal abuse Mr. Ramsey might hand out. She took a deep breath and crossed the threshold.

Amos Ramsey lay in a huge, four-poster bed with a hat hung on each post. Clad in long underwear, he had clearly been covered with a muslin sheet and a thin quilt, but the bedclothes were now strewn on the floor. He thrashed about with jerky movements, muttering nonsense about angels and cursing encyclopedically.

Faith gave a cry and ran to the side of the bed. She pressed one hand to his face, which she found hot, dry, and quite red. "Oh my, oh my. Mr. Ramsey, you must have a doctor right away."

Although the man did not answer, he quieted under Faith's touch, grunting incoherently. She blinked to keep back tears. The poor, tormented soul!

"Yes, indeed," Mrs. Perkins chimed in, approaching the

bed from the other side. She clicked her tongue as she touched his forehead. "The man is delirious with fever." She turned to Slim. "What has Mr. Ramsey been eating?"

Slim thought a moment. "Nothing more than we all eat, ma'am—beef and beans."

"Hmm." Mrs. Perkins eyed Mr. Ramsey's limbs. "He's not snake-bit, is he?"

"No, ma'am. There's not been any swelling, and two weeks with snake venom would have seen him dead by now."

Faith looked at Slim, her eyes brimming with tears. "You must send someone for the doctor this instant. He may die."

"I don't know, miss—"

"She's right, Mr. McHenry. You don't want Mr. Ramsey's death on your conscience." Mrs. Perkins made as though to shove Slim out the door, and he backed up.

"He does seem mighty low. Worse than before."

"You're the foreman, isn't that right?" Mrs. Perkins shook her finger in Slim's face. "It's up to you to make decisions when your boss isn't well enough to do so, correct?"

"I—I guess so. Yes, I suppose I'd better do that." Slim turned and stepped into the corridor. He returned immediately. "You ladies will stay with him?"

Faith nodded, and Mrs. Perkins murmured, "Of course. Go along, Mr. McHenry."

He did.

"Who's there? Who's there?" Mr. Ramsey began to thrash again. "I can't see. Who is it?"

Faith caught his hand in hers and patted it. "I'm the school teacher, sir, and this lady keeps the store in town. You're ill, but the doctor will be here soon."

"Damn doctor," Mr. Ramsey said, pulling his hand free. "He won't see my angel."

"Where is it, sir?"

Amos turned his face toward Faith's and squinted. "I don't know you, do I? Damn eyes. Don't work proper." He moved his arm spasmodically, pointing toward the top of the wardrobe. "It's sittin' on top, guarding me. You see it?"

Faith looked. "Of course. Such lovely hair."

"I can't see it clear anymore. What happened to my eyes?"

"You must rest. Mrs. Perkins and I will remain with you until the doctor arrives." She turned to her companion. "We must sponge his face and arms to cool his fever, and get him to drink water. I've learned that much about sickroom care from a relative."

"Good idea. I'll fetch a basin and cloth. The cook will know where they're to be found." She left the room.

Two hours later, Slim brought the doctor into the room.

"Ladies," the man greeted them, removing his hat along with his coat. "Let's see what we have here." He opened his black bag and produced an implement that he placed into his ears and the other end upon Mr. Ramsey's chest. "Ah. Rapid heartbeat. How long has your ticker been racing, Amos?"

"Damn doctor," Amos said. He followed that with his view of the man's parentage.

"Let me see your tongue." The doctor wielded a flat stick in Amos's direction and managed to use it briefly. "Hmm." He raised Amos's eyelids one by one. "Hmm," he repeated.

"Damn eyes don't work right," Amos complained.

"Hmm," the doctor said a third time. "You're feverish."

"We've been wiping his face and arms, doctor," Faith said. "He hasn't cooled much."

"Slim, how long has he been in this state?"

"Couple weeks, doc. He talks about angels in trees and such."

"She's sitting over yonder." Amos raised a jerky hand and pointed.

"How bad is he, doc?"

The doctor took Slim to one side, whispering his opinion, but Faith heard enough.

". . . nursing care, around the clock, if possible."

Letting all social propriety go, she intruded herself into the conversation. "I know the very person to care for him, Mr. McHenry. My cousin is a trained nurse. She can be here in three or four days, if you will send her a telegram."

"Excellent," the doctor said. "Make the arrangements, McHenry. I can't be held accountable for his decline if he's left alone."

FOUR

"**D**earest Clarissa, I'm glad you've arrived safely." Faith hugged her cousin fiercely and had her sit in the best chair. A cowboy calling himself Baldy Babbitt had fetched Clarissa from the train station, and she was to rest here at Faith's house while Mr. Babbitt filled an order for the ranch at the store.

Clarissa looked around as she removed her hat and gloves. "You have a cozy situation here."

"Thank you, cousin. May I bring you a refreshment?" Faith asked.

"Perhaps a glass of water, if you don't mind," Clarissa said. "It's a relief to sit still. Crossing the country on the train cars was quite an experience."

"You have only another hour of wagon travel to the ranch so you won't feel all of that disconcerting movement." Faith brought Clarissa a sandwich on a plate in addition to the water. "Please eat a bite. You must be famished."

Clarissa smiled. "I suppose I am, dear. If truth be told, I am anxious for Mr. Ramsey. You say he is having visions?" She bit into the sandwich.

"He is, and he complains of poor sight. Also, his movements are jerky."

After she swallowed, Clarissa said, "My first thought was that he's suffered a brain stroke, but he has use of all his limbs?"

"Yes."

"And the doctor has no diagnosis?"

"He seems mystified. He's ruled out insect or snake bite, but he doesn't have any other ideas to account for Mr. Ramsey's symptoms."

"I suppose I shall be limited to treating those symptoms, then."

"You're an excellent nurse. I'm confident you will be able to restore the man to health."

"God willing," Clarissa said, brushing crumbs off her bodice front.

Faith smiled. "I'm certain Mrs. Marks will appreciate your arrival. She's the cook, but I hear she's been wearing herself to a frazzle tending to the man over the last few days."

As it was Saturday, Faith insisted on accompanying Clarissa the rest of the way to the Four Rivers Ranch to see her settled.

When they arrived, Clarissa said, "I wonder if Mr. Ramsey has had a change of diet. Perhaps he is eating something that disagrees with his constitution."

"Mr. McHenry thought not."

A convivial woman let them in, and inside, they found the house in an uproar.

Identifying herself as Mrs. Marks, the woman said, "The old boy is having conniptions. He wants his whiskey. Now." She winced at the curses coming from the second floor.

"Strong drink can't be good for him," Faith said.

"Doc says he can have one glass after supper," Mrs. Marks retorted. She addressed herself to Clarissa, saying, "Come along. We'll put your things in your room, ma'am, and I'll introduce you to the old geezer."

When the cousins entered the sickroom, Mrs. Marks made the promised introductions.

"Mr. Ramsey, I'm here to nurse you," Clarissa said. "I'll have your health increasing just as soon as Doctor Quincy determines what ails you."

"Damn doctor said I could have whiskey. Where is it?" Amos demanded.

"You must eat your supper first. Mrs. Marks will bring it presently."

"I'm not hungry. Who did you say you are? Come closer."

"Clarissa Pembroke, sir. I'm the trained nurse Doctor sent for."

"Trained nurse?" He peered at her. "You don't look ugly. Not boney. Not like that one." He gestured toward Faith and smirked at Clarissa. "Are you giving me a bath tonight, nurse?"

"I'll clean you up after you eat your supper," Clarissa answered.

Amos smacked his lips. "Bring the food. I want a shave, too."

"We'll see." Clarissa raised her eyebrows and took Faith into a corner. "I can handle this case. He's full of ginger, but I believe he craves attention. Will you take notes of his actions for me?"

"Yes. I'll sit out of your way."

Faith watched as Clarissa assisted Amos with his meal, then washed him up and trimmed his whiskers.

"You have a nice start to an attractive beard," Clarissa said. "You won't require a shave."

"Hey! I figured you'd dunk me in a tub. I'm paying for your nursing skills, aren't I? I want them used right."

"Mr. Ramsey, the doctor and I will determine the best use of my skills. You needed only a minor cleansing and a trim. Now, let's see about your whiskey."

"Aye, my whiskey."

Mrs. Marks brought a nearly empty bottle and a tumbler. "Good thing Mr. Babbitt bought a new bottle today," she said. "This one is on its last legs." She poured the whiskey and started to hand the drink to Clarissa but stopped and looked into the glass. "That's odd. Something fell out with the whiskey." She put a finger into the glass and pulled out an object. She held it on her palm. "Look at that. What do you make of it, ma'am?"

Faith came over and watched Clarissa examine the gray splinter. "That certainly has no business in the bottle."

Clarissa agreed, picking up the object and working her fingers over it. "Organic, but not smooth. It has broken edges. It's not a tree or plant limb. Is it part of a seed?"

"It may be, although it's a bit large for a seed," Faith said.

"Indeed. How did it get into the bottle?" Clarissa asked.

Mrs. Marks shrugged. "I can't say, ma'am."

Clarissa took the tumbler and poured the liquid into the chamber pot, over Amos's objection. "Where was the bottle kept? Locked up, I trust?" she asked the cook.

"In the common room, in a cabinet. I don't think there's a key anymore."

"Hmm," Clarissa said.

"I want my whiskey!" Amos roared.

"There will be a slight delay," she said to Amos, then turned to Mrs. Marks. "I won't give him anything from that bottle. Please show me where it was kept."

"Sure. I thought it would be used up, so I put the new bottle in its place."

"I'll keep watch," Faith said, motioning toward Mr. Ramsey.

Rance slipped into the house from the back door after finding the cook missing. *Lucky me*, he thought, looking into the room where Amos kept his whiskey supply. *Nobody's here.* He crossed to a cabinet, pulled it open, and took down the bottle.

"New?" he whispered. "Damn!" He'd have to take care pulling the cork, or someone would see that the bottle had been opened. He set to work and, when the cork was free, took a square of brown paper from his pocket and opened it.

He was in the act of pouring powdered seed into the bottle when he heard two women's voices coming from the staircase. He swore, then quickly crumpled the paper and thrust the cork into the bottle. He hit it with the heel of his hand to seal it, put the bottle back on the shelf, and hustled through the door to the kitchen, where he held his breath, not daring to go out the back door yet.

"I feed him the same as before he went strange," the cook was saying. "It's not my food."

"Has he taken a fall that would result in an injury to the head?" the second woman asked. Her voice was unknown to him. Who was this in the house?

Before the cook answered, the stranger asked another question. "Did you leave the door to the cabinet ajar when you brought up the whiskey?"

"I did not." The cook sounded put upon. "I always close them doors."

"Hmm," said the stranger. "Mr. Ramsey will be obliged to forego his liquor tonight. I can't allow him to drink from a suspect bottle."

"Right you are," the cook agreed. "Whoever goes into town next can bring another."

Rance mentally cursed the women, whose sudden descent had caused his careless error. He tiptoed across the kitchen and eased open the back door. With a little luck, he would be the chosen errand boy. He'd have to get a new supply of seeds and smash them up tomorrow.

When Slim saw Hunter and Bray at supper, he felt relieved. The perimeter fence had finally had been repaired; the ranch wouldn't lose cows in that direction.

In the morning, though, he didn't feel as confident, so he asked Curly to ride out with him to inspect the work.

Coming upon abandoned rolls of barbed wire and loose strands hanging on the fence posts, Slim swore. Had Hunter and Bray even come out here? He surveyed the area but found no recent camp spot.

"Them buzzards! Where have they been?"

Curly spit. "When did you send them here?"

Slim calmed himself enough to consider. "Day before the cattle tally came up short."

Curly took out cigarette makings and looked at Slim.

Slim looked at Curly. He closed his eyes, realization heavy on his lids. "Hunter asked the cook to pack food for them so they could fix the fence," Slim growled. "They never did the work. He's stealing cattle from his old man."

The clock hands crept slowly from three thirty toward four o'clock, and Faith almost regretted her choice to become a school teacher. Some of the children had been unruly today, and she could hardly wait to dismiss them so she could retreat to her house and close out the world.

A sound at the rear of the room drew her attention. *Joey, if you're playing tricks again*—But then she raised her eyes to see Rance Hunter at the back of the room, holding onto the doorjamb with a hand clad in a leather riding glove.

"We're gonna have supper together tonight," he said, slurring his words.

Faith caught her breath. Petticoats rustled as girls

turned sideways to see who had come in.

"Get rid o' these kids," he demanded, taking a few unsteady steps into the room.

She drew herself up and started toward him. "School keeps until four o'clock, Mr. Hunter."

"Not today, it don't."

"You're setting these children a poor example!"

"Brats'll grow up anyway," he said, leering at her. He lurched closer and put forward both gloved hands to grasp Faith's face.

"Miss!" Charley said, alarmed.

She winced at the unpleasant mix of the odors of liquor and leather coming from Mr. Hunter's person, and she put out a stiff arm to repel his advance. His chest came to rest against her palm, and he stopped. She pushed him back down the aisle. "You will leave the premises, Mr. Hunter."

The man resisted the pressure on his chest, but he stumbled backward as she pushed harder. He crouched a bit, and his eyes drilled into hers with a withering look. "You'll regret treating me like this," he said. "I'll be the big man hereabouts soon enough."

At the venom in his voice, Faith took half a step backward. What did he mean by his claim? A glance at the look of terror on Lovinia's face made Faith remember her charges.

"You *will* leave," she repeated, resolving to protect the children. She stiffened her voice into brittle shards. "Get out."

He turned and left, and Faith slammed the door and put her back to it as she tried to slow her breathing to normal.

"Are you all right, miss?" Charley asked, standing in the aisle, brandishing a piece of firewood.

Faith squared her shoulders. "He is gone, children. Let's finish the lesson." She marched on wobbly legs to the front of the classroom and faced the pupils. "Now, whose turn is it?"

As soon as the children left school, Faith hurried to the livery stable and rented a horse. She had just enough time to ride to the ranch before nightfall. She needed to speak with Clarissa.

Faith dismounted at the ranch house, opened the door without knocking, shouted, "Clarissa!" and, at her cousin's answering call, dashed into the kitchen.

"He said he'd be the 'big man' soon enough," Faith said as she finished her account. "He terrified the children."

Clarissa folded her arms and looked pensive. "That fits with the foreign object in Mr. Ramsey's liquor. I'm beginning to suspect he's being poisoned."

Faith shook her head in disbelief. "A killer in my schoolroom."

Clarissa motioned Mrs. Marks to join them. "Does Mr. Hunter bear his stepfather a grudge?" she asked the cook.

"Oh yes, ma'am," Mrs. Marks said. "His ma spoiled him terrible. He took her death mighty hard and blames Amos Ramsey for it."

"Enough to want him dead?" Faith asked.

The cook shivered. "Ever looked into them bottomless eyes? I'd say he does." She dipped into her apron pocket. "When I swept up earlier, I found this in the common room under the liquor cabinet."

Clarissa took the crumpled paper and straightened it out. "There's a residue." She rubbed her finger over the paper and sniffed.

"Careful!" Faith said.

"Granular. Not commercial talcum. Not flour or powdered sugar. It's coarse, as though someone used a rock to grind an object down." Clarissa wet another finger with her tongue.

"No," Faith cautioned. "Don't taste it."

"I don't suppose a tiny bit will hurt me."

"It might do," Mrs. Marks said, leaning over to inspect the paper. "That piece there could be a spine from a seed husk." She straightened. "Jimson weed. That'll drive man or beast mad and kill 'em in the end."

"According to our eminent lecturer, Dr. Harley, such a powder, introduced slowly, would make an effective poison," Clarissa agreed. "I must tell the authorities."

"You must tell *Slim*—I mean, Mr. McHenry." Faith felt her mouth go dry. When had she begun to think of him as *Slim*?

Clarissa said, "I will. Now you must get back to town, dear. I suggest you ask for an escort."

Rance pulled Bray out of the bunkhouse, proposing a smoke before bed.

"Those damn women," he said, watching as Bray built his cigarette. "They're on to us."

"Us?"

"They figured out about the poison. We have to get out of here."

Bray lit up. "I haven't drawn any pay yet. Are you going to make up the loss?"

Rance swore. "I'm out of cash. We have to gather up all the cattle we can grab and high tail it for New Mexico."

Bray lifted an eyebrow as smoke curled from his cigarette.

Rance continued. "We'll put a rope through the mossy-back steer's nose ring. The whole herd will follow."

Bray shrugged. "It could work."

Rance rubbed his fingers together. "Ten o'clock tonight, then. Banjo's snoring won't cover bumping around in the dark, so be as quiet as you can. We can't chance getting caught."

FIVE

The next morning, Clarissa introduced a new regimen for Mr. Ramsey: He was to drink a gray liquid she'd concocted from powdered charcoal and milk, and he was to drink it every two hours until she said he'd had enough.

"I'll be gol-darned if I'm gonna take that stuff," he said, snorting in disgust.

"You will drink it down, sir, or I will not be responsible for your care. I believe you have been poisoned, and this remedy will cure that. If you have not been poisoned, it will not harm you. Either way, you *will* drink it."

"The lady means it, boss," Slim said, standing ready to enforce her edict.

Amos grumbled and cursed, but he took the draught, almost gagging at first, then finishing with a shudder. "Poisoned, huh? Who would poison me?" He thought about it for a while, then started to get out of bed, his face dark with anger. "Damn his hide! I knew that weasel was up to no good."

"See? You're better already, sir," Clarissa pointed out, keeping him from rising. "Not from the remedy, but because you haven't been taking the poison."

"I don't need your concoction."

"Yes, you do. The poison is still in your system and must be flushed out. We suspect it was in your whiskey."

"He poisoned my drink?"

Amos tried to hoist himself up, but Slim gently pushed him back. "I'll see to him."

"Go to it, son."

Slim jogged toward the barn until he spotted Curly riding in at a gallop. He waited for him, itching to get his hands around Rance Hunter's throat.

"They're gone," Curly huffed. "The whole herd."

"What?"

"Baldy figures Hunter and Bray took them sometime last night."

"Grab a shotgun," Slim yelled at Curly, who cooled his mount in the yard. "Get all the shells you can find." Slim saddled a horse in record time and added weapons to his gear.

Curly did as he was told while Slim went to the kitchen for any leftover food Mrs. Marks could put together. He came back with several parcels, which he put in his saddlebags.

As Curly mounted, he said, "The whole outfit wants to go after them."

"No. Just you and me." Slim swung into his saddle. "We'll travel faster and make less noise. You lead out."

Curly shrugged and clicked his tongue to start his horse.

"'By the shores of Gitche Gumee,'" began little Lovinia. "'By the shining Big-Sea-Water,'" she lisped. Lovinia was the last pupil on the program. Parents shifted on the hard benches.

Faith's stomach hurt. It had ever since Mrs. Perkins scurried up to her before the program started and whispered in her ear that Rance Hunter had stolen Amos Ramsey's herd and that Slim McHenry had taken out after him.

She inhaled and held her breath. *It can't be true. Mrs. Perkins must stop listening to rumors.* She exhaled.

"'Many things Nokomis taught him,'" Lovinia declaimed, curling her hand into her pinafore pocket.

No, Faith thought. *Keep your hands folded together.*

Lovinia took a deep breath, smoothed her pinafore, then folded her hands in front. "'Of the stars that shine in heaven,'" she continued.

Faith frowned at two boys whispering together at the back of the room. A cold chill enveloped her. *It could be true. Slim would chase Hunter down despite the risk.*

"'Saw the moon rise from the water,'" chanted Lovinia, then hesitated. Her mother made an encouraging sound from her seat on the front row. The girl continued. "'Rippling, rounding from the water.'"

She's nearly finished, Faith thought, her mind wandering despite her best effort to concentrate on Lovinia. *Oh Slim, be careful. Rance is like that rattlesnake—beautiful, but dangerous. Oh, take care.*

Faith blinked as the girl at the front of the room curtsied and smiled, seemingly relieved that her long ordeal was over. The parents and pupils clapped politely, then harder as Faith stood and went to the front of the schoolroom.

"Well done, Miss Bannister," Mr. Evans called.

"Yes, fine work," Mr. Perkins agreed.

"Thank you." At the praise, Faith felt a blush on her cheeks. "On behalf of the pupils of Bitter Springs School, thank you for coming. I'm pleased to show how diligently they have studied and how much they have learned the last few weeks. Refreshments will be served in the schoolyard."

The parents filed outside, where the mothers took charge of serving the food.

Faith sank onto her desk chair and chewed at a snagged nail. *Don't die, Slim. I'll never forgive you if you die.*

"Psst." Slim motioned to Curly from behind the volcanic outcrop. The trail of the herd had skirted the Mormon communities and led through Indian land, but now the terrain had become so rough that he didn't know how Hunter and Bray could possibly push the cows through. The time had come to put a stop to the rustlers before they lost more of Amos's cattle.

"We'll pinch them off here," Slim whispered. "They can't get around that chute without slowing considerable."

"What's your plan?"

"I'll be over behind that black knob and call on them to stop. You cover me."

"Slim—"

"It's got to work. Two beeves went down this morning."

"Shall I use the shotgun?"

"If you have to. It'll make a mess. Don't put me in your field of fire."

Curly scoffed. "Don't plan to. I don't want your job."

Slim made his way down the back side of the outcrop, then crawled up the malapai knob until he had a view of the oncoming herd.

Bray led the way, his rope tied to a ring in the nose of the old steer. The cattle followed, lowing their displeasure at the hurried pace. Slim let himself slip down the knob and stepped out into the trail.

"Stop there, Bray," Slim called, amazed that his voice didn't shake, because his knees sure did.

"What the—" The man went for his pistol and drew faster than Slim would have thought possible.

Slim threw himself to the side. He winced as he hit the ground, but his own pistol was ready in his hand, and he fired back in the man's direction.

Bray was off his horse, pulling it down for cover. Slim tried to push himself behind the knob, but his leg didn't want to work. He glanced down, then back at Bray. "Curly!"

In answer, Curly fired a slug toward Bray, but it went over his head.

Good—not the shotgun. *Keep him pinned down, Curly.* Slim pulled himself behind the knob by hooking his arm around a tree trunk, but he couldn't locate Hunter.

I should have done that first, he chided himself. *I'm not good at this manhunt playacting.*

With several shots aimed at Slim, Hunter revealed his position, but Curly had the shotgun up and swinging. He let it off, and Hunter screamed.

"Give it up, Bray," Slim called.

"Hunter?" Bray shouted.

Hunter didn't answer.

"Damn," Bray said. "There goes my pay." He threw his pistol over the horse's neck and got to his feet, hands in the air.

Slim looked at his leg. *I need to get that bullet fetched out.* The light faded.

Next thing he knew, Curly shook his shoulder, not gentle at all. "Slim!"

He looked up. Curly's head blocked the sun, haloed above them. "What?"

"I stopped the bleeding but couldn't get to the bullet. Come on. Stand up. We'll go to Show Low. They have a doc."

He did as he was told, glad to pass the reins of this

cayuse over to Curly. Bray sat against a pine, trussed up like a Christmas goose. "He looks secure. Where's Hunter?"

Curly tilted his head to indicate a sack tied across a horse. Slim squinted. Not a sack. Hunter.

"He dead?"

Curly snarled, "Yeah. I've got to tote his dad-blamed carcass back to the ranch."

Slim considered Curly's words. Yep. They would need to haul him back; this rocky malapai didn't make a good burial ground. "How we gonna do this?"

Curly looked off into the trees.

"Well?"

"I told the outfit to follow us."

"You what?"

"You heard me. I said to hold back some." He waved his arm. "Come out, boys. He'll get over being mad soon as we get him to the doc."

Charley had brought Faith a telegram after school. When he'd departed, she'd read it once, then clutched it to her breast. Now her badly shaking hands almost prevented her from reading it again. Almost.

MISS FAITH BANNISTER STOP AM CRIPPLED UP FOR A WHILE STOP HOPE YOU WILL VISIT WHEN I RETURN ON TUESDAY NEXT STOP JEFFERSON DAVIS MCHENRY END

He'd spent money to send her a telegram. He hadn't mentioned the extent of his injuries, but he had thought of her in his extremity. She crushed the telegram, hearing the paper crackle. *Thank God he's alive.*

On Monday afternoon, Faith announced a school recess for the next day.

"What's the holiday, miss?" Joey asked.

"I must visit a sick friend."

Joey raised his eyebrows at Curtis. "I told you," he said. "Ma was right."

Faith stifled a groan. *That woman!* She had a good heart, though. "Class dismissed."

She waited a moment to pick up her valise before following the pupils out the door. A horse awaited her at the livery. Tomorrow Slim would return, and she would be at the ranch to greet him. She didn't know what would happen after that.

By the time Curly drove a wagon into the ranch yard the next day, Faith had chewed all of her nails to the quick. She was sure Clarissa could hear her heart thumping as they watched the vehicle approach. How badly was Slim wounded? No one could tell her. Clarissa patted her shoulder. The wagon turned. Slim sat in the back, supported by several blankets. A pretty young woman sat beside him.

Faith gasped, but before she could turn away in dismay, Slim's voice croaked, "Miss Faith," and she had to meet his gaze.

He beckoned to her. Clarissa gave her a push. Faith's legs dragged like wooden fence posts toward the wagon. She stopped and clutched the wagon's sideboard.

Slim gazed up at her and pried one of her hands loose to hold it. He laid his other hand over his heart, like one of her pupils about to recite a poem about everlasting love. His fingers pressed hers insistently. She held her breath. Had her heart stopped? She couldn't hear it in the stillness.

"Miss Faith," Slim said, a little tremor in his voice. "Meet my cousin Betsy from Show Low. She's come along to nurse me back to health." He looked at the cousin and said, "Hoist me up more, Bets," then returned his attention to Faith. "When I'm healed, I'd be honored if you'd allow me to call."

"I'd like that," she whispered as her heart began to thump again, wildly, joyfully.

The next thing she knew, Slim's lips pressed against her cheek, and gladness suffused her entire soul.

"It'll be soon," Slim said. "That's a promise."

ABOUT MARSHA WARD

Photo Credit: Heather Zahn Gardner

Marsha Ward was born in the sleepy little town of Phoenix, Arizona, in the southwestern United States, and grew up with chickens, citrus trees, and lots of room to roam. Her love of the 19th-century Western era was reinforced by visits to her cousins on their ranch and listening to her father's stories of homesteading in Old Mexico and in the southern part of Arizona.

Marsha is an award-winning poet, writer, and editor, with over 900 pieces of published work, including her acclaimed novel series featuring the Owen family. Her fourth novel, *Spinster's Folly*, was a 2012 Whitney Award Finalist in Historical Fiction and won the 2013 USA Best Books Award for Western Fiction.

Marsha is the founder of American Night Writers Association (ANWA) and a member of Western Writers of America and Women Writing the West. A workshop presenter and writing teacher, Marsha makes her home in a tiny forest hamlet in Arizona.

Website: MarshaWard.com
Blog: MarshaWard.blogspot.com
Facebook: Author Marsha Ward

More Timeless Romance Anthologies

For more information about our anthologies, visit our blog: TimelessRomanceAnthologies.blogspot.com

Made in the USA
Columbia, SC
26 October 2023

24944813R00191